Caitlyn's heart fluttered

in recognition. Gideon!

She felt all the air leave her body.

Gideon?

But it wasn't Gideon. It couldn't be Gideon. Even though he moved with the familiar gait of the boy she'd once loved more than life itself. How many times had she mistaken a stranger in the crowd for her long-lost lover? Hundreds? A thousand? More?

The interloper reached the stone pillar where Caitlyn stood, her body trembling, mouth dry.

Her heart was in her throat. Her knees were noodles. Her confused mind was in utter chaos. Her head spun, her vision blurred.

It wasn't Gideon. It simply could not be. She knew it, and yet, and yet . . .

Then he stripped off his helmet, pulled away the goggles.

And Caitlyn stared straight into the eyes of a dead man.

By Lori Wilde

THE WELCOME HOME GARDEN CLUB
THE FIRST LOVE COOKIE CLUB
THE TRUE LOVE QUILTING CLUB
THE SWEETHEARTS' KNITTING CLUB

THE
Welcome Home
GARDEN
CLUB

LORI WILDE

AVON
An Imprint of HarperCollinsPublishers

This is a work of fiction. Names, characters, places, and incidents are products of the author's imagination or are used fictitiously and are not to be construed as real. Any resemblance to actual events, locales, organizations, or persons, living or dead, is entirely coincidental.

AVON BOOKS
An Imprint of HarperCollins*Publishers*
10 East 53rd Street
New York, New York 10022-5299

Copyright © 2011 by Laurie Vanzura
Teaser excerpt copyright © 2011 by Laurie Vanzura
ISBN 978-0-06-198843-1
www.avonromance.com

First Avon Books mass market printing: April 2011

Avon Trademark Reg. U.S. Pat. Off. and in Other Countries, Marca Registrada, Hecho en U.S.A.
HarperCollins® is a registered trademark of HarperCollins Publishers.

Printed in the U.S.A.

10 9 8 7 6 5 4 3 2

To all the loved ones of our servicemen and -women.
Your sacrifices mean so much.

ACKNOWLEDGMENTS

Thank you to all the servicemen and -women who daily put their lives on the line to give the rest of us our freedom. God bless you!

THE
Welcome Home
GARDEN
CLUB

PROLOGUE

*Traditional meaning of striped carnation—
no, sorry, I cannot be with you.*

From the look of things, the good citizens of Twilight, Texas, thought more of J. Foster Goodnight as a corpse than they had as a human being.

Numerous military-themed floral baskets and vases filled with white lilies, red roses, blue delphiniums, and red and white striped carnations with blue bows vied for space with the dressed-in-their-Sunday-best crowd spilling out of the stone pavilion overlooking the Brazos River. But no one cried, most speculated on the lavish contents of J. Foster's will, and quite a few shared a smile or two.

Caitlyn Marsh concurred with the sentiment.

In death, J. Foster had earned her floral shop more money than she'd made her entire last quarter.

While in life, the grandfather of her only child had killed her high school sweetheart as surely as if he'd pulled the trigger.

Even now, eight years after Gideon's murder, just thinking of him as he'd been—whole, handsome, incredibly strong and brave—hurt Caitlyn's soul. Never mind that at age twenty-five she'd already been both bride and widow to someone else, her heart would forever and always belong to Gideon Garza.

In the distance, she heard the faraway droning of a motorcycle engine. The cool spring breeze dispersed somewhat the cloying perfume of too many blooms; ruffled hairstyles and funeral programs with a photograph of the deceased sitting in an overstuffed leather chair, a black Stetson perched atop his head. He had one hand on his Bluetick Coonhound's neck, the other curled around a tumbler of malt Scotch. A fully loaded gun rack, along with various dead animal heads, was mounted on the wall behind him. He looked the epitome of what he was. Rich, privileged, cruel, and proud of it. J. Foster had been the kind of wealthy, hard-ass, good old boy who'd once defined Texas—loud, shrewd, swaggeringly arrogant, and tough as his alligator boots.

No expense had been spared on the flag-draped, cherry hardwood coffin with a MemorySafe drawer to display his cherished keepsakes—the scorecard from the hole in one he shot on his forty-fifth birthday at the Pecan Valley Country Club, old Blue's last dog collar, a cigar that was reportedly Cuban and given to him by LBJ, a navy Vietnam War veteran patch, and a paperback copy of Larry McMurtry's *Lonesome Dove*. The coffin's handles were solid gold and the casket liner was one hundred percent silk, custom-made, a cowboy print depicting an Old West cattle drive scene.

The casket sat flanked by two young navy seamen in white. Ringing the pavilion, standing at attention as erect as the young servicemen, were the Patriot Guard. On their motorcycles, American flags flying, they had escorted the hearse from Shady Rest Funeral Home to the hillside where many of Twilight's servicemen and women were buried. Just the sight of them, stalwart and dutiful, misted Caitlyn's eyes with patriotism. She might have hated J. Foster, but he had served his country, and for that, he'd earned her grudging respect.

The minister delivered the eulogy, but Caitlyn wasn't much listening. She knew what J. Foster was really like, and she didn't particularly want to hear the positive spin the reverend put on his life. Instead, she was calculating how long it would take her and the funeral home assistant to get the flowers, earmarked for the graveside, into the rear of her van while the sound of the distant motorcycle grew steadily louder.

The young servicemen carefully folded the flag with practiced precision. Once their task was complete, the honor guard took over. Three retired servicemen with rifles, simultaneously firing off three shots apiece. The loud, definitive noise jarred Caitlyn, and she winced with each firing as spent bullet casings spit against the cement.

"Taps" issued eerily out across the cemetery. The river running below bounced the sound back until it was difficult to know from what direction the mournful bugling came. The hairs on her arms rose and a lump clogged her throat. Caitlyn swiveled her head, looking for the bugler, but saw instead a black motorcycle traveling the winding road toward the pavilion.

The bugling stopped and she heard the engine again, much louder now.

It was an Indian.

She knew because Gideon had owned a 2000 Indian Chief bought with money he'd earned working as a carpenter's apprentice the year after he'd graduated high school, and she'd loved riding on the back of it, her arms wrapped around Gideon's firm waist, the wind blowing over her skin, the throb of that distinctive machine vibrating up through the seat.

Who was this latecomer?

Closer and closer the motorcycle drew. For a moment it disappeared behind a bend in the road, hidden by a cedar copse. Then it reappeared, just as the two navy seamen handed the folded flag to Goodnight's next of kin, saluted, snapped their heels, and pivoted away.

The Indian pulled to a stop behind the procession of cars parked along the circular drive. Heads turned. A murmur ran through the throng as others noticed the new arrival.

The rider, cloaked in leather, his face hidden behind a helmet and protective goggles, swung off the bike. He sauntered toward the group, everyone transfixed.

Caitlyn's heart fluttered in recognition. *Gideon.* She felt all the air leave her body, heard the blood bounding through her ears.

Gideon?

But it wasn't Gideon. It couldn't be Gideon. Even though he moved with the familiar gait of the boy she'd once loved more than life itself. How many times had she mistaken a stranger in the crowd for her long-lost lover? Hundreds? A thousand? More?

The interloper reached the stone pillar where Caitlyn stood, her body trembling, mouth dry.

He stopped halfway between her and the casket.

Her heart was in her throat. Her knees were noodles. Her confused mind was in utter chaos. Her head spun, her vision blurred. She fisted her hands, gulped for air.

It wasn't Gideon. It simply could not be. She knew it, and yet, and yet . . .

Then he stripped off his helmet, pulled away the goggles, and Caitlyn stared straight into the eyes of a dead man.

CHAPTER ONE

Traditional meaning of hibiscus—delicate beauty.

Three weeks earlier

On that late Sunday afternoon in early February, it took a moment for Caitlyn to realize someone had spoken her name. Her gloved hands were deep in the rich loam, the earthy scent of cool winter soil teased her nostrils with the promise of miracles.

At first she thought the sound was her favorite hen, a beautiful salmon Faverolles named Collette, clucking over a fat juicy worm, so she didn't pay much attention. Digging in the dirt helped her think, and she was desperate for a solution to save her flower shop and the home she loved.

"Caitlyn?"

She raised her gaze, saw the two Elberta peach

trees she'd planted in honor of the two men she'd lost, one her husband, the other the love of her life. Both trees were already boldly putting on buds as if just daring Mother Nature to strike again with a vicious freeze before the official start to spring. Tempting death, those trees, same as her lovers.

"It never pays to take risks," she muttered, dusting her hands and rising to her feet. "Mark my word, you saucy darlings, we'll have no fresh peach cobbler this summer."

"What did you say, dear?"

Caitlyn pressed her palms into the small of her back, stretching out the kinks and shifting to meet the gazes of all ten members of her gardening club standing around her in a semicircle. "Just talking to my peach trees."

"They're going to get blasted, blooming this early." Eighty-five-year-old Dotty Mae Densmore, the oldest of the group, shook her head.

Caitlyn was surprised to notice that Dotty Mae was dressed in a pink shift dress and a matching Jackie Onassis pillbox hat and holding a clutch purse. In fact, all the ladies assembled were overdressed.

Uneasiness cooled the back of her neck. She forced a smile, tried not to let her imagination run away with her, removed her gardening gloves, and pushed an errant lock of hair from her forehead. "That's what I was telling those naughty trees. This streak of warm weather has them busting out like teenagers on spring break. So what's up?"

"We need to speak with you," said Patsy Cross, who was on the town council.

Patsy was a widow like Caitlyn, but at sixty, she was almost three times her age. She also owned the Teal Peacock, a curio store just off the town square. She wore her frosted blond hair cut like Diane Sawyer's, had lost weight recently, and seemed to be smiling a lot more often. She wore navy blue slacks, a tangerine silk blouse, and navy blue ankle boots. She marched with a determined gait, her legs like a general's. After Caitlyn's husband, Kevin, had been killed six months ago, Patsy had been the first one to the house with a box of Kleenex and a casserole dish of King Ranch Chicken. "It's rather urgent."

"Is something wrong?" Her hand crept to her neck as fear burrowed underneath her skin.

"Everything's fine," Flynn MacGregor Calloway soothed. Flynn was just a few years older than Caitlyn, and newly wed to Patsy's nephew Jesse. She was attending college to become an elementary school teacher, and she was one of those instinctively nurturing types who'd picked up on Caitlyn's tendency to become easily alarmed. A riot of dark brown curls surrounded her pretty face. She smiled, showing off a wealth of dimples. Flynn had been the one to offer to babysit Caitlyn's seven-year-old, Danny, during the chaos of Kevin's funeral arrangements. "Town business, and we need your help."

Relief sagged through her. Thank heavens nothing was wrong. She glanced at her watch and saw that she had an hour before she had to pick Danny up from his playdate.

Caitlyn waved them toward the cottage. "Please come in, I'll put on a pot of water for tea."

They trooped inside and gathered around the circular farmhouse table. She hauled in a few chairs from other rooms to have enough seating for everyone.

While she was doing this, quiet Christine Noble, who'd once been an Olympic contender before an accident had crushed her leg, filled the chicken-shaped teakettle with water and put it on the stove to boil.

Christine owned the Twilight Bakery and she and Caitlyn often worked the same events together—weddings, graduations, anniversaries. Christine provided the cakes, Caitlyn the flowers.

In fact, they were working together on the upcoming wedding of one of their garden club members, self-contained Sarah Collier. Sarah was a children's book author recently engaged to Travis Walker, the local game warden, who had a daughter who was a year older than Danny. Sarah had a tendency to keep a low profile. Caitlyn noticed Sarah had taken the chair closest to the door. She and Sarah were the same age, and younger than everyone else in the club.

"Thank you," Caitlyn told Christine.

Christine smiled shyly and limped to the over-sized white rocking chair that Caitlyn had dragged in from the screened porch and waved at the brown paper bag on the counter. "I brought cookies too."

"What kind?" asked Marva Bullock, a beautiful African-American woman in her late forties and the principal of Twilight High. Once upon a time, she'd been Caitlyn's algebra teacher. "I'm wondering if they're worth blowing my diet over."

"Lemon drop," Christine enticed.

Marva groaned. "My favorite."

"As if you need to diet." Raylene Pringle snorted. "You've got a fine body."

Marva patted her belly. "Gotta keep this middle-aged spread under control."

"What for?" Raylene asked. "G.C.? Trust me, men aren't worth the trouble. They'll just leave you in the end."

Raylene had once been a Dallas Cowboys cheerleader back in the Tom Landry heydays. Even at sixty, she'd managed to hang on to her youthful figure. She was blunt, outspoken, and sassy. But lately, since she and her husband of thirty-four years had split up, she'd fallen in a deep funk. She'd stopped bleaching her hair blond and quit wearing her skirts short. Her friends in the garden club weren't sure what to make of this new Raylene.

Marva looked a little alarmed, and when Caitlyn set the platter of lemon drop cookies on the table, she shook her head. "I'll be good and pass on the cookies."

"What?" Raylene asked. "You think being skinny is gonna save your marriage? Men either up and die on you, or when the going gets tough, they jump ship and run off."

No one pointed out that her husband had had a very good reason for walking out on her.

"Ray," Patsy said softly, and put a gentle hand on Raylene's forearm. "G.C.'s not Earl. He's not going to leave Marva."

"Yeah? Well, I never thought Earl would leave me

either. How am I supposed to run the Horny Toad Tavern without him?" Raylene looked as if she was on the verge of tears, and that startled everyone. Normally, things slid as easily off Raylene as rain off a horny toad's hide.

"So," Caitlyn said, swiftly changing the subject. "What's up that couldn't wait until the next garden club meeting?"

"Yes, yes, the reason we're here." Perpetually cheerful Belinda Murphey beamed. She took a couple of lemon drop cookies and munched happily.

Belinda was plump, pretty, and in her early forties. She was also mother to five rambunctious kids and ran the Sweetest Match, Twilight's local matchmaking service. She'd built a booming business by taking advantage of the local romantic legend.

Lore had it that Jon Grant and Rebekka Nash were young lovers from Missouri separated by the Civil War. But they never stopped believing that they were fated to be together. Then one evening at twilight, fifteen years later, they met by chance on the banks of the Brazos River where the town of Twilight now stood. It was rumored that if you threw a coin into the fountain—erected in honor of Jon and Rebekka and located in the center of Sweetheart Park—you'd be reunited with your high school sweetheart. The town made a sizable income each year off the spare change of tourists.

Caitlyn herself was Jon and Rebekka's great-great-great-granddaughter on her mother's side. She and Danny were the last remaining descendants of the Grant-Nash union. But Caitlyn had no idea if the folklore was true or not. The original story had been greatly embellished and fantasy-fueled over the years.

"There's a contest," Emma Parks said.

Emma was petite and bubbly, with gorgeous red hair and a gamine face. The newest member of the gardening club was in her early thirties and a Broadway actress who'd moved back to Twilight and hooked up with her high school sweetheart, Dr. Sam Cheek, the town veterinarian.

The teakettle sang, and Caitlyn switched off the burner. "What kind of contest?"

"A gardening contest," Terri Longoria added.

Terri rounded out the group. Compact and dark-haired, she was in her late thirties, mother to a young son and married to the chief of staff at Twilight General. She ran Hot Legs Gym and she'd once won ten thousand dollars on a reality TV show by eating a bucket of earthworms in under ten minutes. Caitlyn admired Terri's intrepidness. She could never, ever do something like that.

The mention of a gardening contest pricked Caitlyn's curiosity. She poured the hot water into eleven cups and carried them to the table on a tray, along with a variety of teas to choose from—green jasmine, Earl Grey, chrysanthemum, orchid, ginger, oolong, Assam, orange pekoe, chamomile, hibiscus, red tea, and kandy.

She found it interesting how people's choice of tea seemed to reflect their personalities. Shy Christine went for the unassuming pekoe. Practical Patsy favored no-nonsense oolong. Sweet-natured Dotty

Mae gravitated to the chamomile, but she always added a dollop of peppermint schnapps to it, suggesting that she wasn't as gentle as she seemed. Belinda reached for the robust, full-bodied kandy, especially fitting because all her children's names started with the letter K. Vivacious Emma plucked red tea from the mix. Trustworthy Flynn selected the old standby Earl Grey. Daring Terri picked ginger. Independent Sarah prized autonomous chrysanthemum. Bold Raylene chose the stout, malty Assam. And health-conscious Marva drank green jasmine.

Caitlyn herself liked the floral teas, most particularly hibiscus served with a teaspoon of fresh honey. She wondered what that said about her.

"What kind of gardening contest?" she asked, taking the last empty seat at the table after her guests had been served.

"A victory garden contest sponsored by the first lady of Texas!" Belinda exclaimed. "That's why we're so dressed up. Our book club went to Austin for a literary brunch and that's where we found out about the competition."

From her purse, Patsy pulled a spiral-bound pamphlet. "It's a statewide competition. I got my hands on the official rulebook and entry form. I called the town council members and we just had an impromptu conference call to discuss Twilight's participation."

"There are five categories," Terri said. "Best Small-Town Garden, Best Urban Garden, Best Flower Garden, Most Creative, and Most Romantic."

"Oh, and the gardens all have to be organic," Flynn added.

"Considering that Twilight stands for romance, you would think we'd be a shoo-in for most romantic." Marva took a sip of her tea.

"Especially if you were the garden's architect, Caitlyn," Dotty Mae said. "You've got the greenest thumb in North Texas and your own garden is the prettiest in Twilight."

Completely caught off guard, Caitlyn looked around the table at the faces of her friends, and placed a palm over her chest. "You want *me* to plan and execute our town's victory garden for a statewide competition?"

Ten heads nodded in unison.

"But I'm only twenty-five. You're all older than I am."

"And none of us half as talented with plants as you are," Christine declared.

The compliment brought a warm flush to Caitlyn's cheeks. Praise often embarrassed her. She lived a simple life and wanted only two things—to raise a happy, healthy son and to tend her plants.

"Thank you for thinking of me," she said, "but really, I'm still picking up the pieces of my life. Kevin left our finances in ruin. The floral shop is struggling, Danny's having trouble in school—"

"I thought things were better with Danny since Crockett started taking an interest in him . . ." Flynn winked. "And you."

Crockett was the younger son of the richest man in town. Caitlyn wasn't a woman much given to hatred, but if she hated anyone, it was J. Foster Goodnight. She had her reasons, and she didn't owe anyone an explanation. But her feelings toward the father made her leery of the son. Then again, who was she to judge? Hadn't she struggled for years to throw off her own controlling father's influence?

Crockett's baseball memorabilia store was right next door to hers on the square, and when business was slow, he'd pop over to regale her with jokes and stories about his days playing semiprofessional baseball. She had to admit that Crockett could get her to lighten up when no one else could with his lighthearted teasing.

She simply shook her head at Flynn. "Crockett and I are just friends."

"Yeah?" Terri arched her eyebrows and grinned slyly. "That's what Flynn used to say about Jesse."

"You don't want to get mixed up with Crockett," Patsy said. "That boy has only one thing on his mind. I don't trust him any further than I can throw him."

"Crockett's not so bad," Belinda interjected. "He's one of the most popular dates at the Sweetest Match. All the women seem to love him. He does know how to show the ladies a good time."

"I don't know, there's something off about the boy." Dotty Mae frowned. "He reminds me of Eddie Haskell from *Leave It to Beaver*. He's all 'yes ma'am' and 'no ma'am' and 'what a nice dress you're wearing today, Ms. Densmore,' but behind those thick, dark eyelashes you can tell something sneaky is going on."

"Well," Raylene said, "J. Foster did drive his mother into the loony bin with his hard-living ways. That's gotta affect a kid. Those boys were only what? Six and ten when their mother got carted off?"

"His brother turned out fine," Terri said.

Patsy snorted. "Bowie? That man has anger issues. He goes around scowling and grumbling. I don't call that exactly well balanced."

"I think it's a big bluff he puts on in defense against J. Foster. You have to be a warrior to go toe-to-toe with that old man." Terri settled her cup into its saucer. "Bowie has a big heart. He was the first one to donate blood after those tourists were badly hurt in that boating accident a few years back, and I can't ever forget the day he ran out in front of the delivery truck to snatch Gerald up out of the street just in the nick of time. My son would have been killed if it hadn't been for Bowie. Gerald had just learned to walk and he broke free from my grip and just dashed into the road . . ." Terri trailed off, her eyes misted with tears.

Christine patted Terri on the back. "It's okay. Gerald is fine."

"I know, I know, but Bowie Goodnight will always have a soft place in my heart." Terri plastered a hand over her heart.

"Honestly," Emma said. "I didn't really know them, but it sounds like both the Goodnight men have a lot of emotional baggage."

"Amen to that." Flynn reached for another cookie.

"Don't worry, I won't be losing my head or my

heart over Crockett Goodnight," Caitlyn assured her friends. "I harbor no illusions about him."

"I say go for a booty call, I mean have you seen that boy? Butt like a Greek god, face like a cherub, a smile like Satan. Do him and then throw him away like a used tissue. Treat men the way they treat us," Raylene said.

"Raylene!" everyone exclaimed.

Raylene glowered and snapped her fingers. "Hush y'all and pass the schnapps already, Dotty Mae."

"You know, Ray, there's always the possibility that Earl will come back," Belinda murmured. "He does love you."

"Booty call," Raylene said firmly to Caitlyn, ignored Belinda, and tippled schnapps into her Assam. She held up the bottle. "Anyone else want a snort?"

"Let's get back on track. About the victory garden contest," Patsy said, steering the conversation where she wanted it to go.

"Don't get me wrong," Caitlyn said. "It's an honor to be asked and I do thank you, but I just don't have the time for volunteer work. I was even thinking of dropping out of the gardening club because it looks like I'll be taking a part-time job to make ends meet."

Or selling the flower shop.

She shoved that thought aside. Caitlyn loved being a florist almost as much as she loved being a mom and she'd do everything in her power to hang on to the shop. Well, except ask her father for money. Before she stooped to something that desperate, she'd sell a kidney on the black market.

But with her job skills or lack thereof, the only part-time position she qualified for required the utterance of phrases such as "You want fries with that?" She'd been a wife and a mother and Kevin's assistant in the flower shop. That was the extent of her résumé.

"Did I mention that the job pays twenty dollars an hour?" Patsy asked. "Plus don't underestimate the power of publicity. When we win this thing— and with you in charge, we *will* win it—you'll have people flocking to buy flowers from the designer of the most romantic victory garden in Texas."

Patsy's unbridled optimism shot excitement up Caitlyn's spine. But she was nothing if not cautious and she tamped down her enthusiastic mind which was already toying with plot design and flower selection. "It's a paying position?"

"You'd get to dig in the garden and make money at your passion," Patsy enticed.

She wanted to hope, but something didn't sound right. Could her father be behind this offer? She wouldn't put it past him. Caitlyn narrowed her eyes. "Where's the money for my salary coming from?"

"Town council has an overflow fund."

"Why would they use it to fund a victory garden?"

"Because the grand prize is a hundred thousand dollars that would go into the town coffers if we won."

Caitlyn stirred more honey into her tea. "And if we don't win the grand prize?"

"We'd still have a beautiful victory garden to attract tourists. It's a win/win situation." Patsy ran a hand over her lap, flicking away cookie crumbs.

It seemed too good to be true. She didn't trust too good to be true. Caitlyn narrowed her eyes. "What's the catch?"

"Well . . ." Patsy folded her napkin, paused for a long moment, and then took a deep breath. "The town council wants you to design the garden around your great-great-grandfather's carousel."

Gideon had once promised that he would fix up the carousel for her. Refurbish the damaged horses. Get the rusty old mechanisms working again. Gideon had had the hands for it—broad palms, long deft fingers, a way with both wood and engines.

But Gideon was gone, just like her mother.

Ah, here it was—the catch to end all catches. Hope flickered out. "Do we have to use the carousel for the garden?"

"I'm afraid it's a deal breaker," Patsy said. "No carousel, no garden. The town council feels the carousel *is* the tourist draw."

"Couldn't we just make a carousel?"

"It wouldn't have the historical significance. Imagine if we built our garden around the oldest functioning carousel in the state of Texas, that just happened to have been built by the son of the town founders and then lovingly restored to its former glory in a garden nurtured and designed by Jon and Rebekka Grant's great-great-great-granddaughter. It's the stuff of legends."

"No."

"It's really—"

Caitlyn held up a palm, cutting Patsy off. "I'm sorry, I can't help you."

"Could you at least—"

"Not doing it."

"What other options do you have, Caitlyn?" Dotty Mae murmured. "You've got Danny to think about."

Low blow. Caitlyn felt more than a little bit manipulated. They didn't want her. They were only offering her a paying job in order to get their hands on the carousel and her heritage. "Ladies, I'd love to help, I really would. But honestly, I'd rather sell the flower shop before resorting to that."

"If you could even find a buyer," Patsy pointed out. "Real estate just isn't moving in these tough economic times."

"I'm sorry." Caitlyn got up, pushed back her chair. "I have to pick Danny up from his playdate. If you all will excuse me . . ."

"Sure, sure." Everyone got to her feet and headed for the door.

Patsy was the last one to leave. She paused at the threshold, met Caitlyn's gaze. "I do hope you'll reconsider. The victory garden would be a boon to both you and Twilight."

"Thank you again for your offer." She pressed her lips into a firm line. "But I prefer to solve my own problems. I don't need to be rescued and I don't like being used."

"I'm sorry you feel that way," Patsy said, "but the door is still open if you change your mind. We have until next Monday to file the entry form." Then she turned and followed the others.

Caitlyn shut the door behind them, her mind racing. A job creating the victory garden was the answer to her prayers. Too bad it came with strings tied so tightly that a chain saw couldn't shear through them.

CHAPTER TWO

Traditional meaning of poppy—eternal sleep.

Badakhshan Province, Afghanistan

Half a world away, former Green Beret sergeant Gideon Garza stared out across the craggy desert landscape. A black SUV, windows tinted darkly, smoke billowing out from behind the tires, raced toward his encampment.

Trouble coming. He could smell it.

His good hand automatically went to the gun he kept holstered at his chest, and in Pashto, he calmly instructed the children to go inside the tent. They could be mischievous and unruly, but his tone told them he wasn't kidding around. Far too accustomed to sudden danger, the orphans quickly left their games and did as he asked.

He'd been hired by concerned family members to escort the ragtag youths from volatile living conditions in the Pashtun heartlands to the relative safety of the mountains near Faisabad. The orphans' relatives couldn't pay him much, but he wasn't doing it for the money. He made the bulk of his six-figure annual salary providing personal security and translation services to British and American opportunists doing business in Kandahar and Kabul. He was just damn tired of seeing kids with their limbs blown off by land mines.

Yeah, you're a regular flippin' Princess Di.

Right now, he felt more like Clint Eastwood, gun drawn, muscles tensed, eyes steely, stance ready for action. The children behind him, the threat rapidly approaching, the wind at his back. All he needed now was the soundtrack to *The Good, the Bad and the Ugly*, because damn if he wasn't all three rolled into one.

He'd set up the camp in a valley of stone outcroppings. The vehicle wouldn't be able to just drive straight up on them. But it was close enough that he could make out that the SUV belonged to an infamous group of paramilitary subcontractors that, among other things, provided serious muscle to powerful and influential private citizens mucking around in war-torn countries. His competition. Why would they be interested in a handful of scraggly orphans? A chill ran through him at the potential answers. He steeled his spine, clenched his jaw.

The SUV halted at the lip of the rocky rim surrounding his encampment about five hundred yards from where he stood. His mind raced, but his heartbeat was slow and steady. Did he have a fight on his hands? There was only one vehicle. How bad could it be?

The driver's side door swung open and a muscular man stepped out. Buzz haircut, dark sunglasses, desert fatigues, boots, AK–47 slung across his chest, all Mr. Badass. Gideon's mirror image.

Rambo stood casually, but there was nothing casual about him. He mouthed something into a headset clipped to his ear and waited while the back passenger door opened and a greenhorn climbed to the ground.

The greenhorn and Rambo had a short powwow, then the greenhorn turned and headed toward Gideon.

It was almost worth the disruption to watch the balding man in the tailored Italian suit and leather loafers mince his way over the rocky terrain. He slipped several times in his attempt to navigate the hill. If Gideon hadn't been full-on alert, he might have chuckled at the ludicrous sight.

One of the younger boys poked his head from the tent and made fun of the man.

"Get back inside," Gideon said. "Now."

The curious brown face disappeared, but he could hear childish giggles from the other side of the tent.

"Hello," Italian Suit called out in a Texas twang.

"What do you want?" Gideon kept his voice low and even, one eye on the man in front of him, the other on Rambo, who was smoking a cigarette and lounging against the SUV. He could smell the burning tar. It had been a while since he'd heard the accent of his native land, and his suspicion escalated. He leveled the gun at the man's head. "Arms up."

Startled, Italian Suit shot his arms into the air, the briefcase clutched in his right hand banging against his head. "I'm looking for Gideon Garza. You're him, aren't you?"

"Who wants to know?"

"My name is Lester LaVon and I'm from Twilight, Texas."

The hairs on the back of Gideon's neck stood at attention, but he'd be damned if he'd let his fear show. Twilight, Texas, scared him more than Rambo and company. "Long way from home. You aren't in Texas anymore, Toto."

LaVon looked confused. "Huh?"

"You've gone over the rainbow, Lester. There's a field of poppies just beyond that next rise, and people delight in killing overfed white Americans for them. You find any yellow bricks around here, then you better run like hell."

"Why are you speaking in riddles? I'm not following a word you're saying."

Gideon didn't bother to explain his sarcasm. He simply nodded in the direction of the SUV. "Who's your friend?"

"My escort."

"Is he coming down for this little chat?"

"Our business is not his concern."

"Clue me in. What is our business?"

"Must you point that gun at me?" LaVon shifted nervously, arms still extended over his head, briefcase resting on his balding pate.

"Until I know who you are and what you want, yeah, I must."

"I told you, I'm—"

"I don't mean your name. Who sent you?"

LaVon's face flushed and sweat slid down his temple. "If you'll just put away the gun . . ."

The hairs on the nape of Gideon's neck were dancing now. Trouble, trouble, trouble. "Who sent you?" he repeated, but from LaVon's shifty behavior, he already knew the answer.

"Umm . . ." LaVon licked his lips. "Your father."

"I don't have a father. His name was left off my birth certificate."

"J. Foster Goodnight."

"Ah, you mean the jerkwad who ignored my mother and me and then denied who he was when I confronted him."

"He's sorry about that and he wants to make amends."

Gideon snorted. "I don't believe you, and furthermore, I don't give a damn if it is true."

"Look, can I put my hands down now? This briefcase is getting heavy."

Gideon was not inclined to trust him. Then again, Gideon wasn't inclined to trust anyone. At twenty-seven, he'd already seen far more of the dark side of life than most men three times his age.

Moira Simon, the British relief aid worker he visited whenever he crossed over the border, had once told him he possessed the eyes of a very old soul. He didn't believe in new age mumbo-jumbo, but her words had unsettled him. He *felt* very old.

Tilting his head, he sought out Rambo again. The hired gun was taking a leak against the back tire of his own vehicle. What a dog. But if he was relaxed enough to do that, he wasn't expecting immediate danger.

Gideon let out his breath and nodded, but kept his gun leveled at the intruder. "You can put your hands down, but do it slowly."

Inch by inch, LaVon lowered arms that trembled with exertion. "May I sit?"

Gideon indicated a large flat rock with a nod of his head. LaVon sank down on it, pulled a handkerchief from his breast pocket, and sopped his sweaty brow.

"Goodnight flew you all the way to Afghanistan?" He knew his biological father had both the money and political means to make that happen, he just couldn't figure out why. Especially after all this time. He didn't for one minute believe it was to make amends as LaVon claimed.

"He did."

"How did you find me?"

"J. Foster kept up with your career. He knows what happened." LaVon glanced pointedly at Gideon's prosthetic hand.

Feeling both exposed and violated, Gideon narrowed his eyes. "Well isn't that nice? I suppose this is where you expect me to get all teary-eyed over Daddy Dearest?"

"Your father is not well, Sergeant Garza."

"Why are you telling me this? He's got two legitimate sons. Let them take care of him."

"He wants to see you before he dies. I have money in my briefcase to pay your travel expenses."

"I'm kind of in the middle of something." Gideon waved a hand at the orphans peeking from behind the tent flap, staring with interest at the white-skinned interloper in foreign clothing. "I couldn't leave if I wanted to and I don't want to."

LaVons gaze slid over the orphans dismissively. "But your father, he's dying—"

"I don't give a shit," Gideon interrupted.

"I came all this way." The lawyer worried the strap of his briefcase. "J. Foster is going to be very disappointed."

"Not my problem."

"So what do I tell him?"

Without batting an eye, Gideon said coldly, "To rot in hell."

On Monday morning after she dropped Danny off at school, Caitlyn paced outside the stately Victorian on the ritzy end of Ruby Street. It had been eight years since she'd set foot in the home she'd grown up in, even though she'd tried, really tried, to bridge the gap between herself and her father. He was the holdout, hard-nosed and unbendable and condemning. She'd made one mistake, and although close to a decade had passed, he was still punishing her for it. Punishing Danny too. And whether he knew it or not, Judge Richard Blackthorne was punishing himself.

Such heartbreak he'd caused with his lack of forgiveness.

She fisted her hands. *Come on, you can do this. Remember, it's for Danny's sake.* Everything she'd ever done, from fleeing this house in the middle of the night, to marrying Kevin, to staying in Twilight even though the pain of staying here was at times almost too much to bear, had always been about her little dark-haired boy with the soulful eyes so much like Gideon's. Part of her kept hoping against hope that her father would relent and her son could finally know his grandfather.

Yesterday, she'd told Patsy and the other ladies from the gardening club that she would not consider taking the job if it meant asking her father for the carousel. The honest reason was that she simply couldn't take another rejection from him. There were only so many times a woman could grovel with no results before she gathered up her self-respect and closed the door on all possibility of absolution.

She'd spent a sleepless night tossing and turning and thinking about not just the twenty-dollars-an-hour, part-time job that could help solve her problems, but about the joy of creating a victory garden honoring Twilight's war heroes.

And one hero in particular.

Gideon.

Caitlyn laid a palm over her heart. Would the pain of losing him ever subside? She thought of all he'd missed. The excitement of learning he was going to become a father, the joy of seeing his child, their son's first words, Danny's first steps, his first day of school.

Over time, she'd taught herself to not think of him constantly, to accept her loss and be content with what she had, and for the most part, she was successful. There'd really been no other choice. She'd done it for Danny's sake. Just as she was doing this.

Her soul ached in mournful remembrance. Time might have blunted the old wounds, but it hadn't healed them. Her throat constricted. It wasn't as if she was asking her father for money. The carousel was her heritage. A legacy from her mother's people. He had no right to keep it from her.

How do you know he'll keep it from you? You've never asked him for the carousel.

She'd never asked because she understood how her father operated. He would use any leverage at his disposal to control her.

Judge Richard Blackthorne believed right was right and wrong was wrong. His black and white worldview might make him a decisive adjudicator, but his steamroller superiority flattened any mere mortal stupid enough to disagree with him. Not once had she ever seen him compromise or admit a mistake. The local lawyers lived in terror of him.

The thing about her father was how difficult it was to keep him in perspective. He stood five-foot-ten, yet people swore he was much taller. Maybe it was because most folks found it really difficult to look him in the eyes. His stare was unrelenting, as if he could see every dark secret of your soul. He had the town buffaloed. If a person wanted to hold his own with Judge Blackthorne, he had to keep in mind that the judge wasn't as omnipotent as he seemed.

Squaring her shoulders, Caitlyn took a deep breath, opened the wrought-iron gate, and marched up the cobblestone sidewalk to the wide wrap-around porch. She knocked on the door, and it was all she could do to keep from turning tail and running away.

Remember, this isn't about you. This is about Danny and the town victory garden and memorializing Gideon's honor and sacrifice.

She didn't know the pinched-face, razor-backed housekeeper who answered the door. Caitlyn's demanding, impossible-to-please father went through servants like strippers went through pasties.

"Yes?" The woman stood a good four inches taller than Caitlyn's five-foot-four and she had her graying hair pulled back in a tight bun. She blocked the space between the partially open door and the frame, a perfect threshold guardian obscuring Caitlyn's view into the foyer beyond. This housekeeper might last awhile.

"I'm here to see Judge Blackthorne."

"He's already left for the courthouse."

Relief rushed through her, but as much as she wanted to do so, she couldn't throw in the towel that easily. "I'm his daughter."

"I know." The woman gave her a half-lidded reptilian stare.

A long silence stretched between them. Caitlyn weighed her options. Come back later, or wrangle with the woman? She put on her best customer-service smile and lied through her teeth. "I'm sorry I missed him."

"He'll be back for lunch."

She knew that. Her frugal father rarely took his meals away from home, unless someone else was buying. She started to ask the housekeeper if she could have a peek in the backyard barn, but realized the woman would not grant her permission.

"Thank you for your time." She turned away.

"He's really lonely, you know," the woman said.

Caitlyn paused, hand on the porch railing, and swiveled her head around.

"You ought to come see him once in a while. Like a good daughter should."

She didn't appreciate being lectured. The woman knew nothing of their relationship, or how hard Caitlyn had tried to reach out to him in the past, only to be repeatedly rebuffed. "My father and I don't see eye-to-eye."

"Someone has to mend the rift."

She wondered what the housekeeper would say if she knew that Caitlyn had called her father from her hospital bed after she'd given birth to Danny to tell him he had a grandson and he'd hung up on her. "Or not."

"Or not," the woman echoed, and then without saying another word, she shut the door and clicked it locked.

Caitlyn heard the sound of her heartbeat in her

ears, thudding hard and slow. A ripple of anger rolled over her. She didn't know for sure whom she was mad at. The housekeeper, her father, or herself. She kneaded her temple with her fingers, felt a headache coming on.

She hurried down the porch steps, but stopped when she reached the sidewalk. Without even making a conscious decision, she did not head for the street, but instead pivoted and stepped around the side of the house.

The oversized barn, painted kelly green, squatted at the back of the sloping acre lot, surrounded by a thicket of aged oaks. Ignoring the apprehension that tightened her chest, she marched toward the barn.

What if he'd moved the carousel? Worse, what if he came home and caught her back there without his permission? He'd probably call Sheriff Hondo Crouch and have him arrest her for trespassing.

That thought was almost enough to send her scurrying back to the safety of her flower shop, but something kept tugging her forward. She reached the barn. A padlock dangled from the hasp. Was the combination still the same?

The lock lay cold against her palm. Caitlyn was startled to see that her fingers trembled as she dialed in the date of her birthday.

It was a great relief when the lock yielded, but gratitude swiftly gave way to cold feet. The barn was dark, the windows smeared with years of grime that let in only a small slant of morning light. The air smelled musty and sullen.

Quickly, she slipped over the threshold and

pulled the door closed behind her. She hadn't been inside this place for twenty years. In the silence, she could hear the whisper-soft ticking of her wristwatch. Somewhere in the neighborhood the sound of a hammer slamming into boards echoed.

The hulking shadows of carved animals sat stacked in rows. On the far side of the barn arced the curve of the wooden platform, dismantled into four sections. Steel poles, bound into bundles, were propped in the corner. The mechanized parts hung suspended from the ceiling or housed in bins. Oil stains dotted the cement floor. Her breathing was the only sound in the cramped space.

A trail of red splinters led her to the horse, his decapitated head dangling from a leather bridle. His sightless eyes staring into nothingness.

Caitlyn squatted beside the horse, tears bunching up in her throat. She reached out a hand to stroke the curling black mane threaded through with orange poppies. Paint flaked off on her fingers, sparkled like stars.

"Blaze," she whimpered, and the past rushed up to slap her.

Even though she'd been only five years old when it happened, Caitlyn remembered her mother's death with a clarity born from abject grief. Her mother, fair-haired Angelica, as lovely as her name—soft-spoken, kindhearted, full of laughter.

"It's spring, Caity," her mother had said, giggling, one Saturday morning. "You know what that means?"

Caitlyn had nodded, even though she didn't.

"It's time to start up the carousel."

Back then, the carousel had been located in Sweetheart Park. It was a gift from the Grant family to the town of Twilight. Angelica had dressed Caitlyn in a frilly pink dress complete with a petticoat, pink butterfly barrettes in her hair, and pink patent leather Mary Janes. She had been so proud of those shoes that were so shiny that she could see her face reflected in them.

She and Mama had walked hand in hand to the park. The carousel was three rows deep, with fifty-three menagerie animals—including twenty jumping horses and another twenty standers, one gigantic lion perfect for siblings to ride together, six prancing deer, four ostriches, and two giraffes—and four golden chariots. The polished wood floor shone brightly in the sunlight.

The ride operator greeted them with a low bow as if they were royalty and ushered them into the carousel ahead of everyone else. "Right this way, Mrs. Blackthorne."

A small crowd had gathered. Mostly other mothers with children eager to ride the carousel on opening day.

"You're a Grant," Mama had said to her. "You get first pick."

Those words had made Caitlyn feel like a special princess. She recalled racing to the back and trying to climb aboard a red horse sculpted with a flying black mane.

Angelica had smiled and given her a boost up. "This was my favorite horse when I was a little girl," she'd murmured. "I named him Blaze."

Tulips near the pond were blooming. Yellow and pink. The air smelled fresh, happy with the scent of flowers and her mother's perfume, attracting the lazy buzz of bees. Organ music played from the speakers mounted inside the stationary part of the carousel.

Row, row, row your boat.

Angelica wrapped one arm around Caitlyn's waist, and placed her other hand around the smooth metal pole for balance as the other mothers and children climbed aboard.

Excitement gripped her when the rotating platform lurched forward and "Row Your Boat" turned into "Roll Out the Barrel."

Round and round the carousel went. Up and down, Caitlyn rode Blaze. She laughed and laughed as the breeze rushed over her skin, tousled her hair.

What magic!

The carousel whirled, picking up speed, going faster and faster. The tight grip her mother had around her waist loosened. Caitlyn started to get scared. She closed her eyes and clung to Blaze's mane. "Mama?"

Her mother made a small, strangled cry.

Caitlyn's eyes flew open and she looked over to see that her mother's face was the color of paste and her eyes had rolled back. Angelica clutched her head with one hand and in the next instant plunged face forward onto the rotating platform.

"Mama!" she screamed.

"Roll Out the Barrel" kept playing merrily. Children kept laughing. Horses kept jumping.

Caitlyn tried to climb down to get to Mama, but her pretty little pink patent leather Mary Jane got hung in the stirrup. She flipped upside down, her petticoat in her face, her hair fanning out over Mama's body, her ankle twisting in the stirrup, her arms flailing.

Blindly, Blaze continued to prance, yanking Caitlyn up and down, up and down.

Suddenly, everything halted.

The carousel ground to a stop. Blaze froze in midstride. The music died with a strangle. Caitlyn's foot came loose and she fell to the platform beside her mother.

She peered into her mother's wide open eyes. They looked so empty. Just like Blaze's did now. Caitlyn reached out to touch her mother's cold face. "Mama?" she whispered.

People were shouting, running. Some ran away from her, some toward her. A man grabbed Caitlyn around the waist.

"Mama!" she'd screamed, and kicked as the man carried her off. "Mama, wake up, wake up!"

But her mother never woke up. An ambulance appeared and two men whisked her away on a stretcher. Later, her father came and took her home to stay with the housekeeper, and then he went away again.

Late in the middle of the night, her father came back. Caitlyn had waited for him on the stairs, but he didn't see her. He moved past her, headed for the back of the house. She followed him, but he stared straight ahead, not seeing her. He went into the barn and found an axe. He slung it over his shoulder and marched away into the darkness.

Caitlyn wanted to call out to him, but something stopped her. She crept silently behind her father as he walked up Ruby Street, headed in the direction of the town square and Sweetheart Park beyond. Underneath the bulbs of the streetlamps, she could see his face twisted in a scary expression.

The light from the full moon glinted off the gold trim of the carousel. The animals looked ghostly, unreal. Grass dew dampened the hem of Caitlyn's pajamas. Fear rippled over her. She twisted a lock of her hair around one index finger and twirled it, while simultaneously popping her thumb into her mouth. Mama had told her big girls didn't suck their thumbs and she'd been trying so hard to be a big girl, but Mama wasn't here and her father couldn't even see her.

Was she invisible?

Then Daddy did something horrifying. He stalked up onto the carousel platform, swung the axe, and chopped off Blaze's head.

Caitlyn screamed, shrill and deafening.

"What are you doing here?" Her father's brusque voice yanked her back to the present.

Caitlyn blinked up at him. She was sitting cross-legged in his barn in the dark, with Blaze's head cradled in her lap. She probably looked psychotic.

She put the horse head aside, got to her feet, dusted her palms together. She hadn't been to his house in eight years, but she saw him every day as he crossed the courthouse lawn walking to and from work. He always carried a walking stick. Not because he needed it to lean on, but because he thought it made him look stately.

In the beginning, when she'd first left home, she'd try waving at him, but he'd stared straight ahead, never meeting her gaze, acting like he hadn't seen her. Then one day, she'd brought Danny with her into his courtroom, hoping to force her father to acknowledge her, but then Danny had started to cry and he'd had the bailiff escort her out.

Her father had made her feel invisible, so she'd stopped waving, stopped speaking, stopped trying to get him to have a relationship with his grandson. He'd shut them out of his life. It had been his choice. His treatment of her had made it uncomfortable for Caitlyn to stay in her hometown. But Twilight was in her very DNA, and she couldn't imagine living anywhere else. So she'd stayed and made the best of things, even if it meant feeling the icy silence every time she spotted him on the street or in a store.

"I thought you were in court," she said.

"Greta called me. The trial hasn't started yet."

"Greta?"

"My housekeeper."

"She's not from Twilight."

"No. She's of Czech descent. Her people are from West." This conversation was so like her relationship with her father. Cool, impersonal.

Caitlyn had learned a long time ago that the best way to handle the judge was to state your case. Of course that usually meant having to accept no for an answer. "I came for the carousel."

They stared at each other, the air tense. Dust motes rode the slant of light between them, showing cobweb veils draped over the wooden animals. In the distance a dog barked.

"The carousel is mine. Mother left it to me." She fisted her hands at her sides. "I'll get a lawyer if I have to." The threat sounded so hollow. Probably because it was. Even if she had the money to hire a lawyer, no one in town would dare go up against Judge Blackstone.

Judge.

Whether it was a noun or verb, that's how she thought of him now. Not Father, certainly not Dad. Judge. Because that's all he'd ever done. Judge her ruthlessly when she'd been unable to live up to his impossible standards.

The judge plowed a palm down the length of his face and suddenly looked weary. "That won't be necessary. You can have it."

All the fight went out of her then. She hadn't expected it to be this easy. Why was it so easy? She smelled a trap. What was she missing? Somewhere, there had to be strings attached. "You're going to give it to me? Just like that?"

"All you had to do was ask. No need for trespassing and breaking and entering."

"I am your daughter."

"It's been a long time since you acted like it." He sounded so sad that it startled her.

In that moment she could have said something, could have taken a step toward him, put her hand on his arm, changed the way of things. But she did not. She was exhausted of trying to rebuild the relationship he'd so ruthlessly torn down. Apparently, in his mind, he was the wounded party. She was tired of shouldering all the blame and leery of getting rejected again.

"I'll have a delivery truck bring it by your house in the next week or two," he said.

Caitlyn nodded stiffly. "Thank you."

He kept standing there, studying her, the four-foot gap between them as wide as Texas. Then without another word, he turned and walked away from her, just as he'd done the night he'd murdered Blaze.

Judge Richard Blackthorne sat at his desk staring out the window at the flower shop across the street. For eight years, he'd sat here and watched his only child come and go. Watched her, but been unable to span the ocean between them.

He'd been appalled when she'd run away from home and married Kevin Marsh. The man had been twelve years Caitlyn's senior and a widower. A nothing. His people less than ordinary. The only thing he'd had was the flower shop, and that had been mortgaged to the hilt. But Marsh had taken his daughter in, given her bastard a name. Many times over the years, Kevin had leaned out the door of his place of business, leveled a glare at Richard's office window, and shot him the bird.

Marsh hadn't had any class, but he'd had gumption. Richard could have slapped him with an obscenity fine over the finger, but he hadn't wanted to stir the pot. God only knew what Caitlyn had told the man.

She probably told him the truth. That you tried to force her to get rid of Danny.

Richard took off his glasses, rubbed his eyes. In retrospect, that hadn't been one of his smarter moves. Because of it, he'd paid a high price. Lost his daughter and the chance to know his grandchild. But he wasn't going to admit that he was wrong. She was the one who'd made the huge mistake. Getting pregnant at seventeen by that scummy Gideon Garza.

Ultimately, he blamed that cursed carousel.

He should have torched the damn thing a long time ago. Why had he kept it all these years, stuck in the barn in his backyard? Rusting in the dark like some dirty secret.

It was a good question and he didn't have an easy answer. He'd tried chopping it up, decapitating Angelica's favorite horse in a fit of rage. He would have kept chopping if Caitlyn hadn't screamed and shattered through his anger and grief.

Rationally, he'd understood that the silent aneurysm lurking in Angelica's brain had burst. That the carousel hadn't killed her. But when the doctor said the centrifugal force of the spinning merry-go-round might have precipitated her death, Richard had lost all power of reason.

His beautiful young wife had inherited not only

the carousel from her prominent, affluent family, but also the propensity for brain aneurysms. It was what had killed both her great-great-grandmother Rebekka Nash Grant and Angelica's father. He couldn't lash out at those ghosts, so he'd taken his revenge on the one thing that symbolized his wife's ancestry.

The carousel.

He hadn't stopped to think that it was Caitlyn's heritage as well, but after Angelica's death, he'd been diligent about keeping his daughter healthy. He paid for an annual CAT scan and MRI for her out of his own pocket because insurance wouldn't cover it. He'd kept her safe. Guarded her with every resource at his disposal.

He'd been tough on her, yes, but it had been for her own good. He couldn't believe she'd blamed him for everything. It hurt that she didn't understand how he'd been operating from a place of love, wanting only the best for her. Yes, he was strict. Yes, he put discipline ahead of hugs. But a child needed to learn right from wrong.

If he gave in, loosened his principles, what would that say? In essence, he would be condoning her choices, and he simply could not do that. You followed the rules. That's how the game was played. That's what he was all about.

Except a small part of him whispered, *Where has following the rules gotten you? Estranged from your daughter, no relationship with your only grandchild. Lonely and alone rambling around in that big house. You followed the rules, kept up your principles, and you still lost the love of your life. Your code of honor hasn't saved you.*

If he dared to admit it, he often felt humiliated that he'd swallowed the letter of the law, hook, line, and sinker, and taken such an unbending stance. He had believed in the false promise that a just God would reward his adherence to the rules.

Richard reached for the glass of water on his desk, hoping to wash away the taste of resentment, bitterness, and regret. He was mad at the world and even madder at himself, because deep inside his core, he feared he'd somehow sold out his daughter, and for a very poor price.

CHAPTER THREE

*Traditional meaning of begonia—
beware, I am fanciful.*

Two weeks after Lester LaVon's surprise visit, Gideon ambled into the relief aid camp on the Pakistan border. He'd gotten the orphans to their relatives in the mountains and he was ready for some R&R. Which basically constituted hanging out with Moira for a few days. Of course, that meant she'd put him to work.

He grinned. She always put him to work, but he didn't mind. Work kept him from dwelling too much on the past. Left alone for too long, he had a tendency to hide inside his own head, and brooding took him to dark places he didn't need to travel.

Gideon found Moira in one of the medical huts, bandaging the stump of a child who appeared to have lost his leg to a land mine. Tears of pain and loss welled in the young boy's eyes. Involuntarily, Gideon ran his right hand over his left arm where it was joined to the cyborg-esque, military-funded bionic myoelectric hand. His own stump throbbed in empathy.

Inwardly, he was annoyed with himself for the vulnerability. The kid didn't need anyone's pity. Neither did Gideon.

He'd lost the arm a few inches below the elbow two and a half years ago, and he was used to the phantom pains. Pain he could handle. It was the limitations that got to him. He'd been left-handed, after all, and he'd never stopped feeling at a disadvantage even with his state-of-the-art prosthesis.

Moira glanced up, met his gaze. The minute he looked into her face, he knew something had changed. Her usually calm blue eyes were stormy; her bright smile taut and faded.

"Gideon," she said softly in her melodically harsh Scouse dialect that revealed her distinctive Liverpudlian roots. "I'll meet ya in my hut straightaway."

He scowled. Something was definitely different. Under normal circumstances, she would have invited him to give the boy a pep talk, do a little show-and-tell with his mechanical hand.

She made a shooing motion. "Be off, big man."

For a long moment, he simply stood there wondering what was going on. His relationship with Moira was casual. They'd both wanted it that way. But even so, he couldn't suppress the concern stomping around inside him. Was she going to break things off with him? Finally, not knowing what else to do, he turned and shambled away.

Once inside her domicile, he sank down on the end of the narrow bed with the cheap mattress that was too small for his big frame, and scanned the sparse space. Not many personal effects in here. Toiletries on the small bureau made of stout cardboard. A few snapshots of the kids she'd helped, displayed on a makeshift desk of plywood and cinder blocks; a notebook computer plugged into the precarious wiring system. Beside the computer and pictures sat a potted plant of red begonias. He recognized the plant because they'd once grown in profusion in his mother's front yard. When he was a kid he'd thought they were called Be Gone You.

Did Moira have another admirer?

He didn't feel jealous. They weren't exclusive. They both knew their relationship wasn't headed anywhere. It was what it was—comfort, solace, the commingling of two lonely strangers in a strange land. But he *was* curious.

A few minutes later, Moira stepped into the hut.

His desire, fueled by the thought that another man wanted her, sent Gideon to his feet. He pulled her into his arms, cupped her butt with his right palm, and planted a kiss on her lips.

But she didn't melt into him as she usually did. Instead, she ducked her head and turned away. Yet she took his right hand, interlaced her slender fingers with his thick ones, and led him back to the bed.

"Sit," she murmured.

He obeyed. She stepped between his knees, cradled his chin in her palm, and tilted his face up to meet her gaze.

The hairs on the back of his neck lifted. Something wasn't right.

"How are the nightmares?"

"Okay," he mumbled.

"Don't lie to me, Gid."

"I'm not. They're down to once or twice a week."

Moira sighed. Her eyes softened at the same time her mouth tightened into a straight-across slit. Her expression made him feel suddenly bleak.

"What is it?" he asked.

"I'm afraid I have bad news."

Here it comes. She was giving him the heave. He forced a smile. She was a good woman—warmhearted, altruistic, kind. He didn't want her to feel badly about dumping him. He'd known it would happen eventually.

"Whatever you have to tell me, it's okay." He reached up to run his palm over her shoulder.

She looked at him with such pity that his gut kicked.

"Just say it," he said. "I'm a rip-the-Band-Aid-off kinda guy. Not a fan of the slow pull. End the torture with one clean, sharp yank."

"I know, but some news should be broken gently."

A sudden thought occurred to him and he gulped. "You're not . . . are you . . . pregnant?"

How could she be pregnant? They'd been very careful. She took the pill, he always wore condoms.

She laughed. "No, Gideon, I'm not pregnant."

"What is it then?"

"It's about your father." She paused. Wet her lips. Gentled her voice to a whisper. "I'm afraid he passed on to the other side."

It wasn't what he'd expected her to say. He just sat there, not processing. "Passed onto the other side?"

"A call for you came in from some lawyer named LaVon. He didn't know how else to reach ya and hoped we could get the word out."

Gideon hauled in a deep breath. So it really was true.

She lowered herself to her knees, her shoulders between his thighs, and met him face-to-face. Her eyes darkened with concern. "Gid? Are ya all right?"

He didn't answer. He didn't know what to say.

Moira wrapped her arms around his waist, rested her head on his chest, and squeezed him tightly. "I'm so, so sorry."

His throat burned and his muscles hardened to stone. Her words held no meaning. It was as if she was speaking in a foreign tongue he had not perfected.

"I know it's shockin'," she cooed, walking her hands up to the back of his neck. She rested her forehead against his and gazed into his eyes. "I remember how awful it was when I heard my da had died. I fell to my knees sobbing. Ya don't have to hold it in, Gid. I'm here. You're safe." She hugged him tighter. He could smell her familiar earthy scent.

Gideon said nothing.

"Did ya hear what I said?" she whispered after a long silence.

"I heard you."

"He died of pancreatic cancer in the wee hours of the mornin'. His funeral is on Saturday. That'll just give ya time to get back to the States."

J. Foster Goodnight, the man who sired him and tossed him aside, the man he'd resented his entire life, was dead, and yet Gideon felt . . . *absolutely nothing.*

Gently, he untangled Moira's arms from around his neck, slipped from her embrace, set her aside, got to his feet. "Thanks for telling me, but I'm not going to his funeral."

In the silence of the small hut, Moira's sharp intake of breath echoed loudly. "Ya don't mean that."

"I do."

"Trust me on this, no matter what your relationship with your da was, ya need closure."

"No, I don't."

"I've never asked ya any questions about the past and I've respected those boundaries because I don't want to speak of mine," Moira said. "But would ya care to say what you're feeling?"

Empty. That's all he felt. Empty and hollow. The old anger was gone. So was the regret. In its place, nothing. The nothingness of it made him feel not there. And that caused him to feel very far away from Moira and her sympathetic eyes.

He reached his hand to the button of her shirt. "I'd rather just make love to you."

Moira wrapped her hand around his. "You tell me something about yourself and I'll let you have a button."

Her skin was so soft, so warm. He'd been sleeping alone on the ground for many weeks. "You drive a hard bargain, Moira Simon."

"Your father?"

"He never acknowledged he was my father. There's no reason to mourn him."

She let him undo the top button. "That sounds like reason enough to me. Look at what he missed out on. Getting to know a wonderful man like you."

He ignored the compliment and went for the second button.

"Ach, no. Secret first."

"My father was already married when he got my mother pregnant," he said, not wanting to talk about any of this, but hungry to press his lips against Moira's heated flesh. "She worked as a maid in his house. Give me another button."

She held her fist closed over the second button. "Your da was rich?"

"The wealthiest man in my hometown. Meanwhile I grew up in poverty."

"Poor pet." She let him have the second button.

He could see her cleavage. Sweet peaches. He focused on those enticing breasts. Who cared about J. Foster?

"That must've been so hard on ya."

Gideon shrugged. "I didn't learn he was my father until after my mother died when I was nineteen." He went for the third button.

Moira clucked her tongue. "Not yet."

"I really don't want to talk about this."

She buttoned the second button back up. The woman couldn't be derailed.

"Okay, okay."

Slanting him a sly smile, she undid the button again. He could feel her warm breath on his skin, he tried to kiss her but she shook her head. "A deal's a deal."

"I don't know why you want to know this."

"It's not for me. It's for you. Don't keep things bottled up. Let it out."

"If I tell you the whole sordid story at once, can we go to bed?"

"I'm listening."

"I confronted him. He denied he was my father. In the way of a stupid punk kid grieving his dead mother, I lashed out, wanting to make him pay, and I set his barn on fire." Gideon balled up his fist, the dark memory poking him.

For better or worse, his life to date was a consequence of those youthful knee-jerk reactions. He wondered if all people felt this disappointed with themselves, the things they'd done, the irrevocable paths they'd chosen. The minute he'd lit that match, set it to the gasoline, he'd realized he'd forever lost the chance to right himself. That he could spend his whole lifetime trying and never be the man he wanted to be—a man good enough for Caitlyn Blackthorne.

Caitlyn.

The thought of her blew over him like an Arctic breeze.

The man he wanted to be would not have confronted Goodnight in the first place. He would have taken the high road, honored his mother's memory by letting the past be past. Been noble instead of angry. Been smart instead of driven by vengeance.

Gideon felt like a fraud. In the army, he'd been a Green Beret, held up as the best of the best, and yet he was a lowly bastard, not good enough for the likes of Judge Blackthorne's daughter. He thought he'd moved beyond it all. Forgotten about the unfortunate circumstances of his birth. He thought he'd let go of Twilight and tucked Caitlyn into the far reaches of his mind.

"What happened?" Moira whispered.

Now that he was telling the tale, he couldn't seem to stop. "I was arrested, brought up before the judge, who was, surprise, surprise, a golfing buddy of my father's." Gideon ran his palm down his face.

"Your hometown is very small?"

"Population six thousand." The moment was branded into his brain. Him, with his court-appointed lawyer, standing in front of Judge Blackthorne's bench. "I was given a choice. Join the military or go to jail for arson."

"So ya joined the army."

He smiled without mirth, held out his mechanical arm. "And sealed my fate."

"And you've never seen or talked to your da since?"

He shook his head, and then told her about his visit from Lester LaVon.

"Maybe your da left ya some money. Maybe in his old age he felt badly about what he did to ya and he wanted to make amends."

"Too little, too late."

A disappointed expression carved a wrinkle in her brow. "That's not like ya."

"What?" The woman had no idea what he was really like. They were just bed buddies.

"The bitterness."

"You don't know me well enough to make that assessment."

"Go ahead, lash out, I can take it." She was rubbing his shoulder, trying to knead out the tension.

"You don't owe me your understanding."

"There's something more, isn't there?" Moira challenged. "Another reason you're not going back to Twilight. I mean your da is dead, after all. He can't do anything more to ya now."

"Let's change the subject." He didn't want to think about Caitlyn, much less talk about her. He leaned down to kiss Moira. "I came here to see you." He reached for the last buttons on her shirt.

Moira held her palms up. "I won't be taking advantage of a vulnerable man."

"You're kidding."

Solemnly, she shook her head. "You've held it in too long. Who is she and what did she do to muck ya up so badly?"

The air left his lungs like a thief in the night, sneaking out in a tiptoe swirl, leaving him sucker-punched and breathless. "Who said there's a she?"

Moira leveled him a knowing glance filled with feminine intuition. "What was her name?"

He sank back on the bed again, all the energy drained from his body. "Caitlyn," he whispered, realizing it had been years since he'd said her name out loud.

Saying it was like scrubbing salt across a wound once thought healed, only to discover the flesh was still freshly flayed. Hell, they'd been together for only a few months. He should have forgotten all about Caitlyn. But he hadn't.

He'd seen terrible atrocities in battle. As a warrior, he'd done some dark things himself. But even the moment when his hand had been blown from his arm was not as clearly vivid as when the letters he'd written her, telling her how much he loved her, had all come back unopened and marked "Return to Sender." Until he'd finally wised up and stopped sending them. That was when he realized he was on his own. That she'd washed her hands of him.

"You loved her very much."

"Yeah," he admitted. "Once."

"Have you tried to contact her? Reconnect?"

"Hell, no."

Moira shook her head. "Stubborn man."

"I don't grovel. If a woman doesn't want to be with me, I'm not going to chase after her like a lapdog hungry for affection." He clenched his jaw.

"You love her still."

He shook his head. "No, I don't."

"Maybe not," Moira said, "but still she has a hold on ya. You're never going to loosen that grip until you face her again."

He shrugged, but in his heart, he knew Moira was right.

* * *

Over two weeks had passed since Caitlyn's father had promised to have the carousel delivered to her house. She'd accepted the job of designing and overseeing the victory garden. The contest entry paperwork had been filled out and sent in. Supplies and seeds had been ordered, but still no carousel.

Like it or not, she was going to have to confront her father again, and she'd been stewing all morning over the best way to go about it.

Caitlyn was in the back of the shop snipping stems off some roses when she heard the bell over the door tinkle. She set down the flowers, smoothed her damp hands over her smock, and stepped to the front of the building.

Crockett Goodnight was standing there looking like he'd been kicked in the teeth. His hair was disheveled, his face was the color of cookie dough, a day's growth of beard ringed his jaw. His shirt was untucked and wrinkled, his stare vacant.

"Crockett?" She walked toward him. "What's wrong?"

The expression in his eyes broke her heart. "My . . . my dad just died."

"Oh," she said, and put a supportive arm around his shoulders. He wobbled on his feet. She might have hated J. Foster Goodnight's guts, but a death in the family was a death in the family. "Here, sit down."

Caitlyn took Crockett's arm and guided him to a wrought-iron patio chair. "How are you holding up?"

"I'm good, I'm okay." He nodded, shoved his fingers through his disheveled hair. "I'm a mess."

"You can talk to me."

"Can I, Caitlyn? Can I really?"

Did she truly want this intimacy with him? They'd been dancing around a flirtation for weeks, Crockett was funny and handsome and he knew how to have a good time. He was exciting to be around, but there was something about him—and not just the fact that he was J. Foster's son and Gideon's half brother—that held her back. He was too fun-loving, too exciting, too handsome. And then there were those rare dark moods when he'd come over to her shop, full of doom and gloom and despair, talking about what an awful place the world was. It didn't happen often. Just a few times in all the years she'd known him, but it did make her wonder.

She should step back, murmur words of sympathy, and send him on his way. Instead, she said, "I'm listening."

"I wasn't there when he died." Crockett fisted his hands against his knees. "I was out drinking with my buddies. I should have been there, but I wasn't there."

"You couldn't have known." She stood beside him, placed a hand on his shoulder, and felt odd about it.

"I did know. The nurses told us not to leave. Bowie stayed. But I . . . I couldn't deal with it, Caitlyn. You know what I mean? It was just too much." He leaned into her, his head resting against her breasts. He wrapped an arm around her waist, and a soft sob escaped his lips.

Caitlyn stiffened, uncomfortable with the familiarity, but not knowing how to extricate herself. She'd invited him to talk. She was stuck with the consequences.

"I'm a terrible son."

"You're not a terrible son," she felt obligated to say. She didn't know. Maybe he had been a terrible son. Then again, from what she'd seen, J. Foster had been a terrible father.

"I want you to handle the flowers for the funeral. We want lots of flowers. Red, white, and blue. My dad fought for his country. He deserves a military sendoff. And begonias. Can you plant red begonias in his honor in that victory garden you're planning? My daddy loved red begonias."

Red begonias? Why not? They were attractive, hardy plants strong enough to endure the sweltering Texas summers. Considering, that was, there would be a victory garden. Through the plate-glass window, she cast a quick glance at the courthouse.

"Sure, sure," she said. "I can do that."

"You're very special, Caitlyn," Crockett murmured. Somehow his hand had migrated from her waist to her rump. "Very, very special."

She shook her head, shook off the compliment. Not because she didn't like it, but because she did. She wasn't giving in to Crockett's smooth flattery. Even if he wasn't Gideon's half brother, there were a hundred other reasons not to get involved with him—his reputation, for one thing, and the fact that Danny adored him, for another. If she got involved with him and it didn't work out, her son would be devastated.

His thumb was kneading the small of her back. She reached around to grab his wrist. "Crockett, please," she protested.

But she got no further. The next thing she knew, he had tugged her into his lap and he was gazing into her eyes.

"Crock—"

His mouth cut off her words.

As kisses went, it wasn't bad. Nothing like the wild, passionate kisses she'd shared with Gideon, but far superior to Kevin's gentle pecks. Firm, moist, teasing. He tasted like whiskey and that was a turn-off, but his father had just died. Tossing back a shot or two, even in the early morning, wasn't that shocking.

What did shock Caitlyn was that for a fraction of a second she simply gave in to the pleasure. To the warmth and comfort of human connection.

Get up!

She struggled to get off his lap at the same time he tried to deepen the kiss, parting his mouth, letting his tongue trace over her lips. His arm tightened around her waist, pressing her into his lap, and she could feel the unmistakable bulge of his erection.

Okay, she'd heard that grief could manifest in a lifeward drive, but he'd just crossed the line. They were in her shop, for heaven's sake, in broad daylight, and even if they weren't, she didn't want this.

She pushed her palm against his chest and turned her head, wrenching her lips from his.

At that same moment, the bell over the door tinkled.

"What the hell!" a man exclaimed.

The next thing she knew, someone had Crockett by the scruff of the neck, yanking him up and spilling Caitlyn from his lap. Her butt hit the floor, but she sprang to her feet, twisting her head around to see what was happening.

"What are you doing?" Bowie Goodnight roared. While blond, fine-boned Crockett had taken after his mother's side of the family, Bowie was dark-haired and rough-hewn like J. Foster—hulking shoulders, hawkish nose, eyes black as pitch. He had a good four inches of height on his brother. He held the back of Crockett's collar fisted in his hand, and looked like he wanted to kill him. "Our father hasn't been dead six hours and you're kissing some slut."

"Caitlyn's not a slut!" Crockett's nostrils flared. Arms windmilling, fists knotted, he swung at Bowie, but his blows fell on empty air.

Bowie shook him like a vicious dog shaking a dead cat. His eyes held a scary, empty expression, as if he'd lost all power of reason. Mental illness ran in their family. Their mother had been confined in a top-notch mental health facility for years. Some claimed that J. Foster had driven her there with his drinking and whoring and gambling. But the official word was that Charlotte Goodnight had a severe bipolar disorder poorly controlled by medication.

Hand to her throat, Caitlyn stepped behind the counter.

"Take it back!" Crockett demanded, kicking and flailing.

"You're a male whore," Bowie said. "Just like Dad. Going from slut to slut."

"I'm not like Dad," the younger Goodnight howled. "I'm nothing like him."

Caitlyn had grown up an only child in a quiet household. Kevin had been a soft-spoken man. Danny was an only child. She had no experience with sibling rivalry, but she could tell this fight had nothing to do with her and everything to do with age-old conflicts between these two brothers.

Crockett let out a string of vile curse words and connected a fist to Bowie's jaw.

The fight was on.

They grabbed each other around the throats and went down on the ground, knocking over flower stands, smashing planter boxes, breaking clay pots. They were grunting and slinging accusations.

"You gutless coward, you couldn't even stand by his bedside while he took his last breath," Bowie howled in the midst of the punching.

"Why should I stand by him?" Crockett gasped. "He was never there for me. Never came to a single Little League game. Didn't even congratulate me when I took Twilight High to State."

"So you can swing a bat." Bowie punched. "Big effing deal. What do you want? A freakin' medal? You never took any interest in the ranch."

"How could I?" Crockett gouged. "You had your nose three feet up his ass."

"He loved you best." Bowie delivered a punishing smack to Crockett's temple. "I could never measure up to perfect little Crockett."

"Are you insane? He was always telling me to be more like you." Crockett sank his teeth into his brother's wrist.

Bowie howled and kicked Crockett halfway across the room. A rubber tree plant imploded upon contact.

"Stop it!" Caitlyn commanded. "Stop it right now!"

Completely focused on each other and the rage they'd been holding on to for decades, they ignored her.

They grunted and hit. Groaned and jabbed.

"Fine. I'm calling the sheriff and letting him sort you two out." Caitlyn went for the phone, called Hondo Crouch's office, and then quickly told the dispatcher what was happening.

"I'll send him right over," the dispatcher said.

Caitlyn hung up, spun back to the altercation. Part of her just wanted to slip out the back door and let the two of them have at each other, but this was her shop and she was standing her ground. "Hondo's on his way over," she warned, but she might as well have been whistling the "Star Spangled Banner" for all the notice they took of her.

"Dad was a total asshole," Crockett yowled as Bowie methodically punched him in the eye.

"A complete prick," Bowie agreed, and then let out an *ooph* as Crockett belted him in the stomach.

"He cheated on Mom with that Mexican whore." Crockett spit out a stream of blood.

That statement caused Caitlyn's stomach to clench. They were talking about Gideon's mother, Linda Garza. Caitlyn did not want to hear this. Both Gideon and Linda were long dead, but they were talking about Danny's grandmother.

"He used to whip us for being too loud." Bowie had Crockett in a chokehold.

But just when she thought the older brother had bested the younger, from seemingly out of nowhere, a switchblade knife flashed in Crockett's hand. A metallic snapping sound slit the air as the blade sprang from the hilt.

Crockett laid the blade against his brother's throat.

Caitlyn gasped.

Sheriff Hondo Crouch came barreling through the door like John Wayne, hand resting on the butt of the duty weapon holstered at his hip.

"Stop it right there, you fools."

Bowie released his brother. Crockett pushed a button and the blade disappeared into the handle of the knife. They rolled over, sat in the middle of the floor huffing and puffing and bleeding while Hondo confiscated the switchblade.

Her shop was in shambles. Bodies of plants and flowers lay sprawled in spilled dirt and shattered pot fragments. Twisted roots stuck out at odd angles.

Petals lay crushed. Leaves scattered. Her precious foliage was naked and damaged.

"My flowers," she whispered, and sank down in the wrought-iron chair.

Bowie and Crockett exchanged sheepish glances. Hondo cleared his throat. He held out a hand, helped first Crockett, and then Bowie to his feet. "I know you boys just lost your daddy, but there's no excuse for this. Unless you want to go to jail, here's what's going to happen. You are going to clean this place up and then you're going to pay Mrs. Marsh for damages." He shifted his gaze to Caitlyn.

Glowering, Bowie pulled a wad of one-hundred-dollar bills from his pocket and peeled off several. Caitlyn stared in surprise. Who walked around with that much cash tucked into his pocket?

"Mrs. Marsh," Hondo said, "why don't you take an early lunch? I'm gonna sit right here and supervise the cleanup."

Not knowing what else to do, Caitlyn nodded, tucked the money into her purse, and headed out the door for the bank. Her hands were shaking and her breath came in shallow gasps, and although she couldn't articulate what she was feeling, she couldn't help thinking that with J. Foster's death, big changes were in store for Twilight.

CHAPTER FOUR

Traditional meaning of white lilac—
my first dream of love.

Riding the motorcycle—which had been in a storage pod at DFW airport for eight years—down Highway 51 on that Saturday morning in early March, Gideon drove through the low fog squatting over the Brazos River Bridge that joined Parker County to Hood. In an instant, he was enveloped in a gray mist so thick he couldn't see more than a foot ahead of him. Moisture clouds swirled into his lungs along with the scent of the river.

For a moment, he could not breathe, suffocated by the past behind him and the uncertain future stretching ahead. For that whisper of a second, he was suspended in frosty animation, the water vapor weighting him down, holding him trapped. Then just as quickly as he was doused, the clouds vanished and he broke through to the other side.

And there it was before him. The town he'd fought so hard to forget.

A canopy of pecan trees formed a tunnel, ushering him past the "Welcome to Twilight, Friendliest Hometown in Texas" billboard. He guided his Indian Chief over the train tracks past the old train depot restored to its former 1870s glory. The depot now housed the Twilight Visitors Bureau. A mile beyond that lay the town square.

The entire town square, which had been listed on the National Register in the 1970s, was a portal into Texas history. All the buildings were the original limestone structures that had been lovingly restored and turned into shops and restaurants catering to the tourist trade. He could almost see cowboys tying their horses to hitching posts, or gunslingers drawing off on each other in the middle of the street.

On the other side of the square sat Sweetheart Park, so christened in honor of the town founders, Jon Grant and Rebekka Nash. Caitlyn's ancestors. In the center of the park was a fountain statue of two lovers embracing. A tributary of the Brazos ran through the park, dotted with wooden footbridges, lush gardens, and a big white gazebo.

The town made happily-ever-after promises it couldn't keep. It was rife with true-love legends. Throw a penny into the town fountain and you'd be reunited with your high school sweetheart. Carve your name into the Sweetheart Tree and you'll be together forever. For one stupid moment, he considered stopping and tossing a coin into the fountain, but he'd never been whimsical or superstitious and he wasn't about to start now.

Gideon was surprised to note that the place hadn't changed much in eight years. The only obvious alteration was that the old Twilight Theatre was gone. A vacant lot, gaping like a missing tooth, stretched out between an insurance office on one side and a hair salon on the other.

Most of the establishments were still the same. The Funny Farm restaurant, Rinky-Tink's Old-Fashioned Ice Cream Parlor, Marsh's Flower Shop, Ye Olde Book Nook. He drove on past the square, took the road that led to Shady Rest Funeral Home, and saw posted on the marquee that his father's funeral was scheduled for eleven A.M.

He felt nothing. Until he reached his ultimate destination.

The Twilight Cemetery.

His mother's grave was overgrown with weeds. It saddened Gideon to realize Linda Garza's death had been just as lacking as her life. He ran his fingers over his mother's tombstone etched with the dates of her birth and her death and the simple words: *Loving Mother to Gideon.*

"I'm sorry, Mom," he muttered, grabbed a handful of weeds, and started pulling.

He'd dressed all in black leather, his motorcycle helmet on the ground beside him. He'd come back after all, drawn by shame and regret and sorrow. So much damn sorrow.

And J. Foster Goodnight was the cause of most of it.

Anger seethed inside him. Moira had been wrong. He would find no closure here. Only more questions waited for him here. He grabbed another fistful of weeds and yanked.

Gideon thought of the day he'd discovered who his real father was. At the time, it had been the worst day of his life. It still ranked up there in the top three. His mother had died in his arms, a victim of liver failure. A consequence of the hepatitis C she'd contracted. As she drew her last breath, she'd whispered J. Foster's name.

It was the last thing she ever said to him.

His mother might not have walked the straight and narrow. She had made a lot of mistakes in her life, but she'd been a damn good mother. She'd been kind and patient and understanding. She'd never raised her voice. Yes, she'd run with the wrong crowd. She'd drunk too much, perhaps done other things she shouldn't have done, but she'd never neglected him. He'd always come first.

Then when he was going through her things, getting ready for the funeral, he'd found that letter. She'd written it years before, sealed it in an envelope, left it in the lockbox tucked under the foot of her bed. The letter had been short and succinct. She'd told him how much she loved him. Praised him for being a good son. And then she'd dropped the bomb that forever altered the course of his life. She'd confessed that when she worked at the Goodnight ranch, she'd had a torrid affair with J. Foster, and Gideon was the result of that encounter.

He could still recall the cold chill that had fallen over him. The denial. Then the rush of hope. In utter foolishness born of naïveté and longing, he'd hopped on his motorcycle and driven to the Goodnight ranch. He hadn't expected to be welcomed unconditionally. He wasn't that dumb. But, armed with the letter, he had at least expected J. Foster to admit who he was and do right by him. Maybe pay some of the child support money he'd never paid.

Instead, J. Foster had called his mother horrible names, among them a liar. Gideon had said he was going to get a lawyer and demand a paternity test. J. Foster's eyes had narrowed and he'd slapped Gideon across the face. Gideon had doubled up his fists, ready to fight back, but J. Foster's legitimate sons, Bowie and Crockett, had been there to mete out a beating and throw him from the house.

Battered and bruised, he refused to take no for an answer. He'd gone back. They'd beaten him again.

Barely able to stand, he'd gone back a third time with the same results.

At this point it was no longer about getting recognition from J. Foster. Clearly, the man was an asshole of the highest order. Rather, it was about avenging his mother. She'd been in love with J. Foster. Or so she'd told him in the letter. Although Gideon couldn't imagine how that was possible. Who could love such a coldhearted prick?

He'd waited until dark the next day, then he'd

sneaked onto the ranch. Initially, he hadn't planned to burn down the barn. His intention was merely to keep coming at J. Foster until the man admitted who he was and what he'd done, but somewhere along the way, he'd realized that was not going to happen.

Vengeance had taken complete control of him, and the next thing he knew, he'd released all the horses and was torching the barn. He watched it burn from the shadows. Watched Bowie and Crockett and J. Foster and their ranch hands work frantically to put it out. Watched while the volunteer fire department joined the fray. Then he'd hobbled back to town, drunk an entire bottle of whiskey by himself, and passed out in his bed.

He was awakened later by the sounds of then Sheriff Clinton Trainer knocking on his door.

That had been the beginning of the end for him and Caitlyn.

Gideon bit back the ugly memories. He'd never once thought his grief over losing his mother would end up costing him the love of his life. But it had.

The memory of the second worst day of his life flitted around him.

It was burned into his mind, the way Caitlyn had looked the last time he'd seen her. Standing in the moonlight in Sweetheart Park where they'd rendezvoused, wearing a thin cotton summer dress that showed off every inch of her sexy seventeen-year-old body. Her blond hair, which was normally pulled back into a perky ponytail, hung loose down her shoulders, her pert breasts rising high with each breath she took, her creamy skin gleaming.

God, she'd once meant so much to him. Beautiful, poised, calm on the surface, but underneath she was a deeply passionate woman. He'd been crazy in lust for her, but what he'd felt went much deeper than the hot, physical yearnings of youth. He'd been stone-cold in love.

What did she look like now? Was she still just as beautiful? Still just as reserved, with that fiery inner spark she let very few people see?

He glanced at his watch. A quarter to eleven. He straightened, rose to his feet. His mother was buried in the lowland part of the cemetery, next to the highway, where they interred the people who could not afford the good lots on the hill overlooking the Brazos River.

Willow trees hid the graves from the road, but he could see the cars starting the procession up the winding hillside. He swallowed, tasted the bitterness of loss and hatred. He'd hated J. Foster for so long, it felt odd to lose it now.

He studied the cars as they passed. Cadillacs and Lincolns in the lead. Then came a florist van, a ponytailed woman behind the wheel.

Something struck his heart, made him take a second look.

Caitlyn?

But the van had already passed out of sight. Surely, it wasn't Caitlyn. He must be seeing things. What would she be doing driving a florist's van?

Curiosity had him by the short hairs, but he would bide his time. The military had given him the gift of patience he'd sorely lacked. Soon enough, he would arrive on that hill, in a staged entrance, and all hell would break loose.

Car after car passed. It looked like the entire community of six thousand was motoring up the hillside. When they buried the wealthiest man in town, it attracted folks, whether they mourned the deceased or not. Everyone secretly hoping he or she would be mentioned in the will. Gideon had no illusions on that score. Anyway, he didn't want anything J. Foster had to offer. He was here to make sure the old man was dead, and that was it.

And to see Caitlyn.

It wasn't something he outwardly acknowledged, but damn him, yeah, he hungered for a look at the woman who'd broken his heart.

A moment later, the hearse came into view. Black, sleek, and moving slowly, and followed by a white limousine. Gideon's muscles tensed. His gut soured. His father's last ride.

How many times had he wished things had been different? That J. Foster had been the kind of father who would welcome him into the fold. But the world didn't work that way. Gideon had discovered that acts of kindness were usually self-motivated. He didn't deceive himself about human nature. People, by and large, were a worthless lot.

What remained of his left arm throbbed from the riding he'd done. He could have taken off the mechanical arm, but he didn't want the town to see him as half a man. Not today, anyway. Today was his coup de grâce. He wanted to look like the frickin' Terminator.

He waited until the last of the cars had trickled past, and then he swung onto his motorcycle and started up the hill, anticipation surging his blood.

The engine vibrated with a steady sound, carrying him closer and closer to his destiny. By the time he reached the top of the hill, a bugler was blowing "Taps." The limo and hearse were parked in the middle of the circular drive at the stone pavilion.

People dressed mostly in black sat on the stone pews or ringed the outside perimeter. The Patriot Guard stood at attention, flags flying. Looking at the guard tugged at him. Even here, under these circumstances, he was military through and through. Never mind that army had discharged him after he'd lost his arm. The military was the only thing that had saved him from certain ruin. On that score, Judge Blackthorne had been right.

You look pretty damn ruined to me. Blown-off arm. Bad attitude. Where's the redemption in that? The voice in his head sounded exactly like J. Foster. Cruel, taunting.

He shoved the voice aside, parked the motorcycle behind the hearse. He saw heads turn as he got off the Indian and then sauntered down the aisle toward the flag-draped coffin.

Gideon wasn't sure what he expected to feel. Triumph? Spite? Rejoicing, perhaps? But he did not feel any of those things. He stood numb, detached, barely involved in his surroundings.

Murmurs ran through the crowd.

He stopped, turned, and then he saw her standing between a stone column and the coffin, off to the side of the general gathering, not far from where the funeral home director stood.

Caitlyn.

He was hyperaware of her. As attuned to this woman as if he'd just been told that memorizing everything about her was a top secret mission. She glanced up, turned his way. Their eyes met, and his knees went to water.

Caitlyn.

Thinner, but compelling as always. She wasn't the most beautiful woman he'd ever seen, but she was the most captivating. Once his eyes lighted upon her, it was impossible to peel them off. Her pride was in her regal bearing, the stubborn set to her chin. Her soft blond hair was caught back in an elegant clip. A black skirt fell to the curve of her shapely knee. A light dusting of makeup brightened her cheeks.

He felt simultaneously aroused, self-conscious, and . . . *staggered*.

The old magic was still there. Still there? Hell, it was stronger than ever. How was that possible?

Her hands were clenched and he saw the column of her throat move as she swallowed. Gulped? What was she feeling?

He had an overwhelming urge to touch her. Gideon stripped off his helmet and stared into the face of the woman he'd loved since he was nineteen years old, and he felt the earth crumble beneath his feet.

Even though he'd told himself a million times he was over her, he didn't expect this. If he'd taken bets on his emotions under such circumstances, he would have expected a little anger, some resentment, maybe a pinch of sarcasm—irked, peeved, jaded, wronged. Yeah, any or all of those things.

But what he hadn't anticipated was the potent rush of homesickness, immediately followed by a strong wallop of stupid, irrational joy. One look in her startled blue-green eyes, and he was intoxicated as surely as if he'd downed an entire bottle of rich, red Cabernet.

Caitlyn.

The woman who haunted his desert dreams.

He gazed at her sweet, strawberry-hued lips and wanted so badly to crush his rough mouth against hers that he could barely breathe. Even after eight years, he still remembered the flavor of her—fresh, innocent, loving. She'd once tasted like salvation, offered promises of redemption to a bad boy from the wrong side of town. Through three tours of duty in the Middle East, he'd hungered to sup from those lips again, but he'd never believed it could happen.

Still couldn't.

"You . . . it's not . . . possible . . ." Her face blanched pale of all color and she looked utterly terrified.

Her abject terror was a knife to his gut. He must look as horrific as he suspected. Could she somehow tell about his arm, even though he wore the prosthesis, gloves, and a long-sleeved leather jacket? Torment wrung him out. He should have followed his instincts. He should not have come back.

"You . . . you . . ." Caitlyn stammered.

"Caitlyn," he murmured.

"No." She raised her hands warding him off. "It can't be true." Then her knees gave way, her eyes rolled back, her body went limp, and she pitched forward.

Just before she hit the ground, Gideon caught her with his good arm and held her tightly to his chest. He could feel the erratic beating of her heart, and he feared that when she'd looked him in the eyes, she'd seen that his soul was black as soot.

Caitlyn heard the sound of murmured voices and realized she was lying on something cold and hard. The overwhelming smell of flowers washed through her nostrils—the soft, perfect scent of roses, mingled with the whisper of baby's breath and the bold perfume of stargazer lilies. But underneath it all, she smelled white lilacs.

White lilacs. The flowers Gideon had brought her for their first date.

Her mind felt fuzzy, foggy. She frowned, tried to think, and then it all came rushing back.

Gideon.

She'd seen Gideon standing before her dressed in leather, motorcycle helmet tucked under his arm. But it couldn't be Gideon. Her eyes must have been playing tricks on her. Gideon had been dead for eight years.

"Caitlyn?"

The voice calling to her sounded so familiar even though she hadn't heard it in a very long time. Was she dreaming? Hallucinating? What was happening to her?

Slowly, she pried her eyes open, blinking against the brightness of the sun. Her head was cradled against someone, but her gaze wouldn't focus.

"Caitlyn, are you all right?"

Noises. People talking excitedly in hushed whispers.

She shook her head. Her vision cleared, and she saw him all over again, peering down into her face. Her head was in his lap.

Gideon!

Eight years fell away. Her heart caught fire. Her stomach churned. Head reeled. How was this possible? Gideon was alive and cradling her in his lap.

Unless . . . unless . . . unless she'd just died of a brain aneurysm at J. Foster's funeral. Was she dead? Was that what had happened? Had she been felled by the condition that plagued her family history? Was she dead and in heaven with Gideon?

The thought brought instant joy, but then she thought of Danny. No! She could not be dead. She refused to be dead. She would not leave her baby boy to grow up an orphan. Her father would get custody. Judge Blackthorne raising her son with his iron fist.

Caitlyn bolted upright. "No!"

Every head at the pavilion swiveled to stare at her. Her temple throbbed and she reached a hand up to rub the tender spot. Then she looked over to see the man in leather kneeling on the floor of the van beside her. A tingle of emotion rushed through her as their gazes met again.

Gideon. It *was* Gideon. But he did not look the same. Had he carried her to the van?

Caitlyn stared into the face of the boy she'd once

loved. He stared back, scalding her with his eyes. A boy no more, fully a man. No, not just a man but a warrior, hardened and battle-weary, but his inky black hair was as wild as it had always been. No buzz cut, no control, finger-combed off his forehead in a regal mane.

Their gaze was a chain, linking them together.

Gone was the roundness of his youthful face. In maturity, his jaw had strengthened and his cheeks had thinned out. Fear passed through her. Was he really here? Or was she seeing a ghost? She got out of the van, where Gideon had apparently carried her, staggered to her feet, and squinted in the glare of bright sunlight.

Before she had time to fully assess what was going on, she was surrounded by a crush of people. Dotty Mae, Patsy, Raylene, Emma, Sarah, Flynn, Belinda, Marva, Terri, Christine. Everyone was talking at once. Caitlyn heard a high humming in her ears, and she couldn't take her eyes off Gideon.

Her words stacked up, a logjam in her throat, so many coming at once she couldn't get any of them out. Questions. So many questions.

Gideon was alive.

But how? And why hadn't he come home before now? Why hadn't he ever contacted her?

"Is it really you?" she whispered.

"Yeah," he said, his lips pulling tight. "It's me."

He did not seem happy to see her. She stared, incredulous, not really believing this was happening. She had to be dreaming. In real life, people did not come back from the dead.

She wanted to say more, but got no further, because he abruptly slid from the back of the van and left her standing there. Her friends were talking at once, while at the same time the funeral director was trying to return everyone's attention to the ceremony in progress. Gideon walked over to the coffin and stood there for the longest time just staring down at what was left of his father.

In her dreams, whenever Caitlyn imagined that Gideon had lived, she fantasized about the life they would have had together with their son. But she'd never, ever expected to see him again. She'd wanted it, prayed for it, dreamed and dreamed and dreamed about it, but she'd understood that hoping and wishing and praying didn't make a thing so. She'd learned that well enough from the loss of her mother.

But now here was the impossible suddenly made possible. Even though her entire body was trembling from her big toes to the very hairs on her head, she moved toward him, her friends trailing behind her as if to be there to catch her when she fell. They were saying things, but none of their words registered. Nothing registered. She could not get over the profound knowledge that Gideon was not dead. How could she ever have believed it was so?

She felt the old, familiar pain grip her. Gideon had lost out on so much. He'd died never even knowing he had a son. Caitlyn swallowed, strengthening herself against the tears that hovered behind her eyelids whenever she thought too long about Gideon.

It had been eight years, but at times, the grief was

just as fresh as if it had just happened. She could still remember that awful day when Hiram Malone, the private eye she'd hired to find Gideon, met her in the park with the file folder in his hand. She'd known before he'd ever said a word. He'd sat down in the park swing beside her. She'd been eighteen by then and four months pregnant, wearing blousy tops to hide her growing midriff from her father, knowing that soon he would guess the truth.

"It's bad news, isn't it?" she'd whispered, bracing herself.

But there was no bracing for the words that robbed her of all hope. Malone spoke softly. She barely heard him over the creaking of her swing. She was rocking, back and forth, back and forth. Knowing, dreading, fearing.

"Gideon Garza died in battle serving his country," Malone had said. "He was a brave and honorable man."

She'd sat there for a moment, praying she'd heard wrong. "No."

"Yes." He'd opened the folders, pulled out papers.

It couldn't be. How could it be? Gideon had been her destiny. Her soul mate. Her one true love. If he was dead, then she was dead. Her life was over. She wanted to die.

And then for the first time, she'd felt Danny move. A fluttering inside her belly. Soft, but distinct. Movement. Gideon's son. A piece of him was living on inside her.

The moment was so surreal she could not absorb it all. Emotions of every kind and facet poked and prodded her. Anger, hope, regret, joy, fear, sadness, exhilaration. It was a mad jumble that set her pulse to jumping and her stomach rocking.

She stood on the precipice. Her inner urge was to fling herself into Gideon's arms, but he looked so changed. It had been eight long years, and she no longer had any idea who he was. And if he wasn't dead, why hadn't he come home before now?

He swiveled his head, cast a glance at her from the corner of his eye. Tentatively, she reached out a hand to finger his jacket, but he jerked back.

"Don't," he snapped.

Hurt, she dropped her arm.

His eyes narrowed. His jaw hardened, but his tone softened. "Just don't."

Pain at his rejection cut deep. What was wrong with him? What had happened to make him so hard? It must have been something terrible. She didn't know what to do. It was all too much. Seeking the only thing she knew that could ground her, she pivoted and went back to the van. *Danny*. She had to get to her son.

Caitlyn slammed the back doors closed, climbed into the front seat, and with fingers so numb she couldn't feel the keys, she started the engine and drove away.

CHAPTER FIVE

*Traditional meaning of almond blossom—
hope and watchfulness.*

Wedding ring. On the third finger of her left hand.
Simple gold band. The realization solidified in Gideon's mind like cement.

Caitlyn was married.

Feeling like he'd lost the last hope worth living
for, Gideon stared after the retreating van, as did
everyone else in the pavilion. After Caitlyn disappeared from sight down the winding road, people
converged, peppering him with questions.

"Where have you been?"

"We heard you were dead."

"Why haven't you come home before now?"

"Goodness, Gideon, you're better-looking than
ever."

In the past, he might have enjoyed the attention, but not anymore.

He raised his palm, growled. "I came to see J. Foster Goodnight put into the ground. I'd appreciate it if you'd leave me in peace until that task is accomplished."

But of course, it wasn't going to be that easy.

His older half brother, Bowie Goodnight, stalked over and shoved his face into Gideon's. He smelled like a distillery and wore an expensive black suit with a fat paisley blue tie that made him look like a 1970s undertaker.

"You're not wanted here," he ground out through gritted teeth. "Leave."

"Actually," Gideon said coolly, "I'm afraid to burst your bubble. But our old man invited me."

"Bullshit!" Bowie curled his hands into fists, leaned inward, crowding Gideon's personal space. "And you're *not* my brother."

Gideon cocked his head at Lester LaVon, who was hovering at the fringe of the crowd. "Tell him, LaVon."

Lester nodded, his balding head shining sweatily in the sun. "It's true. Your father sent me to Afghanistan last month to find him."

Bowie looked like a wasp had flown up his nose. "But why?"

Lester shifted, tugged at his tie. "Because Gideon is his youngest son, and J. Foster named him in the will."

The words Lester spoke didn't really register with Gideon, but they had a powerful effect on Bowie and Crockett. They were yelling at once, throwing a tantrum right there at their daddy's funeral.

"This is outrageous," Bowie shouted. "Not to be tolerated."

"I'll sue! I'll sue!" Crockett waved his hands. "He's not getting one red cent of our inheritance."

Gideon stared at the coffin. *Was this what you intended, you ornery old coot? To have your three sons at each other's throats? Are you and Satan sharing a snout full of whiskey and laughing your asses off?*

"Settle down." LaVon pushed his palm down in a calming motion and looked chagrined at the stupidity of his mistake in announcing details of the will at the graveside.

Gideon could have taken a moment to bask in the sweet irony of the situation, but Bowie was red-faced and spewing spittle as he repeatedly shouted, "Leave, leave, leave." He could stay put and fight with high-octane Bowie, or he could get on his motorcycle and go after Caitlyn.

Because one look in her eyes and he'd been jettisoned back to the past. All the old feelings had swarmed back, stronger than ever, and he hated it. He'd sworn never again to be that vulnerable, never again to open himself up to such heartache.

God, why had he returned? He didn't give a damn about the contents of Goodnight's will. And he'd mentally cut his ties to Caitlyn years ago. He'd been happy enough in Afghanistan. Why had he mucked it up? Moira had been so wrong. Closure was the last thing he'd found in Twilight. All he'd done was split open a raw and achy wound, only to discover it was abscessed to the bone.

He shouldered Bowie aside and headed for his motorcycle, but he'd taken only a few steps when an old man stood up from the last pew.

"Garza," the man called.

Judge Blackthorne's hair was grayer, his jowls thicker, his shoulders sloped, but his eyes remained eagle sharp.

All the old fury—and the need to prove himself to this town and this man—came whipping back. His good hand curled into a fist. He'd lost his other hand in a large part thanks to Judge Blackthorne, who'd backed him into a corner. He wasn't blaming Blackthorne for his actions. Gideon *had* set that barn fire. But Blackthorne had given him no wiggle room, made no allowances for Gideon's extenuating circumstances. He met the old man's eyes with a dagger-sharp gaze.

Blackthorne did not flinch. "If you know what's good for you, you'll stay away from my daughter," he barked. "Get out of town now."

Gideon had an urge to brush up against him hard. Slam his shoulder into the old man with enough impact to spin him on his ass. But if nothing else, the army had taught him impulse control. A lesson he'd sorely needed.

Instead, he simply narrowed his eyes, drilled a hole straight through the judge, and dared, "Or what?"

Caitlyn paced her kitchen and wrung her hands. Not knowing where else to go or what else to do, she'd raced home from the funeral, leaving the van parked haphazardly at the curb in front of her house. She hadn't even stopped at the babysitter's to pick up Danny. She needed time to process what was happening. To get her head straight. To calm her racing pulse.

Gideon was alive!

How could he be alive? She'd hired a PI. He's shown her the paper trail. Gideon was dead.

Except that had been no dead man cradling her head in his lap in the back of her van. He'd been warm and strong and very much alive.

Her heart soared, wanting desperately but very afraid to believe in this fragile dream. How many people who'd lost loved ones had dreamed dreams like this? Their beloved returned to them, whole and safe. She bit down on her lip, felt both exquisite joy and intense anxiety threading through her.

Gideon was alive.

The first rush of questions hit her. But what did this mean? Where had he been? Why had the PI lied? Had it been some kind of mistake? Or was her father somehow behind it? Then the second wave of questions crashed. What about Danny? How did she tell Gideon about Danny? How did she tell Danny about his father? Everyone in Twilight believed that Kevin was her son's father. To protect him, she'd let Danny believe it too, planning, one day, when he was old enough and the time was right, to tell him the truth about his real father. What was she going to do about this?

The thought made her feel liquid and jittery.

The magnitude of what had happened hit her in fresh waves. She stopped pacing, wrapped her arms around her waist, sank her spine down the length of the counter cabinet until her butt touched the cool tile floor.

Gideon was alive.

Memories tumbled through her. Their first date: a canoe ride on the river followed by a picnic of bologna sandwiches and fresh-picked pears. Their first kiss shared underneath the Ruby Street viaduct. The time they'd conceived Danny in the wee hours of the morning on a blanket in Sweetheart Park.

How was she supposed to handle this? She didn't even know who Gideon was anymore. At the cemetery, he'd looked so imposing. Like a warrior straight off the battlefield. Emotionless, detached. Had he lost his humanity? Was he still in the military? Where had he been? How long was he staying?

It was all too much to absorb.

She pulled her knees to her chest, pressed her forehead to her knees. Her emotions ran the gamut from giddy joy, to tentative hopefulness, to abject fear, to downright panic. What if Gideon wanted to take Danny away from her?

Don't let your imagination run away with you. He doesn't even know about Danny.

No, but someone in Twilight was bound to tell him soon enough. She needed to do it first. Except how did you tell someone something like that? Someone you thought dead and buried for eight years?

Good to see you again, glad to know you're not dead. Oh yeah, and by the way, you have a seven-and-a-half-year-old son who has no idea you're his father.

But in the midst of her panic, a small inner voice whispered, *What if Gideon still loves you? What if he's happy about Danny? What if he wants to be a family?*

How beautiful, that what-if scenario! She wanted to believe it was a possibility, but she couldn't afford to kid herself or assume anything. They'd both grown and changed. Neither of them were the kids they used to be. Becoming a mother had altered her in fundamental ways, and she was certain that being a soldier had changed him.

Without warning, the tears were upon her. Tears of sadness and hope. Tears of relief that he was alive. Even if they couldn't pick up where they'd left off, she was so happy that he wasn't dead.

She wished she hadn't been so shocked and run away. She wished she'd gone against her innately cautious nature and just flung herself into his arms, and told him how much she'd missed him, how she'd loved him. But she hadn't done that and there was no chance to redo their first meeting since he'd risen from the dead. It was already set in stone, her reaction.

He can't blame you for that. He had to know how much it would rattle you, his showing up for J. Foster's funeral dressed like that.

He *had* presented an unsettling image. He should have given her some warning. Written a letter, picked up a phone. She was listed in the phone book. Not that hard to find.

You're listed as Caitlyn Marsh, not Caitlyn Blackthorne. He doesn't know you're married.

Maybe he did know she was married. Maybe that was why he hadn't called. Maybe he did know she was married and hadn't heard that Kevin had died. And where had he been for eight years? Why hadn't he come home before now? Why hadn't he tried to contact her?

Oh, this dithering was getting her nowhere. She needed to talk to him. Caitlyn hauled in a deep breath. Yes, okay, she'd talk to him. But not right now. She needed time to rehearse things in her head, get a plan together for how this was going to go. Get a—

A knock at the back door broke off her thoughts.

She sat frozen.

Another knock.

Get up. Go answer the door. Reluctantly, she forced herself up off the floor.

A third knock.

She peeked through the blinds, and there he was. Gideon. Standing on her back porch. The sight of him nailed her feet to the floor. Her breath slipped from her lungs. Gooseflesh traveled the length of her forearms, spread across her shoulders and down her back.

How had he found out where she lived?

It was a stupid question. This was Twilight, where everyone knew everyone. It wouldn't take a black ops agent to find her. All it would take was for him to pop into any store on the town square and call out, "Does anyone know where Caitlyn Blackthorne lives?" He wouldn't even have to know her married name. Or even *if* she was married. Then again, if he didn't know she was married, wouldn't he have just gone to her father's house? Maybe he did go to her father's house and Greta had directed him here.

Another knock. "Caitlyn."

The sound of her name on his lips sent adrenaline shooting through her like a bullet, blood circulating through her veins with a breathtaking ricochet. She wrapped her hand around the knob and wrenched open the door.

He stood there looking down at her. She'd forgotten how tall he was. Six-foot-three, his shoulders as broad as oak tree branches. Unable to meet his gaze, she focused on his chest. Even through the bulk of his unzipped leather jacket, she could tell his chest muscles were honed, chiseled.

"Caitlyn." His voice was soft as the spring breeze, in sharp contrast to his hard eyes, his hard body, his hard everything. Soft, and yet much deeper than she remembered.

Their past was an electrical current connecting them, surging with a force that was both compelling and utterly terrifying. Her entire world shifted, changed. She drew in a breath and heard his own harsh intake of air.

Slowly, she raised her head. His gaze slammed into hers, more powerful than ever. She inhaled sharply, felt his stare pierce her lungs. They just

looked at each other. Neither one making a move.
Both hung on the horns of indecision. Him on the
outside. Her on the inside.

"You're not dead," she said after what seemed
like an eternity.

"Neither are you."

She frowned. "You thought I was dead?"

He shook his head. "I thought all kinds of crazy
things when you sent my letters back."

Misery gripped her. She put a palm to her forehead, let out her breath. He'd written? "You sent
letters?"

"You're telling me you never got them?"

"You sent letters?" she repeated, unable to believe
it. Her fingers ached to reach out and touch him, to
skim over his face, but she remembered how he'd
reacted, how he'd told her not to touch him when
she'd tried it at the cemetery, so she held back. In
fact, she tucked her fingers into her armpits to keep
from touching him.

"I did."

"I never got any letters."

Gideon swore darkly. "Your father."

Caitlyn jumped back at the anger in his tone.
He was so big and he was virtually a stranger to
her now. Yes, she'd once known him well, but that
was a long time ago. She did not know this man
standing in front of her. He seemed so changed. The
Gideon she remembered had been a lot more emotional, a lot less controlled. He'd been full of passion
and dreams and a strong determination to remake
the world into a better place. This guy, this guy . . .

His eyes were hooded. His body language guarded. This guy had been remade by the world, not the other way around. An idealistic boy had left Twilight, but a hardened, cynical man had returned. She could see it etched in his face—the ugly things he'd seen, the loss of his innocence, the disturbing new values and beliefs formed by war and heartbreak.

He smelled differently too. Once upon a time, the aroma of his exuberant passions had clung to him. He'd loved tinkering with his motorcycle, woodworking, carving, making things with his hands. The scent of pine and oak and maple, of wood polish and lemon oil had defined him. To Caitlyn, his old fragrance had represented safety, comfort, home.

This new smell spoke of change. It was foreign, strange—almond blossoms and turmeric, cardamom, cumin, caraway, cinnamon, and sticky dates. Scents of the Middle East now owned him—exotic, dangerous, alien.

His stare was more intense than the noonday Texas sun in August—bold and hot and vivid. She had to turn her head away or be forever scarred. Briefly, she closed her eyes, but she could still see him. Still smell the almond blossoms.

"Why didn't you call?"

"What? And have you reject me over the phone? No ma'am. The letters returned unopened was kick in the gut enough."

"But I didn't get your letters."

"How was I to know?"

"I left home," she explained. "Just weeks after you went away."

He pushed at a crack in the cement with the toe of his motorcycle boot. Her gaze followed his movement, fixed on that heavy leather boot.

Should she invite him in? It was the polite thing to do, but the thought of being closed up with him inside her small kitchen was too overwhelming to consider. She didn't know him anymore. Not really.

"So your father was the one who sent the letters back."

"I guess that's what happened," she agreed. She certainly didn't put it past the judge.

"And you really thought I was dead?"

She nodded, raised her gaze back to his face again. Could he see it in her eyes? How his death had destroyed her? His expression was impassive, hiding whatever he might be feeling. Was he even feeling anything? Had the army turned him into an automaton?

"Why did you believe that?"

"I hired a PI to find you."

"You looked for me?" He swallowed hard, his shoulders tensed visibly.

"Yes. The PI showed me proof that you were dead. He said you'd been killed in a roadside bombing."

"I wasn't killed."

"But you were involved in a bombing?"

"Bombings. More than one. The first time, in Baghdad, I suffered a severe concussion resulting in temporal lobe retrograde amnesia," he explained.

"Oh. I bet that was weird."

"Worse than weird. You feel . . ." He paused, speaking of himself in the second person, keeping the experience universal, unspecific. " . . . lost."

She placed a hand over her mouth, unable to think of anything to say.

"It took months for my memory to fully return, and when it did . . ." He paused. "There were some things that I still did not remember clearly."

"Did you remember me?"

"In my dreams." His smile was vague, humorless. "I'd dream of you and wake up feeling confused and empty. It took a while to piece everything together, but with time and therapy I recovered most of my memory, although I still can't recall the hours just before the bombing."

"How long did it last?"

"Over a period of several months."

It seemed so odd, talking like this, catching up as if they were old high school pals who had met in the grocery store and were chatting over Fruit Roll-Ups and Hamburger Helper. Surreal.

"Are you still in the army?"

He shook his head. "Medical discharge a couple of years ago. After the second bombing."

She shifted, hugged herself tighter, glanced down again. The toe of his boot was still working on that crack. Was he trying to open it up so he could fall in? "What have you been doing since?"

"Personal security and translation services to foreign businessmen in the Middle East."

"Translation services?"

He shrugged. "Turns out I have a knack. I suppose growing up bilingual helped. I pick up languages really quickly and the military took full advantage of my skills. I speak both Afghan languages, Dari and Pashto. Plus I'm also fluent in French, Italian, Kurdish, Arabic, Hindi, and Farsi as well as Spanish."

"Impressive," she said, because she did not know what else to say.

"It's helped me make a good living."

"That's wonderful."

Silence fell between them. He was studying her with an intensity she found unsettling.

"So you," he said, and waved a hand, and that was when she realized he was still wearing leather gloves. "You've got your own house. And a flower business?"

"Yes." She nodded.

"You always loved flowers." His tone softened.

"I still do."

Another long silence.

"Do you remember the first flowers I ever brought you?" He spoke so quietly she almost didn't hear him.

"White lilacs. I'm surprised you remember."

He smiled, but it didn't reach his eyes. "So, did you get to college? Get that degree in botany you wanted?"

"No."

"Why not?"

"Life got in the way."

"It has a way of doing that."

"Uh-huh."

The silence stretched into eternity.

"Well," he said.

"Well," she echoed. "I'm glad you're not dead."

"Me too."

Neither one of them knew what else to say.

"Listen," she said at the same time he said, "Look."

They laughed uncomfortably.

"You go first," he said.

"No, you."

"I was just going to say that I'm in town for the reading of J. Foster's will. Apparently he left me something." Gideon snorted. "Imagine that. He probably left me his toilet seat."

Encouraged to see a small glimmer of his old sense of humor, she smiled. "I'm sorry for your loss."

"Hey, it was no loss to me."

"I guess the inheritance is the reason you came back?"

He shook his head. "I didn't even know about that until I got here, but a friend told me I couldn't really move on with my life until I got some closure with my past, and I realized she was right. What better way to get closure than to see them put Goodnight in the ground?"

She? Caitlyn was appalled to discover she felt jealous. She had no right to feel jealous. She had no claims on Gideon. The bond they'd once shared had been severed long ago.

"Anyway," he continued, "I was wondering if you'd like to go to dinner one night, catch up."

It sounded so normal, so sensible, but there was nothing normal about this situation. Her lover had come back from the dead.

"I got married," she blurted.

"I saw the ring." He looked at the wedding band. She hadn't taken it off after Kevin had died because it thwarted men from hitting on her.

"I thought you were dead. The PI told me you were dead. What was I going to do?" She knotted her fists.

"You don't owe me an explanation," he said.

She studied his face but she could read nothing there, nothing to give away what he was feeling.

"Bring your husband along with you to dinner. I'd love to meet him."

"My husband died six months ago."

"Oh." His face remained expressionless, impassive. She could read Braille easier than she could read him.

"He was struck by lightning while roofing our flower shop. It's been tough. He didn't leave any life insurance—" She broke off. "But there's no reason to burden you with my troubles."

"You married Kevin Marsh?"

"Yes."

"Funny."

"What?"

"I never would have guessed you would marry someone like Kevin." He sounded displeased.

"What was wrong with Kevin?" she asked, feeling suddenly defensive. He had no right to judge her choice of mates. He'd been the one to ruin things between them by burning down J. Foster's barn. If he hadn't done that, he would not have started the awful chain of events.

"Nothing at all. It's just that he was very—"

"What?" she snapped, not understanding why she felt so irritable.

"Don't take this the wrong way. I liked Kevin. He was a good guy. He cut me a break on the flowers for my mother's funeral. It's just that he was so . . . ordinary."

"What's wrong with ordinary?"

"Your father made it clear enough that his daughter was way too good for ordinary."

"Things change." Caitlyn knew she was going to have to tell him about Danny. She was dancing all around the topic, but she just couldn't bring herself to come right out with it. She needed to think this through, figure out the best way to break the news to Gideon that he had a son. To let Danny know that Kevin had not been his biological father.

She might have just gone ahead and spilled the whole thing, timing be damned, if at that moment a large moving van hadn't rumbled into her driveway.

"Going somewhere?" Gideon asked, arching one eyebrow.

Caitlyn shook her head, but, grateful for the interruption, she moved toward the driver, who was swinging out of the cab.

"Hello," called out the burly man with a handlebar mustache.

"You must have the wrong house," she said, waving a hand at the moving van. "I didn't order movers." She felt rather than saw Gideon come up behind her. He had her back. It was a disturbingly comforting thought.

The man consulted his clipboard. "You Caitlyn Marsh?"

"Yes."

"Then this delivery is for you."

While they were talking, two more men had climbed from the cab and had gone around to open the back door of the eighteen-wheeler tractor that was taking up Caitlyn's entire driveway. She followed the driver to the back of the truck. Gideon fell into step beside her.

She rounded the corner of the vehicle and peered inside. There lay the pieces of the carousel. The animals, the mechanics, the frame, the platform, all stuffed inside the truck. Her father had finally come through.

"Please sign this." The driver extended the clipboard toward her as his assistants started to pull out items. One of the men had hold of Blaze's severed head.

"Wait a minute." Caitlyn raised a hand. "Can you guys take this delivery to the vacant lot on the square? That's where we're building the garden."

"Sure," the mustached man said.

"What this all about?" Gideon asked.

"It's for the victory garden the town is building in your honor."

CHAPTER SIX

Traditional meaning of aconite—
misanthropy and poisonous words.

Caitlyn's words caught Gideon like a hard left jab to the jaw and he'd never thought to defend against it.

Twilight was constructing a victory garden to honor him?

A surprise ripple of chagrin, pleasure, and embarrassment ran through him. He'd spent the last eight years hating this town and everyone in it only to find out they were honoring him with a garden.

He hitched in his breath. Then again, apparently they'd all thought he was dead. It was easy to make nice with dead people. As evidenced by the throng at J. Foster's funeral. He shouldn't feel touched. Rallying around a serviceman was the thing to do. It was symbolic, not personal.

Besides, he'd done nothing to earn the star treatment. He'd simply performed his job. He didn't see himself as a hero.

The delivery van backed out of her driveway. "I'm going to walk over to the town square," Caitlyn said. "Would you like to come with me?"

"Sure," he said, and they took off after the moving van. The square was only a quarter of a mile away.

They walked side by side in silence.

"Have you considered staying in Twilight?"

"What?" He'd been so caught up in his thoughts he hadn't heard her.

"Why not stay awhile?" She canted her head, her blue-green eyes searching his face. "Unless you've got commitments somewhere else?"

Did she have any idea the effect she had on him? He recalled how she'd been in high school, so dreamy-eyed and sensitive, with her head in the clouds. No, not clouds. Flowers. Her thoughts were usually so wrapped in flowers that she didn't notice that heads turned when she walked by. Even now, she still gave off that naïve, soft-focused aura that roused his protective instincts. Hell, what was there to protect her from but him?

Did she want him to stay? Better question, could he risk staying? "Why?" he hedged.

"We need someone to repair the carousel. Once upon a time you even promised you'd restore it for me. Remember?" Her smile was soft, beguiling. "And you were always so good with your hands. If you were staying in town . . ."

His laugh came out in a barking snort.

Her startled eyes widened. "Did I say something funny?"

She hadn't noticed his hand. Of course not, he was still wearing his motorcycle gloves. He'd kept them on primarily because he hadn't wanted her to know. Had wanted to postpone the inevitable.

She put out her hand to touch him, but he side-stepped it. She looked hurt again, just as she had at the cemetery.

Why couldn't he let her touch him? Maybe it was because he knew that if she touched him he wouldn't be able to hold on to his stoic façade. That he'd come completely apart at the seams. The thought scared the shit out of him. He'd held his tender emotions in reserve for so long he didn't even know if they were still there. Maybe that was really what terrified him. That he'd lost the ability to love.

"What's wrong?" she whispered.

Just rip off the Band-Aid. Show her. Get the horror over with.

"I'm sorry, but I'm not your man."

"What?" Confusion clouded her features.

"I can't refurbish your carousel."

"Because you're leaving town."

"Because I *can't* do it."

"Nonsense. Remember that jewelry box you made me for my seventeenth birthday? I still have it."

Why did that news make him feel so buoyantly sad? "I *was* good with my hands. Past tense. Not anymore."

Her nose crinkled. "What do you mean? You can't forget a talent like that."

"No, but you can lose it." He was being coy with her, which wasn't his style, but he couldn't seem to make himself just pull off the glove and show her. They'd reached the town square. The van had pulled up into the vacant lot and the workers were unloading the contents.

"How?" she asked.

He anticipated the stunned look on her face that would quickly turn to revulsion when he pulled the glove off. He knew how it would go. The only two women who had not turned away from his deformity were an army nurse with a weird kink for amputees and Moira, who'd seen so many land mine casualties it no longer fazed her. "Remember when I said I'd been in more than one bombing?"

"Uh-huh." She brought a hand to her mouth and fear came into her eyes. Those innocent eyes that should never know about stuff like this.

He took a deep breath. Here was the moment of truth. Standing in the vacant lot, surrounded by wooden carousel animals ravaged by time and burly workmen going about their chores. "It happened in a village outside Kandahar. I was a newly minted Green Beret, on a special ops mission targeting high-level Taliban insurgents."

Caitlyn's gaze never left his face, but he couldn't look at her or he wouldn't be able to continue with the story. He shifted his gaze to the budding mimosa trees on the courthouse lawn. This place was so damn Norman Rockwell. He didn't belong here. He never really had.

"There was a little girl." He spoke dispassionately as if it had happened to someone else. "She dropped her doll in the street."

Caitlyn was shaking her head, already jumping to the obvious conclusion. "No," she whispered. "Don't tell me there was a bomb in the doll."

He nodded.

"Oh, Gideon."

"In spite of my training, some stupid impulse took hold of me. I grabbed up the dropped doll, called to the girl, and—" He stopped, unable to say anything else.

This was where the rubber met the road. The time had come to stop talking and just show her. He tugged off his left glove, revealing his artificial hand. Then he took off his jacket, and rolled up his sleeve to where the prosthesis connected to his stump.

Shock etched her features, just as he knew it would, but the revulsion never came. Instead, she looked him straight in the eyes and said, "All the more reason for you to refurbish the carousel. You can't let this define who you are. The job is yours if you're up for it. That dinner you invited me to? Why don't you come to my house instead? Monday night. I'll make meat loaf, your favorite. We've got a lot to discuss."

After Gideon had left and the movers had unloaded and stacked the carousel parts in the middle of the lot, reality finally sank in. Gideon had lost his left hand—his dominant hand—and she'd just invited him to rebuild her carousel. Not only that, but she'd also asked him to dinner because she had her own metaphorical bomb to detonate.

Danny.

Speaking of her son, she was over an hour late picking him up. On the way over to the babysitter's house, she practiced saying the words out loud. "Gideon, this is your son, Danny. Danny, this man is your real dad."

She groaned and snagged her own gaze in the rearview mirror. "This is not going to be easy."

When she got to the sitter's house, she was surprised to find Crockett Goodnight on the front lawn in his funeral suit playing catch with her son. He had his jacket off and his shirtsleeves rolled up and his tie tucked into his front pocket. She got out, shaded her eyes with her hand.

"Hey, Mom!" Danny called, easily snagging the ball Crockett sailed his way.

His two front teeth were missing and he was at that ungainly stage where he seemed to be all elbows and knees. She walked over to settle a hand on the back of his shoulder. He smelled of freshmown grass, dandelions, and the oil he rubbed into his baseball mitt every night.

"Hey yourself." She glanced at Crockett. "What are you doing here? Shouldn't you be at your father's wake?"

"I couldn't go back to the ranch with all those chubby-cheeked, casserole-bearing ladies clucking their tongues and gossiping about Dad. And I couldn't face the thought of my empty condo, so I took a walk and saw Danny out here in the yard trying to play catch by himself."

"Crockett says I'm a natural." Danny beamed.

"Does he now?"

"I wish my dad was here," Danny said. "I wish he could see what a good player I am."

For one startling second, Caitlyn thought he was talking about Gideon, but then immediately realized he meant Kevin. "I know, buddy."

"Crockett's dad died too."

"It's a sad thing to have in common."

Crockett gave a hangdog look for Danny's benefit. He still had a black eye and bruises from his fight with Bowie in her flower shop. She remembered how he'd pulled the switchblade knife on his brother, and an uneasy feeling slid down her spine. As much as Danny enjoyed throwing the ball around with Crockett, she was thinking maybe that wasn't the best idea in the world. Especially now that Gideon was back.

Gideon was back.

Her heart fluttered. She felt it then, a rush of heat and hope and anticipation. Gideon had always been able to make her hot and bothered with one simple look, and nothing was different on that score. But what did it mean? He was so changed.

It might sound bizarre, but she found the changes in him incredibly sexy. When he was young, he'd been something of a loose cannon—impulsive, edgy, wild. She supposed, for a good girl who'd always toed the line, that was the attraction.

This new Gideon was controlled, steely-eyed, immovable. What had once been unfocused youthful energy was now deadly intense concentration. He was even more dangerous than he'd been then, but somehow, she wasn't afraid of him. In fact, around him she felt safe, protected.

And highly aroused.

From the moment she'd looked into Gideon's eyes at the cemetery pavilion, an undercurrent of dark sexual attraction ran like a deep flowing river beneath all the other emotions of disbelief, shock, hope, and anxiety. Eight years of believing him dead, of mourning him, missing him, of yearning to kiss him again, to hold him, to touch him, make love to him coalesced into throbbing, primal need. He was the only man she'd ever really wanted.

Crockett came trotting over to the van in his easy, carefree lope. Sweat glistened his skin. A charming smile curled his lips. A smile that seemed far too upbeat for the occasion. "Could I talk to you in private for a sec, Caitlyn?"

"Danny," she called out. "Run tell Amelia I'm here to pick you up." Her son went for the front door of Amelia Mullin's cute Cape Cod.

"What is it?" she asked once Danny was out of earshot.

"I've got season tickets to the Rangers game. I was hoping you and Danny might join me on opening day."

"Are you asking me out?"

"No, no." The look he sent her said, *That is, unless you want me to ask you out.* "You're a good friend, Caitlyn. One of the few people in this town I can converse with on an intellectual level."

"I appreciate the offer, Crockett, but this victory garden project eats up all my spare time."

"Yeah, okay, I get it, you're a busy woman." He shrugged and widened his grin. "But if you change your mind, just let me know. We could have a really good time."

If he'd asked before the unsettling switchblade incident with Bowie, before Gideon had come back to town, she just might have said yes, but not now, not ever. "Thank you for asking."

Danny came zooming up, rescuing her from more conversation.

"Well, I've got to get Danny home."

Crockett's smile hung like faded clothes on a wash line. She could almost feel his disequilibrium. But what did she expect? He'd just buried his father today. He stuck his hands in the pockets of his designer slacks, restlessly jangled his keys. His shoulders pulled downward in a lonely slump. She wondered why he stayed in Twilight. He seemed so out of place here. Was it the same reason she'd stayed? His roots ran too deep to pull them up.

She had an urge to touch Crockett's arm, to tell him everything was going to be okay, but she didn't want to lead him on.

Because Gideon was back, and even though things were strange and strained between them, the one thing she knew for certain was that her feelings for him had not changed.

She wanted him just as much now as she had eight years ago. Maybe even more so. To think they'd lost so much time together and her father was to blame.

The anger she'd struggled to keep under control made her nose burn. She'd put it off for too long.

The time had come to confront her father about his unconscionable actions. She could no longer allow him to get away with what he had done. It was time he paid for his sins.

Sunday morning after J. Foster's Saturday funeral, Richard Blackthorne sat in his usual pew near the front of the First Presbyterian Church of Twilight. He'd been attending the church for thirty-four years. Caitlyn had stopped coming here after she'd moved out and married Marsh. She'd turned Baptist on him, going to Marsh's church on the other side of town. To avoid him, he knew. Today's service was on transgressions, and he couldn't help thinking of Caitlyn.

Richard had just stood up with the rest of the congregation, hymnal in hand, ready to sing "The Old Rugged Cross," when he felt soft fingers clamp down on his shoulder from behind and smelled the light lavender scent of his daughter's perfume.

"I need to see you," Caitlyn whispered in his ear.

An undertow of panic caught him low in the gut, snatched at him, ripped. He kept singing, pretending he didn't hear her.

Her fingers tightened. "Now."

Sweat dampened his collar, but the room wasn't hot. He was alarmed to realize his hands were trembling.

"I'll be waiting for you on the front steps," she said, and then took her hand from his shoulder.

A second passed. He turned his head and saw his daughter disappearing out the back door.

For a moment, he thought about not going, but Richard wasn't a coward. He put his hymnal into the slot behind the pew in front of him, then apologized and excused himself to the end of the aisle. He arrived out in the bright morning sunlight to see Caitlyn pacing back and forth at the top of the steps.

He frowned, acting affronted to hide his fear. "Why have you dragged me from my worship service?"

She stopped pacing and stared at him, her mouth grim, her lips so pale they were almost white, as if she'd been biting them hard and long enough to drain away the color.

"I always knew you were a hard man, but this, this . . ." She swept her arm, clearly at a loss for words.

"I don't know what you're talking about," he lied.

"Even for you. Low. So low."

He felt his internal boxing gloves go up, desperate to defend himself and the things he'd done. Aggressive now that his secret manipulations were coming out. He knew. The minute he'd seen Gideon Garza pull up on that motorcycle, Richard knew he'd lost all hope of redemption.

Eight years ago, he'd crossed a very big line. He'd lost control of his own righteous indignation. He'd forced Garza into the army. Tried to force Caitlyn into a home for unwed mothers who were giving their babies up for adoption. It had all been for her own good. That had been his justification and he'd stuck to it.

"You paid that PI to lie, to forge documents so that I'd believe Gideon had died."

"He was badly wounded in a bombing. He had amnesia. No one thought he would live," he admitted.

"You were counting on him not getting his memory back. You were sure you were going to get away with your deception."

He had been at that.

Caitlyn snorted, shook her head. "And when he wrote to me, you sent his letters back to him, making him think I didn't care. How could you have been so cruel?"

"Sometimes," he said, "the end justifies the means."

Her face flushed red and she sank her hands on her hips. "You're a hypocrite. You're always talking about what's right and doing the right thing and not compromising your principles, and look, just look what you've done. You've violated everything you stand for."

She was right. Every word out of her mouth was the truth.

"I just . . . I just . . ." He couldn't speak, couldn't push air through his vocal cords.

Caitlyn razored him with a hard-edged glare. "You just what, Father? Realized that for all your condemning of others, you are no better than anyone else? Full of faults and flaws."

Agony fisted his chest. He was bad, defective, broken. He wanted so badly to be good, to be an example for the community, to do everything the right way. He was an abject failure, as a father and as a man. But he couldn't admit it. He couldn't bring himself to say the words out loud. Couldn't ask her to forgive him. To do so would mean utter annihilation of who he was at his core. An upright man. A pillar of the community. A model citizen.

"An apology would be nice," she said. "But I can see that's too damn much to hope for. You don't even care that you cheated Gideon and Danny and me out of a life together."

"I just wanted to stop you from ruining your life." Why couldn't she see that? Why couldn't she understand his position?

"What's wrong with the life I have? I have a job I love. A healthy son. Friends and neighbors I can count on. What's so bad about that?"

"You could have had—could have been—so much more, Caitlyn. I—"

"No." She raised her palm. "You know what? You don't get to pass judgment on my life. Not anymore. I'm done fretting about what you think of me. You've made your bed, Judge. I hope you're happy with *your* life."

Then she turned and left Richard standing there feeling more lonely and ashamed than he'd ever felt in his life.

Gideon took a room at the Merry Cherub, a popular bed-and-breakfast not far from the lake. He'd enjoyed sleeping on soft clean sheets again, eating down-home cooking. Both were a far cry from what he was accustomed to. It felt odd, being back in the States, but nice in a way he hadn't expected.

On Sunday, he'd rented a boat and spent the entire day on the river, trying to reorient himself to his surroundings, make sense of his feelings for Caitlyn, and prep himself for the reading of J. Foster's will.

"Mornin', Gideon!" Patsy Cross called out to him as he walked past her store, the Teal Peacock, on Monday morning.

That took him aback. When he was a teenager, she'd reported him to the sheriff for having too loud a muffler on his motorcycle, now she was all smiles.

"Good morning, Mrs. Cross."

"It's so nice to have you home."

"Thank you."

He'd walked only a few steps when another shop owner warmly welcomed him home and then another and another. People clapped him on the shoulder, shook his hand, told him how much they appreciated his sacrifice for their freedom.

It felt odd to be "in" with the folks of Twilight, instead of on the outs as before. He probably should have expected the accolades. People loved a wounded war hero, but he hadn't been prepared for how their admiration would make him feel.

In the past, he'd felt like a foreigner in his hometown, the kid from the wrong side of the tracks, the one who didn't fit. He'd dreamed of someday doing something impressive to earn the respect of those who'd turned up their noses, turned their backs.

Now that he was something of a celebrity, everyone wanted to snag his attention, sing his praises. Embarrassment settled on him as on a scolded dog. He didn't like the spotlight. He was being thanked for doing dark things and it felt wrong.

Once he hit the town square, he was surprised at the number of tourists crowding the streets and then he remembered it was spring break in Texas. In country, too busy worrying about staying alive, a solider forgot about the way things were back home.

Home.

The smell of fresh-baked cinnamon rolls curled under his nose. He could almost taste the sweet, spice-infused yeast dough. The cool breeze sighed past his ears, sending the wind chimes in the chinaberry tree on the courthouse lawn singing. Colorful flowers bloomed in window boxes and baskets hanging from lampposts. Hummingbirds whirled and bickered over honeyed blossoms.

On the corner sat Marsh's Flower Shop; he had to walk by it to get to the courthouse. He pulled in a deep breath and ambled past the window. He really hadn't intended on turning his head, peering in, but a force he couldn't control compelled him to peer inside past the display of roses and lilies and chrysanthemums.

There she was sitting on a small wrought-iron bistro table, arranging flowers in a vase. Beside her sat a woman about Caitlyn's own age. Caitlyn raised her head and their eyes met, pinning Gideon's boots to the sidewalk.

She had on a purple top that clung to the curve

of her breasts. Bedazzled, he stood there with his mouth half open.

Eight years had only added fuel to the fire. He wanted her even more than he'd wanted her back then, and that was saying something monumental. The heat of Caitlyn's gaze had him standing taller, thrusting out his chest, posturing like a damn peacock.

He couldn't wrap his head around the notion that he'd made it back to Twilight, that she hadn't rejected him as he'd imagined. That she'd thought he was dead. But how could he just slip back into a quiet life in a quiet town? He'd been on dangerous missions, had walked among the enemy, had learned their language, become enmeshed in a culture so foreign to this one that there was no way he could even express the differences.

Hope filled him. Hope and longing and greedy need.

The morning sun filtered into Caitlyn's shop, lighting up the flowers surrounding her, bathing her in a rosy romantic glow. She rocked his world with thoughts of what-if.

Her gaze burned into his, her eyes as searing as lasers. Hell if she didn't look as hot and bothered as he felt. Impulse, the thing that had gotten him into so much trouble as a young man, had him aching to stalk right into that flower shop, pull her into his arms, and kiss her until neither of them could breathe.

Gideon's head reeled. His gut clenched. And a certain part of his anatomy heated up in a thoroughly enjoyable way.

But he'd learned a lot in eight years, primarily self-control. He no longer acted on impulse. He'd been schooled in how to wait patiently and weigh all the pros and cons before taking action. The lessons had saved his life on more than one occasion. Yet the impulses still lingered, still welled up to fill him with so much longing he had to do an epic battle with himself to merely give her a smile and a mocking salute.

And then Caitlyn did the damnedest thing.

She raised her fingers to her lips and blew him a kiss.

"Caitlyn?" Sarah Collier's voice broke through the trance that had settled over her after she'd seen Gideon on the street outside her window and blown him a kiss. She had no idea why she'd done it. She wasn't given to frivolous impulse.

Caitlyn blinked at her friend. "Uh-huh?"

"I think I've found the perfect flowers for my wedding," Sarah said, tapping the floral catalogue spread out on the bistro table in front of them.

Caitlyn studied the picture, shook her head. "No, not aconite. Not for a wedding."

"But I love the hooded shape of the petals, and my wedding colors are purple and white."

"Aconite stands for misanthropy and poisonous words."

Sarah wrinkled her brow. "Isn't that a bit superstitious?"

"Do you want to take a chance on your wedding day?"

Sarah gave that some thought. "No, you're right."

"How about orchids instead? They're classic."

"What's the meaning of orchids?"

"Magnificent love."

"Well, I guess that settles it then. How did you ever learn so much about flowers?"

Caitlyn shrugged. "I've always been fascinated by them."

"Was that part of what attracted you to Kevin? Your shared interest in flowers?"

She had to admit that it was, and the fact that Kevin had first offered her a job and a place to stay and then later offered to marry her and become a surrogate father to her son. She'd needed a safe haven, and Kevin had needed someone to nurture.

"Hey," Sarah said. "You stopped wearing your wedding ring."

Caitlyn's thumb went to the bare ring finger on her left hand. She'd taken it off after Gideon had come back to town.

"Does this have anything to do with the devastating, good-looking stranger who had you fainting at J. Foster's funeral?" Sarah hadn't lived in Twilight when Caitlyn and Gideon had been an item.

"What have you heard?"

"The gossip is flying," Sarah admitted. "Gideon is your first love and you thought he was dead?"

Caitlyn nodded.

Sarah admired her own engagement ring and sighed softly. "I have to say it's been my experience that there's no other love like that first one."

"This town is founded on that supposition," Caitlyn murmured.

"So what's holding you back from a heartfelt reunion?"

"Eight long years. A war between us. He's changed a lot. And I have a son to raise."

"Do you think you'll be able to find your way back to each other?" Sarah asked.

"Honestly, I don't know. Both of us are so different now."

"You're afraid to get your hopes up, huh?"

"Yes," Caitlyn admitted.

"He hurt you once and you're afraid he'll do it again."

"Something like that."

"It was touch and go with Travis and me for a while there," Sarah said. "The past can complicate things if you let it, and I know from Travis that things aren't so cut-and-dried when you have a child to consider."

"That's true," Caitlyn agreed. She still hadn't figured out the best way to break the news about Danny to Gideon, and he was coming to dinner tonight.

Sarah reached across the table and laid her hand on Caitlyn's. "Well, whether it's with Gideon or someone else, I hope you get your happily-ever-after. You've been through so much. You deserve it."

Caitlyn smiled, touched by Sarah's heartfelt statement, but not wanting to dwell on it. Sarah was right, she was afraid to hope for happily-ever-after. "So are you ready for me to order those orchids?"

CHAPTER SEVEN

Traditional meaning of mimosa—sensitivity.

Lester LaVon's office was located in the Twilight courthouse. The last time Gideon had been in this building, he'd been in handcuffs, brought up before Judge Blackthorne on charges of burning down his father's barn.

It smelled the same. Musty as the old white stone walls. The hardwood floors creaked beneath his feet, the sound echoing in his ears full of ugly memories. He could still remember how fast and hard his heart had pounded. How the metal handcuffs had bitten into his skin.

Oddly, his phantom limb ached. Funny, how his wrist still hurt even years after it was gone. Pain. It was an odd thing all around. Unpleasant, miserable, but at least when you were hurting you knew you were alive. He thought of those dark days after the bombing, when he'd lain writhing in the dark. Then the horrifying realization that his left hand was gone.

He suppressed the shudder that passed through him, kept his face impassive, his head high, shoulders straight in proud military bearing. He was Green Beret. Yes, he was out of the service now, but that identity was the only thing that had saved him from himself, and he leaned on it in times of stress.

The office at the end of the corridor had "Lester LaVon, Attorney at Law" stenciled on it in gold lettering. Gideon paused at the door, his hand on the knob, preparing himself for what was going to happen next. He'd be facing Bowie and Crockett Goodnight.

His half brothers.

When he was a kid, he'd badly wanted siblings. He'd often beg his mother to get married, have more children. She would just laugh and kiss the top of his head and tell him if she had more kids it would take away from the love she could give to him. His heart would light up when she'd say that and he wouldn't broach the subject again for weeks. Finally, he'd stopped asking. But he'd never stopped wanting brothers and sisters.

Then, after his mother died and he'd discovered he had brothers, he'd been momentarily joyous.

But they hadn't accepted him. Just as J. Foster had denied Gideon was his son, Bowie and Crockett denied they were his brothers. He didn't expect that anything had changed in that regard.

Except that on his deathbed, J. Foster had sent his lawyer to Afghanistan to find him. He'd apparently decided to finally recognize Gideon and mention him in his will.

Gideon wasn't expecting much and he didn't want anything from J. Foster except the public admission that Gideon was indeed his son.

The door hinges squeaked when he pushed into the office. A plump thirty-something executive assistant sat behind the desk. She smiled and directed him to sit in the lobby.

He didn't want to sit. Sitting made him feel restless, confined. He was accustomed to traversing mountainous desert terrain. Sleeping in tents, inhaling dust. The niceties of polite society were an encumbrance. He didn't know how to play the game. He'd been a soldier his entire adult life.

The woman was boldly studying his artificial hand. When most people realized you were missing a limb, they would quickly glance away. He wondered if she was a devotee or merely curious.

Devotees (officially known as acrotomorphiles) got sexually turned on by amputees. He'd gotten involved with a devotee right after he'd lost his hand. Raquel had been a military nurse on his rehab unit. At first, he didn't realize she was attracted simply because he *was* missing a hand, he'd just known she hadn't turned away in revulsion. But he quickly realized his attachment to Raquel was getting in the way of his emotional healing.

He'd broken things off with her, but it had made him hypersensitive to that particular sexual predilection. Some amputees were all for devotees. But being valued for simply what he was missing had made Gideon feel like a freak.

"Are you a soldier?" the woman asked.

He really didn't want to get into a conversation with her. He nodded.

"Middle East?"

He grunted this time, but that only seemed to encourage her.

"My brother's in Iraq. His second deployment."

Gideon relaxed. That's why she'd been staring. "I did one tour in Iraq, two in Afghanistan."

"Thank you," she whispered.

He said nothing. What did you say to someone who thanked you for getting your hand blown off?

The office door opened again and Bowie and Crockett walked in. They stopped dead when they saw him in the lobby. Their eyes narrowed in unison, and he felt the sting of their collective hatred. Coolly, he met their glares. No one said anything.

A tense minute passed.

"You may all go in now." The executive assistant waved at the closed door.

Gideon stepped forward at the same time Bowie and Crockett did. He didn't want to walk beside them, so he took a long stride and reached LaVon's office first. Taking control, he wrenched open the door and stepped inside. LaVon sat behind his desk, reading glasses perched on the end of his nose, a stack of papers in front of him. He got to his feet as Crockett and Bowie came in behind Gideon.

"Gentlemen," LaVon said, coming around the desk to shake their hands. "Thank you for coming."

Bowie scowled at Gideon.

He had to admit that he looked a lot like the oldest Goodnight brother. They'd both had inherited J. Foster's thick dark hair, deep brown eyes, heavy five-o'clock shadow, and muscular build. But Gideon was a good two inches taller than Bowie, who stood over six feet. Crockett on the other hand was smaller, wiry, and of average height, five-nine or -ten. If someone who looked at the three of them was told that one of the brothers was a bastard from another mother and was asked to pick him out, he would have instinctively chosen Crockett.

"He's mentioned in your father's will," LaVon said.

LaVon appeared a lot more powerful here in this office where he was king than he had in the Afghan desert with a briefcase sitting on his bald head. Here he was in charge, and Gideon was the one who felt out of place in the world of litigation and law. He was on LaVon's turf now.

"Please have a seat." LaVon waved at the Western-style furniture surrounding his desk. A heavy love seat made of mahogany and covered in expensive leather along with matching chairs. The rugs were cowhide. The lamps were constructed of deer antlers. In the corner sat a small wet bar. LaVon crossed over to it. "Anyone want a drink?"

"Bourbon and branch," Bowie said.

"I'll have a vodka tonic," Crockett added.

LaVon looked at Gideon.

Gideon raised his palm. "Nothing for me."

"You sure you don't want some fortification?" LaVon asked, telegraphing Gideon a look he didn't understand.

"I prefer to keep my wits about me."

"Hear that, Crock?" Bowie said to his brother. "He's calling us witless."

So that's how it was going to be? Gideon chose to ignore the remark and sank down on the love seat on the opposite side of the room from the plush upholstered chairs where Bowie and Crockett landed. He rested his right ankle across his left knee, spread his right arm out over the back of the couch, making himself look bigger, taking up space and carefully settling his mechanical hand onto his left upper thigh. He might be missing a limb, but he wasn't going to let that be a weakness.

LaVon poured the drinks, came back across the room, passed them out to Bowie and Crockett, and then went to resume his position behind the desk. Ice tinkled in Crockett's glass as he gulped his drink. Bowie held his in a tight fist.

LaVon cleared his throat. "The will has to go through probate, but here's how your father wished for his fortune to be divided up."

Bowie tensed.

Crockett leaned forward.

LaVon adjusted his reading glasses.

Gideon remained perfectly still.

" 'To my oldest son, Bowie,' " LaVon read, " 'I leave all my vehicles. The 2009 Cadillac XLR-V, the Hummer H3 . . .'" LaVon kept on, listing the eight cars and trucks J. Foster had owned. "'And one hundred thousand dollars in cash.'"

Bowie grinned until LaVon said, "'To my second son—'"

"Hey, whoa, wait, hold it," Bowie interrupted.

"Yes?" LaVon peered at him over the top of his glasses.

"That's it? He just left me the vehicles and a measly hundred grand?"

"That's it," LaVon said.

Bowie looked poleaxed. "No, that can't be possible. There has to be some mistake. I'm my father's ranch foreman. I took care of everything. He has to have left me the ranch."

"He did not."

Bowie let loose a string of curse words that would have shocked a sailor. He leaped from his seat and reached for the will on LaVon's desk.

But LaVon was much quicker than he looked. Nimbly, he yanked the will away before Bowie could grab it. "Please return to your seat, Mr. Goodnight."

"I will not return to my seat. This is an outrage! How could he have left the ranch to that little twerp?" He waved a hand at Crockett. "He doesn't give a shit about the ranch. All he cares about is getting drunk and chasing women and coaching Little League in a desperate bid to recapture his glory days."

Crockett was on his feet now. "Screw you and the horse you rode in on, Bowie. Dad lavished you with everything. Finally, he recognized that it was my turn."

Bowie doubled up his fists, glared at his brother. Crockett stuck out his chin, just daring Bowie to deck him. Children. They were acting like spoiled children.

LaVon sighed. "Don't make me call security."

Gideon just watched. He didn't have a horse in this race.

"He didn't leave the ranch to you either, Crockett," LaVon said.

"What?" Crockett whipped his head around, stared at LaVon, incredulous.

"Sit back down, both of you," LaVon instructed.

Reluctantly, the brothers returned to their seats, still throwing daggers at each other with their eyes.

Once they were seated and quiet again, LaVon continued reading. "'To my son Crockett, I leave the house on Galveston Island and one hundred thousand in cash.'"

"That shithole!" Crockett howled. "It got trashed during Hurricane Ike."

"It's worth more than eight damn old cars," Bowie groused.

"Is that it?" Crockett asked. "The beach house and pocket change?"

"There's some of his personal items he's split among you boys," LaVon said. "His clothes, his tools, his books, his golf trophies."

"Well, who did he leave the ranch to?" Bowie said. "And the rest of the money? Our old man was worth over thirty million dollars. If he gave it to some goddamn charity, I swear I'll fight this thing tooth and nail. He can't buy his way to heaven at this point."

LaVon's gaze swung to Gideon.

"Oh, hell no," Bowie exclaimed.

" 'To my youngest son, Gideon, by Linda Garza,' " LaVon began.

The hairs on Gideon's arms prickled. Apprehension folded him in a tight hug.

" 'I leave the Rocking J Ranch located on Highway 51 between Twilight and Weatherford, the ranch house, and all the contents thereof, not already allocated to one of my other sons. Along with the ranch house I leave the bulk of my monies.' " LaVon paused. "That's eleven million in cash, stocks, and bonds."

"No, no, no, no!" Crockett yelled, and jumped to his feet.

"Sit down," LaVon said, "I'm not finished reading."

"I won't sit still and listen to this. That's our money. Bowie's and mine."

"J. Foster thought otherwise."

"Cancer was eating up his brain," Crockett said. "He didn't know what he was doing."

"Gideon *is* your brother." Lavon ruffled the papers.

"No he's not. Dad denied it when *he*"—Crockett drilled Gideon with a hard stare—"showed up at our house years ago."

"Your father lied." LaVon pushed his reading glasses up on his head.

"How do we know he's not lying now?" Bowie said inanely.

Gideon sat there, still as a stone, watchful, primed for anything. His muscles were coiled, ready to spring.

"It's his last will and testament," LaVon said.

"Why would he leave everything to this poser?" Crockett grumbled.

Bowie had gone all quiet, and that worried Gideon worse than his outburst. An outburst was a gut reaction, kneejerk. But quiet meant he was thinking. And thinking spelled trouble.

LaVon flipped the glasses back down on his nose and continued to read. " 'I realize that the sons of my marriage to Charlotte Van Zandt will not be happy with the distribution of my wealth, and this is the only place I am going to make an explanation. You were born with platinum spoons in your mouths. You had the best of everything. More toys than you could play with. More food than you could eat. You went to the finest colleges that money could buy. You drove fast cars, dated fast women. You ended up with no respect for anything. Crockett, you don't work the ranch. You idled away your days. You're shallow as a pie pan and fickle as a butterfly. Bowie, you're filled with anger, but you have nothing to be mad about. The bitterness has made you hard. But the son I denied. The son I turned away. The son I refused to recognize became one hell of a man. He challenged me and when I sent him away, he bravely took vengeance by burning down my barn. Now, that I respect.' "

"Shit," Crockett drawled, his eyes gleaming with hatred. "I could've burned down his barn if that's what it took to get him to fork over his fortune."

Gideon was so shocked, he forgot to keep an eye on the seething Bowie. His jaw dropped, his airway constricted. He could feel his toes curl against the soles of his boots, heard the soft whirr of the overhead ceiling fan churning. From his peripheral vision saw a mockingbird settle into the mimosa tree outside LaVon's window. J. Foster had not only recognized him, but left him almost his entire fortune. Unbelievable. His breath whispered through his lungs. He blinked, shook his head. Wondered if he was dreaming.

LaVon continued. "'I asked my friend Judge Blackthorne to put Gideon between a rock and a hard place. Go to the military or go to jail. Gideon went into the army. He was shipped first to Iraq and then to Afghanistan. He excelled at everything. Discovered he had a knack for languages and became a translator. He had the drive and determination born of poverty and hard circumstances. He became a Ranger and from there, a Green Beret. He served his country well, and for that I am extremely proud. I am also ashamed of myself and the way I treated him.'"

It should have felt good to hear all this. Why didn't it feel good? Instead, Gideon felt only mild surprise. On his deathbed, J. Foster had sought redemption. Now, was he expecting Gideon to get all cozy about dear old Dad just because he'd left him a pile of money? It didn't change anything. J. Foster had let him grow up without a dad. Had treated him like crap. Had turned his back on Gideon's mother.

No, Gideon wasn't the least bit interested in his money. He'd spent the last few years making money hand over fist in the Middle East, and while he might not be rich, he had a very nice nest egg saved up. He didn't need a damn thing from Goodnight.

"This is bullshit," Bowie raged. He jumped up and slammed a fist on LaVon's desk. "Fix this, Lester. I don't care what you have to do. Just fix it."

"It was your father's wishes."

"The old man was out of his mind with pain." Bowie shoved a hand through his hair. "He can't give our money to this . . . this . . . one-armed Mexican." He said it like it was the vilest insult he could dredge up.

Gideon laughed. It was ridiculous. He didn't want Goodnight's money. Didn't want to be here with his lovely siblings. He'd only come because Moira had convinced him it was the thing to do. Bad move. Bad judgment. A mistake all around. He'd tell her that once he got back.

That's not the only reason you returned. There was the matter of Caitlyn. Where did he stand with her?

"Don't you dare mock me." Bowie whirled on him, moving across the floor with startling quickness.

But Gideon was a warrior. In a second, he was on his feet, and when Bowie reached him and cocked his arm back to deliver a stinging blow, Gideon caught his wrist, turned his body into Bowie's, and in one smooth move, put the other man on the ground and rested his boot snugly against Bowie's throat.

Bowie's eyes rounded to the size of Oreos. The artery in his neck pounded visibly.

Gideon stared down at his brother, felt absolutely nothing. No love. No hatred. No disgust. Nothing but complete disinterest. "I could crush your windpipe in a nanosecond," he said. "You're alive only because I want you to be alive."

All the color drained from Bowie's face.

"I don't want your father's money or his ranch or anything that belonged to him. I care about a sand flea on my ass more than I care about J. Foster Goodnight and his sons. You keep your daddy's money."

"Really?" Crockett said. "You mean it?"

Bowie lay completely still underneath Gideon's foot. He knew the threat wasn't idle.

"It's not that simple," LaVon said. "There's paperwork to be filled out, legal procedures to follow them . . ."

Gideon swung his gaze to LaVon but kept his boot to Bowie's throat. He didn't want any blindsides. "Then do what you have to do to give my *brothers* what's coming to them."

Then with that, he turned and walked away.

CHAPTER EIGHT

Traditional meaning of daylily—motherhood.

Gideon arrived at Caitlyn's house on Monday evening more nervous than he'd been when he dated her eight years ago. Back then, he'd had to fight Judge Blackthorne's disapproval. Now, he had to battle his own demons, which were even harder to deal with than Caitlyn's father. He wanted so much to hope that they could pick up where they'd left off, but he wasn't dumb enough to believe things hadn't changed. Eight years was a long time and even if Caitlyn wasn't different, he certainly was.

But they weren't exactly dating, were they?

He held a bouquet of daylilies in his hand. Since she was the only florist in town and he hadn't wanted to give her flowers that he'd bought from her, he'd driven to the next town over. The scent surrounded him, made him feel strangely weighed down, like he was moving through water.

Having chosen not to wear his prosthesis, and suddenly regretting that decision, he kept his left arm behind him, his right hand with the lilies clutched in it.

The friendly smell of meat loaf greeted him before he even pressed his thumb to her doorbell. He was early and he knew it, but he hadn't been able to wait any longer.

"Just a minute," Caitlyn called out.

He heard the sound of an oven door springing closed. Becoming a Green Beret had sharpened his senses. He'd learned to listen, really listen, to the sounds beyond the obvious, to smell the complicated layers of a scent, to detect subtle differences in textures and temperatures, to taste with discernment. Heightened sensory skills could keep you alive.

The door flew open and Caitlyn stood there, her hair caught back in a high ponytail, curling tendrils escaping to float around her face. She wore a floral apron over a pair of tailored slacks and a beige silk blouse. What a glorious sight for a hungry soldier's war-weary eyes.

"Hey," he said.

"You're early."

"Is that a problem?" He inclined his head, grinned. "I could go and come back in ten minutes."

"Of course not."

"I brought you some . . ." Feeling nineteen again and as suave as a sand pebble, he thrust the bouquet of daylilies at her. "Here."

"Thank you," she said breathlessly, but she had a strange expression on her face.

He pressed his palm against the nape of his neck. "Did I do something wrong?"

"Wrong?"

"Are you allergic to lilies or something?"

"No, no," she denied, but she was holding them tentatively.

Then he remembered that she'd once told him that flowers had hidden meanings. He gulped, wondering what in the hell covert meaning people attached to daylilies. Obviously, from the way she was acting, it wasn't something all that good.

"C'mon in." She ushered him inside. "I'll just put these in water. They'll make a lovely centerpiece for the table."

He followed her inside and she closed the door behind him. He cast a glance around the room, checking out his surroundings, noticing everything. The denim sofa that had seen better days, the hand-knitted afghan thrown across the back, the oak hardwood floors covered by a floral-patterned rug, the small television set in the corner opposite a desk playing host to a notebook computer, and next to that a bookcase overflowing with books. It was a small room, comfortable and cozy.

The delicious aroma of meat loaf was even stronger in here. Underneath it, he picked up the scent of buttery mashed potatoes, rustic carrots, and yeast rolls. Awkwardness stole over them.

"You look beautiful," he said.

She pushed a tendril of hair back from her face,

her cheeks pinked, and she glanced away. She'd never been comfortable with compliments. Had never considered herself beautiful. She might not be a classic beauty, but in Gideon's eyes she was a goddess. She had the smoothest skin, and he knew she was diligent about using sunscreen. Some might consider her nose a bit too strong for a woman's face, but he thought it kept her features from being too soft and gave her a sense of purpose.

"Let's go into the kitchen," she invited. "You can toss a salad."

"Putting me to work already, huh?"

"Yes." She took the salad bowl from the refrigerator pinned with kitschy magnets that held childish crayon drawings in place. And he couldn't help wondering who'd drawn them. She set the bowl on the cabinet along with a pair of tongs and a bottle of Italian dressing. "Toss away."

It had been a very long time since he'd been in a civilized kitchen, helping a woman cook. It felt as alien to him as sleeping on the ground in a desert mountain range would feel to her. Gideon did as she asked, pouring a moderate amount of dressing onto the salad and tossing it.

Caitlyn bent to pull the yeast rolls from the oven, and he couldn't help casting a surreptitious glance at her butt.

Man, she still had a world-class ass. That had not changed one bit.

She raised her head, caught him staring at her rump. Quickly, he returned his attention to the salad tossing.

A fresh silence fell between them, as uncomfortable as the first one. He wished this were easier, that things felt more natural between them. But that's not how it was.

Was this a bad omen?

"So," Caitlyn said as she buttered the rolls. "How did the reading of the will go?"

"You're not going to believe this."

"He left you a chunk of the ranch," she guessed.

"He left me all of it."

"What?" She laid down the butter knife, turned to stare at him.

"And eleven million dollars."

"Gideon!"

"I'm not accepting it."

"Why not?"

"I don't want anything that belonged to J. Foster."

"That's some grudge holding."

"Maybe."

"Does this mean you won't be staying in Twilight?"

"I don't know," he answered honestly. "I'm still getting accustomed to America all over again."

"Oh," she said. Did she sound sad or was it just his imagination? "It must feel very different, coming home."

"You have no idea."

She put the rolls and the salad on the table, then turned back to him. "What was it like over there?"

He shrugged. "You couldn't imagine it if I told you."

"Try me."

He laughed.

"You don't think I'm capable of understanding?"

"Your life here"—he paused, swept his hand at her kitchen—"is the opposite of my life in Afghanistan."

"In what way?"

"In every way imaginable." It made him aware of just how different they were. How isolated he was.

"May I ask you something personal?"

He tensed, not knowing what to expect. "As long as I have the option of not answering."

"All right."

He stepped closer, loomed over her to see if he could stem the tide of nosy questions. "Then fire away."

She didn't back up. In fact, she raised her chin in a determined gesture. "Why didn't you come home after you were discharged? After . . ." She glanced at his missing hand.

How could he begin to explain that one? People talked easily of duty and honor and freedom, but few understood the real price that servicemen and women paid so those on the home front could live free. Gideon tightened his jaw, felt everything tighten inside him, but he didn't step back, just stayed there, standing close, inhaling her sweet scent that smelled of lavender and fresh-baked bread.

How did you wash the ugliness from your soul? Was it even possible? He'd been trained to kill. How did a man return to a quiet life filled with lavender and homemade bread? It seemed so beyond his reach. Such sweet peace.

And yet, when he looked in Caitlyn's eyes and saw the caring and acceptance shimmering there, he wanted so badly to believe in possibilities. In happily-ever-after miracles.

But he knew better.

How he wished that he could undo the past, unsee the things he'd seen; undo the things he'd done. But no matter how he wished it, the stain on his soul could not be washed clean. It struck him then that he was too damaged for her, his mangled arm just an outward manifestation of the emptiness inside him. There were things he simply could not tell her. Things he desperately wanted to protect her from. Like the ugly world lurking beyond the protective boundaries of Twilight, Texas. She had no clue what was out there. Nor did he ever want her to know. He would carry that burden forever, never let her shoulder it with him. It was the price he paid as a Green Beret.

"Caitlyn," he whispered, "I can't do this."

"Do what?" She appeared genuinely confused. Was he that baffling?

"Be normal."

"It's not that hard. Just act normal."

"Fake it?"

"Until you make it. That's what everyone does."

"It's not that simple."

"Why not?"

"I can't begin to explain." He found himself moving away from her. He was the one who couldn't handle the proximity, not she.

"Don't pull away from me. Don't shut me out."

Gideon thought about a man he'd been forced to kill up close and personal in hand-to-hand combat. Thought about the look that had come over the man's face as he'd taken his last breath. He'd looked oddly peaceful, as if he welcomed the escape of death. Such dark thoughts didn't belong in this cheery yellow kitchen.

"I . . ." He swallowed hard. "I have to. I can't . . . I've got to protect you."

"So let me get this straight. By denying what you're feeling, you think you're somehow protecting me?"

"I know I am because you can't handle what I am. What I've become. I have nightmares—"

"Why don't you let me decide what I can and can't handle?"

She was so naïve. He reached out and ran his thumb along her jaw. "You are so sweet. So loving. You have no idea what the world is really like."

She tilted her head up, met his gaze. "You think I haven't suffered? You think I haven't seen loss?"

"You can't begin to imagine what I've gone through."

"So tell me. Let me help shoulder your burden. Let me in, Gideon."

He shook his head and turned his back on her, forced out the words in a harsh whisper. "I can't. It's too hard to talk about."

"Gid . . ." The pleading in her voice was a knife to his heart.

"I just can't . . ." He paused. "Soil you with the dirty details."

"Soil me?" Caitlyn laughed. "Gideon, I'm not some delicate flower. I'm stronger than you can possibly imagine. I know what I've been through here can't compare to what's happened to you, but things haven't been easy for me—"

"You lost your husband."

"Yes, but that's not all." She hitched in her breath. "Sit down. We need to have a talk."

"What about dinner?"

"It can wait." She pulled out two chairs from the table and sat.

Gideon sank down opposite her; he felt vaguely nauseous, but had no idea why. He dropped his left arm, hiding his missing hand from her underneath the table. Why the hell had he not worn his prosthesis? On the window ledge, he spied a tiny red Hot Wheels roadster. The crayon drawings on the fridge. The toy car. Of course, why hadn't he realized it before?

"There's something I need to tell you," she said. "It may come as something of a shock."

"You have a child," he said.

She blinked. "Yes."

As if on cue, the back door opened and a boy's voice called, "Mom, Mom, guess what—" The child's words broke off when he saw Gideon. He looked to his mother as if to say, *Who's this guy?*

"We've got company for dinner, Danny," she said.

The second Gideon stared into the child's eyes, his head spun and his world upended. His breath scraped across his teeth, coming out wary and weighted. He heard his heartbeat thudding in his ears, felt it hammering at his throat, tasted it surging adrenaline into his mouth.

The boy looked exactly as he had looked at that age. Brown-eyed, black hair with a cowlick that stuck up in the back, ears a little bit too big for his head.

Involuntarily, Gideon reached his hand to the top of his ear, felt his heart stutter in his chest, a battered old pump breaking down. The kid looked to be around seven or eight years old. Gideon did a quick bit of math. It was entirely possible the child was his.

That realization was a heart-stopper.

"Mom?" the boy said. "Why are you crying?"

Caitlyn was crying? Gideon swung his gaze back to Caitlyn. She was swiping at her eyes with both hands. The moment crystallized like a drop of amber preserved forever in time.

The kid notched up his chin as his mother had done earlier. Freckles dusted the bridge of his nose. He got those from his mom too.

Seeing the boy, recognizing for the first time that he was his, hit Gideon like a pile driver. He stared at Danny.

Danny stared back, his small eyebrows lowered in an intense frown, and stepped forward, his little hands knotted into tight fists. "Did you make my mommy cry?"

"No," Caitlyn said. "I'm not crying. He didn't make me cry."

Instantly, Gideon was jettisoned back in time, engulfed by a memory he'd completely forgotten. He'd been a bit younger than this boy was now. Maybe five years old and standing in the kitchen of the trailer house he and his mom had lived in near the train tracks behind the feed store. He could smell the grainy dust of that long-ago air, thick with the odor of hay and oats, corn and cottonseed.

A man had been sitting at the kitchen table, wearing only a white undershirt and boxer shorts; a black cowboy hat perched on the table. His mother had been straddling the guy's lap, her dress hiked up around her thighs, her arms threaded around the man's neck. He recognized the memory man he'd long forgotten. J. Foster Goodnight.

Gideon blinked away the memory, met the boy's stare. He didn't want any child to feel the way he'd felt in that moment. Like someone was taking his mother away from him. He struggled to figure out what he was feeling, what he was going to say to her, to the kid. He knew what it was like to walk into a room and find your mother looking chummy with a man you didn't know—a kick to the gut, a stab to the heart.

"Danny," Caitlyn said, her voice coming out too breathless and high. "I want you to meet Mr. Garza."

Danny swiveled his head toward his mother, his eyelids lowered, dismissing Gideon. "Crockett invited us to the Rangers' opening game. It's the first Saturday in April. He's already bought the tickets. Can we go?"

Crockett Goodnight. His half brother. Had he

asked Danny to the game just to needle him? Right, you self-absorbed jerk. He didn't trust Crockett any further than he could throw him, but that was being too suspicious. Shit, he didn't know how to act anymore. He'd been in country for eight years. His hometown was more foreign to him than the Middle East. And his son was a total stranger.

"Don't be rude. Say hello to Mr. Garza," Caitlyn admonished.

The kid dipped his head, kicked the tile floor with the toe of his sneaker.

Gideon thought of the times his mother had forced him to be nice to her boyfriends. He'd hated it. Not that he was Caitlyn's boyfriend. Not that she had a string of boyfriends. He knew her. She wasn't like that.

Correction, the old Caitlyn wasn't like that. He didn't even know this woman.

No, she hadn't changed that much. She'd always been true blue, the kind of woman a man could count on. The kind of woman he'd once needed to show him that all women were not fickle when it came to love.

"It's okay," Gideon said, even though inside him something withered.

Five minutes ago, he hadn't even known he had a son, now he was a father. Funny, how parenthood worked. Everything changed in an instant. You didn't want your kids to suffer the way you'd suffered. You wanted to spare them everything unpleasant. This new feeling was strange and yet wonderful. He tested it in his mind. Dad. Pop. Pa. Father.

It made him wonder then how his own father could deny who he was. In the end, of course, J. Foster had finally recognized him, but it had come years too late. Regret was a steamroller, flattening everything in its path. He was a screwed-up cliché. Loose mother, father who refused to accept him.

"Tell Mr. Garza hello," Caitlyn insisted.

Gideon shook his head, narrowed his eyes, sent the silent message, *no*. He didn't want the kid to feel obligated to be nice. That would only make the boy resent him more.

Danny snaked a quick glance at Gideon. "Hello," he mumbled, then glanced back up at his mom. "So can we go with Crockett?"

Caitlyn shook her head. "You know I have to work on Saturdays."

"Why can't I go with him by myself?"

"Because you're too young."

"You treat me like a baby!" Danny shouted. "I'm not a baby. I'll be eight in a couple of months."

"Well, right now you're certainly acting like a baby, throwing a temper tantrum."

Danny folded his arms over his chest and scowled darkly.

Gideon felt a jolt clean to his toes. Danny's gestures exactly mirrored his pout attitude when he'd been his age. Mad at the world and everyone in it. "I'll take him."

Where the words came from, he didn't know. They just popped from his mouth, making promises he couldn't keep.

Caitlyn met his eyes. "Are you sure?"

Spend the afternoon at the ballpark with his half brother whose inheritance he'd usurped and the son he hadn't known he'd sired? That was one for the record books. He shrugged, tried to show he was game for anything. "Yes."

Danny threw his hands in the air. The look of exasperated surprise on his face was so comical Gideon almost laughed. "Great, you won't let me go alone with Crockett, but you'll let me go with Crockett and some guy I don't know?"

The kid had a point. He was sharp as a razor. Much smarter than Gideon had been at that age.

"Okay, you can go," Caitlyn said, "but only if Mr. Garza goes with you."

The scowl was back. "Who are you?" Danny asked.

It was the perfect opportunity to simply say, *Your dad.* But of course he couldn't do it. Instead he opted for "An old friend of your mother's. You can call me Gideon."

"Well, you're not my friend."

He understood perfectly where the kid was coming from. He'd been in his shoes. He couldn't blame him for his attitude. But neither could he deny the way it made him feel. Unwelcome, unwanted, on the outside peering in. The guy who'd never really belonged anywhere except in the army.

But Danny belonged. His great-great-great-great-grandparents had founded this town. You couldn't get any more entrenched in Twilight than that. Here was something Gideon couldn't relate to. What it was like to be part of a larger-than-life legacy.

And yet, your father was J. Foster Goodnight. Kin to Charles Goodnight, one of the key figures in Texas history. But that was different. He'd never been claimed as a Goodnight. Not until this morning.

"If you want to go to the game," Caitlyn repeated, "it's with Gideon or not at all. The choice is up to you."

Danny jammed his hands in his pockets. The black cowlick, just like one Gideon had, stood up at the back of his head. "Yeah, okay, all right, he can come with us."

Gideon didn't know what to say, so he didn't say anything. It looked like he had a date for the first Saturday in April, but it wasn't the date he'd expected.

"Go wash up now," Caitlyn said. "It's time for supper."

Danny studied Gideon with caution, but then he nodded solemnly, turned, and left the room.

"We have a son?" Gideon whispered, truly feeling the reality of it for the first time. "You and me? We have a son?"

"Yes," Caitlyn confirmed. "Danny is our son. But he thinks Kevin was his father. Everyone in town believes it too. I wanted to make things easier for Danny, and Kevin agreed. I didn't want Danny to—"

"Grow up a bastard."

"I wasn't going to say that."

"Were you ever planning on telling him about me?"

"I was. I suppose. I am. I—"

"You were ashamed of me."

"No! God, no. Never." She got up, paced, wrung her hands. "I remember how you told me what a tough time you had growing up, never knowing your father. Feeling like you never belonged. Like no one cared. I simply wanted Danny to feel loved. Kevin was so good with him and I thought you were dead."

Gideon stood up too. "So you lied to our child."

"You don't have any right to get angry with me. I tried to find you when I discovered I was pregnant, but you'd left no contact number and then later, when I scraped together the money to hire a PI . . ." She waved a hand. "It's all water under the bridge. What's done is done. What we have to decide is how do we proceed from here."

"Yes," Gideon said harshly. "Easy enough for you to say. You haven't just found out you've got a child you knew nothing about."

"We can start again, Gideon. Build a new life."

God, how he wished it was true. He loved her more than words could say, but he'd learned that love wasn't enough. "It's not that easy, Caitlyn."

"You're making things harder than they have to be. You were always like that," she said, "determined to do things the hard way."

It was an accurate criticism, but he didn't appreciate her pointing it out now. He was a father. Gideon still couldn't wrap his mind around it. He had a son.

Gideon experienced this new knowledge in every cell in his body, every muscle fiber, in the center of his bone marrow. He had a son. He had a legacy.

He thought of J. Foster. Goodnight blood ran in his veins. Blood that had helped develop Texas. The same blood ran through Danny. Bigger than life, pulsating, hot, and adamant. Gideon was a Goodnight. Danny was too. The boy deserved his inheritance.

Gideon knew what he had to do.

Because having a child changed everything.

Dinner was a tense affair.

No one spoke over the meat loaf and when Danny asked if he could be excused, Caitlyn quickly said yes. She needed time alone with Gideon to get this straightened out. Every time she looked at him, all she could see was raw masculine power and surging testosterone. He was upset and she understood it, but they needed to work past the anger and blame, and figure out their next step.

"I'll make a pot of coffee," she said. "We can sit out on the porch swing and talk this through."

Gideon nodded, stony-faced. She wished she knew what he was thinking. Once upon a time she could look into his eyes and know every thought that passed through his mind. But those days were gone.

Lost forever?

She turned to the coffeepot, felt the heat of his gaze on her. Was he staring at her backside again? She hadn't missed the look he'd sent her when she bent over the oven. A smile tipped her lips. Maybe he wasn't as stony as he wanted her to believe.

Then again, a mischievous part of her thought, maybe he was. Caitlyn's cheeks warmed. Here she was scandalizing herself.

"Pie?" she asked when the coffee was ready. "I picked it up from the Twilight Bakery on the way home. It's apple. I remembered it used to be your favorite."

"Designed to butter me up for the news that I had a son?"

"I didn't know any other way to break it to you." She balanced the pie plates onto two cups of steaming coffee. He held the door open for her so she could walk out onto the porch. She set the cups down on the small white wrought-iron table beside the porch swing and pulled two forks from her apron pocket.

Gideon sank down onto the porch swing. His weight sent the chains creaking. She handed him a pie plate and tried not to notice how he had carefully settled it onto his thigh. She should have thought this through. Eating on a porch swing was a balancing act for people with two hands. She pushed his coffee cup to the edge of the table so he could reach it, picked up her own cup and plate, and went to sit beside him.

The minute her bottom brushed the wood she completely regretted the suggestion altogether. He was so close to her. So close she could see his coffee-bean-colored irises and thick, dark eyelashes. So close she could feel his body heat as warm as honeysuckle vines in the sun. So close she could smell the alchemy of his scent—a tangy mixture of sage, daylilies, and rugged man.

She felt drawn into a mystical spell of fantasy. Three days ago she could never have imagined sitting here with the love of her life. Maybe this wasn't real, but some kind of bizarre waking dream.

"I thought that somehow you guessed," she said. "Or someone had told you I had a kid and you put two and two together."

"What made you think that?" His eyes were clear and focused on her.

Caitlyn dropped her gaze, worked a chunk of pie off the slice with her fork. She noticed he wasn't eating, just watching her. "The daylilies. They represent motherhood."

"I didn't know."

"Weird coincidence. Why did you choose them?"

"Their color reminded me of your lips."

"Oh." She reached up a finger to brush piecrust crumbs from her mouth.

The sun was setting, casting a soft orange glow over low-lying clouds. The light slanted across Gideon's face and his skin seemed to almost shimmer. She wondered if her skin appeared the same way. Tingling with life.

"So about Danny," he said.

Yes, about Danny.

Gideon paused for a long moment, and she could tell he was having a hard time putting his feelings into words. "He didn't seem to warm up to me."

"You're a stranger. He doesn't know you. It takes him a while to warm up to strangers."

"Takes after you."

She bristled, felt as if he was judging her. "There's nothing wrong with being cautious."

"I never said there was."

"You used to tease me about it."

"That was before I knew how dangerous the world can be. You're right to be cautious."

"I worry that I might make Danny too much of a fraidy cat. Especially without a father around. I want him to be strong and independent."

"He's got a father around now."

"You've decided to stay in Twilight?" She held her breath and realized that either way, she was afraid of his answer.

"I am now. Danny changes everything. I've decided I'm going to accept J. Foster's inheritance."

"That's an about-face."

"I have a son to think about."

Caitlyn smiled. "Bowie and Crockett are going to be steamed."

"That's not my problem."

"They'll fight you."

"Tulip," he said, "have you ever known me to back down from a brawl?"

Tulip.

The nickname he'd given her so long ago. She hadn't heard it in eight years. "I'm happy to hear you say that."

"What? That I'm ready to fight?"

"That you plan on being around for Danny."

Gideon scowled. "Did you ever have a doubt?"

"I didn't want to assume anything."

"I've already missed almost eight years of his life, I don't want to miss a minute more."

"We have to discuss how to break the news to him. We can't just come out and say it. He's already been through so much with Kevin's death. He's having a hard time at school. I think we should take it slow. Let you two get to know each other first."

Gideon's scowl deepened. "I don't agree, but you're his mother, you know him best, so I'll defer to your wishes."

Caitlyn let out the breath she didn't even know she'd been holding. "Thank you. That's one reason I wanted to hire you to refurbish the carousel. So you'd have a reason to be around us."

"I don't need an excuse to be around you, Caitlyn." He drilled her with his gaze. "I want to be here."

"Well, I need the pretense of an excuse and we do need someone to repair the carousel."

"All right," he said. "I did promise to get that carousel running for you one day."

"You remember that?"

His eyes met hers. "Tulip, I remember everything about you."

Joy jiggled her heart. "We've only got one hurdle."

"What's that?"

"Convincing the garden club that you're the right man for the job."

After Gideon left, Caitlyn couldn't sleep. She put Danny to bed, tucked him in, read him a story, and then went to her own room. But after hours of twisting and turning and tossing, she was only more awake than ever. Finally, she got out of bed, slipped into her thick, worn sweater, and stepped out onto the back porch.

A full moon hung in the midnight black sky, fat and yellow. In the distance a whippoorwill called and its mate answered. The sweet scent of hyacinth wafted through the air. She could hear the bullfrogs down by Sweetheart Park start in with the late night strumming noises. Spring was almost here—ripe and rich and full. Spring was always her favorite time of year when the bulbs burst forth with bright pastels, making everything misty and romantic like a Monet painting. She liked Easter with its pageantry and symbolism. Loved dying hen eggs and hiding chocolate bunnies in the fresh green grass for Danny to find.

But this year, everything was different. This year, Gideon had risen from the dead.

It was still incomprehensible to her. That the man she thought long buried had returned. She wished this was a fairy tale or a movie where all they had to do was take one look into each other's eyes and melt, arms twined in an endless embrace. But it wasn't.

A lot of time had passed. They'd both grown and changed. They weren't the people they used to be. She couldn't profess her undying love for him, much as her heart might long to do so, because she no longer knew him. He'd been to war. He'd killed people. She didn't have to ask. She saw it in his eyes. Saw the harshness that pulled down his mouth. A mouth that had once laughed so much it seemed impossible that it belonged to the same guy.

And she had Danny to think about. She couldn't allow her heart to lead her head. She no longer had that luxury. She was a mother, and nothing was more important to her than that.

But he's your son's father. It's part of the same whole. Without Gideon there would be no Danny.

Who was this new Gideon with the piercing dark eyes and the bitter laugh that held no humor? He'd always been a bold alpha male, but the military had heightened and ingrained those traits until he was almost unrecognizable. Where had the young man she'd once loved with every cell of her body gone? And could she ever get him back?

Without even posing the question, she knew the answer was no.

So what was going to happen now? Where did they go from here? She had to form some kind of relationship with him, had to accept who he'd become and let go of the image she'd carried of him in her head for years. He was Danny's father, and the boy deserved to know his dad.

She hugged herself, blew out her breath, and remembered that split second of unspeakable joy when she'd looked into Gideon's eyes at J. Foster's funeral and realized he was alive.

That single emotion had been pure bliss, but now she felt too much. Emotions warred inside her—hope and fear, concern and sadness. She wanted to feel the joy again, but it had slipped out under the weight of the other feelings, squashed and weary.

The thing was, she never wanted to hurt again like she'd hurt when the PI had told her Gideon was dead. It had been the most crushing despair of her life. Worse even than her mother's death. She'd been five at the time and hadn't really comprehended what forever meant. But she'd known well enough when Gideon died—

But no, he had not died. He was here and it was an unbelievable miracle.

Caitlyn had a million impulses, none of them healthy, all of them rash and reckless. She could not afford to act on either hope or joy. She had to be calm, coolheaded, practical. Just the way she'd been when she'd married Kevin. Knowing it was not a love match, but understanding that he was a good and decent man who would take care of her and the child she carried. He had claimed Danny and reared him as his own.

She stood on the porch, mesmerized by the moon, trying to make sense of her life, taking stock of the options left open to her.

When it came down to it, one question kept circling her mind.

Just how damaged was Gideon?

CHAPTER NINE

*Traditional meaning of sunflower—
homage and devotion.*

The gardening club buzzed with the news that J. Foster had left his entire fortune to the dark stranger on the motorcycle. Not everyone in the club had known Gideon before, and the old-timers filled the newcomers in on the juicy details.

The club met every Tuesday evening at the event room in the public library. On the Tuesday following J. Foster's funeral, they gathered to finalize ground-breaking plans for the victory garden. Caitlyn was scheduled to present her design, and the group had asked the county extension agent, Newt Bandy, to stop by and give them advice on prepping the soil.

The spot donated for the victory garden had been underneath a building for over a hundred and twenty-five years, and the soil would need special preparation to make it suitable for growing.

Caitlyn stepped into the room, flip chart tucked under her arm, Danny in tow. She knew he'd be bored, but she'd been unable to find a babysitter, so she'd swung by the video store to rent him a game for his Nintendo.

"If you're good," she said, setting him up at the back of the room, "we'll stop by Rinky-Tink's for ice cream on the way home."

"I'll be good," Danny promised.

She kissed the top of his head, smiled at his little boy scent. How she loved being a mom. It was a hundred times better than she'd ever imagined it would be. She couldn't wait for Gideon to discover the joy of being this child's parent. "That's my boy."

"Evening, Caitlyn," Newt Bandy greeted, slipping into the chair beside hers.

Newt had been a good friend of Kevin's. He was a slope-shouldered man, closer to forty than thirty, with the kind of grin that made you feel as if you were sharing a secret when he directed it at you. He was losing his hair, and as a cover-up, he never took off his cowboy hat. Idly, she wondered if he slept in it.

She could have had the opportunity to find out. He'd asked her out a few months after Kevin's death, but she'd turned him down. For one thing, she wasn't attracted to him. For another thing, she didn't want to slip from one dependent relationship into another. She'd relied too much on her husband. Kevin had been a much-needed prop to get her out of her father's house, but now she needed to learn to stand on her own two feet. She was twenty-five, high time she started carving out a life of her own. One not defined or confined by a man.

That was another concern she had about renewing her relationship with Gideon. He was an alpha male just like her father. Would a dynamic like that undermine her struggle for independence?

"Hi, Newt." She returned his warm smile, but kept her body language aloof. She didn't want him to read anything into her friendliness other than what it was. "Thank you for coming to speak to our group."

"My pleasure." Newt beamed and scooted closer.

As president of the club, Patsy called the meeting to order promptly at seven o'clock. "I know Belinda isn't here yet, but we need to get this show on the road, and who knows when she'll drag in here. First order of business, we need a name for the garden. Something snappy that will capture the judges' attention."

Dotty Mae raised a hand. "How about the Lost Loves Garden?"

"That sounds so sad," said Emma. Her husband Sam's first wife had been an RN killed in Iraq by an IED while on her way to deliver medicine to orphans. "What about something a little more upbeat?"

"What about the Twilight Memorial Garden?" Marva suggested.

Raylene wrinkled her nose. "Too blah."

"Soldier Fields?" Christine proposed.

"That's leaving out the navy and air force veterans," Terri pointed out. Her husband, Ted, had received his medical training in the air force.

A few more names were bandied about, but nothing they could come to a consensus on. And then Caitlyn ventured a suggestion based on Gideon's homecoming. "What do you ladies think of the Welcome Home Garden?"

They all tried it out, saying it several times, and no one shot it down.

"Hey," Flynn said. "We could wrap the trees with yellow ribbons."

That resulted in an enthusiastic response from the group and some off-key renditions of Tony Orlando and Dawn, and then they took a vote.

"All in favor of calling it the Welcome Home Garden, raise your hands," Patsy said.

Everyone raised her hand. It was unanimous.

Patsy banged her gavel. "Welcome Home Garden it is. On to the next order of business. Caitlyn, how are the design plans coming along?"

Caitlyn stood up. Behind her came the cheery sounds of Super Mario Bros. ramping up a level on Danny's Game Boy. She walked to the podium, settled her flip chart onto the easel. "I've finished the preliminary sketches and my father finally sent the carousel over."

Patsy nodded. "I saw them unloading at the lot on Saturday afternoon."

"You need to get a temporary shelter built to house it," Newt interjected. "Keep it out of the weather while it's under construction. Discourage vandals."

"I've already got one coming," Patsy said. "Now we have to find someone who can restore the thing. That project is going to be as big as the garden itself. We'll need a lot of hands."

"I've got plenty of hands," Belinda Murphey called out as she came through the door, her five kids in tow.

"Great, she brought her army," Patsy muttered under her breath.

Danny spied the Murphey kids and jumped up from his seat. By their sheer number, Belinda's children caused chaos wherever they went. "Y'all go outside and play. But stay on the lighted basketball court."

Danny hung at the door looking like he really wanted to go outside with the other kids, but knowing better than to go without Caitlyn's permission. She nodded at him. "Go on."

He raced up to the podium, handed her his Game Boy to put in her purse, and then zoomed off with Belinda's brood. Once the kids were gone and everyone from the garden club had assembled their chairs in a semicircle around the lectern, Caitlyn opened the flip chart.

She'd painstakingly spent hours designing and drawing up the plans, using colored pencils to illustrate the carousel positioned in the middle. She'd divided the garden into four circular quadrants—fruits, vegetables, herbs, and flowers, encircling the carousel and spiraling outward in a circle like ripples on water.

The traditional victory gardens of World War I and II were food-based, meant to feed the locals and boost morale, but Caitlyn couldn't bear the thought of excluding flowers from the mix. What lifted the spirits more than saucy bright flowers in bloom? Besides, the contest rules had not restricted the gardens to edibles only.

Almost every night since they'd filed the paperwork with the state to be entered into the contest, she worked well until after midnight, long after Danny had been in bed. On paper and in her mind, the garden had bloomed, a testament to her dedication to the project.

And to Gideon.

But that had been when she'd thought he was dead. The garden had been a memorial. Yes, it was supposed to represent all the servicemen and women who'd served for Twilight, but in her mind, she'd been thinking only of Gideon.

"My gosh, Caitlyn, that's beautiful," Marva said.

"If you can plant the way you can draw," Terri said, "we're hands down going to win."

The carousel was the showstopper. Blaze featured front and center on her illustration, his beautiful head reattached, the poppies in his mane freshly painted, his eyes flashing as he jumped high on the shiny brass pole. It was how she remembered him. Before the aneurysm stole her mother from her. Before her father decapitated him with an axe.

All around the carousel were the flowers: taller ones in the back, shorter ones in the front. She planned a variety of plants to attract butterflies for all their stages of life—milkweed, violets, phlox, gaillardia, tuberosa, blazing stars, purple coneflowers, black-eyed Susans, bee balm. She picked other flowers for their vibrant colors or intriguing petal pattern and orchestrated their combination for the most dramatic effect—caladium, cosmos, hibiscus, impatiens, roses, salvia, red begonias, zinnias, and sunflowers.

Particularly sunflowers. They stood for homage, just as the garden did. The plants would flourish by early June, just in time for the contest judging.

"We'll have benches between the four circular gardens," Caitlyn explained, using the laser pointer on her key chain to illustrate. "And a few birdbaths scattered throughout, along with wind chimes and gazing balls and a sundial."

"Wonderful idea," Belinda said.

"The second section will contain herbs and spices," Caitlyn went on. "Rosemary, lavender, lemon balm, basil, comfrey, oregano, sage, mint, thyme, dill, allspice."

"It's going to smell like my grandmother's pantry," Marva said. "I can't wait."

"Third tier will be fruit—strawberries, blackberries, raspberries, rhubarb. Fourth tier, and largest, is for the vegetables; yellow squash and zucchini, bell peppers and tomatoes, onions and potatoes, carrots and Swiss chard, cucumbers and radishes, pole beans and black-eyed peas, spinach and beets."

"We're a shoe-in for Most Romantic garden in the state of Texas." Belinda breathed dreamily. "I can't wait to get started."

"That's good because we need to get a move on fast," Caitlyn said.

"I've talked to the high school ag teacher and he's giving extra credit to the kids who help out in the garden. I should have a roster to you by the end of the week," Marva said.

"I've also got a list of local churches who have eager volunteers," Patsy added. "This is a community project. Your main role, Caitlyn, will be to oversee it all."

Newt stepped up to examine her flip chart. "I don't know why you ladies asked me here. Caitlyn knows exactly what kind of plants will do well in North Central Texas in the summer, and she's incorporated them into an eye-pleasing design that really works."

Caitlyn's cheeks heated at his compliment. "We need you because I'm not a soil expert, nor do I know everything there is to know about organic gardening. And since that ground has been lying fallow underneath the old Twilight Theatre since 1875, it's going to need a lot of TLC to get this garden to grow. Can you tell us where to start?"

Newt took the podium and Caitlyn sat down. He launched into what they'd need to do to prep the soil. She busily took notes while her fellow garden club members asked lots of questions.

When he finished, Patsy Cross took over. "Okay, Caitlyn's got the design in place and we all agree it's beautiful, but to follow Robert's Rules of Order, let's vote on it. All for using Caitlyn's plan, raise your hands."

Ten hands shot into the air.

"It passes. We approve Caitlyn's design. Now," Patsy said. "There's the not so small matter of the carousel. Restoration is not going to be easy and we have a tight timetable to stick to. First order of business is to hire someone to refurbish the carousel. I know Marva can round up some of the high school kids from the woodworking and engine repair classes to help with the grunt work, but we need someone in charge. Someone with exemplary carpentry skills. Any suggestions?"

Caitlyn stood up. "I hope I didn't overstep my bounds, but since you put me in charge of the garden, I've already hired someone."

"Oh?" Patsy said. "And who is that?"

"Gideon Garza."

The group gaped at her.

"Gideon?" Dotty Mae asked. "Is he even staying in Twilight?"

"I doubt it," Raylene said. "He turned down his inheritance. I'm surprised he hasn't left town already."

"He's changed his mind," Caitlyn said. "He's staying and he's accepting his inheritance."

"Whew," Flynn said. "That's going to have some repercussions."

Caitlyn didn't comment on that. "Gideon is masterful with his hands. He's got mad woodworking skills. You've all seen that intricately carved jewelry box he made for me."

"Gideon might have been good with his hands once," Patsy said, "but that was a long time ago.

And now he's only got one hand. We need someone with two good hands for this project."

Anger flared through her. "That's discrimination. Just because he's disabled doesn't mean he can't do the job."

"We're talking about a job that requires working with your hands and he's only got one."

"I'm for giving him a chance," Belinda said.

"As someone in the disabled camp herself," Christine threw in, "I'm backing Gideon. He can do anything a two-handed guy could do. It might take him longer, but we can recruit Marva's students to help."

"And what if he fails to live up to our expectations?" Patsy asked.

Caitlyn lifted her chin. "Then it's on me."

Patsy shrugged. "All right." She met Caitlyn's eye. "All in favor of hiring Gideon to take the job of refurbishing the carousel, raise your hands."

The motion passed with only Patsy voting against him.

It was official. Caitlyn and Gideon would be working side by side in the victory garden.

While the garden club was meeting, Richard Blackthorne was taking his supper at Froggy's Marina Bar and Grill on the Brazos River. It was Greta's night off and he had a coupon for a half-priced fried chicken dinner. The dining room was packed, and because he hadn't wanted to wait—he was accustomed to taking his evening meal precisely at seven—he'd agreed to be seated in the bar area.

Crockett Goodnight was sitting at the bar nursing a long-necked Miller, one eye on the preseason baseball game playing out on the television monitor mounted over the bar. He wore khaki pants and a button-down crisp white shirt with the sleeves rolled up, looking collegiate casual. He'd gone to the University of Texas on a baseball scholarship and then come back home to open his own business selling baseball memorabilia. This was the Goodnight brother Caitlyn should have gone for. Not that rascal Garza who'd dragged her down to his level.

"Hello, Judge." Crockett smiled.

Richard put a hand on his shoulder. "How you boys holding up?"

"As well as could be expected."

He wasn't good at the sympathy stuff. So he just grunted and said, "Give it time."

The waitress seated Richard at a table for two positioned behind Crockett. Richard had just given her his order when Bowie came loping in to join his brother at the bar. He didn't look over at Richard. His shoulders were tense, his dark hair disheveled, a deep scowl carved into his brow. He didn't even glance Richard's way as he took the seat next to Crockett.

"So what the hell is up with Lester?" Bowie asked his brother. "Why did he ask us to meet him here?"

Crockett shrugged and pushed a bowl of peanuts toward his brother. "He said he's got news about Garza. Peanut?"

His curiosity piqued, Richard found himself eavesdropping.

"No." Bowie snorted. "I hope it's good news. Like Garza is on his way out of town, never to return."

Richard had to agree. He wanted Garza gone as much as the Goodnight boys did. At a time when he and Caitlyn had started to make forward progress in their relationship—she'd come to his house, after all, for the first time in eight years and asked for the carousel—Garza had shown up to set it back to square one.

He knew it was only a matter of time before Caitlyn figured out he'd paid Malone to lie, to make fake documents that showed Garza had died. If she hadn't figured it out already. He'd seen Garza's motorcycle in her driveway yesterday evening when he had gone for his nightly constitutional and walked past her house as he always did.

"Bourbon and branch," Bowie ordered from the bartender and rubbed his temple. "Better make it a double." To his brother, he said, "Can you believe Garza? Just giving the ranch back to us?"

"What I can't believe," Crockett said, "is that Dad left him the ranch in the first place. What in the hell happened?"

"The old man was hopped up on painkillers. That's all I can figure."

"Well, he about gave me a heart attack. Good thing Garza is stupid as a post and too proud to realize it." Crockett circled a finger around the lip of his beer bottle. "Thank God for that."

Bowie grunted but said nothing.

"There's Lester." Crockett nodded in the direction of the lawyer loping toward them.

LaVon nodded at Richard, Richard nodded back.

"Let's get a table," LaVon said, his briefcase tucked under his arm. "So we can talk face-to-face."

Shoot. Now he wouldn't be able to overhear their conversation.

But luck was with him. The table behind Richard's opened up and the waitress seated them there.

"So," Bowie said, once the waitress had departed. "What's up?"

Lester took a deep breath. "I've got some bad news for you boys."

Richard got a feeling like a spider crawling down his back.

"What is it?" Bowie asked.

Some fool put money in the jukebox and Willie Nelson started admonishing mothers not to let their sons grow up to be cowboys. Frustrated, Richard was forced to turn his head to the right in order to follow the conversation going on behind him.

"Garza changed his mind," Lester said.

"What do you mean?" Bowie growled.

"He's decided he wants to accept his inheritance after all."

"Son of a bitch," Bowie exclaimed, and thumped the table with a fist. "I knew it. What happened?"

"He just said he'd given it some thought and he'd changed his mind."

Bowie swore again.

"Okay," Crockett said. "What's our next move?"

"You can take him to court. Hold the will up in probate for months, even years."

"Yeah, yeah," Bowie said. "That's what we want

to do. Take him to court. Dad wasn't in his right mind when he signed that will."

"Honestly, what are our chances of winning?" Crockett asked.

Lavon spread his palms. "Look, boys, your daddy was of sound mind—"

"Not that sound! Giving our inheritance away to some bastard he sired with a Mexican whore," Bowie exclaimed. "You've got to show he didn't know what he was doing when he made out that will."

"But he did know," Lester said. "I can't lie about that."

"So what do you suggest we do?"

Lester slanted him a look. "I'm afraid you boys can no longer afford my services. Unless you sell those vehicles or that beach house he left you."

Bowie's rage—reliable as a match head against sandpaper—lit like a fuse. Richard could feel his seething a table away.

"It's not fair! I was at our father's bedside for the last four months, taking care of him during his final days. Me. I'm the one. I stayed home and helped him out with the ranch when in reality all I ever wanted was to be a pilot. And then this bastard Garza comes and steals away the one thing we have left. The Rocking J."

"There's got to be a way around this," Crockett said. "Do you know for absolute certain that Garza is our half brother?"

"J. Foster admitted it. That's reason enough. Of course, you'll demand a paternity test, but I figure it will just prove J. Foster is Gideon's daddy." Lester cocked his head, cut a bite-sized chunk from his steak swimming in cream gravy. "But honestly? I'd cut my losses." He chewed. "Make the most of what your father did leave you."

"What if we don't want to do that?"

"It is your right to contest the will," Lester said.

"But you don't think we can win?"

"Not likely. But you can tie things up in probate court for a long time. Damn, this is good chicken fried steak. Eat up boys, my treat."

"That's our only option?" Crockett snorted.

Lester raised an eyebrow. "You could make nice with Garza, maybe he'll cut you in."

"Fuck that," Bowie said. "I've got another question."

"Yes?" Lester smacked his lips around a second bite of chicken fried steak.

"What would happen if Gideon was to die before the will was probated? Would the money go to us?"

"According to J. Foster's will, if Gideon dies before he inherits, the money goes to you boys."

"Well hell." Bowie smiled. "Why didn't you say so in the first place?"

"Unless," Lester said, "he has heirs. Does Garza have any heirs?"

"Not that we know of," Crockett answered.

There was that spider-crawling feeling scurrying down Richard's spine, because Gideon did have an heir. A little dark-haired boy named Danny.

Richard's grandson. And he had the strangest feeling the child had just been threatened.

CHAPTER TEN

*Traditional meaning of Carolina rose—
love is dangerous.*

For long stretches at a time, Gideon dwelled on thoughts of Caitlyn and the boy. On Saturday night, a week after he'd come back to Twilight, he lay alone on the extra-firm mattress at the Merry Cherub, just a few blocks away from Caitlyn's house. He imagined her tucking their son into bed, reading him a story, putting a glass of water nearby in case he should wake up thirsty in the middle of the night.

It was not just thoughts of Caitlyn and Danny that kept him awake. Since his return to his hometown, the nightmares had come back in full force. Almost every night, he did battle in his sleep, viciously killing and slaying his enemies, with two good hands, only to wake up in a panic, gasping for air with the fresh realization his hand was gone. It had gotten to the point where he was afraid to sleep.

Anxiety fueled the nightmares. Or so the shrink he'd been forced to see had told him. Control the anxiety; control the dreams. But how could he control the anxiety? He was still adjusting to the fact he was a dad and trying to fit into a place where he'd never belonged.

No matter how hard he tried, he couldn't make himself fit in. It wasn't that the people weren't friendly and welcoming in Twilight, because they were. Too welcoming, in fact. Everyone wanted to talk to him, buy him lunch or a cup of coffee or a beer. They wanted to hear his stories. He just didn't want to tell them.

It wasn't that he didn't want to try to be part of the community. Rather, it was as if he'd left a part of himself on the battlefields of Iraq and Afghanistan. The good part, the part that knew how to connect, make nice, play the game, be a member of the team. It seemed to be the part of him that had been connected to his left hand.

Was that where your humanity dwelled? In your left hand? Once it was gone you couldn't ever really connect again? Did other soldiers feel like this? Or was he unique? Wasn't he supposed to embrace his homecoming? When a soldier was in country, that's all he ever thought about. The place he'd left behind. But now he was back, he found himself displaced.

Knock it off. Stop feeling sorry for yourself. She gave no indication that your disfigurement bothered her.

Maybe not, but it bothered him.

He'd tried to drown it out by working. He'd started in on the carousel full throttle. He'd already gotten the mechanics of the carousel working again. The gears and cogs and pulleys had been the easy part. Next week, he and high school volunteers were going to set up the base in the middle of the garden.

Now came the art and the craft of restoring the animals to their former majesty. That was going to take a lot of time.

Gideon threw back the covers and got dressed. It was after eleven, but even on a Saturday night the bed-and-breakfast was silent. He tiptoed from the Merry Cherub, and then walked along the empty streets, breathing in the stimulating night air that smelled heavily of the lake. He had no plans other than to roam, burn off some restless energy, until he came to the town square and saw her.

Caitlyn.

Standing in front of the vacant lot, head tilted, arms on her hips. She wore blue jeans, a pink long-sleeved cotton T-shirt, grubby sneakers, and gardening gloves. A tiller sat off to one side. The lot stretching in front of her had been freshly tilled around where they would set up the carousel base. She looked hot and sweaty and dirty. He had an urge to make her even hotter and sweatier and dirtier.

Oh yeah. Involuntarily, he licked his lips.

She must have heard his approaching footsteps, because she turned toward him, peered into the darkness. "Evening," she said.

The wind carried her scent to him—womanly,

musky, earthy—and his nostrils twitched. He felt like a lone wolf on the hunt. Hard, horny, and ready to mate. "What are you doing out so late?"

"Couldn't sleep so I thought I'd get some real work done, now that you guys have gotten the mechanics of the carousel up and running. We start planting tomorrow." She waved at several sacks of seeds and budding containers stacked against the wall of the temporary storage barn that workmen had erected a few days before. The lettering on the side of the plastic wrapping read "Carolina Roses," along with a picture of a white flower that didn't look much like a rose to Gideon.

"Why didn't you call me? I would have helped."

"I don't have your number."

That's where she was wrong. She had his number a long time ago. "Give me your cell phone," he commanded.

She arched an eyebrow. "Excuse me?"

"I'll put my number on your speed dial. You need it in case something happens with Danny."

She took her cell phone from her hip pocket—he couldn't help following her movements and noticing exactly how nice her fanny looked in those jeans—and passed it to him.

He flipped it open and with one hand deftly programmed his number in at the top slot on her speed dial, demoting . . . He peered at the screen. Someone named Emma.

"There you go." He handed the cell back to her.

His thumb brushed against her knuckles and he heard her sharp intake of breath. He realized his own breathing was erratic. His body hot and bothered.

"Where is Danny, by the way?" he asked, staring at her lips.

"What? You think I left him at home alone?"

"Don't get testy."

She shot him an irritated glance. "Danny is spending the night with his best friend, Charlie."

"You know," he said, "I don't even know Danny's full name."

"Daniel Dane."

"You gave him my middle name." A flush of pride rushed through him.

She nodded. "I wanted to name him Gideon, but figured that was too much of a giveaway."

"Yeah," he said.

That was hard to accept. She hadn't wanted anyone to know he was Danny's real father. In a way, he understood. It was easier for her to let everyone believe Kevin Marsh was his Danny's dad, but understanding her motives didn't stop him from hating them.

A moment of silence passed between them.

"Caitlyn," he said.

"Yes?"

God, when she pursed those lips it was all he could do not to grab her and kiss her until she begged for more. "I wish things had turned out differently."

"Is that an apology?" Her tone mocked him. "You never used to apologize."

"And you never used to be so smart-mouthed." He grinned.

"Things change," she said.

It was a cliché, but a profound one.

"You want some help packing up?" He waved a hand at her tools strewn about the lot—hoes, rakes, twine, the tiller.

"Yes, thanks."

The streetlamps cast them in an eerie, ghostly purple-white glow. Moths circled the lights, dipping and swirling. He knocked dirt clods off the blades of the tiller before loading it into a metal shed. His gaze lifted from the tiller. The feel of metal cool against his skin, he studied Caitlyn's strong, slender back, her shoulder blades moving beneath her cotton shirt as she worked.

She'd always loved plants. Whenever he brought her flowers, which hadn't been often on his meager salary working as a stock boy at Branson's, she'd been delighted. He'd picked wildflowers for her once and she'd been just as impressed by that as she had by the store-bought variety.

Gideon guided his gaze back to getting the tiller ensconced in her shed, his emotions clouded and confused. He wanted her, God, how he wanted her, but he didn't feel he had a right to claim her. She'd thought he'd died and she'd done what any good mother would have done. She'd picked up the pieces of her life and moved on. Providing for her son the only way she knew how—by marrying Kevin Marsh.

Jealousy pushed up hard against his rib cage, making his chest hurt. Kevin had gotten to hold her in his arms, press his lips to hers, make love to her. Gideon swallowed, narrowed his gaze.

"Gideon?" Her voice was soft.

He didn't want to look at her. He was terrified she'd see the despair inside him. Or worse. The emptiness.

Slowly, he raised his head.

She was standing in front of him, a bottle of water in her hand. She extended it. "I thought you might be thirsty."

Their gazes clutched. Or at least his clung to hers, but then that made him feel desperate. So he closed the shed, locked it, and took the water.

"Thanks," he said gruffly, and twisted the cap off the bottle.

Her tongue peeked out to moisten her lips. He tried not to notice, but it was impossible not to acknowledge the gesture. Innocent enough on her part, but it flooded his system with testosterone.

He'd imagined this moment a million times. Being back with Caitlyn. In the early days of his exile in Afghanistan—for that's how he thought of it now, banishment from the one person who'd meant more to him than life itself—he'd thought of her constantly. Then when his letters came back unopened he'd stubbornly hardened his heart and her memory had begun to fade until he'd stopped fantasizing about her.

But he hadn't stopped dreaming.

On those dark nights when he cobbled together a few hours of uninterrupted sleep, his treacherous mind would spin dreams of her. Caitlyn, coming to him, standing in the doorway of his subconscious, wind blowing her hair about her face in soft wisps, her eyes filled with longing just as they were now.

If it had been a million years ago, he would have dropped the water bottle to the ground, reached up, snagged his arm around her waist, and pulled her to him. He would have moistened those tempting lips for her.

But too much time had passed.

She'd been married and widowed. She'd given birth to his child without his even knowing about it. He'd been on the other side of the world, losing an arm, losing his humanity. He had nothing left to give her. A kiss would make promises he wasn't sure he could keep.

So he tipped back his head and drank, letting the cool water slide down his throat. Allowing the liquid to substitute for the nectar he really wanted. Caitlyn's sweet lips.

"I should head home," she said, wrapping her arms around her.

The night wind had kicked up and blew cold against their skin. She shivered. But Gideon's goose bumps weren't from the breeze, rather his skin prickled from being so close to her, wanting her but not knowing how to have her again. Not knowing if he could. If he even should.

Things could never go back to the way they had been.

"I'll walk you," he said.

"There's no need. Twilight is safe as a cocoon."

She was probably right. "I'll walk you," he said, making sure his tone brooked no argument.

For a long moment, she said nothing, just peered into his eyes, and he thought she was going to buck him on it, but finally, she nodded. She'd always been cautious. In their youth, he'd been the reckless one. The war had tempered that impulsiveness. Recklessness on the battlefield could get you killed. Recklessness had indeed almost cost him his life. His phantom limb gave a twitch, reminding him that he had not conquered his impulsiveness. It was there. Lurking. Ready to stir up trouble.

He stared at her, fascinated by the unruly tendrils of blond hair escaping her ponytail to frame the angular edges of her face. She looked so fierce with her shirtsleeves rolled up, but in that fierceness he spied the vulnerability she struggled to hide. She was still his soft, innocent Tulip underneath it all. So achingly sincere.

"Okay." She nodded. "You can walk me home."

The full moon shone overhead as they left the square and started toward Caitlyn's house.

"Let's cut through Sweetheart Park," she said, surprising him.

She left the pavement, her feet angling for the grass. He followed her to the cobblestone path leading to the wooden footbridge stretching over the narrow tributary of the Brazos that ran through the park. She paused on the bridge, rested her hands on the wooden railing, and took a deep breath. Moonlight illuminated the stalwart oak, pecan, and elm trees that dominated the park. The air smelled heavy with the scent of water. A clump of white ducks slumbered in a group along the banks. Gideon wondered what prevented a predator from attacking them. What kept Twilight ducks so safe?

"What are you thinking?" she murmured.

He shrugged. "Nothing."

"You were frowning so intently. Like you were mad at the world."

"I was thinking how vulnerable those ducks were," he said. "Just sitting out here in the open. A dog could come by or a raccoon or a coyote."

"Animal control is pretty vigilant and the park is well patrolled. It is on the road to the sheriff's office."

"Still . . ."

"The ducks do the best they can," she said. "What else can they do? They live their lives and—"

"Die."

"Everything dies."

"But not many things come back to life," he said, not knowing why he said it.

"No." Her whisper was so low that he almost didn't hear her.

"Caitlyn," Gideon whispered, still really unable to believe that this was real. That she was here with him and it wasn't some dream.

She reached up to stroke his shoulder, a gentle palm, soft and light.

His body roared to life, throbbing so strong with a blinding-hot need to possess her. He wanted this woman more than he wanted to breathe. His dick hardened to stone.

His erection was so hard he could barely catch his breath. He wanted her more than he'd ever wanted anything in his life. His blood raced with the thought of making love to her, but how prudent was that? He was damaged beyond repair and it wasn't simply because of his missing limb. His psyche had been mutilated and there was no way to repair it. He could not unsee what he'd seen, could not undo what he'd done.

Ironic really, that the same issue that tore them apart as teens still stood between them, albeit in a different guise. They came from different worlds. Back then the rift had sprung from the fact she was the daughter of the judge, the great-great-great-granddaughter of the town founders, and he was the bastard child of the richest man in town and a Mexican woman of low moral character. She'd lived in one of the most elegant houses in Twilight. He'd grown up in a shack across the railroad tracks. She was gentle and cautious and sweet. He'd been rough and reckless and impecunious. She'd kept her emotions under wraps; he expressed himself without reservation.

Now the rift was even wider because all that history was still there, but added into the mix was the sorry state of affairs that he was disfigured, both outside and in. He'd seen the worst the world had to offer. She was wrapped in the cocoon of her safe little world. She'd never ventured beyond the bounds of Twilight. He was world-weary. She was innocent. He was coarse. She was refined. He was broken. She was whole.

"Gideon," she whispered. "Talk to me."

He didn't want to talk to her. The crude, hard, masculine side of him wanted to strip off her clothes, lay her down on the cool, rich soil, and make love to her right there in the park. But of course, he couldn't do that. Wouldn't do that. She deserved honor and dignity and respect. No matter how much his body throbbed for her, he couldn't take her, not like this.

Her pink lips parted and she stared deeply into his eyes. "Gideon."

In a time warp, they were transported, back eight years to when they were teenagers, so hungry for each other they couldn't resist the hormonal pull of their bodies.

He stepped closer, not even sure what he intended, and she didn't move away.

"When I thought you were dead . . ." she said.

Gideon heard the words clog her throat, heard her pain, could see she teetered on the verge of tears. It ate him up inside.

"Oh, Gideon, your death ruined everything."

Caitlyn wasn't going to cry. She refused to cry as the memories of the past washed over her. It didn't matter now. The past was gone and he was back.

"Tulip," he murmured.

"I'm okay, I'm all right." She took a deep breath, gave a shaky laugh. "I just can't get enough of looking at you."

He looked pleased, but worried. He ducked his head, but his deep chocolate eyes never left her face. "What do you see when you look at me?"

"You look . . . deeper."

His laugh was short and shallow. "What does that mean?"

"Layers. You've got layers. You used to be simple, easy to read. And now you're as complicated as a bottle of expensive wine."

"Red or white?" he teased.

"You're making fun."

He measured off an inch with his thumb and forefinger.

"I get the feeling that if I don't watch myself I'll be sinking in quicksand."

"Complicated and deadly. Yeah, that about sums me up."

"I don't mean it like that," she said. "What I mean is you're out of my league."

He laughed again, more robustly this time. "You've always been out of *my* league, Caitlyn Blackthorne Marsh. Just ask your father."

She canted her head, studied him. Other than the hand, what was it about him that was so altered? He was more textured now. Like the accent wall in her kitchen that she'd added plaster mud to and dabbed with rags to create an Old World look. He had on desert camo pants, his black leather motorcycle boots, and a red flannel shirt unbuttoned to reveal a black T-shirt underneath. Beard stubble darkened his strong jaw. His hair was longer on top and shorter on the sides, but certainly not the severe buzz cut most former soldiers favored.

Her gaze dropped to his hand. To the prosthesis with black plastic fingers in sharp contrast to his flesh-colored skin. He had a watch strapped to the artificial hand, which struck her as incongruous. But why not? Machinery strapped to machinery.

His gaze followed hers to his hand, and then he went back to her face. She could tell right away it bothered him far more than it bothered her. All she cared about was having him back, but his dark eyes sheltered demons she knew nothing about. She could see them lurking beneath the surface.

There was that quicksand again, shifting beneath her feet.

"Caitlyn, you are the most beautiful woman I have ever known." His words were music, soft and sensual. He was luring her in, saying exactly what she needed to hear.

"I'm not." Embarrassed, but flattered, she raised a hand to her cheek. Even when a woman knew she wasn't all that beautiful, she loved hearing her man say it.

Her man.

Was he still her man? Did she want him to be? She still loved him, yes. No doubt about that. But could she handle the heavy baggage he carried with him?

So much had happened. So much had changed.

"You are beautiful," he said, and she could hear that he meant it. "When I look at you—" He broke off. He'd always had trouble expressing his feelings. He was terrified of being vulnerable. Even if he couldn't say it, she knew.

"Gideon," she whispered, knowing she shouldn't be crumbling so easily.

They needed to take this slowly. Find out how they still fit, or even if they did. Danny was between them now and he could not be taken out of the equation. Their son's needs came first.

Gideon stepped closer, encroaching on her space, looming. He didn't talk. He acted. He was so big. Six-foot-three, two hundred pounds, all muscles and man. Beside him, she felt, well, like a delicate tulip at five-four and a hundred and twenty pounds. He was solid as a brick wall and hot as a radiator and one hundred percent male.

His dark eyes glittered in the moonlight, telling her that he had something wicked on his mind. Oh, the naughty things he used to do to her body! She could only imagine that his rugged life away from her had taught him even more erotic tricks.

Her knees trembled and she drew in a shaky breath.

He wove a spell over her with his eyes, pulled her in. There were a million things they needed to say to each other. Questions to ask, questions to answer. Fears to be overcome. Doubts to conquer. But underneath the hesitancy and confusion, the shock and surprise of their new lives mingling with the old, pulsed a primal undercurrent that could not be denied.

They were soul mates.

His mouth came down on hers with the weight of years behind it. He wrapped his arm around her waist, pulled her to him. She went up on tiptoes, greedily trying to get as close as she could.

They inhaled a single breath, tasting the rapture of each other.

Welcome home, welcome home. She tried to show him with her mouth what she was thinking.

At first his kiss was tentative, searching, but it quickly escalated to something frantic and hot and electric. Time had not eroded the chemistry—in fact, it seemed to have stoked their former heat to a raging blaze. She parted her teeth, invited him deeper.

They fell on each other, into each other, mouths seared, hands touching, caressing, kneading. Both of them ignoring the fact that they were out in the open in the middle of the night. The magic spun about them like fireflies, pulled them deeper into the spell. Happily-ever-after was a seductive myth.

Caught up on the current, they drifted on the river of bliss. She cupped his cheeks between her palms, holding him, cherishing the feel of him. Then she moved her hands up, threading through his hair, holding on while he plumbed her mouth with his tongue.

Her lips tingled. She let out a shuddery breath and he absorbed it. Every inch of her body was inflamed. Had any kiss in the history of the world been this perfect?

A heightened sense of awareness stole over her. She was aware of everything. The pressure of his lips, the smell of the water, the feel of his skin against hers, the light of the moon shining down on them. And for an instant, everything was perfectly, absolutely clear, and she felt free for the first time in her life.

She wished she could freeze this moment, stay like this forever suspended in Gideon's embrace, forever capturing this fleeting moment of utter joy.

Finally, he let out a low groan and pulled his mouth from hers. "We have to stop."

Why? Why? Why did they have to stop? It felt so good.

Too good. He was right. If they didn't stop, they'd hop headlong into something they weren't ready for, especially with Danny being away for the night. It would be so easy to take him home, bring him into her bed. Too easy.

Just like old times.

Except it was not just like old times.

The yearning to turn back time was so strong. To start fresh, start anew, but no amount of yearning could change things.

He wasn't the man he used to be. She wasn't that girl—love struck and dependent.

The moment was already gone, the sweet haze of desire dissipating in the cool breeze. She had to be rational. She had to be an adult. She had a child to think about.

Their child.

Danny belonged to him too. Was it so wrong of her to dream of being a family? Of a grand reunion. Was that so impossible?

The haunted expression in Gideon's eyes said it was. He was already breaking away from her, stepping back, and distancing himself.

Was he so damaged that there was no fixing him?

"You don't know," he said.

"I don't know what?" she asked, moving toward him.

He raised his palm, blocking her, shutting her out. "I'm not fit for you, for this."

"What are you talking about?"

He shook his head. "You don't know."

"Then tell me." She reached out, but he turned away.

"I . . . I have to go."

Then he walked away with a hurried, stiff-legged stride, leaving Caitlyn wondering just what it was that she'd done so wrong.

CHAPTER ELEVEN

*Traditional meaning of tulip—
symbol of the perfect lover.*

For the first time in a long time, Gideon felt the need for a drink.

After running away—yes, like a coward, he'd run away when things had gotten too hot to handle—from Caitlyn in Sweetheart Park, he stalked into the Horny Toad Tavern desperate for something to take his mind off what he'd just done.

Impulsively, he'd kissed her. Before she was ready for it. Hell, before he was ready for it. He'd thought he'd conquered his rashness, that the army had drilled that character flaw out of him. He hated this, his inability to control his impetuous impulses.

If he moved too fast, he could royally screw up this thing with Caitlyn, because he didn't do anything in small measures. Throughout his life, it had been all or nothing. Moderation hadn't been part of his mindset.

Uncontrolled impulse had gotten him into trouble time and time again. It led him to burning down J. Foster's barn, to joining the army, to losing his hand.

He stared down at the prosthesis, opened the hand, closed it, felt nothing. The i-LIMB was a vast improvement over his previous prosthesis. This hand built on myoelectric principles could move each digit individually. The fingers stayed locked into position until he triggered movement through an open signal by flexing the muscles just above where his arm had been amputated. Now, he was able to pick up a Styrofoam cup without crushing it and he was grateful for that improvement. Advancing technology offered the hope of even more progress on the horizon. One day, he would be able to trigger movement just by thinking about it.

Enough time had elapsed since the bombing that he'd dealt with the major psychological issues, but this was the first time he'd left the Middle East since it had happened. Coming home, being in a different environment, it was like getting accustomed to the loss all over again.

"What'll you have?" asked the bartender.

"Shot of whiskey," he said.

When he first joined the army, when Caitlyn had first sent his letters back—correction, when her old man had sent the letters back—he'd taken refuge in the bottle. Drinking to excess in a mad attempt to block out the emotional pain. But then he'd realized that wasn't the path he wanted to continue down. If he couldn't have Caitlyn, he'd throw himself into his work, heart and soul, and he couldn't do that if his mind was on drinking. So he'd stopped.

After losing his hand, he'd gone through another bout of self-pity–induced drinking, but with therapy, he'd come to grips with what happened. Gideon stared into the glass of amber liquid. Did he really want to start down that road again?

"That'll be five dollars," the bartender said.

"I'm buying."

Gideon looked up to see Sheriff Hondo Crouch standing beside him. When he'd lived here before, Hondo had been a paramedic working for the ambulance service.

Hondo slapped a ten-dollar bill down on the counter. "Club soda for me, Jim."

Gideon pushed the sawbuck toward Hondo. "Keep your money, Sheriff."

"Ah," Hondo said. "You're in the moody, broody phase. I thought that might be the case when I heard you'd met Danny."

"Where'd you hear that?" Gideon tossed the whiskey down his throat. It burned nice and smooth. A welcome friend.

"My lady friend Patsy Cross is in the garden club with your lady friend."

He started to protest that Caitlyn wasn't his "lady" friend, but he let it go.

Hondo nodded at the barstool beside him. "Do you mind?"

Gideon shrugged. "Suit yourself."

Hondo settled on the barstool.

"Another." Gideon caught the bartender's eye, pointed at his whiskey glass.

"You sure you want to do that?" Hondo asked. "Alcohol is never the answer. I know. I've tried to find the answers in there too many times."

"Yeah? So what's the question?"

"You want to know why you didn't die." Hondo flicked his gaze at Gideon's prosthesis. "You want to know how the hell you're expected to fit into polite society now that you've been to the darkest place a man can go."

Gideon couldn't argue.

"I was in 'Nam." Hondo took a drink of his club soda, stared at the colorful array of liquor bottles on the shelf behind the bar. "POW."

"Shit." That raised the hair on Gideon's arm. He couldn't imagine being a POW.

"I came back home battered, bruised, wanting to die, and wasted out of my mind."

"On what?"

"Heroin."

"That shit is serious."

"Tell me about it. I lost everything and I do mean everything, except . . ." He nodded at Gideon's hand again. "A body part."

"How'd you kick the junk?"

"It took me three stints in rehab and lots of group therapy to finally shuck that monkey off my back."

"And yet here you are, sheriff of Twilight."

"I've been clean for over twenty years and this town believes in giving people second chances."

"Is that directed at me?"

"Should it be?"

Gideon downed the second shot of whiskey. He was feeling more in control now. Less panicked. So he'd kissed Caitlyn. It didn't have to mean anything. Yes, he'd been impulsive, but it wasn't something he couldn't correct. All he had to do was not kiss her again.

Yeah. Like that was easy.

"It's got to be a kick in the gut, coming home, realizing you have a son you've never met who'll soon be eight years old."

"I thought everyone believed Kevin Marsh was Danny's father."

"Hell, a blind man could tell that redheaded Irishman wasn't Danny's biological father. The kid looks exactly like you. Everyone just pretended for Danny's sake."

"Caitlyn thinks she's got everyone fooled."

"The real question you should be asking yourself is how do you become a father to that boy? Most dads get on-the-job training. They're there in the beginning. They're thrown right in, sink or swim. You don't have that advantage on your side."

It was true. He did not. Gideon cocked his head. "How do you know so much about it?"

"Because I've been where you are."

"You had a kid you knew nothing about?"

"That's right. But I didn't find out about Jesse

until he was twenty-eight years old. You've got a twenty-year head start on me, Gideon. Count your blessings."

"Yeah, right because I have so many of those."

"You are extremely blessed. The woman you've always loved is a widow. You could have come back and found her still married to Kevin. You've been given a second chance to woo her. A chance to heal those old wounds. Don't blow it."

"Who says I'm blowing it?"

"That empty shot glass in front of you."

"So you just thought, what? You'd come over here and give me the benefit of your vast wisdom?"

"I'd just hate to see you make the same mistakes I made. How are the nightmares?"

Stunned, Gideon stared at him. "How do you know about the nightmares?"

"All vets have them to one degree or another, and you with the hand, I figure yours have got to be pretty bad."

"Do they ever go away?"

"Over time. For the most part. Now and then one still creeps in. But don't let the night terrors run your waking life."

Gideon felt at once appreciative and resentful. It was nice of Hondo to come over here and give him a pep talk, but he hated being told what to do. Another one of his negative personality traits. Extreme stubbornness.

"Okay, since you seem to know it all," he said, "just how do you propose I put my life back together?"

Hondo moved the shot glass away. "First lay off that stuff."

"Then?"

"Take your time and prove to your woman that you're worthy of her. Don't rush her. Let things evolve organically. Show her that you're going to stick around. That she can rely on you. But don't be possessive. Give her space."

"In other words be a wimp." Gideon motioned the bartender to refill his drink. He liked the way the alcohol took the edge off, made everything soft focus and rosy.

Hondo laughed. "Nothing is further from the truth. A strong man knows how to let his woman be strong in her own right. You don't have to protect her or take care of her."

"Then what the hell is my function?"

"Just be there for her and your boy too. Take it one day at a time."

"Wow, that's some profound advice. Where'd you read it? In a fortune cookie?"

Hondo put his hand over the shot glass, blocking the bartender from tippling in another shot. "In AA."

He met Hondo's stare, felt himself grow simultaneously hot and cold. The bartender stepped back. Hondo stayed leaning across the counter, his hand over the shot glass.

Gideon had a choice to make. Accept things the way they were and try to do something about it, or drink himself into oblivion.

"You want me to get you another glass?" the bartender asked when it became clear that Hondo was not going to move his hand.

Gideon shook his head. "No, I'm done."

Hondo clapped Gideon on the shoulder. "Wise choice, son, wise choice. Now, first thing tomorrow morning, you go see your lady friend and you tell her what she needs to hear."

Even though at that moment he resented the hell out of Hondo for his interference, Gideon knew in his heart the sheriff was absolutely right. Caitlyn had always been a cautious woman, and now that she was a mother, she was even more so. Only time could win her heart.

If he wanted to rebuild his life, he had to prove to her and his son that he would be there for them, no matter what.

Caitlyn woke, as she always did, just before dawn and immediately thought about what she'd fix Danny for breakfast, but then remembered that he'd spent the night at his friend Charlie's house. She could go back to sleep if she wanted. No one was about. Nothing to roust her.

It wasn't often that Danny had a sleepover and she was unaccustomed to the quiet. Besides, she couldn't stop thinking about Gideon and what had passed between them last night.

Had he actually kissed her? Or had she dreamed it? She reached up to finger her puffy lips. Not a dream. He *had* kissed her. Kissed her hard, and she'd felt it clean to her soul.

What did it mean? Just as quickly as he'd kissed

her, he'd pulled back, mumbled something cryptic, and practically run away.

She got out of bed, stretching. Arms over her head, spine curled, her ears cocked for sounds of Danny awakening. *He's not here. He's at Emma and Sam's spending the night with Charlie.*

"Enjoy having the morning all to yourself," she said, and resolved to do so. She put a pot of steel-cut oatmeal on to cook, and in the misty gray predawn went out to feed the chickens.

"Good morning, ladies," she called to her nine Buff Orpingtons and sprinkled out the grain. To the Faverolles, she spoke French. *"Bonjour, Collette, comment allez-vous aujourd'hui?"*

Collette with her beautiful collar of cream and brown feathers came over to peck affectionately at the toe of Caitlyn's rubber boot. Caitlyn filled up their water trough and let them out into their run. Then she picked up the basket she kept draped over a nail and went to the nesting boxes to gather eggs.

She used to allow the hens to free range the acre lot, but a pair of Cooper's hawks had taken up residence in the wooded lot across the road and she'd lost three Buffies to the raptors before she could build the enclosed run.

"I'm so sorry about the loss of your freedom, my darlings," she apologized.

They clucked and scratched and didn't seem the least bit concerned. Smiling, Caitlyn took the ten perfect brown eggs and headed back to the house. Her oatmeal was ready. She made a cup of hibiscus tea, put honey in both it and the oatmeal, and sat at the kitchen table to watch the sun finish pushing up over the horizon.

She closed her eyes, breathing deeply of the morning air, and said a prayer of thanks.

After she'd eaten, she realized she could squeeze in an hour working at the victory garden before picking Danny up at Sam and Emma's, hurrying home for a quick shower, and then heading out again to Sunday school and church. She dressed in jeans and a long-sleeved white cotton blouse, sneakers, and a blue sweater so old the elbows had gone threadbare. It was her favorite sweater. Too faded now for public use, but perfect for gardening. Perching a straw hat on her head, she rubbed a dollop of sunscreen on her face and the backs of her hands and walked to the victory garden.

This early on a Sunday morning the streets lay quiet. A couple of neighborhood dogs barked as she strolled past, but she didn't see anyone else out and about. Most of the coffee shops wouldn't open until six and it was a few minutes shy of that, but she could smell doughnuts in the air. Christine Noble was busy behind the counter of the Twilight Bakery.

Maybe she'd pick up a box of doughnuts on the way home as a special treat for Danny. She didn't let him have junk food very often, but she'd been feeling a bit guilty for not spending as much time with him as she normally did.

Yeah, that's great. Give your kid doughnuts to make up for lack of attention. Okay, she promised herself. She'd take him fishing this afternoon.

Idly, she wondered if Gideon would like to come,

but squelched the thought. She couldn't foist father-hood on him. She had to let him take things at his own pace. She imagined it must be a huge shock, suddenly learning that you were a father and had missed the first seven and a half years of your child's life.

The doughnut guilt morphed into another kind of guilt. She shouldn't feel bone-deep remorse. She hadn't intentionally kept Danny from his father. She'd thought Gideon was dead. There was no one to blame. No one, that was, except for Judge Black-thorne. Sooner or later, she was going to have to have it out with her father over that. His actions were unconscionable.

Her shoulder muscles tensed and she forced her-self to take a deep calming breath. She was so busy trying to relax and get her mind off Gideon that she didn't see him until she was already at the garden. He was crouching in front of the base of the car-ousel, painstakingly securing the wooden platform with carriage bolts. He'd made amazing progress on repairing the carousel's mechanized parts over the past week.

Caitlyn paused, but Gideon glanced up and spied her before she had a chance to retreat. Her pulse revved. Why did she have a strong urge to turn and run away?

His eyes were red-rimmed, his hair disheveled, his T-shirt wrinkled as if he'd slept in it, his jaw un-shaven. He looked gruff and rough and abrupt, and the minute she laid eyes on him her heart fluttered ridiculously.

She smiled, raised her hand. "Good morning."

"Morning."

"You're up early."

"Same could be said of you."

"How'd you sleep?" she asked.

"Fair enough."

Liar. It looks like you haven't slept a wink.

"How about you?" He met her gaze. "How did you sleep?"

Well, other than those erotic dreams I had about you all night long, not good at all. If he could lie, she could too. "Great!"

Okay, that sounded too chipper.

He didn't say anything else and she walked over to the storage shed. She opened it up, took out gardening gloves, trowels, shovels, kneepads, and several sacks of seeds. She needed to get the seeds in ground ASAP. It was already the second week in March and she was running behind in her planting schedule.

She got straight to work. Last week had been about prepping the soil. This week was about sowing the seeds. She took the hoe and made little furrows in the freshly tilled soil.

Behind her, she could hear Gideon's hammer banging in the carriage bolts. It came off strangely loud in the quiet morning, punctuated by mockingbird trills. She felt her back heat and without even turning her head, she could tell Gideon was staring at her. Warmth built in the center of her stomach.

He's not looking at you and even if he is, so what? It doesn't mean anything.

But what did it mean when all she wanted to do was turn and ogle him? How strange it was, this distance between them. Once upon a time they'd been as close as two people could be.

Why did it feel so awkward now?

Once upon a time, you were teenagers. Young, dumb, knowing nothing about how life really worked.

For one brief, sweet second, she wished she could turn back time, be seventeen again and so madly in love with Gideon that everything she ate tasted like candy, every time she looked at the sky she saw rainbows, and every song she heard was a love ballad. How she wished they could be transported back to the time when the future held promise, before it had been set in stone.

This is your chance to make a clean start, begin again.

Caitlyn wished it was that simple. She was a single mom now and her life wasn't her own, and Gideon . . . well, he had more issues than the *New York Times*. He needed to unpack some of that baggage before they could even dream of anything more.

Gideon was bent over, his butt in the air, muscles taut beneath the denim of his jeans. Sudden lust had her by the throat, squeezing tight with a powerful response. She ached to trace her fingers over those jeans straining across his very fine ass.

Now, that doesn't sound the least bit motherly. For shame, Caitlyn, what are you thinking?

She was thinking she'd love to know if his butt

still felt the same. If she dug her fingers into his flesh, would she feel the same hard lines and honed angles she'd once caressed?

Her mind wandered to thoughts of their past lovemaking and she forgot to pay attention to what she was doing. The smell of earthy loam was in her nose as she dug, aerating the soil. She spied the rusted chain peeking from the dirt. Hmm, what was this? She set her hoe aside, got down on her knees, saw a jagged edge of metal.

"That's odd," she said.

"What?" Gideon turned his head her way.

"There looks to be something underneath the dirt." She reached down. "Like some kind of metal—"

"No!" Gideon yelled. "Don't touch it."

But it was too late. From her peripheral vision she saw him come racing toward her just as the metal thing sprang from the dirt and clamped around her left lower arm.

She heard the horrific snap, stared down at her arm, saw blood bloom around what appeared to be an antique bear trap biting solidly into her flesh. She didn't immediately feel the pain. For one ignorant second she just stared, wondering how she'd gotten caught in a bear trap of all things.

That's when the surge of blinding pain hit.

"Oh, oh," she gasped.

Blood poured over her hand, and the excruciating pain knocked her back onto her butt. Numbly, she reached out and tried to pry the trap off her, but Gideon was there.

He didn't even ask what had happened. He just took action. Somehow, she didn't know how he did it with only one hand; he managed to pry the bear trap off her. She thought once it was off the pain would at least become bearable, but the release of pressure made it hurt even worse as bright red blood came spurting from the wound.

Uh-oh, this was very serious. Her life flashed before her eyes. She was going to die.

Gideon yanked a red bandana from his back pocket, twisted it thin, and wrapped it tightly around her arm just above the jagged, gaping flesh. She screamed against this fresh pain.

"I'm so sorry, baby," he cooed. "But I've got to stop the bleeding. Hang on, hang on."

The next thing she knew, he was cradling her against him, half pulling, half carrying her toward the Twilight Bakery.

The smell of doughnuts was nauseating now. *Dear God, please don't let me throw up.*

He pushed open the door to the bakery with his butt. "We need your help!" he shouted to Christine.

"Oh my, oh goodness!" Christine cried.

Caitlyn felt faint, blood dripping hot and sticky down her arm, her head spinning wildly. *Dammit, I'm going to die before I ever get the chance to get Gideon naked one more time.*

Fate was surely a bitch. Bringing them together only to tear them apart all over again. Done in by a bear trap. Who knew it would end like this? She could see the headlines in the *Twilight Caller*: *Judge Blackthorne's Daughter Dies in Freak Gardening*

Accident. And here she'd always figured an aneurysm would do her in.

"Stay with me, Tulip," Gideon whispered softly.

"What should I do?" Christine asked.

"Drive us to the hospital," Gideon commanded.

"Yes, right, sure, just let me get my keys and turn off the ovens."

Christine turned off the ovens, grabbed her keys, and came rushing toward them with a stack of clean hand towels.

"Thank you." Gideon accepted them from her and wrapped a towel around the wound.

Caitlyn had to bite down hard on the inside of her cheek to keep from screaming. If it hadn't been for Gideon holding on to her, she would have passed out.

Christine ushered them to her Honda Civic parked at the back of the bakery and opened the backseat.

Gideon slid inside, taking Caitlyn with him. She felt so exhausted, wrung out, and rested her head against his shoulder on the short ride to Twilight General. She breathed in short, panting gasps. By the time they reached the hospital, she was lightheaded, feeling oddly sleepy, and blessedly her arm had gone numb.

Gideon carried her into the ER, she didn't know how he managed it, but he did.

"We're twins." She giggled goofily, not even really sure what she was saying.

Gideon grunted as the nurses ran toward them. "How do you mean?"

"Messed-up lefties."

"You're going to be fine," he said. "Few stitches. Good as new."

He guided her into the wheelchair, held on to her bleeding wrist as one of the nurses wheeled her into an examination room. They helped her transfer from the wheelchair onto a gurney and they took over from Gideon. It was only then that Caitlyn saw he was covered in her blood and his eyes were dark with concern.

"Get Dr. Longoria in here stat," one of the nurses yelled to the front desk. "We've got an artery involved."

Things were getting really blurry now and she felt dreamy in a cloudy way. Like cotton candy, fluffy and sweet and empty.

"Good thing you made a tourniquet of that bandana," the nurse told Gideon, "otherwise she would have bled out."

People crowded into the examination room, running around doing stuff. She thought someone started an IV in her right hand, but she couldn't be sure.

"Caitlyn," the nurse said, "how we doing?"

"It doesn't hurt anymore. In fact," she whispered, "it feels like I'm floating."

"Caitlyn?" She heard Gideon's voice. He might have been standing in front of her, but she couldn't really see. "Hang on, don't leave me."

But leave him she did.

Gideon's heart leaped into his throat as Caitlyn's eyes rolled back in her head. He knew she'd lost a lot of blood. Fear slammed into his heart. This wasn't good, not good at all. The medical staff gathered around and kicked the brakes of the gurney and pushed her down the hall.

"Sir," one of the nurses said. "You have to stay here."

He looked up to see they were just outside the operating room.

"Have a seat in the waiting room. Someone will be with you shortly."

He'd been in many skirmishes. Had seen a lot of blood. Had bled a lot himself. He'd almost died when he'd lost his arm. He knew what she was going through. The initial numbness and denial, quickly followed by the fear and pain, and then finally as death hovered, the easy acceptance, the slipping away.

His chest tightened and he couldn't speak. He just nodded and stepped to the waiting area. Other visitors were in there and they stared at him in horror.

He looked down, saw he was covered in Caitlyn's blood. Stunned, he stood frozen, and it wasn't until a nurse put a hand to his back and handed him a pair of green scrubs that he moved into action.

"You can use the staff lounge to clean up and change," she said kindly, and showed him where to go. "Then we'll need you to fill out some forms for us, answer some questions."

"Yeah, sure, okay."

He stood under the hot water for a long time, reliving the moment when he'd heard Caitlyn exclaim "oh" and he'd looked up to see blood spurting from her hand in what he knew was arterial spray. The sight had chilled him to the bone and he'd run as fast as he could, staying calm, staying in control for her. But now that the moment was over and she was in the hands of the medical professionals, all the strength and courage abandoned him.

To keep from coming completely unraveled, he turned his thoughts to the bear trap. The thing was rusted, ancient. Probably a hundred years old. How had it gotten into the victory garden, set and loaded? It couldn't have been there all this time. The land had just been tilled. The trap would have been discovered at that point. He knew a booby trap when he saw one.

No, someone had planted it there.

Intentionally. And very recently at that, sometime between last night and this morning.

But who?

And why?

Gideon was determined to find out and hold the culprit fully accountable.

CHAPTER TWELVE

Traditional meaning of purple hyacinth—
I'm sorry, please forgive me.

Richard Blackthorne was sitting near the front row of the Twilight First Presbyterian Church when his cell phone rang.

"Caitlyn's in surgery at Twilight General," Hondo Crouch said. "I just thought you should know."

Richard's old heart staggered, stumbled. "An aneurysm?"

"No—"

"What's wrong?" he interrupted, rising up out of his seat, catching the disapproving eye of Pastor Dupree, who had a thing against cell phones in church.

"She got her hand snapped in a bear trap."

"What?" Richard frowned and leaned more

heavily on his cane than he normally did. "I can't hear you. I thought you said she got caught in a bear trap."

"I did."

Several people were glaring at him now, heads turning as he walked past. Usually attracting that kind of negative attention would embarrass him, but he was too worried about Caitlyn to care. "How in the world did she get her hand caught in a bear trap?"

"That's what I'm trying to find out," Hondo said. "Someone set it in the garden."

"Intentionally?"

"It looks like it."

"To hurt my Caitlyn?"

"I don't know who it was directed toward. Probably some ill-conceived prank gone bad. Just wanted you to know she was in surgery. The damn thing severed an artery and if Gideon hadn't been there to stop the bleeding, she would have died."

"My Lord." Richard's knees started to buckle and he might have fallen down right there in the foyer of the First Presbyterian Church if Greta hadn't appeared at his side and slipped her arm around him.

"Judge?" Her face pinched with worry.

"Drive me to the hospital."

"Are you sick?"

"Not me. It's Caitlyn." He pulled back from her grasp. He didn't want anyone to think he was weak, that he couldn't get around on his own steam. Hell, he wasn't even that old. Yes, he'd been almost forty when Caitlyn was born. But he was only sixty-five.

Not that old at all these days. He easily had another good ten years left on the bench. It was just the damn arthritis that had his knees playing out from time to time.

"Give me your keys," Greta said.

Richard fished in his pocket, found his keys, and handed them to her. The heavy wooden doors of the church closed behind them.

"Wait by the curb," Greta said. "I'll bring the car around."

He stood there feeling like a fool, wishing he hadn't asked her to drive him. He wasn't crippled. He was just well . . . *shaken*. To hear that Caitlyn could have died. Had almost died except for Garza. The man had saved her life.

Richard had wondered what was going on with them. They seemed to be circling around each other, not sure what to make of their new relationship. He'd been watching the flower shop and the progress in the victory garden from his office, and he'd listened to the local gossip in the coffee shops. People were taking bets on whether Caitlyn and Garza were going to get back together or not.

While he stood there wondering why it was taking Greta so damn long, the sweet, honeyed scent of spring teased his nose and he glanced down at the base of the mimosa tree. A profusion of densely packed, bell-shaped purple flowers enlivened the air with their perfume. Impulsively, he bent down and plucked a handful.

Greta pulled up in the Lincoln and leaned over to open the passenger side door so Richard could get in. He slid into the seat and pulled the door closed behind him. She had the air-conditioning on, even though it was only March. Probably one of those hot flash things. He shivered and directed the vent away from him and onto her.

She didn't ask him any more questions. Which was one of the things he liked about her and why he didn't say anything about the annoyance of the cold air. The woman knew how to keep her mouth shut. A rare trait among women, in Richard's estimation.

Within a few minutes, they'd arrived at Twilight General. Greta marched in ahead of him, went straight to the front desk. "What room is Judge Blackthorne's daughter in?"

The clerk typed on a computer keyboard. "We don't have anyone listed under the name Blackthorne."

"Caitlyn Marsh," Richard said, his hand still clamped around the overly sweet-smelling flowers. He was starting to regret having picked them. "Her name is Caitlyn Marsh."

"She's in recovery, sir. You can wait for her in the PACU waiting area at the end of the second floor hallway. A nurse will come get you when it's okay to visit." The woman leaned over the desk to point down the hallway. "If you go down this corridor—"

"I know where it is," Richard said impatiently. "I've spent my entire life in this town. I was here before this hospital was built."

The clerk looked affronted. "Well, excuse me for breathing."

Being in this hospital made him irritable. It wasn't

just the cloying smell of antiseptic and disease that clung to the walls. It wasn't just the fact that generally, if you were coming to this place, things weren't going so well for you. Rather, the recovery room waiting area was where he'd gotten the news that his beloved Angelica hadn't survived brain surgery. Being here jettisoned him back twenty years and he did not want to go there.

Dear God, if anything happened to Caitlyn, he wouldn't be able to live with himself. His stubbornness had cut her out of his life. They'd been estranged from each other for far too long. He'd missed getting to know his grandson, missed holidays and celebrations, all because he couldn't bend, couldn't keep up with modern times and mores.

Couldn't forgive.

He reached the recovery waiting area, Greta at his side, the purple flowers getting sweaty in his clenched fist, but when he started to step into the room, he spied Gideon Garza looking as big as a redwood tree. He didn't remember Garza being so big.

Along with Garza were a few of the local old busybodies who couldn't keep their noses out of other people's business. Dotty Mae Densmore, Patsy Cross, Raylene Pringle. And there was that young woman with the crippled leg who ran the Twilight Bakery. Richard frequented Mindy Lou's Pie Shop, so he couldn't remember the bakery woman's name.

Richard's gaze met Garza's. He didn't flinch or back down. He was accustomed to being in control.

Garza's eyes blazed fire. He had tree-trunk upper

arms folded over his chest, his artificial left hand tucked under his right armpit. Richard remembered when he'd been in his courtroom and he'd told him he had two options. Prison or the military.

Richard had been so full of shit. A good lawyer could have gotten him off on the arson charges. Garza had no priors. But he'd been a dumb kid who couldn't afford a good lawyer and Richard had wanted to get him as far away from his impressionable young daughter as possible. He hadn't realized he'd been too late. If he'd known Caitlyn was pregnant, most likely he wouldn't have run Garza off. In spite of J. Foster strong-arming him.

Garza stalked over to him.

Richard stood his ground, cane in one hand, flowers in the other.

"I'm not going to throw you out on your ass, Judge," Garza said. "Even though you deserve it for the shit you pulled on us. But because I'm a father now too, I'm going to let you stay. So sit down over there and keep your mouth shut."

Anger blasted through Richard. "You have no right to talk to me like that, young man."

Garza's face was stone. "I have every right. You robbed me of eight years with Caitlyn and Danny. Because of you, I lost my hand. We figured out that you paid Malone to lie. That you sent back the letters I wrote her."

Richard's chest tightened. He was very aware that everyone in the room was staring at them. "I did what I thought was best."

"Yeah? Well, you don't get to manipulate other

people's lives. It's not your place to play God. I know being a judge has gone to your head, given you a power trip, but I'm not that dumb kid you had over a barrel."

Richard was impressed. Maybe he'd misjudged Garza. After all, J. Foster had changed his mind about the boy in the end.

"But to prove I'm not like you, I'm not going to stop you from seeing your child. Assuming, that is, that she even wants to speak with you."

"I just . . ." Richard straightened his shoulders, cleared his throat. "I just wanted to say thank you for saving her life. Hondo told me she would have died if you hadn't been there."

The women in the room all looked stunned, including Greta. What? He could be nice when he wanted to. Was that such an alien thing?

Garza seemed taken aback as well. "I didn't save her because I was doing you a favor."

"I know that."

Silence fell. The only noise came from the coffee-maker in the corner.

At that moment the door to the recovery room opened and the nurse stuck her head in the waiting room. "Who's with Caitlyn Marsh?"

"We all are," Patsy Cross said.

"Only one person at a time. You make up your minds who's coming in."

Richard looked at Garza. "I'm her father."

"I saved her life."

"Touché," Richard said. "You go in first."

"Age before beauty," Garza suddenly conceded,

and gestured toward the door. He took a seat in the waiting room beside the bakery woman.

Well, this was an unexpected turn of events. Richard wondered what Garza was trying to pull. *Maybe he's not trying to pull anything. Maybe he's just trying to mend a rift. Ever think about that?* No, because Richard wasn't a rift mender. The idea was foreign to him. He believed in sticking to his guns, no matter what. He'd always been that way, but he'd gotten more entrenched after losing Angelica.

"It's not a trick," Gideon said. "I'm not the kind of guy who keeps a father from his child."

Ah, so that was his game. Needling. Fine. As long as he knew where Garza was coming from.

Once he stepped through the door into the recovery room—these days they called it post anesthesia care unit—he felt a bit overwhelmed. Staff in scrubs scuttled to and fro. Ventilators made heavy breathing sounds like wet lungs sucking air. The place smelled of a strange gaseous odor and Betadine and something faintly singed. The patients were lined up in rows on gurneys, all hooked up to oxygen and IVs and monitors.

"Mrs. Marsh is over there, sir," the nurse said, and indicated the second bed on the right.

He crept closer, feeling very out of place. The nurse pulled a curtain around him and Caitlyn to give them some privacy from the beehive of activity going on around them.

"Go ahead," the nurse said. "Talk to her." Then she disappeared on the other side of the curtain.

Caitlyn's eyes were closed and Richard didn't know how to start. He sidled closer, stared down at her pale face. Her left arm was swathed in bandages. Through a needle in her right arm, she was receiving a blood transfusion. She must have lost a lot of blood in order to need a transfusion. His heart stumbled again, the way it had when Hondo first told him she'd been taken into surgery.

"Caity?" he said tentatively. He hadn't called her that in years. "It's Daddy." He hadn't said that in years either.

Her eyelids fluttered open and she pinned him with blue-green eyes so much like her mother's. "You're here."

"I am."

"Did I die or something?"

"Almost." He nodded.

"I was right," she whispered.

"Right about what?"

"I figured I'd have to be on my deathbed for you to get over your mule-headed snit and come see me."

"Oh, Caity," he said, tears suddenly welling up in his foolish old eyes. He never cried. Why the hell was he crying? She was fine. She was going to pull through. She was okay. No need for tears. He was a judge. He did not cry.

"It's okay, Dad. I'm going to be okay. Everything is going to be okay."

Dad. She'd called him Dad. Not Father. Not Judge as she'd taken to calling him after he'd banished Garza. Dad. He rubbed the knuckle of his index finger across the corner of his eye.

"I got these," he said, and held out the purple flowers. "For you."

"Purple hyacinth. They smell so sweet."

Was that what they were called?

She broke into a beautiful smile. "Yes, Dad, yes, yes. I forgive you. You're forgiven. All is forgiven. Thank you for having the courage to come here and bring me purple hyacinth."

Richard startled. What? He hadn't asked for her forgiveness. But she looked so happy he couldn't backpedal now.

His daughter, however, was perceptive. "Oh," she said, the light dimming in her eyes. "You didn't know."

"Know what?"

"That giving someone purple hyacinth means *I'm sorry, please forgive me.*"

This flower gifting was complicated. Angelica used to know all that hidden flower meaning malarkey too.

"Of course I knew," Richard bluffed, not wanting to admit the truth. That it was by pure quirk of fate he'd finally asked for his daughter's forgiveness.

"I'm moving in with you," Gideon announced as he helped Caitlyn get into her van later that same day.

"Excuse me?" She arched an eyebrow at him.

Caitlyn had just been dismissed from the hospital with a prescription for pain pills and antibiotics and instructions to take it easy and visit her family physician in a week. Amazing how soon they kicked you out of the hospital these days when you didn't have any insurance, even though Gideon had paid her bill in full. She'd tried to argue with him, but he'd put his foot down on that as well. And even though she'd kept grumbling about repaying him, he could see the relief in her eyes knowing she didn't have a big hospital bill looming over her head. It made him feel good to help.

"Whether you like it or not, I won't take no for an answer. You'll need help running the household, taking care of Danny."

"Oh? And how many children have you taken care of?"

He didn't tell her about the orphans he'd rescued. The kids he'd gotten to safety. It would sound like bragging and he didn't expect praise for what he'd done. Shunned it, even.

Instead, he simply smiled, shrugged. "One little seven-and-a-half-year-old. How hard could it be?"

"You'll see."

"So you agree that it's a good idea for you to have some help."

She glanced at his arm and he just knew what she was thinking. How much help could a cripple be? The maimed leading the maimed.

His smile vanished and he felt blood rush to his head.

Caitlyn's bandaged arm was propped on the console armrest. Her friend Emma had brought her some clean clothes to put on and told her not to worry about Danny, that she and her husband, Sam, would happily keep him overnight again, but

Caitlyn wanted Danny home with her. That's where they were headed now.

"Yes. I need help. I admit it. Happy now?" she asked.

Was she just saying that to make him feel better? "You don't like asking for help."

"Do you?"

"No."

"So you get where I'm coming from."

"It doesn't mean you're weak to ask for help," he said.

"Just remind yourself of that from time to time."

"Go ahead, give me a hard time, you're not chasing me away."

She cast a sideways glance at him. He pulled to a stop at a traffic light. "Was that weird about my father or what?"

"Unexpected."

"He asked me to forgive him."

"Really? That doesn't sound like Judge Blackthorne."

"Well, not in so many words, but he brought me purple hyacinth. If you give someone purple hyacinth, it means you're asking for forgiveness."

"You sure he knows that?"

Caitlyn grinned. "He does now."

Gideon laughed. "I love to see you smile."

"I love to hear you laugh. You don't do it nearly often enough."

They looked at each other.

"I think we have a mutual admiration society going here," Caitlyn said.

Hell yes. He admired her something fierce. But was admiration enough? Could it span the chasm eight years apart from each other had created? This was their opportunity to find out. They'd be living in close quarters. Really getting to know each other all over again.

"Turn here. Emma and Sam's house is the second one on the right." Caitlyn pointed. "If you are going to move in—"

"I am," he said in a tone that brooked no argument.

"We need to get something straight."

"What are the conditions?"

"You'll be staying in the guest bedroom."

"Well, I had assumed as much, but I didn't realize you thought that I thought otherwise," he teased.

She wrinkled her nose at him. "Does that sentence even make sense?"

"We can't confuse Danny."

"Right."

"We need time to figure all this out."

"So we're in agreement. No sex."

Gideon licked his lips, swallowed hard. He didn't like making promises he wasn't sure he could keep. "No sex."

"Whew." She let out a breath. "I'm glad we got that ironed out."

"How are we going to explain what happened to Danny?" Gideon nodded at her arm. "And about me moving in?"

"We'll just tell him the truth. That I got hurt while gardening, warn him off of sharp tools, and tell him you're going to stay with us for a few days to help out until I'm feeling better."

The truth. Good policy. He had a great deal of respect for the way she'd raised their son. He wanted to tell her that, but he didn't know if he could get the words out without choking up. She had done a damn fine job with Danny. Kevin too.

Jealousy gnawed at him. He hated the pettiness that made him jealous of a dead man. It occurred to him then that Kevin might have been jealous of him. He'd been Caitlyn's first love and a dead (or so everyone had thought) war hero. Had Kevin felt incidental? Damn emotions anyway. All they did was get a guy into trouble. That's why he tamped them down, tried his best to ignore them.

"This it?" He nodded at the cute two-story house on the acre lot with a black and white Border collie sitting on the front porch. Caitlyn's house was on the next block over.

"This is it."

He stopped the van and Caitlyn started to get out, but Gideon put a restraining hand on her shoulder. "Stay put. You're still weak. I'll go get him."

"I don't want him to feel uncomfortable. He's only met you once."

"Settle down, Mother Hen. He can see you from here. And besides, it's about time he got to know me."

A flush of pink colored her pale cheeks. "You're right. I know. I'm just feeling a little shaky."

A wallop of tender emotions sledgehammered him. Caitlyn didn't even seem to know it, but she was one tough cookie. Gideon felt heat rise to his own face. He felt so precarious with her. He wanted her more than words could say, and yet he was afraid. Not because he was scared of her and the things she made him feel, but because he was scared of himself and the things he was incapable of.

Like living a normal life.

Quickly, before she could see the fear in his eyes, Gideon turned and walked up the cobblestone path to pick up the son who didn't even know who he really was. Wondering just how on earth he was going to survive living in the same house with them.

CHAPTER THIRTEEN

Traditional meaning of yarrow—healing.

After making grilled cheese sandwiches and tomato soup for their evening meal and insisting Caitlyn take a pain pill and get some rest, Gideon was at loose ends. Danny had hardly spoken to him. He was holed up in his room playing with his handheld video game device.

Gideon was not a man who could just lie around and watch television or surf the Internet. He liked to keep his body busy as well as his mind. He had to have something to do or go nuts.

"Danny?" He knocked on his son's bedroom door. Son. The word still got to him every time it popped into his head.

There wasn't an immediate answer. Gideon waited patiently, but just when he thought he was going to have to knock again, Danny opened the door and peeked out, his eyes leery, the dark cowlick sticking up at the back of his head.

"Yeah?" he asked.

Gideon remembered being that age, scared little kid trying his best not to show it. And like Danny, it had been just he and his mother. He knew the responsibility that fell on a boy's shoulders when he had to assume the role of man of the house at a young age.

He also knew what it was like to find a strange man in your house and the resentment he'd felt when some guy tried to play daddy to him and tell him what to do.

There had been a revolving door of men as Linda looked for love in all the wrong places. Not that Caitlyn was in any way the same as his mother, but to a kid, an interloper was an interloper.

"Hi," Gideon said, then felt dorky as hell for saying it.

Danny just blinked at him.

Great way to win him over, Garza.

Gideon took a deep breath. "Your mom is sleeping and I wanted to work on the carousel animals, but they're all over at the victory garden . . ." He almost told the boy that he had to come with him because Gideon wasn't leaving Danny alone in the house while his mother was asleep and under the influence of pain pills, but he quickly realized that would not be an effective tactic. He thought about what would have motivated him at that age to help one of Linda's boyfriends. "Could you give me a hand dragging a couple of the animals back over here?"

Danny raised his chin. "What's in it for me?"

Ah, so he had a little mercenary on his hands. The kid took after him in more ways than just physical appearance. When he was Danny's age he'd figured if he was going to have to put up with Linda's men he might as well get paid for it. Gideon pulled five dollars from his wallet.

"Make it ten and you've got yourself a deal," Danny said.

"You drive a hard bargain." Gideon peeled off another five spot.

"And I want a ride on your motorcycle."

"We're taking the van. The carousel animals won't fit on the motorcycle."

Danny looked at him like he was a moron. "I know that. I meant later."

"If your mother gives her permission, I'll take you on the motorcycle," he promised.

"She won't give her permission."

"How do you know?"

"She calls them death machines."

"Let me work on her."

"Really?" Danny gave him a genuine smile.

"Really."

They went to the victory garden, took a couple of carousel horses from the shed. Several members of the garden club were there planting in the waning twilight. Gideon was relieved to see someone had cleaned up Caitlyn's blood.

The garden club ladies made him stop and chat for

a bit, asking about Caitlyn's condition and raising speculations about who could have loaded the bear trap and planted it in their garden. They'd come to the consensus it had to be a contest competitor from a neighboring town, because they'd concluded that no one in Twilight was capable of such a thing.

Gideon shook his head at their insular innocence. How trusting they all were.

"Gideon," Patsy said. "You tell Caitlyn not to worry about the shop. I'll run it for her until she's feeling better and we'll all take turns taking her shifts in the victory garden."

"That's very nice of you, Mrs. Cross."

"Here," Dotty Mae said, and gave him a basket of small red flowers that grew in a thick clump. "This is yarrow. It's good for healing and such a cheery color. I know it will lift her spirits."

"Thank you."

"You're doing a fine job on the carousel by the way," said another one of the women whom he didn't know.

"I'm enjoying the work. And speaking of—" He gestured at the carousel horses waiting to be loaded into the van.

"Yes, sure. You have a good night and tell Caitlyn we're all praying for her speedy recovery."

Gideon thanked them again for their concern and rounded up Danny. His son—there was that magical word again—helped him load and unload the horses and carry them into the workshop that had once belonged to Kevin Marsh.

He rested one horse on a metal worktable, balanced the other between two sawhorses. Once upon a time he'd promised Caitlyn he would repair the carousel and restore her family heritage. He smiled, remembering how much joy that promise had brought her.

"I wish I could carve things," Danny said, running a hand along one of the horses. "But my mom won't let me have a pocketknife. She says I'll cut myself."

"She's just being a good mom."

"Yeah, but how will I ever know how to use a knife if she never lets me have one?"

"You do make a good point," Gideon said.

"So you'll talk to her for me?"

"About letting you have a knife?"

Danny nodded.

The urge to say yes to anything the kid asked was a strong one. He had so much to make up for, but he knew just giving in to Danny was not the best way to parent. So he didn't answer, but instead patted the metal stool beside the worktable. "Hop up here and I'll show you how to restore a carousel horse. And when we get to the part where we need to carve something, I'll show you how to use my knife."

"Really?" Danny's eyes glowed.

The expression in his son's eyes started a warm glow inside Gideon's gut. "Sure."

Danny scrambled up onto the stool. He was close enough for Gideon to smell him. It was a unique aroma, part Caitlyn, part Gideon, part Danny's own bona fide scent.

Gideon reached over to the radio parked on the

windowsill. "Let's have some tunes. What kind of music do you listen to?"

"I like Toby Keith."

"Country-and-western."

"Uh-huh."

Gideon fiddled with the dials, tuned in a country-and-western station. "Watching You," a song about a father and son by Rodney Atkins, was playing. The timeliness of the tune squeezed his heart and brought home the fact he'd already missed so much. The loss hit him like a blow to the gut. He clenched his jaw, steeled himself against those soft emotions. He couldn't tear up in front of the kid.

But Gideon made note of everything, wanting to hang on to this memory for all time. Danny had on faded blue jeans with a small hole in one knee and a red and blue striped T-shirt and grubby sneakers. He was a lean kid, almost but not quite skinny. His shoulders were fairly broad for a seven-and-a-half-year-old, but Gideon had no doubts he'd grow into them.

"Where do we start?" Danny asked.

"First comes the sanding," Gideon said. "Do you know how to run a hand sander?"

Danny shook his head. "My dad said I shouldn't ever touch his tools."

My dad. The words were like a bucket of ice water thrown over his little father-son fantasy.

"Well, you're getting older now," Gideon said, ignoring the possessive urge to tell him that he was his father, not Kevin. "You have to learn how to handle tools sometime, right?"

Danny beamed. "Right!"

Gideon showed him how to put sandpaper onto the hand sander and how to tighten the strap around his hand. "Okay, now be prepared, the sander is going to vibrate and jerk your hand around. You need to press down to control it, but don't press too hard."

"Okay." Danny nodded.

"You need to put on a pair of goggles to keep from getting something in your eye." Gideon plucked a pair of goggles from where they hung on a nail sticking out of the wall. He slipped them on over Danny's head, tightened the band to secure the goggles in place. "How's that?"

"Good, but what are you going to wear?"

"You're the one working with tools. You get the goggles."

"That makes sense. What next?"

"Run the sander lightly over the horse to knock off the old paint. Start with the big areas first like the saddle and work down to the small, hard-to-get places like his hooves."

"Gotcha."

"You ready for me to turn on the switch?"

"Can I do it?"

The kid was so eager for independence. Caitlyn had been too protective, but he understood why. She'd lost a lot in her life—her mother, him, her husband, her relationship with her father. She had a need to cling to what she had, but at some point, a boy had a need to break free from the apron strings, to explore his world and build up his self-confidence.

"Sure," Gideon said. "Go right ahead. Just be prepared for it to try to run away from you."

Danny turned on the sander and laughed with delight as it charged over the back of the horse. "This is fun!"

Gideon reached for the sandpaper and went after the other carousel horse, rasping sandpaper over it by hand. He kept one eye on Danny, making sure the kid was okay. A hand sander was pretty harmless. Even if he lost control, at worst, he'd get skinned up.

They sanded together, father and son, in the workshop. Country-and-western music played on the radio. The fluorescent light overhead buzzed softly in time to Danny's sander. Paint flakes and dust filled the space, flew off in all directions. Danny concentrated like a brain surgeon. He poked his tongue through the gap between his teeth, eyes focused intently.

It reminded Gideon of when he'd first discovered the magic of tools and how they could help him shape and create things. He'd made a cutting board for his mother when he was Danny's age, then later, when he was older and had acquired more knowledge and tools, a rolling pin. Not that his mother had ever baked pies or even cooked for that matter. She'd been a McDonald's and TV dinners kind of mom. But she'd really been proud of that rolling pin. She'd used it to smack up bags of ice for her drinks.

Funny, the things that made an impression.

Danny was making good progress on the horse, sanding off the saddle, heading down the flank in a matter of minutes. It struck Gideon that the child might have inherited his gift for woodworking, and the pride that swelled inside his chest was both surprising and overwhelming. Overwhelming because if Danny had inherited his good qualities, what bad qualities had he also taken from his dad?

Dad.

Such a friendly word. A word he'd never imagined would apply to him. He'd thought he was too damaged. Too messed up to be a good father.

You are messed up, but you don't have to stay that way. The thought tumbled through his head, fleeting, but insightful. He didn't have to stay this way.

Oh yeah? There's nothing you can do about that missing arm. It isn't growing back. But he was more than an arm, wasn't he?

"Hey," Danny called out over the noise of the sander.

"What is it?"

"It's not working so good anymore."

"You need to replace the sandpaper," Gideon said. "Turn it off and load another piece on there like I showed you."

Danny flipped off the switch, pushed the goggles up on his forehead, shook out his arm. "It makes my skin feel like an itchy jumping bean."

Gideon laughed. "I warned you that it would vibrate."

Danny scratched his arm vigorously.

"It'll stop doing that once you get used to a sander."

"You know a lot of stuff," Danny said.

"It's because I'm old."

Danny cocked his head to study Gideon. "You're not *that* old."

"Thanks." He smiled.

"You were in a war, right."

Gideon nodded. "I was."

Danny got really quiet. His gaze flicked cautiously to Gideon's face, and in that moment he looked exactly like his mother, filled with worry and hesitation. "Did you ever kill anybody?"

Gideon sucked in a deep breath. How did you tell a child the truth about something like that? "Sometimes a soldier is forced to kill in order to protect innocent people."

"From bad guys?"

"From bad guys," he confirmed while at the same time wishing life was really that simple. Bad guys against good guys. Right against wrong. Good against evil. But he'd seen bad people do good things and good people do bad things, and he knew in the end it was difficult to tell who was who.

Danny's gaze shifted to his hand and Gideon could see what question was coming next. "Did someone try to kill you?"

"Yes."

"What happened to your arm?"

"I picked up a bomb."

Danny looked at him like he was nuts. "Why did you pick up a bomb?"

"I didn't know it was a bomb. It was inside of a doll that a little girl dropped. I picked it up to give it back to her and it blew off my arm."

That was heavy duty. Maybe he shouldn't have been so honest. How could he explain that someone had wanted him dead so much that he would put a bomb in a child's doll and risk killing his own kid in some misguided zealous plot?

Danny hooted. "You got bombed by a girl?"

His laugh surprised Gideon, but Gideon immediately saw the humor in it. "I did."

"A tiny little girl."

"A tiny little girl."

"That must have been embarrassing."

"Yeah." He was so relieved that Danny saw the funny side of it and not the darkness. He certainly hadn't gotten that trait from either Caitlyn or Gideon. Perhaps he'd picked it up from Kevin, whom Gideon remembered as an easygoing guy with a sharp appreciation for the Three Stooges brand of humor.

"Did the other soldiers tease you?"

"Not so much. I did lose a hand."

"Oh, yeah." Danny's face sobered. "Can I touch it?"

"The artificial hand or my stump?"

"Both."

Gideon rolled up his sleeve, revealing how the prosthesis attached to his arm. Danny lightly ran his fingers over it. "Cool, it's like a robot hand."

"It is." He showed Danny how the hand worked, and then he took it off, opening himself up to the kid, showing his vulnerability.

Danny eyed the stump. "It looks kind of bad."

"You should have seen it before it healed."

Carefully, Danny touched the seams of where the

old wound had been stitched together. The scar was white now. Danny's gentle touch stirred dormant nerve endings and Gideon felt . . . what did he feel? It was a rush of sensation he didn't know how to describe.

"Does it hurt?" Danny whispered.

"Not anymore. But sometimes I get phantom pains."

"What's that?"

"My fingers and hand still hurt sometimes."

"But they're gone."

"That's why it's called phantom pain. It's like my brain hasn't told my nerve endings I don't have a hand anymore."

"Weird."

"Yeah it is, kind of."

"I hope I never have phantom pains."

"I hope you don't either," Gideon said vehemently.

"So what did you do before you were a soldier?" Danny asked, dropping his hand.

Relieved that the examination was over, Gideon slipped the artificial arm back on, rolled down his sleeve. "I've always been a soldier. Well, except when I was a kid. I made things out of wood."

"Like the carousel?"

"Well, I never completed a project this big, but yeah, like a carousel."

"Mom says this carousel is part of my heritage."

"It is. Your great-great-great-grandfather built this carousel himself way back in the cowboy and Indian days."

"But I never knew him, right?"

"Right." Gideon smiled at a kid's concept of time. "He died a long time before your mother was ever born."

"My dad died." Danny suddenly looked sad.

"I heard. I'm sorry about that."

"I miss him."

"I bet you do."

"He used to take me fishing. Sometimes my mom would even come along."

"Sounds like fun."

"Do you know how to fish?" Danny asked.

"I used to go fishing in Lake Twilight when I was your age."

The boy met his eyes. "Do you think you could take me fishing sometime?"

"Danny," Gideon said. "Nothing would please me more."

CHAPTER FOURTEEN

*Traditional meaning of red camellia—
you're a flame in my heart.*

Caitlyn was tired of napping, reading, and watching television. She'd stopped taking the pain pills because they were making her groggy. Her hand throbbed like the dickens, but the pain brought with it the realization of just how much suffering Gideon had gone through with the loss of his arm. And she liked the reminder. It helped her understand him better.

It was nine o'clock on Tuesday morning. Patsy Cross would be opening up the shop now. Caitlyn knew the store was in good hands, but she couldn't help worrying. Gideon had fed Danny and gotten him off to school and then he'd brought her breakfast in bed. Toast and scrambled eggs with orange juice. A woman could get used to this kind of pampering.

The flowering red yarrow Dotty Mae had sent brought a smile to her lips as she got out of bed, pulled a housecoat on over her pajamas, and, balancing the breakfast tray as well as she could with her right hand, carried it into the kitchen. Once again, she was struck by the difficulty Gideon faced performing simple everyday tasks.

The empty kitchen was cleaned perfectly spick-and-span, white tile counters and appliances gleaming. The air smelled of pine-scented cleaner. She felt oddly touched that Gideon bothered to clean so thoroughly. Most guys wouldn't have bothered. Not even Kevin, who'd been pretty good about keeping house. He might wash dishes, yet he'd overlook the crumbs strewn across the counter.

But Gideon had cared for his ailing mother for several years before her death. Her heart gave a soft twist. He might not be quick with the tender words—or even any words at all—but he showed her how he felt with his kind deeds, and when she thought about it, that was more romantic than an emotional treatise.

"Gideon?" she called. Her cottage was only twelve hundred square feet, if he was inside, he would have heard her.

She stepped out onto the back porch. The cool breeze ruffled the collar of her housecoat. The sun warmed her cheeks. She pushed her hair back from her face, saw that the door to Kevin's detached workshop stood open.

She moved toward that open door and peeked her head into the workshop. She hadn't been in it since Kevin's death because she hadn't had the mental energy to deal with going through his things on top of everything else.

Gideon sat on a wooden stool, his back to her, deeply engrossed in his work. Caitlyn leaned her right shoulder against the doorjamb; her bandaged left hand cradled against her chest, and watched him. He was painting something, his head tipped down to the work in front of him, but that wasn't what surprised her.

He was using his artificial hand, holding the paintbrush between the robotic digits and awkwardly rotating his elbow to get it to move, painting the red camellia behind the carousel horse's ear. He wasn't letting his disability get the best of him. He was trying to make his prosthesis function like a real hand with something as precise as painting.

Caitlyn gulped, her own damaged hand aching in empathy. Stupid really. As if her mishap with the bear trap could compare to what he'd suffered. She tried to imagine what it was like for him. This big, powerful man maimed and disfigured, learning how to do the simplest things all over again—tying his own shoes, putting toothpaste on his toothbrush, doing up buttons.

"You're doing so good!"

Gideon jerked back and dropped the paintbrush, a trail of red smearing over the horse as the paintbrush went down.

"Oh, I'm so sorry." She rushed toward him. "I didn't mean to startle you."

"I've messed up the paint job," he said tersely. "I'll have to start again."

"It's my fault."

"Don't apologize," he growled. "It's a sign of weakness. Besides, you didn't cause it. I had a spasm in my elbow."

For a moment, she felt hurt, and then she realized he was just lashing out because he'd been embarrassed. She pressed her lips together.

"What are you doing out of bed?" he asked gruffly, reaching down to pick up the dropped paintbrush, but he used his right hand.

"I'm bored and I hurt my hand, not my legs or my brain."

"You're bleeding."

"What?" Caitlyn looked down to see the blood had seeped through her bandage.

"You were supposed to keep it elevated," he said.

"I'm so—" She broke off before saying "sorry."

"That's my girl." He grinned.

It felt so good to hear him say that, to see him smile. He made her feel special, just like he used to. But that was a dangerous thing, because she wasn't who she used to be and neither was he. They couldn't fall back into old patterns or rely on old ways of communicating. For all intents and purposes this was a new relationship, and she had no idea where it was going or even if it was going anywhere. There was so much negotiating to be done, so many things they had not talked through. Yes, they were Danny's parents, but beyond that . . .

"C'mon." Gideon tossed the paintbrush in a jar of turpentine sitting on the window ledge. "Let's get that seen to."

He took her right hand in his and led her back to the house. It felt so good, this handholding, so simple and yet so fraught with tenderness. But she did notice how he'd managed to take the attention off him and put it on her.

That's not fair. You were bleeding.

Yes, but he hadn't hesitated in deflecting her observations about his painting with his artificial hand. Clearly, he did not want to talk about it, or even let her know that he was experimenting with improving his fine motor control. Why not?

He was never one to open up and talk about what was on his mind. You know that. He'd always had a difficult time with sharing his emotions.

"Where do you keep your first aid kit?"

"Medical supplies are in my bathroom closet."

He took her through her bedroom, past her rumpled bed that she hadn't even tried to make one-handed, and into the adjoining bathroom, which suddenly seemed very small with Gideon's big frame in it.

"Can you hop up here?" He patted the counter-top.

"It's kind of hard one-handed."

"Tell me about it. Here, I'll help you up."

He gave her a boost and she settled her tush onto the cool tile. She was suddenly very aware that she was in her pajamas. Yes, they were cotton "mom" pajamas, nothing sexy, but they were still pajamas.

Gideon rummaged in the cabinet, extracted gauze, medical tape, hydrogen peroxide, and a Telfa nonstick dressing. He took his time carefully unwrapping the bandage and maneuvering his body so that he blocked her from seeing the cut.

"How's it look?"

"You're gonna have some scarring."

"Let me see."

"You sure?"

"I have to see it sometime."

Reluctantly, he moved aside.

She braced herself, but still, the jagged scars encircling her wrist looked vicious. Blood had caked around the sutures, with fresh blood still oozing at the seams. The surgeon had neatly sewn it all back together, but Gideon was right, she was going to have some ugly scars.

He startled her by leaning over and kissing her inner arm near her elbow. "I'm sorry you hurt."

"Hey," she said. "No saying you're sorry. It makes you look weak."

He straightened, smiled down at her. "You're throwing my words back at me?"

"I guess I am."

"Ha, I get the last laugh. I'm the one who's going to wash out your wound." He tucked a towel underneath her arm and unscrewed the cap from the hydrogen peroxide. "This is going to sting."

Gideon gently trickled the cool liquid over her wrist.

She hissed in her breath as the solution fizzed and bubbled and did its job, but it wasn't pain that had her drawing in air through clenched teeth, rather it was her intense awareness of him, his scent, his muscular body, his dark hair in contrast to her pale skin. He bent his head and it oh so barely brushed against her breasts. Instantly, both her nipples hardened to tight little pebbles.

Stop it. Stop it. But she couldn't.

After the hydrogen peroxide had washed away the blood, he carefully laid the nonstick dressing over the sutures, and then wrapped it all up with a thick layer of gauze. "There you go."

Her hair had fallen across her face and she didn't dare look up. Afraid he could see the stark desire in her eyes. She could feel the rise and fall of his chest.

"Caitlyn."

She raised her head. He was staring at her and she was staring at him.

They were breathing in tandem. Rough, jagged gulps of air.

His lips were so close to hers, hard and angular and masculine. He smelled of hydrogen peroxide, wood shavings, and turpentine.

The tugging pull of pleasure-pain burned deep within her. She'd never felt this level of intense arousal, this brand of raw, aching need. She needed relief and he was the salve.

The next thing Caitlyn knew she'd flung her arms around his neck and she was kissing him like it was the end of the world and they were the last two people in it.

It was hormonal insanity. That was the only excuse she had for it. Her sex contracted tightly, begging for him.

"I'm so hard for you," he rasped.

As if she couldn't tell. The bulge behind the zipper of his jeans was like concrete.

She kissed him frantically.

He came back at her like an explosion.

His fingers kneaded her ass, pushing her firm against his pelvis. When she slipped her tongue into his mouth, he slid his hand underneath her pajama top to lightly pinch an erect nipple.

Gideon kissed her back, his mouth matching her ferocity. Caitlyn wrapped her legs around his waist and clung on for dear life. He thrust his tongue inside her mouth, feeling as if he could never be sated no matter how long he drank from her.

He wanted to cling to this moment forever, hold on with both hands.

That thought jolted him. He didn't have two hands to grab on to happily-ever-after with. Just the one. And he suddenly felt inadequate beyond words.

Caitlyn must have sensed the shift in him because she pulled back, stared into his eyes. "Gideon? Are you okay?"

"Fine."

"Are you sure?"

Swallowing against his conflicting desires, he lowered his eyelids to half-mast, stepped away. "I should get back to work."

"No," she said.

He raised an eyebrow. "No?"

"I liked what we were doing. I want more."

"You were the one who made the no sex rule."

"Rules are made to be broken."

"I don't want you to do something you're going to regret later."

"Who says I'll regret it."

"You're still recuperating."

"We could be really careful." She looked at him hopefully.

He groaned and, unable to stop himself, kissed her again.

Her lips tasted of springtime. Like Easter eggs and chocolate bunnies. Sweet and full of hope. She made him hope, and hope was a dangerous thing.

She reached up to thread her hand around his hair, pull his head down lower, deepen the kiss. Her sassy little tongue pushed against his teeth, demanding more, seeking entry.

Damn him, he was weak. With a groan, he parted his lips.

Her delicious tongue slipped inside him. Her grip tightened around him.

In that moment, he felt whole again, and it was a seductive sensation. He slid his right arm around her waist, tugged her as close to him as he could get her.

Her body wriggled against his.

Gideon's cock throbbed, ached, hungered.

The scent of her hair—which smelled like flowers—invaded his nostrils. He took a deep breath, breathing in her fragrance, inhaling her taste. This woman, this woman. He could find no words to describe the level of pleasure she brought him.

Her hair trailed over his cheek, coiling like silk against his skin. Her fingers moved over his spine, exploring, seeking.

He shuddered against her, moved his mouth away, but still held her close. "Caitlyn, no," he murmured.

"Please, Giddy, please," she said, calling him by the silly nickname she'd give him eons ago. *Giddy*.

An image flashed in his mind. One of the times they'd made love. They'd been in her bedroom when her father had been away on a business trip. She was buck naked, straddling his body. His cowboy hat perched atop her head, her pert breasts poking proudly in the air, a sly smile on her face. Boldly—which in their lovemaking up to that point hadn't been like her—she'd eased herself down on his pulsating cock, lifted the cowboy hat off her head, and swatted his thighs with it. "Giddy up, Gideon."

After that, whenever she was feeling particularly sassy, she called him Giddy. It had become their code word for *I want to make love*.

It broke his heart a little, that memory. As did all the memories he had of her. When he looked at Caitlyn, he thought about their past, and thinking about their past made him take stock of everything he'd lost, all the things he could not give her.

Firmly, he put her away from him. "No, Caitlyn, not now. Not today."

She looked hurt. Reached up to trace her fingers over her lips.

He clenched his jaw, hardened his heart. She might be hungry for sex. She might think she really wanted this, but when he took her, he wanted there to be absolutely no regrets.

"I want it to be right," he said. That much was true. What he didn't tell her was that he feared it would never be right. He was too battle-scarred for her. She needed someone who came from her same insular world. Who lived in her small-town cocoon, blissfully unaware of the dangers that lurked beyond the city limits of Twilight.

"When?" she asked, calling him on it.

"I don't know."

"Is it me?" She raised a hand to her throat. "I know I don't have the body I used to have. I'm a mom now and things change, stretch, head south."

"God no," he said, upset that he'd caused her to doubt her femininity. "You are so beautiful. More beautiful than ever."

"Then what's wrong?"

"I'm just not ready."

Her gaze went to his artificial arm. "You haven't been with a woman since . . ."

"Yes, I have, but it didn't mean anything."

"You're saying I mean something to you?"

Didn't she understand that she meant everything to him? But he wasn't about to tell her that. He couldn't bear to lay his tattered heart on the line only to have it mangled again. He couldn't tell her that he feared he was still in love with her. He didn't trust himself, much less her.

"I'm saying the timing is off. We've got a lot of things to deal with before we can even decide if this is what either of us really wants."

She laughed then, a high, brittle sound. "Do you hear what you're saying? For once you're the cautious one and I'm the reckless one. You're holding back and I want to dive headlong into this thing with you."

"That's the problem, Tulip. We can't be diving into anything."

"Because of Danny." She nodded.

"Not just that."

"What else?"

"You still have no idea who I am."

She moistened her lips, and this time, she was the one who took the step back. He could see from the expression in her eyes that it was something she hadn't considered. She was still stuck in the dream of their past, still seventeen, praying for her lover's return. And now that he was here, she was trying to fulfill the fantasy, but he knew it was all a sweet, impossible dream. He knew if she ever saw the monster he kept buried deep inside her, the monster that was capable of killing men without hesitation, she would turn away from him.

He couldn't risk letting down his mask, and if he couldn't let down his mask, he couldn't be with her. His relationship with Moira might have been casual, but at least Moira saw him for who he was, not for something she believed him to be.

He ducked his head, turned away, heard the sound of her high, rapid breathing, and knew that he'd hurt her, but also knew it was for the best.

CHAPTER FIFTEEN

Traditional meaning of asphodel—regret.

"Let's take Danny fishing," Gideon suggested on Saturday after the bathroom incident.

For the most part, they'd avoided each other. For the last three days, Caitlyn had gone over to supervise the progress on the victory garden since Patsy adamantly refused to let her back into the flower shop, citing that she needed two good hands to fill customers, orders, but it took only a sharp pair of eyes and a firm opinion to tell the volunteers what she wanted done.

Gideon had stayed to the guest bedroom when he wasn't playing with Danny or refurbishing the carousel. His rejection had hurt her more than she let on, and she still couldn't figure out what she'd done wrong. Not only that, but she was more sexually frustrated than she'd ever been in her life, with no outlet for it. Every time she looked at him she felt a mix of desire, confusion, and anger. Yes. She was mad, at him for turning her down, at herself for begging.

She would be getting her stitches out on Monday and the only thing that kept her from asking him to move out was the bond he was forging with his son. Danny was quickly coming around, and the first thing he said when he walked into the kitchen each day after school was "Where's Gideon?"

They ended up at an out-of-the way fishing spot where the locals went to escape the tourists. Most of the trees were in full bloom. Red buds and dogwood. Mimosas and oak. The sun shone warm, but the air was still cool. In the field beside the river, a carpet of yellow asphodel with their star-shaped blooms grew in profusion with bluebonnets and Indian blankets.

They carried an Igloo cooler stuffed with sandwiches and cold drinks. Caitlyn's arm still throbbed if she held it down for too long, but she was on the mend.

Danny was excited, talking a mile a minute and running ahead of them to the water's edge. Even though she'd required him to wear a life jacket, she still cautioned him not to get too close.

Gideon put a hand on her shoulder. "Lighten up, Mother Hen. Let him be a little boy."

Caitlyn bit down on her bottom lip. While it had been a relief to have Gideon around to help her get Danny off to school, cook his meals, and put him to bed at night, there had also been a bit of head butting over the past few days, especially after what had happened—or ultimately didn't happen—in the bathroom. Gideon thought she was overprotective, and maybe she was, but Danny was her only child. And she was vigilant by nature.

"Part of your job as a parent is to let him explore his world. Give him confidence to stand on his own two feet."

"So now you're telling me what my job is?" Yes, she was being testy. She knew it, but she just couldn't seem to curtail her temper. Which wasn't like her at all, and that only made her more irritable. Was sexual frustration behind it all?

Gideon carried two rods and reels in his right hand. The bait bucket was grasped in his artificial hand. Caitlyn carried the cooler. Once they reached Danny at the water, Gideon put down the poles and went back to the van for the camp chairs.

That's when Caitlyn looked over and saw the Lincoln parked near a thicket of reeds just off the boat ramp. Her father sat with a hat on his head, a cane pole in his hand. She hadn't seen him since he'd come to the hospital to see her. Her initial instinct was to gather up their stuff and get the hell out of there, because in spite of her having forgiven him, there was still eight years of awkward silence to deal with.

Gideon was on his way back with the camp chairs and he waved at her father. "Afternoon, Judge."

Richard waved his hand.

Looked like they were all going to let bygones be bygones. That was good, right?

Gideon set up the camp chair and an umbrella for Caitlyn to sit under. Then he went to help Danny bait his hook and cast it into the water.

"Mind if I join you?"

Caitlyn looked up to see her father hovering beside her camp chair. "Have a seat," she invited, even though she didn't want to.

He set up his own camp chair and plunked down beside her. "I used to bring you fishing here."

"I know."

"It's a nice tradition."

"It is."

The conversation fell off. Caitlyn shaded her eyes, concentrating on watching Gideon and Danny, not really sure what to say to her father. She could smell his Old Spice and Ben-Gay scent carried over on the breeze. Bees buzzed among the wildflowers growing along the boat ramp.

"How's your arm?"

"It's healing. I get the stitches out on Monday."

"That's good."

More silence. It was an uneasy reunion.

Richard tilted his head in Danny's direction. "He's a good little fisherman."

"Kevin used to bring him here a lot in the summers."

"Kevin wasn't so bad."

Caitlyn whipped her head around to stare at him. "Did you just admit you were wrong about someone?"

"I'm trying here, daughter. Give me a break."

She suppressed a smile. Danny must have gotten a bite because he was yanking back on his pole and hollering with excitement. Gideon put a hand on Danny's shoulder and coached him on how to bring the fish in.

"Gideon's not half bad either."

"You keep that up and I'm going to faint on you," Caitlyn said.

Richard shifted. "You want me to leave?"

"No, no, stay, I'll stop being catty."

"Thank you."

Danny reeled in a palm-sized perch. He wriggled and jiggled with excitement. "Mom, Mom," he said, running over with the fish dangling from his pole. "Look what I caught."

His grin was as wide as Texas, showing off his two missing top teeth.

"My goodness," she exclaimed. "What a fisherman you are."

"Can we eat it for dinner tonight?"

"I'm not sure it's big enough. Remember what the man at the bait store said when he sold Gideon the fishing licenses? You have to measure to see if it's big enough to keep. Otherwise you have to—"

"Catch and release." Danny sounded disappointed.

"The rule is just so that you don't catch any that are too young."

"Mom says it's probably not big enough," Danny called out to Gideon.

"Mother knows best," Gideon said.

Danny stared at Richard. "Who are you?"

"You don't know who I am?"

Danny shook his head. "I've seen you around town. Everyone says you're cranky."

"Oh, they do, do they?"

"Yep."

"I'm your grandfather."

Danny scowled. "No you're not. My granddaddy lives in Michigan."

"I'm your other grandfather."

"How come you're just now telling me?"

Richard looked to Caitlyn, shrugged, but didn't answer Danny.

Anger simmered through Caitlyn and every muscle in her body tensed. She hadn't wanted her father just to come right out and tell Danny who he was. She'd wanted to ease into it. Wanted to see if their relationship was even going to gel before bringing Danny into it at all. Things were slipping out of her control and she didn't like that. Not at all. "Danny, go put the fish back in the river before it dies."

Danny turned and walked back to the water.

"Why did you tell him that?" Caitlyn asked.

"Because I am his grandfather."

"You should have asked me if you could tell him."

"Hey, I stood aside for almost eight years and let you run the show."

"The hell you did! You disowned me for getting pregnant, don't try to put this all on me."

Richard raised his hands. "Clearly, I've made you angry."

"You think?" Caitlyn jumped up from the camp chair. "Gideon, I'm not feeling so well, I'd like to go home now."

"That's right, run away. It's what you do best."

Caitlyn whirled on him. "If I hadn't run away, if I'd listened to you, that little boy would not be here."

Richard gulped. "I was wrong. I'm admitting it. I want a chance to know my grandchild."

"Well, this is not the way to go about it."

"When did you plan on telling him who I was, Caitlyn? When he's twenty?"

"Maybe."

Caitlyn felt a solid hand come down on her shoulder. "Easy, Tulip," Gideon soothed.

But Caitlyn was not in the mood to be soothed. She twisted away from him. "Don't try to placate me."

"Mom?"

Caitlyn turned to see Danny staring at her with those brown inquisitive eyes so much like his father's. "Yes?"

"Is he really my grandfather?"

"I'm afraid he is."

Danny stared at Richard. "How come you never came to see me before?"

"Ask your mother."

"I can't have this conversation right now," Caitlyn said. She was too angry. If she kept talking, she was going to say something she would regret for the rest of her life. "Excuse me."

She stalked off, headed for the van. Behind her, she heard Gideon say to Danny, "Why don't you show your grandfather how well you can bait a hook?"

Blowing out her breath, Caitlyn paced back and forth behind the van. Maybe she should be more forgiving. In the hospital, hopped up on pain pills and anesthesia, she'd forgiven her father, but for him to just come right out and tell Danny who he was and act as if their estrangement was her fault, well, that was beyond the pale.

"Hey," Gideon said softly.

She pushed tendrils of hair from her face, kept pacing. "He shouldn't have told Danny. It was my place to decide when and where that news should be broken."

"Granted, he should have consulted you."

"Yes." She pointed a finger. "Yes, he should have."

"But he does have a right to see his grandchild."

Caitlyn stared at Gideon and her mouth dropped open. "Excuse me? Are you taking his side? The side of the man who lied and connived to keep us apart?"

"He seems to regret it. He's getting old."

"Yes, right, so that makes it cool. What did you think when J. Foster suddenly turned all maudlin on you?"

"It's not the same thing."

"The hell it's not."

"He wants a relationship with Danny."

"I don't give a damn." The pacing was doing nothing to calm her anger.

"It's our son who's going to suffer from not knowing his grandfather. This isn't just about you."

"That man . . ." She pointed a finger toward the boat ramp. "That man down there . . . he wanted to force me to give Danny up for adoption. That's why I ran away. That's why I married Kevin. That's why I have basically ignored my father for the last eight years."

Gideon sucked in an audible breath. "I see your position, but I do think he knows he was wrong."

"He wanted me to get rid of our baby."

"And I'm so proud of you that you didn't do it. God, Caitlyn, you were so brave. I can't imagine how scared you were."

"Terrified. I was terrified. Seventeen. Pregnant. I thought the man I loved was dead. My father turned his back on me because I wouldn't give away *our* baby . . ." She had to stop talking or she was going to start crying.

Gideon waited. Strong, silent, treelike. It got on her nerves.

"Say something, dammit."

"When was it going to be the right time to tell Danny about Richard?"

"I don't know."

His voice lowered, his eyes took on an expression she couldn't read. "When's it going to be the right time to tell him about me?"

"I don't know."

"Well, you need to figure it out. Because while I'm not going to be like your father and just spring the news on Danny, I need to let him know that I'm his father." Gideon's voice was fraught with feeling. "This is important to me."

She'd never heard him speak so passionately. She stared off into the field, saw the asphodels nodding in the breeze. "I can't tell him now. Not on the heels of this new revelation about his grandfather. That has to sink in first."

"How long do you think he needs? A week? A month?"

"You can't put something like this on a timetable. I need to see how Danny adjusts. It's only been seven months since Kevin died."

"Who's really having trouble adapting, Caitlyn? Is it Danny, or is it you?"

"What are you suggesting?"

"That maybe this isn't about Kevin's death or the fallout with your father or your relationship with me."

"No?" She was so mad she could snap something into two pieces. "Then you tell me, what is it about? Because I sure as hell don't know."

"You're scared to death of letting Danny grow up."

He couldn't have shocked her more if he'd reached out and slapped her. Caitlyn put a hand to her cheek. Was it true? Was she in the wrong? She'd spent so many years thinking—*no, knowing*—that she was right, that she hadn't realized she'd become just like her father.

The thought staggered her.

Was she holding on to Danny too tightly, just the way Richard had held on to her? Had she become so entrenched in her position against him that she could see no other alternatives?

"I'm going to go back down there with Danny." Gideon gestured toward the river. "And I'm going to send your father up here to talk to you, and I want you to work this out, for everyone's sake."

It irritated her that he was telling her what to do. It also irritated her that he was right. She blew out her breath, nodded.

Gideon walked to the water and spoke to her father. A few minutes later, Richard walked up the boat ramp toward her.

"Caitlyn," he murmured.

She forced herself to look at him. His hair was grayer than she remembered, his shoulders frailer, but his eyes were still sharp.

"I never wanted to hurt you," her father murmured. "I thought once you had your own child that you would understand—"

"You never wanted me to have my own child," Caitlyn interrupted. "You wanted me to get rid of him."

He opened his mouth, shut it, and then opened it again. "I . . . I was wrong about that."

"Yes," she said. "Yes, you were. You didn't give me any options. You backed me into a corner. You made me choose between my child and you, and it was no contest. I love you, Dad, I always have, but my son comes first. He has to."

"You . . . you still love me? In spite of what I've done?" He looked so sad.

Regret tore at her heart. "Of course I still love you. You're my father."

"I just wanted you to go to college. To finish your education so you could have a better life. So you could find a life mate."

"I'd found him, and if you hadn't sent him off to war, I would have married him. You cheated Gideon and me out of eight years together, then you did the unconscionable and you had Hiram Malone lie to me, write up a false report. You allowed me to believe that Gideon was dead."

"Caitlyn, please understand. I wanted to protect you. I would have done anything to protect you. Just as you will do anything to protect Danny."

"I'd never lie to him."

"But you're lying to him already. You've not yet told him that Gideon is his father. Why is that?"

"I'm not lying," Caitlyn denied, but guilt flickered in her heart. "I'm waiting for the right time."

"Because you want to protect him."

She nodded.

"A lie of omission is still a lie."

"I can't just blurt it out like you just did."

"And you're terrified he'll be upset with you."

"Yes."

"Now you know how I feel about you."

"If you feel this badly, how come you haven't tried to fix it before?"

He spread his hands. "I'm a fallible old man who's

been too vain to admit it. But I want to change. I want to be a part of your life again. Caitlyn, I miss you. You forgave me in the hospital and now I'm holding you to it. I want to know my grandson before it's too late. I heard he's on spring break. Please, let him spend a couple of days with me. I'd like to take him to Fort Worth, show him the stockyards, maybe even take a trip to Six Flags."

"You? At an amusement park? With a soon-to-be eight-year-old?"

"I'll take Greta. She's got two nephews about Danny's age. He'll have a good time."

She was about to say no, she was going to say no, but she turned her gaze to the river, saw Gideon was watching them while Danny fished. His words echoed in her ears. *You're scared to death of letting Danny grow up.*

What she said next was one of the hardest things she'd ever had to say. It was a symbolic untying of the apron strings, a letting go of her child, but she forced herself to say it. "If it's okay with Danny, it's okay with me."

Her father's usually hard face softened. "Caity, darling, you've made me the happiest grandfather in Twilight."

So Caitlyn had feet of clay after all.

Gideon had had her up on a pedestal for so long, it was a bit jarring to see her go off on her father like that, but he also found it oddly encouraging. Caitlyn needed a little dust on her halo. And in contrast, maybe his armor wouldn't look so tarnished.

On the drive home, all Danny could chatter about was his grandfather. After Richard and Caitlyn had finally hashed everything out, her father had helped Danny catch a ten-pound catfish. He'd promised a fish fry at his house the following evening if Danny wanted to come over and spend the night. Richard told him he was welcome to bring his best friend, Charlie, and they could set up a tent in his backyard.

Gideon was happy for the progress that had been made in the family that day, but if he were being honest, he'd admit that he was also jealous. Now, Danny knew that Richard was his grandfather, but because of that revelation, Gideon had to wait even longer to tell Danny that he was his father.

"Mom?" Danny asked from the backseat of the van.

"Yes, honey?"

"Why didn't you tell me Judge Blackthorne was my granddad?"

Caitlyn glanced out the window. Gideon could see the tension in her stiff shoulders. This was still difficult for her. "Because he and I have been very mad at each other for a very long time."

"But you're not mad at him anymore?"

"No."

"That's really cool, because he's got an arrowhead collection he's going to show me and a Swiss Army knife he said I could have and . . ."

Caitlyn opened her mouth, and Gideon knew she was going to protest the Swiss Army knife, so he beat her to the punch and said, "Apron strings."

She glared at him and shut her mouth.

It struck him then that he'd become the peacemaker in this family. Funny, he'd never been in the role of peacemaker before, but going to war made a man value peace. He liked this new role. Liked it a lot.

It made him feel productive. It made him feel good.

But most of all, it made him feel like maybe, just maybe, he had a chance to finally wash off the sins of the past and make a fresh new start.

Chapter Sixteen

*Traditional meaning of orange lily—
hatred, disdain.*

By the time they got home from the outing, Caitlyn was too tired to cook dinner. Not to mention she was still a bit miffed with Gideon for siding with her father.

"Call for pizza," Gideon said, and pressed a twenty-dollar bill into her hand. "My treat. I'm going to swing by the victory garden and install the carousel horses I finished restoring this week. Two down, fifty-one to go."

"All right."

"Should I pick up a DVD on the way home?"

"That sounds nice. Movie and a pizza. See if they have the latest Pixar flick. It's supposed to be a really good one."

"Will do."

Gideon left on his errand. Caitlyn called Pasta Pappa's, placed an order for an extra-large pepperoni pizza, and then sent Danny off for a bath.

The idea of a family movie night had her relaxing and letting go of the negative energy she'd been holding on to since her run-in with her father. She was still nervous about letting Danny spend the night with his grandfather, but it was a step in the right direction. Perhaps the old wounds could be healed.

Caitlyn was setting the table with paper plates and humming softly to herself when a tap sounded at the back door. "C'mon in," she called, expecting Kenny, the pizza delivery boy.

The door opened.

"The money is right there on the hutch." Caitlyn turned. "I—"

The words died in her throat. It wasn't the sixteen-year-old, pimply-faced Kenny Johnstone she was expecting, but rather Bowie Goodnight shrinking her cozy kitchen with his oversized frame.

"Wha . . . what are you doing here?" she whispered, alarmed, blood bulleting through her temples.

Bowie's face looked chiseled from granite, as did his muscular forearms protruding from the sleeves of his black T-shirt, the material stretched tight against his hard biceps. His eyes were narrow black orbs, his nose hawkish. His sharp-edged smile said that he could have gone fifteen rounds with Mike Tyson and won. And he reeked of bourbon.

Immediately, Caitlyn understood how her hens felt when a raptor flew overhead. Panicked. Terrified.

"Hello, Caitlyn," he said in a surprisingly soothing voice that only served to unnerve her more. "I'm here to see Gideon."

"Um," she said, because she didn't know what else to say.

"I heard he was living here."

"Yes. He should be back any minute."

"Wonderful, you don't mind if I wait, do you?" Bowie reached over, pulled out a kitchen chair that, in contrast to his bulk, looked like a dollhouse accessory. She remembered the way he'd attacked Crockett in her flower shop the day J. Foster had died.

She didn't know what to do. "Is there something I can help you with?"

"Nope." Bowie's smile, full of malice and disdain, chilled her to the bone. "This is between him and me."

"Maybe you could come back when he's here." Nervously, she shifted her weight, rested her bandaged hand on the counter; holding it down was making it throb.

Bowie's nose twitched, as if he could smell her fear. "What happened?"

"Huh?" She startled, realized she'd been staring at him as if in a trance.

"Your hand." He nodded at her bandaged arm. "What'd you do to your southpaw?"

"Gardening accident."

He laughed as if she'd said something hysterically funny.

Caitlyn gnawed her bottom lip, and then realized

that made her look anxious, so she forced herself to stop.

Bowie studied her with interest. "You and Gideon are . . . ?"

"Friends."

"Friends with benefits?" He arched his eyebrows, smirked, raked a seductive gaze over her body.

She started to ask him to leave, but then another knock at the back door interrupted her.

"My guess is that's the person you were expecting before," Bowie said.

Caitlyn ignored that, crossed the room to snatch the money off the hutch, and opened the door. Kenny was waiting with a ready smile. "Hey, Mrs. M—" He broke off when he saw Bowie. "Hey, dude, is that your camo Hummer parked in the back alley?"

"It is," Bowie said.

"Sweet."

"Sweet doesn't begin to cover it."

"Badass?"

"Ten different kinds of badass," Bowie assured the ungainly teen.

"Dude, my girlfriend would go apeshit crazy if I showed up for a date in that thing."

"I'm sure."

Kenny slipped the pizza box from the warming container. She noticed Pasta Pappa's had changed the logo on the front of the box. For some bizarre reason they'd replaced the original disc shape with an orange lily twined around a slice of pizza. Then she remembered the wife of the new owner of Pasta

Pappa's was named Lily. Inanely, she wondered if she should tell her that an orange lily represented hatred and disdain.

"How much does one of the beauties go for?" Kenny asked, referring to Bowie's Hummer.

"Don't know. I inherited it."

"Awesome!" Kenny's voice went up an octave.

Caitlyn wished both men would leave her house. "If you'll excuse me," she said. "I think I'm going to call Gideon and see what's keeping him."

"You go right ahead." Bowie got up and ambled toward the pizza box. "You won't mind if I have a piece." He said it as a statement, not a question. "Want a slice, Kenny?"

"Naw dude, I'm burned out on pizza. Working at an Italian restaurant will do that to you."

Bowie picked up a slice of pepperoni. His proprietary manner angered her. Caitlyn hurried to the purse she kept hung over the doorknob in the hallway and took out her cell phone. Quickly, she punched in Gideon's number.

It rang six times and then went to voice mail. *Crap.*

"Gideon, this is Caitlyn. Bowie Goodnight is here in my house. Just opened the door and walked right in. He says he wants to see you, and by the way, I think he's drunk." She wanted to let Gideon know she felt uneasy with him in her house, but she was afraid Bowie could overhear the conversation. "Could you come on home as soon as you get this message?"

She hung up and reluctantly went back to the kitchen. Kenny was still there, peppering Bowie with questions about the Hummer.

"He on his way?" Bowie asked.

"Yes," she lied.

"That's good. We've got a lot to talk about."

"Which is?" she asked boldly.

"Between me and Garza." Bowie took another slice of pizza from the box.

It pissed her off that he was eating their pizza, but she was honestly afraid of him and what might happen if she told him to stop.

"Hey," Bowie said, and wiped a string of mozzarella from his chin with the back of a hammy hand. "This is really good. Got any beer?" He ambled over to the refrigerator, opened it up. "Pizza always goes down better with a cold beer."

Gideon had bought a six-pack of malt beers a few days earlier. Five still sat in the fridge. Bowie took one, twisted the top off. "You want one? You look like you could use one. Your forehead's all scrunched up." He mimicked her frown.

Caitlyn shook her head.

"You want one?" he asked Kenny.

"Yeah."

"He's only sixteen." Caitlyn glowered.

"Oops, sorry, no can do, kid," Bowie said in a way that let Caitlyn know that if she wasn't in the room, he would have given a minor alcohol.

"Well," Kenny said. "I better get back to the restaurant. My boss keeps me on a short chain."

"Poor you," Bowie said, and drank half the beer in one long swallow.

Kenny sidled out the door and Caitlyn tried to think of a diplomatic way of asking Bowie to leave without antagonizing him. It had been a very long time since she'd been unnerved. A couple of years ago one of the Alzheimer's patients had escaped from the local care facility and come rushing into the flower shop, acting erratic and accusing her of trying to kill him. She felt the same way now as she had then.

Just a minute after Kenny had departed, Gideon came rushing in the back door, a steely expression in his eyes. "Goodnight." He spat out the name like it tasted bad.

"Well, looky who's here," Bowie drawled. "If it isn't the favored son."

"Let's take a walk outside." Gideon reached for his elbow, but his half brother slung him off.

"Don't you touch me."

Gideon got in his face. "Don't *you* come threatening me and my family."

Unexpectedly, Bowie grinned. "Hey, who said anything about threatening you." He looked over at Caitlyn. "Did I threaten him?"

Gideon tensed. "Outside."

Bowie looked like he was going to argue, but then he nodded and echoed, "Outside."

The minute Gideon had Bowie outside the house, he squeezed the other man's arm with all the strength in his fingers. "Don't you ever pull any bullshit like that again."

"What?" Bowie grinned, letting him know the iron-claw grip didn't faze him. "I just dropped by to see my long-lost brother and have a nice little chat with his gorgeous girlfriend. So sweet and innocent."

"You stay away from her," Gideon said.

"Or what? You'll kill me?" Hatred shone in Bowie's eyes. "You might as well kill me. You've taken the only thing I care about."

"Don't push me, fuckwad." Gideon slammed him up against the side of the house, put his elbow to his throat, shoved his face into Bowie's. "Don't let the hand fool you. I was a Green Beret."

"Look," Bowie said. "I didn't come here to start any trouble."

"You've been drinking."

"Yeah? So what?"

"You walk into our home without being invited. You terrify my . . . Caitlyn."

"I didn't terrify her. I just helped myself to pizza and beer. Rude maybe, but terrifying? I don't think so. I am your brother after all. LaVon got the DNA results back. It's official. We're kin."

"Is that what you came here to tell me?"

"Among other things."

"What other things?"

Bowie held up both hands. "Honest to God, I just want to talk."

"So talk."

"I want to buy the Rocking J from you."

"It's not mine yet. You're contesting the will, tying it up in probate. You're free to live there until the will is duly probated."

"It's not enough. That ranch means everything to me and I can't—*won't* lose it."

"There you go with the threats again. That's not the way to get what you want."

"Then what is? You tell me? What's your currency, Garza?"

"My family. You threaten them again and next time I won't be so understanding."

"Your family? Caitlyn's not your wife, Danny's not your—" Realization dawned in Bowie's eyes. "Hot damn, Danny is your son. Why didn't I see that before? Of course. He looks nothing like Kevin. He looks like a Goodnight."

Apprehension settled on Gideon's shoulders. He'd just made a huge mistake by giving away Danny's identity.

"Pretty ironic when you think about it. You're J. Foster's bastard child, Danny is yours."

Venomous anger shot through Gideon. He felt it boil through his veins, furious and fierce. In that moment, he was total warrior, all civility forgotten. Let out of its cage, the monster reared up in him, blind and unreasonable. He grabbed Bowie by the arm, twisted it around his back and pulled it up high and tight.

Bowie yelped.

Gideon yanked him toward the Hummer parked so arrogantly in Caitlyn's driveway.

Bowie stumbled, screamed as Gideon kept yanking his arm, unrelenting and unrepentant. He swung open the door of the haughty vehicle and shoved Bowie inside. "Get out of here right now and don't let me ever catch you on Caitlyn's property again. Or you'll be crying out to God to save you from me."

Bowie started the engine, put the Hummer in gear, and backed it from the driveway with a screech of tires. Breathing hard, Gideon turned to see Caitlyn standing in the doorway. She'd seen everything he'd done. Witnessed just a tiny part of what he was capable of.

Dread took hold of him then. Dread and doubt and insecurity. Would she turn away from him? Tell him to leave? Say that he was too violent to be around her son?

He waited, unmoving, unable to read her thoughts on her face.

Then she stepped across the space between them, slipped her arm around his waist. "C'mon in," she murmured. "And I'll heat up the pizza."

Gideon made her feel safe in a way that Kevin never had. Easygoing Kevin would have probably sat down and had a beer with Bowie, clueless as to why Caitlyn had felt threatened.

But Gideon was different. One look into her face and he'd known. He hadn't hesitated. He'd dragged Bowie into the yard and made it perfectly clear that kind of behavior was not welcome in this house.

Caitlyn sneaked a glance over at Gideon. They

were all three sitting on the couch, Gideon on one side, Caitlyn on the other, and Danny in between. Danny was laughing at some cartoon antics on the television screen, but Caitlyn wasn't paying any attention to the movie. She had a feeling Gideon wasn't either.

The electrical energy between them was almost palpable. Gideon had his right arm stretched out across the back of the couch. Intentionally, Caitlyn stretched her left arm out beside his.

A minute passed. They sat there, arms touching, their son between them.

Caitlyn became aware of a tickling sensation at her wrist. She didn't look over as Gideon lightly traced his fingers along the line of her scar. The sutures hadn't come out yet, and the area was still sensitive. Yet his touch was so gentle, the contact felt good, soothing. He could be so forceful—as he'd been with Bowie—while at the same time he could be so incredibly tender with her and Danny.

But today, something had changed.

In him.

In her.

In them both.

The next morning, Danny went to his grandfather's house for a two-night stay. It was hard for Caitlyn to let him go, but she did it. Not only for her son's sake, but also for her own. By doing so, she took the first step toward healing the rift that had begun so long ago.

Danny smiled and waved good-bye as he drove off with the judge in his Cadillac. Caitlyn's heart wrenched.

Gideon put his arm around her waist, leaned in close, and whispered, "You're such a good mother. I'm so proud of you."

"Yeah well, I need something to keep me from thinking about it. Let's go work on the victory garden."

They spent the day at the garden, Caitlyn tending plants with the volunteers, watering, weeding, fertilizing, while Gideon worked on the carousel with his own set of young volunteers from the high school. They worked until well after dark and came home exhausted.

Caitlyn headed for a long hot soak in her tub. Gideon commandeered Danny's bathroom for a shower. She shut and locked the bathroom door behind her. Sitting on the side of the tub, she adjusted the faucets to the right temperature and let the water flow. When the tub was filled, she stripped off her gardening clothes and sank down into the warm, inviting water. She picked up the bar of lavender soap, held it to her nose, inhaled the relaxing scent, and laid her head back against the cool porcelain. Closing her eyes, she luxuriated in the moment. Through the walls she heard the shower coming on in the other bathroom.

She imagined Gideon standing naked underneath the spray. Her heart slammed against her rib cage at the thought of his hard-muscled body. Her nipples hardened and her breasts swelled. Heat pooled deep inside her.

Just thinking about him made Caitlyn feel achy and wet and hot.

In her daydream he looked at her with the ravenous eyes, his manhood thick and swollen with desire for her.

You're making yourself crazy. Stop it.

But she didn't want to stop it. She wanted to climb out of the tub, rush into the other bathroom, and slip into the shower with him. Shaking with need, she got out and dried herself off. Did she dare act on impulse?

Before she could make up her mind, she heard the shower cut off and the bathroom door close. She stood listening to her heart beating loud and fast in her ears. She couldn't make herself move, even though she wanted to make love to Gideon more than anything in the world.

She put her hand on the doorknob, but didn't turn it. What if she couldn't measure up to his memory of her? What if he was disappointed in her stretch marks and breasts that had nursed a baby? What if she wasn't sophisticated enough for him?

Fear held her in a tight grip. In the end, she stepped away from the door, moved back, put on her nightgown, and slipped into bed.

And lay in bed for hours, staring at the ceiling, wondering if she was ever going to have the courage to ask for what she needed. Finally, she fell into a fitful sleep.

At ten after three in the morning, she was yanked awake by a tortured scream.

Gideon!

She leaped from her bed, raced from her room and into the hall. His cries were ear-splitting now, as if he were being tortured. She burst into the guest bedroom.

Moonlight shone through the open curtains, illuminating the strange sight in front of her. Gideon was on his knees in the middle of the bed, totally naked, pummeling his pillow with his fist, howling and gnashing his teeth like a wounded animal.

"Gideon!" she cried. "What's wrong, what's wrong?"

He swiveled his head and stared at her with eyes so empty a dark shiver of despair lanced her heart.

That's when she realized he was still asleep and apparently in the throes of a vicious night terror. Just what had he seen in Iraq and Afghanistan? What horrors ate at his soul?

"Gideon?" she whispered.

"Who's there?" He frowned, shifted around so he was now sitting in the middle of the bed.

"It's me, Caitlyn. Wake up, you're having a nightmare."

"Caitlyn?" His face softened.

She crept forward and tentatively stretched out a hand to touch his shoulder.

He flinched, drew back.

"Gideon, you're home, you're safe, you're back in Twilight."

"Caitlyn?"

"Yes. I'm here." She eased down on the bed beside him.

"Caitlyn." His eyes glistened in the moonlight and he looked at her with such utter desire, it took her breath. "Caitlyn."

"Are you awake now?"

"Yeah," he said hoarsely.

"Do you want to talk about it?"

He shook his head.

"Your nightmare seemed so awful. Have you ever talked to anyone about it?"

Again, he shook his head. "Can't."

"Please, please let me in. All I want to do is help."

"All I want to do is kiss you."

She didn't have to look down to see his erection, it was growing between them, but he was using sex to derail her from questioning. She knew he didn't like to talk about his feelings. And she imagined it must be extremely hard to relive what he'd suffered. "The nightmares aren't going to go away unless you talk about them."

"Women."

"What?"

"Women always want to make you talk about your feelings. What good does that do?"

"You won't know until you try it, will you?"

He sighed.

"Do you have post-traumatic stress syndrome?"

"Why do people have to label it? What's the point of labeling it? Labeling doesn't define it."

"You're talking. This is good. Keep up the talking."

"How can I tell you about it? I can't bring that darkness into your world."

"It's in your world and you're already in my world," she pointed out. "If you tell me, at least I can understand why you scream and beat your pillow in the middle of the night."

His erection had disappeared. He wasn't trying to use sex to deflect talk anymore. This was good. This was progress.

"I'm not who you think I am. I'm different. I've changed."

"Change doesn't have to be a bad thing."

"It is for me."

She heard the rasp in his voice and saw the vulnerability in his eyes that he tried to cover up with that tough warrior thing. "I can still see you in there," she whispered, reaching up to cup his cheek with her palm. "The boy I used to know hidden beneath all the sorrow and loss and pain."

He winced, pulled away from her touch.

Ouch. She tried not to let it show that his rejection hurt. She understood. Okay, not really, but she wanted to understand. "Gideon? What is it? Tell me what you're feeling."

He'd always had trouble expressing his feelings, but she could see him trying. He was trying for her. "I was hoping—"

"What?" she asked after a few seconds passed and he didn't continue. "What were you hoping for?"

He shook his head. "I guess I hoped we could somehow turn back the clock, but I see now that was a foolish thought."

"No, no, not foolish." She laid her hand over his. "Not foolish at all."

He didn't move. Didn't look at her. But he left his hand there, underneath hers.

"Just say it, Gideon. What's the worst that could happen?"

He met her gaze and his eyes were tortured. "That you'd kick me out. Tell me you couldn't bear to look me in the face because of what I'd done."

A cold chill passed through her. What had he done? "Nothing you could do would ever make me turn away from you," she said bravely, and reached out to lay her palm over his heart. "I know who you are deep inside. Tell me, Gideon, who are you fighting in your nightmares?"

"Me," he said. "I'm trying to kill me."

His words sucked the air from her lungs. "Trust me," she whispered. "Trust me with your darkest secret."

Gideon's eyes misted and he clenched his jaw. "It's the bombings and losing my hand and . . ."

"There's more." She said it as a statement, not a question.

He turned his head, stared at the wall, and for one hopeless minute she thought he was not going to open up to her, but then finally, he spoke in a voice so soft she could scarcely hear him. "During my first tour of duty, I was sent into a house where they suspect Saddam Hussein had hidden weapons of mass destruction."

Gideon paused but Caitlyn didn't fill the silence. She waited. Giving him the time and space he needed.

"There weren't any weapons there. We'd finished sweeping the house and we were leaving. I was the last one out."

Caitlyn reached out to run her hand over his upper arm.

Finally, he turned back and looked at her. "He came out of nowhere. He'd been hiding in a secret panel in the ceiling. He just literally dropped on top of me."

She moistened her lips, unable to imagine what that was like.

"He had a knife. We engaged in hand-to-hand combat." Gideon held up his left arm. "Obviously, it was before I lost the hand."

Another long pause stretched out.

"It's okay," Caitlyn said. "You don't have to say anything more."

Gideon wiped his hand over his mouth. "I killed him." He pressed his lips together. "It was my life or his. But then once the heat of the battle was over and I looked down, I saw he was just a boy. A kid. Probably no more than fifteen."

"Oh, Gideon, you didn't know. You were only a boy too. Nineteen. Scared."

He laughed a shaky humorless laugh. "It was as if in that moment, I killed myself. Gideon Garza from Twilight, Texas, was dead and a killer was born."

Caitlyn wrapped her arms around him and rocked him as she would have rocked Danny after a nightmare, and he let her. Obviously needing the comfort of her body.

She kissed him on the forehead, and then moved

to his lips and he responded. Kissing her back with a heat born of the desperate need to blunt his emotional pain with the physical passion of sex.

And Caitlyn welcomed him.

In answer, he wrapped his arm around her waist, drew her to him, and kissed her as if both their lives depended on it.

CHAPTER SEVENTEEN

*Traditional meaning of marvel of Peru—
flame of passion.*

The passion born from confession soon developed into full-blown lust for only each other. Gideon's kisses left her breathless and hungry for more, more, more.

When she was seventeen, she couldn't imagine anything more powerful than Gideon Garza's kisses. He'd hypnotized her, entranced her. Making love to him had been the most exquisite sensation she'd ever experienced. It had been more than just physical, although he certainly knew how to make her body hum. But what catapulted *their* lovemaking to the dizzying heights was the love they'd shared. It had been raw, primal, undeniable, unique.

Later, with Kevin, she'd been struck by how

truly wonderful things had been with Gideon. She'd known it was great at the time, but it was not until she was with Kevin that she discovered precisely how special her bond with Gideon was. Her husband had been a man of mild passions. He'd lived simply, loved simply, nothing grand or earth-shattering. She'd been placated by the ease of it, knowing she could never again have what she'd had with Gideon.

And now here he was, back from the dead and loving her the way she'd never been loved. Not even when they were teenagers.

He'd learned a few things over the years he'd been away. His skill amazed her. He was a better lover than men with two arms. He took his time, not rushing. That was different. Back then, he'd taken her in a heated rush, and while she'd enjoyed the excitement of that headlong dash, this slow tempo suited who she was today. A woman, not a girl.

Gideon trailed his fingertips over her skin, feather light and warm. Little pools of heat burned everywhere he lingered.

A hushed sound of pleasure slipped from her lips and she lowered her eyelids, embracing the moment.

"You like that?" His voice was husky.

"Mmm." She purred.

He kept it up, the gentle stroking. His hand became a paintbrush, swishing back and forth, back and forth, combing her nerve endings with layer upon layer of sensation.

She luxuriated in his caress. It felt so perfect. Too perfect, perhaps. She never wanted it to stop. Never wanted to get out of bed. She wished she could freeze time or put it in a bottle. Hold it still so she could savor this moment endlessly, forever. They'd missed so much. She didn't want it to slip by so fast. Now she understood why he'd made her wait, why he hadn't wanted to hurry. Nothing wrong with a quickie, by and large, but their first time together after their eight years' separation should indeed be special.

He lowered his head and ran his tongue over her forehead, licking where he'd just caressed, dampening her skin gone red-hot from the rubbing. The man's tongue should be labeled a lethal weapon. It was undoing her in a hundred different ways. Her heart rate sped up. Her toes curled. Sweat pearled between her breasts. Her breathing was so shallow she couldn't understand how her lungs continued to function.

He took the hem of her nightgown in his hand and slowly pulled it over her head, then dropped it to the floor. She was naked underneath.

One by one, he dropped kisses up her arm to her shoulder, then from her shoulder to the hollow of her neck. His lips pressed against the pulse fluttering there like an exhausted runner after a marathon. And they were just getting started!

"Tulip," he whispered.

The sound of that nickname poured honey over her ears. *Tulip*.

It shot her right back to seventeen and the first time they'd made love.

It had been on a blanket between a tall thicket of juniper bushes in Sweetheart Park. They'd had trouble finding a place. Her father was strict, and Caitlyn had been afraid of what he would do if he caught Gideon in her bedroom. And at his house, his sick mother had been in the next room. That would have been really bad manners.

So they'd settled on Sweetheart Park at midnight on a weekday. She'd brought the blanket, he'd brought the condoms. It had been rushed. They'd both been afraid of getting caught, but it had been glorious. The next day she'd been very sore between her legs, but every time she'd moved, felt the ache, she'd smiled. She was no longer a virgin, having given herself to the love of her life. In spite of the furtiveness, it had felt so incredibly right.

"Giddy," she answered with the nickname she'd given him. She wasn't sure if he really cared for the silly moniker, but it fell naturally from her lips.

He kissed those lips, softly, quietly.

She savored it, closing her eyes, focusing on the moment. He tasted different than he used to taste. Once upon a time, he'd carried a greenish flavor. Like Granny Smith apples. Today, he tasted more like apple pie—deeper, more complex than a single flavor. It suited him, the depth. She feared that she tasted shallow and one note. She'd never been out of Texas. Had never seen the world. She had no idea what was out there, but one kiss from him and she could taste it.

Gideon propped himself up on his left elbow, arranged the blanket to hide his stump. She didn't know how to reassure him, to let him know it didn't bother her. Honestly, she was just so happy to have him back. Battered, scarred. It didn't matter. Gideon was alive and in her bed once more. The world was a wonderful, forgiving place.

He looked down at her, his eyes shining bright. "Eight years ago, I thought you were the most gorgeous woman I'd ever seen. You moved like water, smooth and calming. I wanted to be a part of you so badly. I thought if I could make love to you that some of that cool smoothness would rub off on me."

"Little did you know that cool smoothness was a cover-up for my insecurities. I never felt beautiful until you."

"But I was wrong."

"Wrong about what?"

"You're way more beautiful now than you were then."

"My breasts aren't as perky as they once were."

He leaned to kiss one nipple and then the other. "They nurtured our child. That makes them even more beautiful."

"Ah, you really know how to charm a girl."

"I wish I could have been there," he said. "It rips me up that I wasn't there."

She studied his face. He looked so sad.

"I missed out on so much time with Danny that I can never get back." The pain in his words cut her to the bone.

"Gideon, I'm so sorry." She reached out to run a finger along his cheek.

He forced a smile, trying to hide the pain, but she saw it in his eyes, heard it in his voice. "It wasn't your fault."

"But Gideon, you're not the only one who lost out. Danny and I had to go on without you."

"You're right," he said. "I'm feeling sorry for myself."

"That's not what I meant. You have a right to feel hurt and cheated."

"What's done is done. I can't go back in time and change the past."

"We both made a lot of mistakes."

"Yeah." He looked away.

She cupped his chin in her palm, directed his gaze back to her. "But this isn't one of them. Danny isn't one of them. He might have been a happy accident, but he was never, ever a mistake. That's what my father didn't understand."

Gideon pulled her close to him, buried his face into her hair. "I'm so sorry, Tulip, for all you suffered."

"It wasn't a tenth of what you went through."

They lay there for a long moment, absorbing warmth and comfort from each other, then slowly, Gideon began to stroke her again. First her hair, then her face, then his hand fell to her breasts.

Caitlyn's nipples beaded instantly, jutting into hard little peaks.

He laughed a throaty laugh and then moved to suckle first one knotted bud and then the other. The heat of his mouth shot sparks of desire throughout her entire body. Her belly quivered, her womb tightened. How she wanted him!

For the longest time, he languished there, kissing and suckling, nibbling and tasting her breasts. She could feel the tension building inside her, growing higher and hotter with each flick of his tongue. A long, low moan escaped her lips.

Gideon's adept mouth drew responses from her that she didn't know she was capable of, and when he started to trail his mouth from her breasts southward, she groaned, threaded her fingers through his hair, arched her back upward, and egged him on.

Down, down, down, he went. His slick tongue pausing to tease her navel before sliding lower and lower until he reached the apex of springy curls nestled between the notch of her hip bones.

"Gideon," she whispered.

"Yes, sweetheart?"

"You don't have to do that. I—"

"Shh," he interrupted. "Shh."

She didn't need any more reassurance than that; she let her knees fall open, giving him full access to her queendom. The king was in the house. She smiled up at the ceiling as his hot tongue touched her trigger point.

In a matter of seconds, it quickly became apparent that Gideon had indeed learned a thing or two over the years. Before, when he'd performed this particular act, it had been hesitant and hurried. Now, oh wow, now.

Caitlyn's eyes slipped to the back of her head and her entire body tensed. She clutched the quilt, patterned with the delicate marvel of Peru flowers, in both fists. What a proper quilt for an improper lovemaking.

His tongued danced, flicking quickly back and forth over her straining clit.

Instant heat poured into her womb. Her thigh muscles spasmed around his head. The brush of his hair was soft against her skin. Gideon. Not only alive but back in her bed, doing wild and interesting things to her with his mouth. And what a mouth. Made of pure lava from the feel of it. Molten, devastating, breathtaking.

His tongue quickly became an instrument of torture as he took her to the edge of orgasm and then ebbed away, stirring two simultaneous emotions—urgent desire and rank frustration.

"Oh please, oh please, oh please," she begged.

"Please what?"

"Please, please—"

"You have to ask for what you want," he teased.

"Please make me come. Please, please."

"All you had to do was ask."

Then the torture stopped and he took her where she'd begged him, riding high on the wave of his wicked tongue in a mad drive toward the ultimate pleasure of the flesh.

"Gideon," she cried, and tightened her fingers in his hair.

He chuckled, breaking the headlong rush.

She made a noise of irritation.

He laughed again, then picked up where he'd left off, pushing her up, up, up. A riot of sensation attacked her, buzzing through her bloodstream, pulling her tight and hard into utter rapture.

* * *

Love was indeed lovelier the second time around, Gideon decided as he moved his body inside Caitlyn's.

She lay on her back in the middle of his bed, looking up at him with wide, shining eyes. He loved the way she felt surrounding him, flexing her internal muscles, giving him a feminine squeeze like no other. Even through the rubber of his condom, it was the most amazing sensation.

"More," she whispered. "Deeper."

This was different. Her telling him what she needed. When they were teenagers, she'd followed his lead, going wherever he took her. It had been fine back then, but now he appreciated her giving him instructions, telling him what pleased her.

He cradled his right arm around her head, peered into her eyes, felt her soul touch his. Caitlyn. He'd missed her so much. He'd told her his darkest secret and she hadn't turned away from him.

Slowly, he slid deeper into her.

Caitlyn moaned. "I'd forgotten how big you were."

"I hadn't forgotten how good you felt," he cooed, and continued stroking.

She wriggled her hips, and her movement fueled the fire burning inside him.

"Wicked minx."

"Slowpoke, I want more friction."

"You've gotten bossy."

"Is that a problem?"

"Not at all. Your wish is my command." Gideon picked up the tempo, watched her eyes widen in pleasure.

"Ooh, yes, that feels nice."

"Just nice?" He stroked deeper, harder, faster.

"More than nice."

"How about this?" He pumped into her hard, shaking the mattress, rocking the headboard into the wall. *Bam, bam, bam.* Back in the day, he'd never taken her like this. So fast and hard and animalistic.

But the harder he pounded, the more she groaned. "Yes, yes, yes."

He gave her his all, sinking into her soft flesh all the way to the hilt.

She inhaled sharply, raised her hips, pushed against him. "Gideon, Gideon, I'm coming undone."

He pulled back. "Not yet, too soon."

She balled her hands into fists, rapped them against his shoulders. "Bastard."

"Don't I know it."

"I didn't mean it like that—"

"I know," he said. "It's okay."

She panted. "You're torturing me."

"I know baby, but it's for your own good. You'll be thanking me in a few minutes."

"Prove it."

"Look at the mouth on you." He dipped his head and kissed her while he started his slow stroking again, giving her another leisurely buildup. "You are so wet, woman. So sweet."

"C'mon," she begged. "Let me have it."

"You want more of this?" He increased his speed again and the headboard went back to slamming.

"Give it to me," she begged.

Then she said a word he'd never heard her say, and the shocking sound of it made him throw back his head and laugh at the same time he did exactly as she commanded. Giving her everything he had in him, working her over until she let out a guttural cry and reached up to wrap both arms around his waist, pulling him impossibly deep within.

His cock throbbed. His brain hummed like a swarming beehive. His balls pulled up tight and hard. He felt his seed spill from him at the same moment he experienced the rhythmic undulations of her orgasm clamp down on him hard and tight.

"Caitlyn," he cried, and the same moment she whispered, "Gideon."

They shuddered together in a simultaneous climax so powerful it robbed them of their breath. They clung to each, his mouth pressed against the top of her head, her head nestled against his chest, their bodies fused in the most intimate act a man and woman could share.

He held her as their orgasm ebbed. Held her. Kissed her. Whispered her name over and over.

The pleasure was so intense, the longing so great that it terrified him. He couldn't, wouldn't lose her again.

Because that was his greatest fear, losing her a second time. He didn't think he could live through that again.

* * *

Sometime later, Caitlyn awoke, feeling more alive than she'd felt in years. Gideon was here, back in her bed where he belonged.

Wait, whispered the cautious voice in the back of her head that was so terrified of getting hurt again, *don't jump to conclusions*.

But she couldn't help herself. Last night had been so incredibly amazing, she couldn't help wishing for a lifetime of his lovemaking. Caitlyn rolled over on her side, stacked her hands on top of each other, slipped them under her cheek, and studied him in the soft morning light coming in through the window.

His face was gentle in repose, the tightness softened. His lips were slightly parted. A lock of hair had fallen over his forehead. Just looking at him filled her heart to overflowing.

Gideon. The love of her life.

It was all she could do not to reach out and trace a finger over his features, touch the scar on his cheek, caress the bridge of his masculine nose. Danny would look similar to this when he was grown. They had the same forehead, the angular shape to their lips. Seeing the father in the son tightened her chest with emotion. Love shoved to new heights.

They could be a family.

The thought gave her heart wings. How much she wanted that, but she couldn't suggest it. Not now. Not yet. It was too soon. Both for her cautious nature and for Gideon. He still carried a lot of baggage from the world, and the nightmares he suffered were proof enough of that.

Time. They both needed time to come to terms with the past and to start down the path to a bright new future. There was no rush.

He opened one eye. "You're staring at me."

"I am," she confessed.

"What do you see?"

She put the tip of her tongue to her lips. "I was thinking about how much Danny looks like you."

"And you tried to pass him off as Kevin's child. No one in town fell for it."

"I know," she said. "But they pretended to."

He smiled.

He didn't smile often, but when he did it was like the sun coming out after weeks of hard, punishing rain.

"We could cook breakfast together," he said. "I'll make your favorite, pecan waffles."

"You remembered."

He reached out to trace a finger over her nose. "Of course I remembered, Caitlyn. You were my first love."

"How many loves have you had?" she asked, then immediately amended it. "Scratch that, I don't want to know."

"I've had a few women in my life," he said. "But you have to remember I've been in the Middle East for eight years. Not a lot of opportunity for falling in love."

"Who were the women?" she asked, fearing he was going to confess that he'd been to prostitutes. Not that she could blame him. He was a man, after all, and men had their needs, she just hated knowing the details.

"There was one woman," he said. "Right after the accident, but that relationship was pretty unhealthy. She was a devotee."

"A what?"

"A devotee. It's people who are turned on by those of us who've lost a limb."

"You mean it's a sexual kink?"

"Yeah. They don't love you, they love the fact that you're missing something."

"That's very strange."

He shrugged. "A lot of amputees get mixed up with devotees at some time or another. It's pretty seductive at first. Especially if you've never heard of an acrotomorphile. You think this person is accepting you for who you are, but instead they want you only because you're an amputee. Some amputees don't mind. They think any love is better than no love."

"But it bothered you."

"Yeah," he admitted.

She scooted across the sheet, getting closer, peering into his eyes, peering straight through him. "I accept you for who you are, Gideon. You don't scare me. Your missing arm neither turns me off nor turns me on. It's simply a part of who you are. Like your height and the color of your hair."

"You say that now . . ."

"Do you really have such a low opinion of me? That I would let your disability come between us?"

"It's a lot more complicated than you understand."

"Well," she said, splaying a palm over his chest. "It certainly didn't affect your lovemaking. You're far better now than you were eight years ago."

"You think so?" He looked pleased at her compliment. And well he should look pleased; after last night, he'd outdone himself.

"I've never had such an amazing lover."

"How many lovers have you had besides me and Kevin?"

"That's it," she admitted.

"So really," he teased, "I'm only better than Kevin."

"Hey, you rocked *my* world."

"I guess that's good enough."

"So besides me and the devotee, who else was there?"

"I had a casual fling with a local girl when I was in boot camp. She looked a lot like you. A case of transference, I suppose. If I couldn't have you, I went after your look-alike."

That caused her to feel simultaneously touched and saddened. He'd been searching for her replacement. She hadn't even tried to replace him. She'd known she wasn't in love with Kevin. He'd known it too, but he hadn't been looking for a grand love. He'd had that with his first wife, who'd died of breast cancer at twenty-eight. Kevin had wanted nothing more than companionship and to be a father to Danny. That made her feel sad too. That she and

Kevin had settled for less than they deserved. Still, he'd been a good father, a good husband.

"Then there was Moira."

"Moira?" Caitlyn said, feeling more jealous than she should. Gideon was here with her, no Moira in sight.

"She was a relief aid worker. British, originally from Liverpool. She talked like the Beatles. It was fun listening to her. We were a lot alike, she and I."

Unlike Caitlyn and Gideon, who were night and day. Caitlyn nibbled her bottom lip. "What happened between you two?"

"I left Afghanistan."

"So you just recently broke up." She hadn't expected the vise-grip of jealousy. It was ugly, but she couldn't banish it.

"We were never together. Moira and I were friends with benefits, we both knew it was nothing more."

"Are you sure?"

Gideon smiled. "Hey, wait, are you jealous of Moira?"

"No," she lied.

"You are." He hooted.

"I'm not."

"Then why are the tops of your ears turning red?"

"They're not." She reached up to cover her exposed ear with her palm.

"The tops of your ears always turned beet red when you were jealous. Do you remember Gina

Watkins who used to wait tables at the Funny Farm and flirted outrageously with me even in front of you?"

Caitlyn scowled. "Yes, I refused to eat there after she gave you a kiss at Christmas when you were standing under the mistletoe."

He chuckled, reached over to cradle her cheek against his palm. "Caitlyn, you had no reason to be jealous. I had no interest in Gina. I only had eyes for you."

"Well, Gina Watkins only had eyes for you."

"Why do I get the feeling that if she were here right now, you'd whip her ass?"

"You'd like that, wouldn't you? Women catfighting over you."

"It's just fun getting you riled up," he teased.

"Gina Watkins is lucky she moved out of town."

"I tell you what," Gideon said, wrapping his arm around her waist and drawing her closer. "How about we spend the next hour or so making love and then we can get to those pancakes. And then we'll take you to get your stitches out."

"You're on," Caitlyn said, and pulled him down on top of her.

Chapter Eighteen

*Traditional meaning of ambrosia—
your love is reciprocated.*

For two glorious days they stayed in bed, eschewing their duties at the victory garden. After all, there was more than one kind of victory, and Gideon was long overdue a hero's proper welcome home, going out only to get Caitlyn's stitches removed. When the phone rang, they let the answering machine pick up, after they checked to make sure it wasn't Caitlyn's father calling.

They fully explored each other's bodies and erogenous zones. They gave each other massages and took a bath together in Caitlyn's bathtub. They lit candles, and the air filled with the smell of ambrosia flowers. They raided the refrigerator, for food and for creative sex play, lingering over each and every morsel of food, savoring the flavor. They donned blindfolds and described to each other the different tastes and textures. Sweet and juicy strawberries with fluffy light whipped cream. The sour crunch of dill pickles and potato chips with a turkey sandwich. The spicy hot tang of chicken enchilada soup.

They involved every sense organ in their erotic picnics. Smearing peanut butter and melted chocolate over their chests and then decadently licking it off. Sucking wine through a straw and getting tipsy. Touching lips through a hole in a doughnut and then gobbling up the yeasty treat. And the whole while giggling like the teens they used to be.

It was a magical, carefree two days, and they both clung to it with all their hearts.

And then Danny came home and they went back to being grown-ups, back to Gideon sleeping in the guest room, back to work and back to family life.

And for two beautiful weeks, everything was perfect.

On the first Saturday in April as the seeds began to sprout and reach for the sun-filled skies, Crockett Goodnight came by Caitlyn's flower shop. He hadn't been around much since Gideon had moved into her house and he'd stopped flirting with her. And she was glad for that, especially after the last incident with Bowie.

"Morning, Caitlyn." He greeted her with a wide smile.

"Hello, Crockett."

"How's your wrist?" He glanced at the scar that was still bright pink and savage-looking.

"Much better, thank you."

"Hondo ever figure who set that bear trap in the victory garden?"

"No. There weren't any fingerprints on the trap."

He clicked his tongue. "Such a shame to mar such a pretty wrist. I hope they catch whoever did it and throw the book at him."

"Who says it's a him? Could just as easily be a woman."

He shook his head. "Women and bear traps? Not likely."

"You never know."

"So." He clasped his palms together. "Are you and Danny ready for opening day?"

Until Crockett walked in, she'd actually forgotten about promising Danny he could go to opening day at the Ballpark in Arlington.

"I told you no weeks ago. I can't make it. I have to work."

Crockett's face fell like that of a first grader who'd been told he couldn't have cake for breakfast. "So it'll just be me and Danny?"

"Actually, Gideon is going to use my ticket, if that's all right with you."

Crockett's eyes narrowed and he pressed his lips tightly together, but then he laughed and said, "Sure, sure, that's fine."

"Is it going to be awkward for you? When we first made these arrangements, I didn't know about the details of the will."

Crockett shrugged. "If it doesn't bother Garza, it doesn't bother me."

"It doesn't bother me a bit, Goodnight," Gideon said.

Both Caitlyn and Crockett turned to see Gideon and Danny standing in the doorway. Danny had a baseball mitt in his hand and he was grinning like it was Christmas. But the tension between the two men was palpable.

"I was planning on us leaving a little early," Crockett said. "I have a surprise for Danny. There's a batting practice clinic before the game starts and I signed us up."

"Really!" Danny's eyes shone. "Oh, Crockett, you're the greatest." He ran across the shop to wrap his arms around Crockett's waist.

Caitlyn saw the look in Gideon's eyes as he watched his son hug another man, and it hurt her heart. "Danny, come here and listen to me a minute. I know you're excited but I want you to hear this."

"Yes, ma'am." He heaved an exaggerated sigh and clomped over to her.

Caitlyn crouched down so they were face to face. "Wear your sunscreen and cap. Don't eat too much junk, and most of all . . ."

"Yeah?"

"Have a good time." She kissed his cheek.

"Mom!" He rubbed off her kiss. "Not in front of everyone."

"I guess I'll see you when I see you," she said to Gideon. "I'll be at the victory garden when I close up here. Probably won't be home until after dark."

Their eyes met over Danny's head. How she wanted to kiss him good-bye. But they'd decided to keep things quiet until they were ready to tell Danny that Gideon was his father. From the way the two had been getting along, not to mention how desperately she wanted to kiss Gideon in public, that wouldn't be too long.

"Bye." Gideon winked and followed Crockett and Danny out the front door.

Gideon had been dreading this trip to the ballpark ever since Caitlyn had proposed it, but to his surprise, Crockett acted as if there was nothing contentious between them. He talked mostly of baseball, which was a safe enough topic, except that Gideon had been out of the country so long he knew none of the players.

Danny knew them, though, and it seemed he had every baseball card ever made. His knowledge about baseball surprised Gideon. He hadn't been that interested in sports when he was Danny's age. He'd been much more interested in taking things apart and seeing how they worked.

It took over an hour to get to Arlington, to park, and to get through the gate. The air smelled like peanuts and popcorn and roasting hot dogs. Danny was so wound up that he couldn't stand still. He wriggled and jiggled and talked ninety-to-nothing.

They went first to the field where the pregame batting clinic, taught by former Texas Rangers, was being held. Crockett stepped out onto the field with Danny, but Gideon hung back.

"Come on," Crockett said, and waved him over.

Gideon shook his head. "Not for me, thanks. I'll just watch."

"Hell, you're a war hero, no one would think twice about it."

"Nah, you two go ahead." He saw the way Danny was with Crockett, animated, happy.

For the most part, whenever he was around his son, Gideon felt overwhelmed. He wasn't scared of fatherhood. In fact, he welcomed the role. He'd played it many times to orphans in Afghanistan. But that wasn't what bothered him. What crawled under his skin and burned like a grass burr was watching the easy way his half brother tossed the ball to his child. The way Danny's face lit up when he caught it.

Gideon had lost his dominant hand. He could toss a ball with his right hand, but not very well. He couldn't catch at all with the prosthesis. And as for batting? Forget it. No matter how he might wish it different, he couldn't give his son the things he needed, and Crockett could.

Stop feeling sorry for yourself. The voice he heard in the back of his head was all Moira's, bristly and British, taking him to task.

"Good catch, Danny-boy," Crockett called out. They were pitching the ball back and forth, warming up, waiting for their turn at the bat. "Sling it back, give it all you've got."

Danny cocked back his arm and hurled.

Crockett easily caught it.

"Hey Gideon," Danny said. "Watch this."

Those four little words went a long way in chasing off his gloomy mood. He smiled and turned his full attention on his son.

Once the batting clinic was over and Danny had snagged autographs from some of the players who'd come down on the field, they made their way to their seats. The Rangers were playing the Yankees on opening day so the place was packed.

Gideon was alarmed to discover they were sitting in the upper box behind home plate. Ever since he'd been in that first bombing in Baghdad where he'd suffered a concussion and temporary amnesia, whenever he had to scale heights much over a second story, his equilibrium screwed up. He wasn't afraid of heights. Rather, he got vertigo.

His son was taking the steps two at a time, eager to get to their seats. Gideon was trying to get up the high metal steps carrying the nachos and soft drinks—which Danny had begged for—which was challenge enough without the dizziness.

"You okay, man?" Crockett asked.

"Fine." Gideon grunted.

"You don't look fine."

"It's nothing."

"Here, let me take that for you." Crockett reached for the nachos.

"I said I'm fine," Gideon growled.

Crockett held up both palms. "This is me backing off, dude."

Okay, he sounded like an ass, and while he might not like Crockett, could some of his testiness have anything to do with the fact that his half brother had wowed his son in ways he could not? Gideon had to admit it did. Relenting, he said, "Look, heights make me light-headed."

"Gideon!" Danny called out from the top row of the upper boxes. "I found our seats, aren't they awesome!"

"I'll be fine once I sit down," Gideon said. "And yeah, you can carry the damn soda for me."

"Hey man, look at you. All asking for help and shit."

Just when he was starting to like that guy, he had to say something that made Gideon want to smack him.

Once he was seated, as long as he didn't lean too far over, he could control the vertigo. He tried to keep his mind focused on the game. The weather wasn't bad. The nachos were surprisingly decent, and Danny was having the time of his life.

By the time the seventh inning stretch rolled around, Crockett and Danny were swaying in the aisles with the other fans to the tune of "Take Me Out to the Ball Game." Gideon stayed put.

Then at the top of the eighth, amazingly, a fly ball came their way.

"Catch it, Gideon! Catch it!" Danny yelled.

Not wanting to disappoint his kid, Gideon stood, hand raised, and tried to catch it, but his head swam and he had to sit back down or tumble over the seat in front of him, just as Crockett knocked a couple of people aside to reach up and snag it for Danny.

The crowd around them went nuts. Some cheering, some booing.

Crockett smirked, tossed Danny the ball. "Here you go, kid."

"Woo-hoo!" Danny and Crockett bumped fists.

Grinning from ear to ear, Danny sat back down, turned to Gideon. "Crockett is so awesome. I wish he could be my dad."

The house was quiet and dark when Caitlyn came home from working the victory garden with all the members of the gardening club. It was well after nine. Someone had brought a couple of bottles of wine—probably Raylene—and they'd ended up doing as much sipping as they had weeding. She kicked off her gardening clogs in the mudroom and shut the door behind her. During the course of the day, she'd made up her mind to tell Gideon it was okay if he wanted to tell Danny who he was. She'd thought putting it off would make things easier, but it had not. They might as well just do it, deal with the fallout, and get it behind them so they could take the next step.

And what was that next step? Gideon was already living with her. Marriage seemed the next logical progression. But he hadn't told her he loved her and she surely was not going to say it first. She knew that he did love her. She could see it in his eyes, feel it in his touch, but until he said the words . . . Was she being silly about that? Shouldn't she just go ahead and tell him she'd never stopped loving him? Would that make her seem needy? She didn't want him to think she was needy. Was she needy?

Too much wine for you tonight, Mrs. Marsh.

Were Gideon and Danny home yet? They hadn't come by the garden on their way in. Maybe the game had gone long. Or maybe Crockett just hadn't felt like stopping. He could be like that.

"Gid?" she called softly.

No answer.

She dropped her car keys on the kitchen table and flicked on the light. The sink was empty, the cabinets sparkling. Gideon had cleaned up. She smiled. He made her feel so taken care of.

"Gid?" She stepped into the living room.

It was empty. The television turned off. There was a baseball program on the coffee table, ticket stubs, an autographed baseball, and a little boy-sized Texas Rangers ball cap. That made her smile too. Looked like Danny had a very good time.

She hadn't meant to stay out so late, but she'd been having such fun and they'd gotten a lot of work done in spite of—or maybe because of—the wine sipping. She felt tired, but it was the good kind of tired, obtained from hard work and camaraderie.

She opened the door to Danny's bedroom, but his bed was empty, the covers turned back. She looked into the master bedroom. They weren't there either.

A soft uneasiness slid over her. Not alarm, not concern, but the slight tugging that something was different. Off. Then she turned the knob of the guest bedroom and stepped inside.

Gideon lay on his left side with Danny curled against his belly. They were both fully dressed and sound asleep.

Her heart lurched and a third smile tugged at her lips. They looked so happy, so peaceful together, this father and son. For the longest time she simply stood in the darkness, the only illumination coming from the kitchen light.

She watched them and realized their chests were rising and falling in tandem breathing. They looked so much alike with their dark hair and tanned skin and identical noses. Finally, she crept forward, intending on easing Danny away from Gideon without waking him. She leaned over, slipped an arm under his little shoulder, and then suddenly, there was a gun in her face.

She didn't know where it had come from. Hadn't even felt him move. One minute it wasn't there, the next it was.

It must have been under his pillow, that's all she could figure. The barrel was at her nose and her heart was thumping like a piston. Her knees were water.

"What the fuck are you doing," Gideon snarled. He stared at her but his eyes were unseeing, his hand wrapped around the pistol grip. He was in the throes of another nightmare.

Fear was a living thing in her chest. He wasn't awake, she realized. In his sleep, he'd pulled a gun on her.

She stayed frozen, terrified to move, terrified to set him off, terrified to even try to wake him. Sweat dripped off her forehead, rolled down her nose. She couldn't stay like this. The gun in her face, Gideon's vacant expression sending her gut into spasms.

"Gideon," she finally whispered. "Wake up, it's me, Caitlyn."

"Mom?"

Oh Jesus, Danny was awake!

"Shh, honey, don't move."

"Mom." His voice was high and reedy. "How come Gideon's holding a gun?"

"He's asleep. He doesn't know what he's doing." Fear was a metal taste in her mouth. Her bones were like rubber.

"Gideon," Danny said sharply, "wake up."

Caitlyn gasped, sucked in her breath, held it.

Gideon's eyes snapped fully open. He stared at her, stared at Danny, stared at the gun in his hand. His mouth fell open. Realization dawned in his eyes.

He flung the gun away from them. Leaped from the bed. "I'm sorry, I'm sorry, oh Caitlyn, I'm sorry."

"Get it out of my house. Get it out now!" she commanded, pointing at the gun lying on her rug.

"I'm going, I'm going." He stabbed his feet into his shoes.

Danny sat on the bed looking nervous.

"You don't have to go, just get rid of the gun. Why do you have a gun?"

"I'm a soldier, Caitlyn. Soldiers have guns."

"Not anymore you're not. You're a carpenter and artist with wood. You don't need a gun."

He snatched up the gun, stuck it in his waistband. Shadows covered his face. He looked as gaunt and haunted as she felt. "I'll come back later for my things."

"Where are you going in the middle of the night?"

"I'll find a motel, don't worry."

"You don't have to go."

"I do. I can't believe . . ." He swallowed, paled. "I can't believe I did that to you."

"I wasn't hurt. You didn't hurt me."

"No, but I could have . . . I—" He had no words left. She could see it in his face. He was torn apart by what he had done and he'd had no control of it.

Then he turned and was gone, fleeing out into the night. After the kitchen door slammed behind him, she heard his motorcycle roar to life, drive away.

"Mom?" Danny said. "What happened?"

She sat down beside him, put her arm over his shoulder, and quietly told him as best she could in language he would understand why Gideon was the way he was.

"I like Gideon. Will he ever come back?"

Feeling wretched to her core, she ruffled her son's hair. "I don't know, honey, I just don't know."

Caitlyn had seen his monster and she'd been horrified. Just as he knew she would be. She was too innocent, too pure to handle the darkness inside him. Gideon didn't blame her. He understood. He had no place here with her and Danny. No place in polite society.

What disturbed him most was the thought that he'd frightened her, that she was scared of him. He was capable of violence. He had harmed people in the name of his country. In the pursuit of duty.

And he could do it again if he had to in order to protect his family.

Except they weren't his family. Not really. Yes, he might be Danny's biological father and he'd lived with Caitlyn for the past few weeks as if they were husband and wife, but he had just been playing at happily-ever-after.

He'd known all along that he would taint it, ruin it. How stupid of him to dream that things could be different. He was who he was and he couldn't change the fact.

Let them go.

It was the only honorable thing to do.

Gideon rode his motorcycle down the silent streets of Twilight, not really sure where he was headed until he got there. The Rocking J Ranch. He did not drive down to the house where Bowie lived, but parked the motorcycle on the side of the road and sat staring at it in the moonlight.

The house was huge, a sprawling ranch-style house with Spanish architecture and a tile roof. As soon as the probate was settled, if he inherited the place, he was going to deed it to Caitlyn. She could keep it or sell it, whatever she wanted to do. He breathed a deep sigh, part relief that the decision was made, part bone-deep regret that he'd let his dark side ruin everything.

Cattle grazed in the fields in the moonlight. Ghostly shapes of a heritage that he had no right to claim.

Now, he was in exile.

He was glad now that he hadn't told Caitlyn that he loved her with all his heart. He'd almost told her during those two magical days when they'd made love almost nonstop. He knew he would never love another the way he loved her.

He had to leave. It would be selfish to stay when he'd brought so much damage and danger into their lives.

But what if you could change? Don't you want to change? For them? For yourself?

He did. He wanted to be well and whole and healed, but it wasn't possible. He'd tried and failed.

And then, he remembered that night at the Horny Toad Tavern when Hondo had told him he would help him if he ever needed it. Gideon knew Hondo was someone who could understand. He'd been where Gideon had been and yet, he'd come out of it. He'd survived.

God, he did not want to go. More than anything in the world he wanted to stay. But he couldn't stay. Not this way.

A twinge clutched him. Love knocking on the door of his heart. Open up and let it in. But how did a guy who'd never really belonged to anyone, never really fit anyplace, do that? The only place he'd ever really felt at home was with the Green Berets, and he'd lost that forever. Here, in Twilight, he felt adrift and he knew it was his own fault.

Danny and Caitlyn were both waiting to love him. He could see it in her eyes when she looked at him. Could tell from Danny's eager smile that he was willing to give Gideon a chance.

He got on his motorcycle and drove, and when he reached the house on the lake, he got out and walked to the front porch. Knocked hard. A few minutes later, the door opened and there stood Hondo in his pajamas.

Gideon looked at him with utter despair and said two simple words. "Help me."

CHAPTER NINETEEN

*Traditional meaning of gladiolus—
strength of character.*

Hondo's plan was simple. No drinking, which was
no real problem for Gideon. Hard work. The carousel restoration covered that. Take relationships slow.
He realized he and Caitlyn had made love too soon.
They'd jumped into the thick of the fairy tale without being fully prepared for the reality.

"You need to romance her," Hondo told him.
"Do all the things you two never got to do before.
Go slow. Make this the best time of your lives."

"I can do that. But how will I know when I'm
ready? When it's right to take that next step with
Caitlyn?"

"Your heart will tell. You'll know when it's right."

"That's pretty vague."

"Trust. Just trust. And when something is bothering you, don't keep it bottled up. Head on over to the VFW hall. Everyone there knows what you're going through. You're not alone, Gideon. We're here for you."

That was going to be a challenge. Opening up to others. But it was a necessary step. It was the main thing he neglected and he knew it. He also turned his gun over to Hondo. If he was going to live a life without violence, he had to lay down his weapons and let down his guard.

"Trust doesn't happen overnight," Hondo said. "But that's okay. Nothing wrong with taking your time."

He took back his old room at the Merry Cherub and spent his days in a labor of love on the carousel. On Sundays, he went to church with Caitlyn and Danny and her father. He sat beside them in the pew and sang from the same hymnal and then he went back to his room at the bed-and-breakfast, and slowly, he stopped feeling weird and out of place.

And as the victory garden grew, so too did the quiet bond now building between him and Caitlyn. A bond born of the present, no longer bound by the ghosts of their past.

A month went by. In the garden, the flowers and herbs and vegetables and fruit flourished while one by one he restored the carousel animals. And in all that time, Gideon did not have a single nightmare.

That's when he realized the healing had truly begun.

* * *

Caitlyn missed Gideon more than she could say, but she understood what he was doing and why and she admired him all the more for having the courage to stay in Twilight and face his demons head-on. Besides, she could see him every day from the window of her flower shop, hard at work on the carousel. In the evenings, she'd bring Danny with her and they'd all toil together with their friends and neighbors, the entire community building the most romantic garden in the state of Texas.

One day in early May, just before the annual Spring Fling Festival, as Caitlyn returned from the grocery store, an odd sensation made the hairs on the back of her neck crawl, and something struck her as wrong.

She pulled into the driveway. Danny was in the backseat playing a video game. She killed the engine and got out, her gaze scanning her acre lot, wondering what had triggered her cautious instincts.

And then she saw that the door to the chicken run stood wide open.

Her heart somersaulted. "Stay in the car," she told Danny, and took off toward the chicken pen at a trot.

The chickens were nowhere to be seen, but overhead, she heard the *kree, kree, kree* of a hawk.

"Chick, chicks!" she called, her stomach tightening. "Chick, chicks!"

But they didn't come running to her call as they normally did.

Kree, kree. The hawk's lazy shadow circled the yard.

Caitlyn raised her fist at the hawk. "You bastard, if you killed my chickens . . ."

"What is it, Mom?" Danny was standing beside her looking concerned.

"Did you open the door to the chicken run?"

Solemnly, he shook his head.

Then who did? The uneasiness that had gripped her when she'd come up the driveway took hold of her again. "Sweetheart, run on over to Dr. Sam's house and see if we can borrow Patches. The chickens have obviously gone into hiding with the hawks on the loose."

"Okay." He tucked his Game Boy in his back pocket and started off at a trot. Sam and Emma and Charlie lived on the next block over. Their Border collie, Patches, had won awards for his herding abilities. He could round up the chickens in no time.

If there were any chickens to round up.

Her throat tightened. It might seem silly to some people, but she loved her chickens and it hurt her when something happened to them. She thought of the three little dead Buff Orpingtons she'd found last fall, not much more than a big pile of feathers once the hawks were done with them. It was just right after Kevin's death, and coming on the heels of that, it had really upset her.

While Danny was gone, Caitlyn went to the garden, still calling, "Chick, chick, chick," hoping against hope they were in there eating up her strawberries, but it was a futile effort.

The hawks kept circling, mocking. Dread took

hold of her. She sank her hands on her hips. "Good thing for you it's against the law to shoot hawks."

Kree, kree.

Nature was a bitch. Caitlyn walked along the honeysuckle thicket growing against the fence on the far side of the chicken run. She heard some rustling in the underbrush, and her spirits soared. "Chick, chick. Chick, chick." She clucked her tongue.

A bold Buffy stuck her head from the undergrowth, and relief loosened Caitlyn's limbs. She thought about going to get some feed, to try and coax them back into the run, but with the hawks out, she was afraid to leave them exposed in the distance between the thicket and the door. She'd wait for Danny and Patches. Surely, the hawks wouldn't try to dive in with all three of them there to shepherd the poultry.

A couple of minutes later, Danny returned not only with Patches, but with Dr. Sam Cheek as well.

"I hear the hawks are giving you fits," Sam said.

"The chickens more than me."

"Patches will have them rounded up in nothing flat," he assured her.

"Thank you so much."

Sam blew a whistle that only the Border collie could hear. The dog immediately sprang into action, running along the fencerow, low and focused. When he approached the honeysuckle, it exploded with movement. Chickens all running full-out for their pen. By the time Caitlyn got to the enclosure, the chickens were inside and Patches was looking at Sam as if to say, *That's it? That's all I get to do?*

Caitlyn did a quick head count and realized one was missing. The one that always stood out in the crowd. Her little Faverolles.

"Collette's not here." She tried to keep the alarm from her voice, but already tears were pushing at the backs of her eyes. *No, please, not Collette.* Unlike the Buffies that she'd gotten from the chicken rescue, she'd raised Collette from an egg. Remembered when she was a tiny chick that could fit in the palm of her hand.

"Not Collette," she whispered.

Sam put a hand on her arm. "Don't fret yet." To his dog, he said, "Patches, find it."

Patches sprang into action again, going back to the honeysuckle thicket, sniffing and sniffing. He sat down, barked sharply.

Caitlyn looked to Sam, saw the bad news in his eyes.

She didn't want her son to see this. "Danny, honey, could you please go unload the groceries from the car?"

"What about Collette?"

"Dr. Sam and I will find her. You go on."

Danny looked reluctant, but he went. The second her son was out of sight, Caitlyn was on her knees, beside Patches, pushing aside the honeysuckle to find Collette. When she saw the blood her heart skipped a bit and she felt a sickness settle inside her. Yes, it was just a chicken, but she couldn't help how she felt. The intense feeling of loss. Dammit, she'd lost so damn much in her life. Not Collette too.

She reached in and gently drew the chicken from the undergrowth. Collette's body was still warm.

And then she felt her move.

Collette wasn't dead!

Don't get your hopes up. She could be mortally wounded. That thought made her feel worse. She didn't want Collette to suffer.

Kree, kree, kree mocked the hawk. Bitches.

Sam reached out to take Collette from her. The chicken opened her eyes, blinked at them.

Gently, he ran his fingers over her body. "The hawk got hold of her, that much is clear. She's missing a lot of tail feathers and she's bleeding, but she must have somehow managed to get away and into the thicket before the hawk could do major damage, but chickens go into shock really easily."

As he spoke, Collette shook her head, flapped her wings.

Joy sent Caitlyn's hopes soaring.

"I'll take her to the clinic and keep her for a few hours just to make sure she's okay."

"Thank you," she whispered. "Thank you so much, Sam."

"No problem." Sam gently tucked Collette into the crook of his arm, whistled to Patches, and started off down the road. He'd just left and Caitlyn was closing the door to the chicken run when Gideon drove up on his motorcycle. He cut the engine, took off his helmet, walked over to where she stood, shoulder sagging against the pen.

"What's wrong?" he asked, his voice dark with concern.

She waved at the sky but the hawks had dispersed, apparently getting the picture that their murderous intentions had been successfully thwarted. "A hawk got hold of Collette."

"Your favorite hen."

Caitlyn nodded, feeling the knot of tears rise up in her throat again.

"But how? Your enclosure is solid."

"When Danny and I got back from the grocery store, the door to the run was standing open."

"Could you have left it open this morning after you fed them?"

"Never."

"Could Danny have opened it?"

"He says he didn't." Her eyes met his.

He stepped to the door. Examined the latch. She'd put on both a hinge lock and triple wooden block closures because raccoons were notoriously clever about undoing locks. And with all the big wooded lots in the area, and the lake nearby, her neighborhood was primo real estate for raccoons.

"It didn't come open accidentally," he said.

"No," she agreed.

"Someone opened it."

"Looks like."

"But who?"

"That's the sixty-four-thousand-dollar question."

Gideon pressed his lips together and a frown creased his brow. She knew what he was thinking.

"Bowie Goodnight," she said, and he didn't deny it.

Collette made a complete recovery, and that weekend was the Spring Fling. Saturday dawned sunny and warm, but not unbearably hot as it could often be during May in North Central Texas.

Caitlyn got up and made breakfast for Danny. Oatmeal with bananas and walnuts in it. Something substantial to counter the junk she knew he was going to want to eat. Cotton candy and funnel cakes. Fried chicken and steak on a stick. Corn on the cob and hot dogs.

She showered while Danny fed the chickens and gathered eggs. She hoped to see Gideon there. He'd said he might drop by the festival and she wanted to look good in case he did. She tried on several outfits but finally decided on a pastel green dress with a floral pattern of gladiolus. It had a flared skirt and a form-fitting bodice.

She'd lost a few pounds since Kevin had died and her breasts didn't quite fill out the cup, but the scoop neckline showed off just the right amount of cleavage. She wore the dress with a pair of espadrilles and pulled her hair back in a loose ponytail. Then she added a little blush to her cheeks, some lip gloss, and mascara.

She and Danny walked to the town square where everything was already in high gear. He was so excited. "Wow, Mom, look. Face painting. Can I get Spider-Man painted on my face?"

"You sure you want to go around like that all day?"

"Yeah, yeah." He nodded.

"All right." She handed him five dollars and he zoomed off to the face-painting kiosk to be turned into a superhero.

"You look beautiful."

She turned her head and saw Gideon standing behind her. He looked pretty darn good himself. He'd gotten his hair trimmed and it lay down for once.

His gaze caressed her, slipping from her eyes to her mouth and then a quick peek at her cleavage before meeting her eyes again. Caitlyn couldn't help smiling. He'd noticed.

"Nice dress."

"Thank you." She ducked her head, felt her cheeks heat the way they had the first time he'd asked her out. It had been at a street fair much like this one. Twilight was always having one kind of street fair or another. Every month there was something planned to draw tourists to their town.

She could tell he was trying hard to be normal and she wondered what was normal for him. She imagined it couldn't be easy for him. Going from the tense, action-packed situation in the Middle East to a Saturday stroll around the square. She'd heard about vets who were so geared up to danger and action that they had trouble assimilating into a normal life. The pace was too slow for them. Too regular. Too routine. They'd been conditioned to live on the edge, and an average existence was too boring. Was that why he'd stayed in Afghanistan after he'd been injured? Was that why he'd never come home before?

He didn't come home because he didn't think you wanted him.

She bit down on her bottom lip as sadness washed over her. She hated to think of it. Him in a foreign country, wounded and alone, believing she'd forsaken him. While she'd been here believing he was dead. So much sorrow.

But the sorrow was gone now and regret wouldn't change things. She resolved to enjoy the moment. It was all anybody really had.

They stood to one side, watching their son getting his face painted red and blue. Their son. They could be a family. Longing pure and raw arrowed through her heart. She wanted that more than she could say. She slipped a hand around Gideon's waist.

"He's a great kid," Gideon said. "You've done a good job."

"Thank you."

He didn't say anything else. He'd never been very chatty. And honestly, neither was she. In the past, they'd shared many comfortable silences. But this silence wasn't comfortable. He was still putting up roadblocks. Boundaries she couldn't cross, and she didn't know how to scale them. What would it take to break through?

It was an unhappy thought. She moistened her lips. Whatever happened between them, he was still Danny's dad. Even if they weren't able to find their way back to each other, to recapture the easiness of their youth, they had a child together, and that would never change.

"It looks like the face painting is going to take a while," Gideon said. "Would you like something to drink?"

"Lemonade would be lovely."

"Lemonade it is."

He went to the lemonade stand, made his pur-
chase, and brought back two tall glasses of lemonade. "Want to sit?" He nodded at a vacant
wrought-iron bench on the courthouse lawn.

"Sure."

They sat, sipping lemonade, listening to the hum
of the crowd who were shopping for crafts, playing games of chance, eating gooey decadent treats
bought from street vendors. It was a perfect morning. She should feel blissfully happy, but life wasn't
that simple. The sun, shifting through the elm trees,
warmed her cheeks. Nearby, a mockingbird trilled a
medley of borrowed birdsongs.

Across the road lay the victory garden. It had been
blocked off from the street with plywood boards to
keep looky-loos from stomping around the tender
plants. Caitlyn found her mind wandering to the
care and feeding of plants.

The silence had stopped being awkward. She felt
more than saw Gideon's shoulders loosen. Heard his
breathing go slower. He was relaxing. Good. Good.

"Caitlyn." Terri Longoria called her name, snapping Caitlyn from her reverie.

"Yes?"

"We desperately need your help."

"What's up?"

"Missy Ivey signed up to man the kissing booth
from eleven to twelve, but she shows up with a cold
sore on her lip. Can you imagine that?"

"Well, you know Missy."

"So can you stand in for her?"

"Um . . . Gideon and I were having an outing

with Danny." The last thing she wanted was to man a kissing booth. The only person she wanted to kiss was the man sitting beside her.

"It's only for an hour. And we need someone young and attractive. It's not like I can grab just anyone."

"Giving away kisses just isn't my thing."

"You won't be giving them away. It's a dollar for cheek kisses, two dollars for on the lips, and no tongue allowed. You can specify cheek kisses only." Terri pressed her palms together in a prayer of supplication. "Please, please. The money is going to charity. Disadvantaged kids."

Why did she have to put it like that? "Terri . . ."

"Please." Terri turned to Gideon. "You don't mind, do you?"

"It's not my place to say. Caitlyn has a mind of her own."

Caitlyn sighed. She liked that he didn't try to tell her what to do, but in this case, she really wished he'd told Terri that he *did* mind. She let out a sigh. "Okay, I'll do it."

Terri hugged her around the neck. "You're a lifesaver."

"Big help you were," Caitlyn teased as she got up to follow Terri over to the kissing booth.

"Hey, you're a big girl."

She went behind the booth, and immediately two old guys from the local nursing home got in line. They paid their dollars and she presented them her cheek. They kissed her and went away bragging. She rolled her eyes, turned to the next person in line.

Gideon. With a hundred-dollar bill in his hand.

"What are you doing?"

"I decided I wasn't mature enough to handle watching other men kiss you, even if they were old codgers who were lucky to still have their teeth."

"Where's Danny?"

Gideon pointed at the temporary arcade set up on the other side of the square. "He's found the games."

"I don't normally let him go off on his own."

"He's almost eight. Let the kid spread his wings a little, Mother Hen."

"I'd just feel better if you were with him."

"We can see him from here."

"He could disappear in an instant."

"This is Twilight. What could possibly happen? Everyone knows him and he knows everyone. He's safe, Caitlyn."

Rationally, she knew that, but she couldn't turn off her worry gene.

Gideon rubbed his finger over the one-hundred-dollar bill. "I'm a paying customer," he enticed.

"I don't have change for a hundred."

"I don't want change."

"You're buying a hundred dollars' worth of kisses?"

"I am and let's get something straight. I'm not interested in those cheek kisses."

"That's all I'm offering."

"No exceptions?"

"None," she flirted. "It wouldn't be fair to give you mouth kisses when that area is off limits to everyone else."

"Okay," he drawled, and lowered his eyelids. "What about other kinds of kisses?"

"What do you mean?"

"How much are butterfly kisses?"

"What are butterfly kisses?"

"You've never had butterfly kisses?"

"No."

He shook his head. "You haven't lived."

"Because I've been in my cocoon."

"So the butterfly hasn't hatched yet."

"That's right."

"How about I give you a preview of the life waiting for you outside the boundaries of your cocoon, Madam Butterfly."

"By giving me a butterfly kiss?"

"That's right."

"How much should I charge?"

"Well," he said, "it's more intimate than a cheek kiss, but not as personal as a mouth kiss. How about a dollar fifty?"

"How about you explain what a butterfly kiss is first."

"You don't trust me?"

"Don't take it personally. I don't trust most people."

"Hazard of being born and raised a rich girl? You automatically assume people like you for your money and not who you are?"

That startled her. Was he right? Was that one explanation for her wariness?

"You'll just have to take it on faith," he said.

"Or give you a pass and kiss the next person in line. She looked over his shoulder to see another customer of the geriatric variety.

"Or you could just trust me." He grinned.

"Okay fine, give me a butterfly kiss." She leaned across the booth, hands gripping the counter.

Gideon leaned into her. He smelled so good. Like nutmeg and sandalwood soap. His face was so close, his lips almost touching hers.

Her breathing came hard and fast. He pressed his forehead against hers, stared straight into her eyes, and then he blinked. His eyelashes caressed her skin. He blinked rapidly. Each time his eyes brushed her skin, she felt a tingling rush of sensation spread over her entire forehead. Silly that she should find it incredibly erotic, but she did.

"That," he said huskily, "was a butterfly kiss."

"Where'd you learn that?"

"My mom."

It was amazingly intimate. He stopped blinking, but he was staring deep into her eyes, not moving, simply looking as if he stood there long enough, he could see the answer to every question he'd ever had.

"Okay," she said, feeling breathless and out of control.

"Then," he said, "there are Eskimo kisses. I know the term isn't politically correct, but I don't know what else they're called."

"Now, I do know what Eskimo kisses are."

"How much do they cost?"

"Let's say a dollar fifty like the butterfly kisses," she negotiated.

"Sounds fair." Slowly, gently, with their faces less than a breath apart, he rubbed his nose over hers.

Caitlyn rubbed back, thrilling to the sensation. It was downright fun, exploring all the ways to kiss.

"Let's not forget angel kisses."

"Where are you getting all this?"

"Told you, my mom. She was an affectionate woman."

"So what's an angel kiss?"

"Close your eyes."

"Gideon . . ."

"Trust me."

She let out a breath of air and closed her eyes. As soon as her visual sense was cut off, the rest of her senses became more acute. She heard the vendor in the next booth scooping ice, could smell cotton candy on the breeze, could feel the wood of the booth against her palms.

And feel the pressure of Gideon's lips as he lightly kissed one eyelid and then the other. "Angel kisses," he murmured.

She opened her eyes, found herself whispering, "What else?"

"Earlobe kisses."

"That'll be a dollar an earlobe."

"Hey!" said the geezer behind Gideon. "Stop hogging the kissin' girl."

Gideon held up his hundred-dollar bill.

"Darn it," the old man said, and wandered off.

"Now where were we?" Gideon asked.

"Earlobe kisses," Caitlyn said, enjoying this more than she should be and turning her head to give him full access to her earlobe.

"Good thing you wore a ponytail."

"Good thing."

Then his hot mouth was at her earlobe. He took it between his teeth, sucked gently.

The sensation was like a lightning bolt straight to her solar plexus. Right there in the middle of the town square at noonday, surrounded by a throng of tourists, Caitlyn got turned on. Like a water faucet. Turned on in a way she hadn't been turned on since the last time he'd sucked her earlobe.

This wasn't wise. This wasn't smart. Her sex was moist and hot. She pulled back, cleared her throat, and dropped her gaze. "That's enough of the earlobe kisses."

"But I only got one lobe," he protested. "And I got a lot of money left."

She presented her cheek. "You can have all the cheek kisses you want."

"One for tradition." He skimmed his lips over her cheek. "Then one with a twist."

"What—"

But she was interrupted when he kissed her cheek a second time and whispered simultaneously, "I want to kiss you in a hundred different places."

She pulled back, felt heat rise to her face. "Gideon!"

"I could have said something much naughtier."

She took the one-hundred-dollar bill from his fingers. "Consider the rest a donation."

"Only if you'll help me out."

"How's that?"

"I've gotten roped into this VFW Memorial Day

picnic and I need a date. Please don't leave me hanging," Gideon said.

"I'd need to find a babysitter."

"You could ask the judge."

"Honestly, this isn't really my sort of thing. I'm more of a homebody."

"It's not my thing either. Go with me. It won't be our thing together."

"So why are you going?"

He raised his left arm. "Apparently I'm the war hero du jour who needs honoring."

"How do you feel about that?"

"I don't like it. I don't consider myself a hero. I was just doing a job, but it seems to make everyone else happy."

"You want to go?"

"I want to take you out."

She met his gaze. "You can do that without dragging me off to the VFW picnic."

"I've agreed to go to the event and I need a plus-one."

"I'll think about it."

"Don't leave me hanging."

"Scoot, you're holding up the line."

"I meant what I said about kissing you in a hundred different places, if that affects your decision any." He held her gaze for a long moment, and then he turned and walked away, leaving Caitlyn feeling very hot and bothered.

CHAPTER TWENTY

*Traditional meaning of pink and white
roses—I love you still and always will.*

When the crowd at the VFW hall greeted him with
"For He's a Jolly Good Fellow" the minute he
walked in the door for the Memorial Day picnic,
it was all Gideon could do to not turn tail and run.

The place smelled of beer, cigars, and barbecue
sauce. A banner hung from the back wall of the pan-
eled room read: "Gideon Garza Hometown Hero."
And a big sheet cake stretched out on the table laden
with food was emblazoned with "We Love You
Gideon."

The attention made him feel uncomfortable.
Not just because he didn't consider himself a hero
but because there were three dozen men in this

room just as worthy of Memorial Day recognition as he was.

People came over to clap him on the back and shake his hand. Repeatedly, he was thanked for his service to his country. As if he'd had a choice. Judge Blackthorne and J. Foster had made sure the army had been his only option. He searched the room looking for Caitlyn, but saw she wasn't here.

"Get yourself a plate and c'mon outside. We've got a nice picnic table under a pecan tree overlooking the lake." Hondo waved at the buffet table and then at the door that led outside to the picnic area.

Feeling out of place without a date, but determined to make the best of it, he loaded up a plate with smoked brisket and coleslaw, potato salad and baked beans, yeast rolls and apple cobbler, and moved to follow Hondo outside.

He'd no sooner settled in than Hondo asked, "How are things with you and Caitlyn?"

"Um, fine." He busied himself cutting the beef brisket into bite-sized pieces.

"Young man." An elderly gentleman wearing a Pearl Harbor cap and pushing a walker with neon yellow tennis balls on the legs sidled up to their picnic table. His hair was the color of a snuff tin, his eyes a faded Old Glory blue. He spoke in a wavering East Texas accent. "My name's Mort Gilchrest and I just had to come over and shake your hand and thank you for your service."

Gideon clenched his jaw against the emotion.

This old guy was the real hero. A Pearl Harbor survivor. Not many of those guys left. He reached out and shook Mort's hand, then saluted him. "It's a real pleasure to meet you, sir, and thank *you* for your service."

The old veteran flicked a glance at Gideon's artificial hand. "I heard about what happened to you over there. I'm real sorry for your loss."

Gideon shrugged. "All part of the deal."

"Yeah," Hondo echoed.

A short silence passed between the three of them. Servicemen who'd all lost a lot in the pursuit of freedom. Nonmilitary personnel could never understand. Which was the point of the VFW. To have someone to talk to who'd marched a mile in your boots. And since Gideon had been coming here, sharing war stories, he'd stopped feeling so alone, stopped having the nightmares.

"I just want you to know, we don't take you for granted," Mort said, then slowly moved away.

Hondo's eyes lit up then and Gideon swiveled to see what he was looking at. Patsy Cross had come through the door carrying a plate in her hand. She spotted Hondo, and a huge smile spread across her face. She strolled over and Hondo scooted down to make room beside him on his side of the bench.

"I still can't believe the victory garden judging is in two days. We still have so much to do. After the picnic, I'm heading back over there to get in the finishing touches."

"Me too," Hondo said.

"I think we're going to win." Patsy smiled.

"Now don't go counting your chickens," Hondo warned.

"Bite your tongue, Hondo Crouch, you have no romance in your soul."

"That wasn't what you said last night," Hondo murmured, and gently tickled her.

"Shh, you old goat, you'll embarrass Gideon."

Gideon washed down his brisket with a swallow of lemonade and wished like hell Caitlyn hadn't stood him up.

"Well, look who just walked up," Hondo said.

"Caitlyn." Patsy waved a hand. "Yoo-hoo. Over here."

Gideon looked over his shoulder and his eyes hugged Caitlyn. Her blond hair was piled atop her head with a clip in a loose, feminine style that gave her an angelic appearance. Her cheeks were pink as if she'd been rushing around, and she wore a yellow print skirt and a simple white cotton V-neck blouse that made her look like one of those prognosticating flowers you pulled the petals off and recited with each dropped sliver, "She loves me, she loves me not."

He felt like he did the first time he'd seen her in high school walking across the quad on that spring morning, books clutched to her chest, a slight smile on her face. She'd reached up a hand to tuck a strand of hair behind her delicate ear, her movements gentle and graceful. For the briefest of moments, she'd glanced up and met his gaze, giving him a glimpse of the most gorgeous blue eyes he'd ever seen and smiled oh so slightly.

And he'd fallen like a meteor crashing to earth. Even though it had taken him two more years to get around to asking her out.

Tulip, he'd thought it then as he thought it now. *There's sunshine in your smile.*

"Yoo-hoo." Patsy waved.

"Hi," Caitlyn said, sounding as breathless as she looked. "I'm sorry I'm late."

She sat down beside Gideon and he could feel her body heat. Close. So close. His gaze zeroed in on her full lips shiny with strawberry gloss. She smelled like strawberries too.

He had an urge to drum his fingers against the table, restlessly bob his knee up and down, for he felt a cosmic force rise up inside him, push hard against his heart. Hondo had said he would know when it was right, and one look in those eyes and he knew. It was right. He wasn't afraid anymore.

"Danny's spending the night at my father's," Caitlyn murmured.

"Got any plans for after the picnic?"

"Got any suggestions?"

He grinned. "Are you free?"

"Are you asking me out?"

"Actually, I'm asking you in."

"What do you have in mind?" She giggled.

"Come to my room at the Merry Cherub at seven P.M.," he said, getting up from the table.

"Hey, where are you going?"

"I have to get ready. This is going to be a night you'll never forget."

* * *

When Caitlyn saw Gideon's bedroom at the Merry Cherub, all the breath fled her lungs. She stood in the doorway, mouth agape, heart thumping, mind spinning, senses buzzing.

For strewn about the room were hundreds of pink and white rose petals. On the bed, on the floor, floating in the spa tub, everywhere she looked. Her eyes misted and she blinked back happy tears. She had seen a lot of flowers in her life, but no romantic gesture like this one. Here lay paradise. "Do you know what pink and white roses mean?"

"Hell yes," he said. "I looked it up to make sure. I love you still and always will, Caitlyn."

"Oh, Gideon."

"I'm sorry I had a meltdown and freaked out on you. I'm sorry about the gun. I'm sorry I withdrew."

"It's okay. You didn't run away. You stayed. You healed. We worked it out."

"You healed me," he whispered. "You and your victory garden and your carousel and our son. I was a shattered man when I came back here and I didn't even know it."

Simultaneously, they breathed in, inhaling the incredible fragrance of roses. The enticing scent of so many petals pushed a rush of heat through her nose and into her lungs, warming her blood, sending red-hot waves of desire radiating straight to the tingling spot between her legs.

Pink and white rose petals. *I love you still and always will.*

She threw back her head and laughed. This, then, was the scent of love. Caitlyn caught her breath, turned. Saw Gideon watching her with heavy-lidded eyes, and she knew he felt it too. This yearning to be joined.

He gave her that old familiar cocky smile that she hadn't seen in eight long years. The carefree smile of a young, untroubled man. What an intoxicating combo. That scent. This man.

His eyes danced with mischief and he came toward her, slowly stripping off his T-shirt, and one look at that fine chest had her knees rocking.

"C'mere," he murmured in a husky, dusky voice, leveled her a soul-stirring stare, and held out his hand.

Dreamily, she moved toward him.

He took her hand and led her to the bed, settled her down on the rose petals, their perfume rising up around them. He lay beside her, kissed her tenderly as if she was a rare and precious thing.

They finished undressing each other. Shoes flying, pants sliding, skirt shimmying, until they were totally naked.

Gideon kissed her hard and long and hot. They lay on the soft, velvety rose petals. Under his deft fingers, her aching body bloomed as spectacular as the victory garden, and she shivered against his rousing touch.

Love swamped her. He was her man. He always had been, and she had to have him now or she would surely die. She pulled his bottom lip up between her teeth and he made a noise of pure masculine enjoyment.

He cupped her face with his palm, dipped his head,

and kissed her with a soul-stealing, grade A, world-class kiss that warmed Caitlyn's heart. The moment was spectacular. He was spectacular. It was her most cherished fantasy brought to life. Making love on a bed of flowers with Gideon, her one true love.

She wriggled into him, her breasts pressed flush against his muscled chest. He ran his palm up and down her arm. She tossed her head and he tracked restless kisses over her tender throat, nestling, nibbling, setting her on fire.

Gently, he rubbed his thumb over one of her nipples until it beaded up tight. "Ah," he said, and dipped his head to kiss that pert peak.

"Uh-huh. A hazy hotness draped over her, thick with sexual urgency. She wanted him so badly she could only whimper.

His tongue played along her collarbone. She shuddered against him. Lightly, he stroked circles on the inside of her arm.

"My lover," she gasped.

"Exactly." He grinned.

The force of her feeling for him caused her to tremble and sweat. Her knees quivered. Her heart pounded. She felt his presence in every cell of her body.

He loved her with his mouth, tonguing her with amazing technique, a slow glide from the sensitive spot behind her knee, around to her kneecap, and up her inner thigh until she was rolling in ecstasy.

She floated, bodiless. She was total awareness, her entire being a giant throb of sexual energy.

He licked lazy circles of heat and she was spellbound. Finally, he edged to the spot where she wanted him to be, the sweet V between her legs. When his full wet lips locked on to her, she imagined she was a succulent summer peach, ripe for the taking.

His moist mouth teased, slowly licking her outer lips. He inhaled her and then caressed her with the sensuous sweep of his tongue. He suckled every fold, lapped at her ridges, and lifted up her bottom to deliver his meal.

She surfed his tongue, owned it. A steady strumming vibration began deep in her throat, emerged as a wild moan. She thrust herself against his mouth, gripped the sides of his head with her thighs.

Her skin was incredibly sensitive, her body tingling and tender. She tried to push him away. It was simply too much pleasure.

But he stayed put, pushing his tongue deep inside her. Then pulling out and moving to the region beyond. This new sensation drove her into a frenzy. Her muscles flexed. Blinding flashes of light. The rushing sound of ocean waves in her head. Uncontrollable spasms rattled her body.

Her world came undone.

Gideon's magic fingers touched and tickled and tingled. Her butt, her inner thigh, her clit. He slid one finger deep inside her wetness, while his tongue continued to strum her feminine notch.

She fell like a shooting star dropping from the midnight sky.

Madly, frantically, they grappled with each other. Time spun, morphed, as elusive as space. She was spellbound, mesmerized, entranced. Embraced by a longing so sweet and severe she couldn't breathe. In delicious anguish, she cried out her delight.

He rocked back on his heels, clasped her to his chest, and held her tight, his hand threaded through her hair, until their crazy hearts calmed.

After they rested, he made love to her again, sinking his flesh into hers. He was her lover and she wanted him desperately and he wanted her right back.

Their bodies joined and hotly fused on the bed of rose petals. *I love you still and always will.* Scent drenched the air—roses and sex—combining, fusing, part of an ancient dance as old as the sun and the moon and the stars.

The entire time he was buried inside her, he stared deep into her eyes, as if he was lost in her gaze and could not find his way out. Did not even want to find his way out.

Two became one.

A single being.

Clinging and trembling.

He filled her up, pushed deep inside her until he could go no further.

In and out, he moved in an even tempo that rocked her soul. He rode her and she rode him until they both came in a blazing, bright, blinding light.

Sometime later, Gideon awoke and lay there listening to Caitlyn's soft breathing. This was the beloved mother of his child. Her head was resting on his chest, and it felt so good he smiled into the darkness and thought about how much he loved her.

"Gideon?" she whispered into the darkened room.

"Uh-huh."

"Do you have any more condoms?"

"Yes."

She rose on one elbow and looked at him. "Do you think that maybe we could go again?"

"There's something I need to ask you first."

"What's that?"

Buck naked, he rolled out of bed. Went to his dresser, pulled out the ring box, knelt on the rose petals strewn across the floor, looked at her face in the moonlight, and said, "This has been a long time coming, Caitlyn Blackthorne Marsh, but will you marry me?"

"Gideon," she whispered, her voice tremulous, her hand splayed to her chest. "Are you sure? Are you really ready?"

"I've never been more certain in my life. I want to marry you. Be with you. For now and always. I want to raise our son with you. Have more babies with you. Please, Caitlyn, without you I'm half a man."

"Oh Gideon, yes, yes. I'll marry you." She flung her arms around his neck and he kissed her for a very long time.

"And tomorrow," he said at last. "Tomorrow we can tell Danny I'm his dad? That we're getting married?"

"Yes, yes, yes."

He slipped the ring on her finger and a joy unlike anything she'd ever known overwhelmed her. "I love you still," he whispered, "and always will."

She pulled him down on the bed on top of her, let out a soft little moan of pleasure, and opened her legs to him.

He slid into her welcoming wetness. The moonlight through the open window shone down on his dear face. She stared into his eyes and moved her body to fit him. She caressed his rugged face with her soft hands, cooed sweet nothings in a lyrical tone. But soon the soft cooing turned to gritty groans and heated gasps. He made her feel like the most cherished woman on earth.

"I love your sexy little sounds," he said. "I could listen to them for the rest of my life and die a happy, happy man."

And when her release came, he twined their right hands together above her head and rocked into her with one fierce thrust.

She arched her back, eager to meet him, and wrapped her legs around his waist, pulling him in as deep as he could go. Their fingers fused, gazes welded as they came in one shattering shudder.

One. Forever. Man and wife.

CHAPTER TWENTY-ONE

Traditional meaning of marigold—cruelty.

Caitlyn awoke at dawn and smiled up at the ceiling. Gideon's legs were tangled in hers. She pinched herself to make sure she wasn't dreaming. This was really, truly real. She was now engaged to the man she once thought dead. She held up her hand, gazed admiringly at her ring.

She would love to roll over and tickle him awake with her mouth to his anatomy, but there wasn't time to luxuriate in their lusty love. This was her last chance to put the finishing touches on her work of art. She was prouder of that victory garden than anything she'd ever done in her life, excluding Danny and Gideon, of course.

But she'd no sooner swung her legs over the edge of the bed than there was a knock at the door. In a scramble, she hunted for her clothes. Gideon sat up, hair mussed.

"What's going on?" he asked.

The knock came again.

"Caitlyn?" Patsy said. "Are you in there with Gideon?"

Her eyes met Gideon's.

"Small-town gossip," he said. "You gotta love it."

"Caitlyn, please open the door, I have terrible news."

Danny!

Caitlyn flung open the door as she stuck her unbuttoned blouse into the waistband of her skirt. On the bed, Gideon drew the covers to his neck. "What is it? What's wrong?"

Patsy looked on the verge of tears. Patsy was one tough cookie. The expression on the older woman's face struck terror in Caitlyn's heart. "You have to come with me now."

Caitlyn grabbed Patsy's arm. "Is it Danny? Has something happened?"

"Not Danny."

"Oh, oh." She couldn't catch her breath. Not Danny. Thank God. Then another awful thought occurred to her. "My father?"

Patsy shook her head. "The garden."

"What?"

"Just come." Caitlyn jammed her feet in her shoes, buttoned up her blouse, and followed Patsy.

"I'm right behind you," Gideon called out.

Patsy's mouth was a thin, tight line as she marched from the B&B and stalked toward the

town square. Caitlyn could barely keep up with
her. Somehow, probably because he'd been in the
military and knew how to hike, Gideon caught up
with them just as they turned the corner to the victory garden. The plywood boards that had been put
up to keep the tourists out were still up, so Caitlyn
couldn't see what had Patsy in such an uproar until
they were upon it.

Patsy pushed back one of the plywood boards.
"Go in."

Caitlyn stepped inside, at first saw nothing but
the backsides of all the garden club members and
then . . .

Devastation.

She halted beside Belinda Murphey, who stood
there dabbing a Kleenex at the tears in the corners
of her eyes. Dotty Mae murmured something, but
Caitlyn heard nothing. It was as if she'd suddenly
gone deaf. Every bit of her attention was focused on
her garden.

Or rather, what had once been her garden.

Everything had been demolished, destroyed,
damaged.

Fragile petals lay stomped into the dirt. Twisted
roots and broken stems were strewn like bodies over
a battlefield. Leaves fluttered, no longer tethered to
the branches.

Shattered pieces of clay pots littered the lot. The
white picket fencing had been kicked over, ravaged
with boot prints. And the yellow ribbons, meant as
symbols of welcome home for Twilight's brave ser-

vicemen and women, had been ripped from the oak trees fronting the garden.

All their hard work, all their hopes and dreams, ruined beyond redemption.

Trembling, Caitlyn pushed forward, dropped to her knees in the dirt, cupped a decapitated rosebud in the palm of her hand, smelled the rich rosy scent. A tear slipped down her cheek, swiftly followed by another and another until tears rained from her eyes. Her heart wrenched. She hadn't felt this devastated since she'd thought Gideon had died.

Her stomach churned and she retched. Who could have done such a horrible, cruel thing?

Belinda handed her a Kleenex and she wiped at her eyes and mouth. It wasn't so much that the contest was lost to them, rather, it was the murder of the beautiful flowers that killed her soul.

"Sweetie, I'm so sorry," Dotty Mae murmured, and put a hand to Caitlyn's shoulder. "All your hard work."

"Did anyone see anything?" she heard Sheriff Crouch ask the crowd. "Hear anything?"

Caitlyn curved her shoulders inward, her head throbbing miserably. She'd wanted this garden so much. First for the money, then to honor Gideon, and after that to prove that she could build the most romantic garden in the state. To show she could be something more than just a small-town girl in her small-town world. Now, even that simple dream had been destroyed.

"Caitlyn." Gideon's voice was low and concerned.

She tilted her head up, met his tender gaze. "Why?"

He reached down his hand, helped her up off the ground. "I don't know, baby," he cooed. "But I'm going to find out who did this and hold them responsible."

"It doesn't matter." She shook her head. "The damage is done. The fruits and vegetables are ruined, the herbs and spices yanked up by their roots. All those pretty flowers."

He pulled her against him, held her tight. "Winning that contest meant a lot to you."

"Yeah," she mumbled. "It did. And even if we didn't win, I would have given it my best, but this—" She swept a hand at the holocaust.

"Shh," Gideon soothed, cradled her head against his chest, softly kissed her temple. "Don't worry. We'll fix it."

Her laugh came out as a sharp bark of despair. "Fix it? How on earth can we fix it? The judging is tomorrow."

"We still have the carousel. They didn't touch it."

"The carousel is nothing without the garden."

"We can find a way through this. All of us. The community working together."

"But how? In one day?" She scanned the wretched lot.

"Don't give up hope." He took her chin in his palm, tilted her head back, forced her to look at him. "If I'd given up hope of one day returning to you, I would never have survived after I lost my arm. I wanted to give up so many times. To stop fighting and just die. But then I'd think of you and I'd rally."

"Even though you thought I didn't care?"

"Yes," he whispered. "You were all I had to hold on to, so I held on as tight as I could."

"Gideon." She buried her face against his chest, breathed in the scent of him.

This man was riddled with contradictions. He was complicated and complex and he was asking her to believe in him, believe in his ability to make this right. She didn't see how he could do it, but she so wanted to believe. He had come back from the dead. Who could say that he couldn't resurrect flowers?

"I have an idea," he said.

She took a deep breath, squared her shoulders. If she'd learned anything from him, it was how to be courageous and face her fears. "Let's hear it."

Everyone in town who could pitch in showed up.

Caitlyn's father offered to keep Danny for another night and even Greta came over to help carry out Gideon's bold plan. Volunteers swarmed the victory garden, working around the clock. Caitlyn refused to go to bed or even take a break.

Through it all, Gideon was at her side.

And when the state judges arrived from Austin at ten A.M. the next morning, Gideon was absolutely sure he'd made the wrong decision.

They had not tried to restore the former glory of Caitlyn's architecture. Rather, they instituted a new, last-minute design for the memorial garden.

The twisted and broken flowers had been left as they were, the fences scattered, the pots busted. But amid the devastation they planted seedlings from Caitlyn's greenhouse.

On the carousel, they'd decorated the animals in camouflage material and smeared their faces with soot. They changed the music in the carousel from the whimsical "Tie a Yellow Ribbon" to "Battle Hymn of the Republic." It was no longer a garden about beauty or romance.

Gone was the softness. The message left behind was hope in the midst of destruction. Healing of raw wounds as evidenced by the seedlings, the new life surviving against all odds. That in spite of chaos and pain, love could survive.

The garden reminded Gideon of the ordinary citizens of Iraq and Afghanistan. Strong and stalwart in the face of much adversity, struggling to live the best they could with dignity and honor in spite of the craziness around them.

Gideon held Caitlyn's hand as the judges first stared in disbelief at the garden, then slowly started picking their way through it.

"They don't get it," Caitlyn whispered.

"It's okay. We tried. After the contest we can get to work on the garden again, put it back the way it should be."

"It was a brilliant idea," she told him. "If we're going to have a victory garden, why not actually show the cost of victory?"

"I'm so proud of you," he whispered.

"And I'm so proud of you."

"No matter what, we've won," he told her. "We've survived. Our love has survived."

When the judges were finished, they gathered in front of the garden. "Who was the architect here?"

Caitlyn stepped forward. "It was originally me but—"

The oldest of the three judges, a tall, academic-looking man with a goatee, smiled. "But you're so young."

"I'm a florist," she explained, "but—"

"You took an amazing chance," the middle judge, an older woman in a straw gardening bonnet, said. "What a creative mind you have. None of the other gardens we've seen have demonstrated this level of complexity."

"What are you saying?" Caitlyn asked, stunned to realize they actually liked the war-torn garden.

"We're saying"—the younger woman carrying a clipboard smiled—"that your garden has won first place in the Most Creative category."

"We won?" Caitlyn blinked, unable to believe it was true. Okay, so she'd been going for Most Romantic, but she'd take Most Creative.

"You did."

The goateed judge wearing a marigold boutonniere handed her the blue ribbon and a gold trophy.

"But I can't take credit for this. The war-torn theme came from Green Beret Sergeant Gideon Garza after a vandal destroyed our garden." Her gaze met Gideon's. "He's the real survivor and he's been teaching us all how to live."

Caitlyn put out her hand to Gideon and drew him over as the photographer readied to snap their picture receiving the award.

The crowd applauded. Gideon felt himself warm from the inside out. Caitlyn had recognized him. The town had recognized him. He was accepted. It felt strange and glorious.

Caitlyn passed him the trophy. "This is yours," she whispered.

"It's ours."

"You pulled my fat out of the fire."

"If you hadn't had those seedlings in your greenhouse, none of this would have been possible."

"For the first time in twenty years, the Grant family carousel is back in operation," Patsy said.

The horses pranced up and down in their camouflage saddles. The loudspeaker played "Battle Hymn of the Republic."

The carousel spun and Blaze raced past Caitlyn looking ferocious with his horsey face smeared with black soot, a green camo-colored bandana tied around his mane. People were laughing and applauding, and for the first time since he'd lost his arm, Gideon Garza felt whole again.

"Gideon." Judge Blackthorne called out his name.

Gideon looked at his soon-to-be father-in-law who was standing to the side of the victory garden celebration. "Do you realize that's the first time you've ever called me by my first name?"

"No." Richard gave him a strange look. "Yeah?"

"Yes."

"My mistake."

"It's okay." Gideon smiled. "We all make them."

"So what did she say?"

On Memorial Day, before he'd brought Caitlyn's engagement ring and decorated his room at the Merry Cherub with pink and white rose petals, Gideon had gone to see Richard and asked for his blessing to marry his daughter. Richard had given it.

"She said yes."

"Long time coming."

"It was."

"I should never have stood in your way. You were young. Too young, I thought. And I didn't think you were good enough for her. I admit my prejudice. But she loves you with all her heart. She's always loved you. Even when she was married to Marsh."

"I appreciate you giving me your blessing."

"I have some more good news for you."

"What's that?"

"I've already informed Bowie and Crockett Goodnight that your father's will is good. All the witnesses have been interviewed. Everything has checked out. I've approved the paperwork. The Rocking J is yours."

Gideon wasn't sure how he felt about this news. He'd never really wanted the ranch, until he'd found out about Danny. Before that, it was really just more about being recognized as J. Foster's son. It seemed sort of anticlimactic. "I'm not sure I know what to do with it."

"Run it, sell it, leave it to your son." Richard looked around the crowd. "Where is Danny?"

"I saw him walk up with you. Maybe he's with his mom." Gideon searched out Caitlyn in the crowd. The minute his eyes landed on her, his heart sped up. His woman. Finally, his for real. For always.

He couldn't wait to find Danny. Tell Danny who he was. Let Danny know he was marrying his mother. They were going to be a family at long last.

Caitlyn met his eyes and broke into a big smile. "Danny?" she mouthed.

He shrugged. "Not with you?"

She shook her head.

Gideon frowned. "Danny!" he called.

But the sound of the carousel drowned out his voice. He turned back to Richard. "When was the last time you saw him?"

"We just walked up here, not ten minutes ago. I'm sure he's around here somewhere. Don't panic."

CHAPTER TWENTY-TWO

Traditional meaning of China aster—jealousy.

They tried calling Danny's cell phone and found it in the seat of Richard's Cadillac. They searched the town square and Caitlyn's house and Richard's house and everywhere they could think of. But an hour later, they had to admit Danny was officially missing.

"We'll find him," Gideon told Caitlyn. "I swear to you, we'll find him. It's time to widen our search area. Let's get the van."

"I'll put out a BOLO," Hondo said, and took off for his patrol car.

Caitlyn gave the keys to Gideon. There was no way she could drive. She was struggling her best not to lose it completely. She'd always been a worrier, and now it seemed her greatest fear had come to pass. Something horrible had happened to her son.

"I haven't kissed him in two days. I was with you on Memorial Day and then I worked all night long last night on the garden. Damn that garden. I put it ahead of my own child." Her stomach roiled. She put a hand to her mouth, willed herself not to vomit.

"I'm here," Gideon said. "We're in this together."

She met his eyes. Thank God for him. She didn't know what she'd do without him. She twisted his ring on her finger, took a deep breath to calm the panic that made her want to scream and cry and break. Gideon's calmness calmed her.

"Try calling everyone you know that we haven't already contacted," Gideon said. "That'll give you something to do. Taking action helps."

She nodded, slipped her cell phone from her pocket, and started making calls. After a few minutes, she gave up in despair. "Nothing. No one has seen him."

"Have you tried Crockett?"

"No, good thought. He didn't open the baseball card shop today. So I didn't see him on the square." She flipped through her contact numbers, found Crockett's toward the bottom of the list.

Just when she thought the call was headed for voice mail, Crockett answered, sounding breathless. "Hello?"

"Hi, Crockett, it's Caitlyn." She was surprised at how calm she sounded. How could she sound so calm?

"Well," he said, "I understand congratulations are in order."

"Listen, I was wondering if you've seen Danny today?"

"Your little garden won an award, huh?"

"Crockett, Danny's missing."

"Funny how you always come up smelling like a China aster, Caitlyn."

Irritation mingled with frustration. It was as if they were having two separate conversations. "Did you hear me? Danny's missing."

"Someone tears up your garden and still, you win."

"Have you seen Danny?"

"And this morning I hear you're engaged to Garza. Did I ever mean anything to you?"

"Crockett, we never dated."

"We kissed."

"You kissed me. I never kissed you back."

"Liar!" he yelled.

The hairs on her arms lifted, and suddenly, she remembered the fight in her flower shop. The switchblade in Crockett's hand, the malevolent look in his eyes directed toward his brother. Bowie and Gideon both got the bulk of J. Foster's DNA. Crockett looked like his mother. His mother who had been in a mental institution for years.

"So tell me, Caitlyn," Crockett said, his voice deadly calm. "Did you say yes to Gideon before or after your father helped him steal my inheritance?"

Every motherly instinct in her blazed with fear and anger. She hung up the phone. "Drive to the

Rocking J now. Crockett's crazy jealous and he's got Danny."

Gideon bulleted the van over the cattle guard leading to the Rocking J, but neither Bowie's Hummer nor Crockett's Mustang was in the driveway.

Caitlyn had the door open before Gideon brought the van to a complete stop. "Danny!" she screamed. "Danny, where are you?"

"Mom!"

His voice sounded so small and far away.

"Danny!" Gideon joined in. They ran toward the sound of his voice. Past the sprawling ranch house that now officially belonged to Gideon. Past the barns and sheds and corrals.

Caitlyn spun in a circle as she walked. "Where are you, Danny?"

"Up here."

They both halted abruptly and looked straight up at the twenty-five-foot-tall spindly metal windmill. Just a few feet below the deadly whirling hung their son.

"I climbed up," Danny said. "But I can't get back down."

"Gideon," she gasped softly, "if he slips . . ."

Fear chilled Gideon colder than Arctic water. "Call Hondo. Tell him the situation," he said, but he knew he couldn't risk waiting. Caitlyn was right. They didn't know how long Danny had been hanging up there. His grip could already be tenuous. His palms sweaty. But that meant Gideon was going to have to climb the windmill. With one good arm, one prosthesis, and a bad case of vertigo.

He called upon every Green Beret fiber inside him as he walked toward the windmill. "Keep him talking, Caitlyn," he said, after she'd already called Hondo. "I'm going to get our boy down."

"Be careful," she cautioned.

"Hey, I'm not going to let anything happen to either one of us. Now that we're about to be a family."

She pressed her fingers to her lips and looked so brave standing there with the wind whipping through her hair. "How long have you been up there, buddy?"

"A long time."

Gideon started up the side of the windmill. He was a big man and it wasn't built to take a lot of weight. The slender structure trembled. White fingers of icy dread wrapped around his heart.

"Mom, it's shaking."

"That's just Gideon. He's coming after you. Hold on, buddy." Her voice was smooth as butter, but he knew that she was just as terrified inside as he was.

"He's too big, Mom. He's making it shake too much."

Even from where he was, Gideon could hear Caitlyn's throaty moan. *No time to waste. Danny needs you. Hurry. Hurry.* He pushed himself, hoping to push past the nerves.

"Danny," Caitlyn said. "How did you get up there?"

"Crockett told me he had a baseball signed by A-Rod and then he was out throwin' it around and it got stuck up on the windmill. He said he was too big to climb up here, but if I would come get it down for him, I could have it. But there's no ball up here and Crockett just got in his car and drove away and left me. Why did he leave me, Mom?"

That question tore at Gideon's heart. He growled like a papa bear. He was going to beat the crap out of Crockett when he got his hands on the weasel. He was having to do some maneuvering to get up the windmill. It wasn't a fast process for a one-armed man. He wasn't high enough for the vertigo to kick in, but it was coming.

"And you can't climb back down?"

"No, Mom, I'm really scared."

"Okay, honey, just hang on. Gideon's coming."

"He gets dizzy when he's high up," Danny said.

Gideon cringed. He didn't want Caitlyn to know that.

Finally, after what seemed an eternity, but was probably only ten minutes, he was within reach of Danny.

"Hey, buddy." Gideon clung tightly to the metal and tried not to look down. He was trying to figure out the best way to do this with one hand without getting both of them killed.

"Hey," Danny said, his voice sounding high and wavy. His energy flagging.

Gideon hated Crockett with every fiber in his body for getting his son up here and taking off.

Crockett better be in the wind if he knew what was good for him.

"Do you think you can turn around and slide down on my back, put your arms around my neck, and let me give you a piggyback ride down this thing?"

"Okay."

"Easy now." Gideon clamped his artificial hand around the metal frame and reached his good hand out to Danny. He prayed like hell the prosthesis was as strong as the manufacturer claimed.

It took a bit of doing, but Danny made it onto Gideon's back. They inched back down. Gideon had to stop occasionally and close his eyes to fight off the vertigo before he could take another step down.

Just as they were a couple of feet from the ground, Hondo pulled up along with firemen and a ladder truck.

"Too little, too late, I see," Hondo said, reaching up to take Danny off Gideon's back.

Gideon's entire body was trembling with exertion but he did his best not to let Caitlyn see his shaky hands. It wasn't too hard. She was wrapped up in hugging their boy.

"We stopped Crockett on the way out of town. He's in the county jail and we'll be charging him with child endangerment for starters. He admitted everything. Bragged about it even. Setting the bear trap, leaving your hen pen open, destroying the victory garden. But all's well that ends well. You and Danny are okay. That's the important thing." Hondo clapped Gideon on the shoulder.

Bowie's Hummer drove into the drive. Looking puzzled, Bowie got out and came over. "What's happening?"

Hondo filled him in.

Bowie plowed a hand through his hair. "He's been off his meds since Dad died. I can't make him take them. Hell knows I've tried."

"He takes medication?" Gideon asked.

"He's bipolar. Same as our mom. He's not nearly as bad as she is, and as long as he takes the meds, he's okay. But when he's off them, there's no telling what will set him off."

"Like Judge Blackthorne ruling in favor of me in the probate case."

"Yeah," Bowie said. "And like you getting engaged to Caitlyn. He's been fantasizing about marrying her, since Kevin died."

"I'm sorry," Gideon said. "I had no idea."

Bowie shrugged. "We tried to keep it quiet. You know how this town likes to gossip."

Now that his son was safe, Gideon was feeling generous. He had a feeling that in the long run, he'd had it much better than his brothers and he'd never even known it. "The fortune's big enough for the three of us. I don't need this ranch. It's yours. We'll get Crockett the help he needs, put his share in a trust, and I'll cash out mine."

"You mean it?" Bowie looked incredulous. "You'd do that? Even after what Crockett did to you?"

"He's got a problem and as long as he gets help, I'll stand by him."

To Gideon's surprise, Bowie wrapped him in a bear hug. "Thank you, brother from another mother."

"We'll talk more about it later," Gideon said. "Right now, I'm pretty anxious to get my family home."

CHAPTER TWENTY-THREE

Traditional meaning of heliotrope—eternal love.

Caitlyn sat by the window watching Danny while he played outside. Since what had happened at the Rocking J, she'd been reluctant to let him out of her sight. Fear heighted her awareness. She'd always been cautious, never a risk taker, but Gideon—he'd always been so brave. So impulsive. He followed his gut and did what he thought was right, whether anyone else did or not. He had a strong moral code, an innate sense of right and wrong. If it hadn't been for him . . .

She shuddered to think of what might have happened to Danny.

"Caitlyn," Gideon whispered. "It's time."

He extended his hand to hers and she sank her palm into his. It felt strong, reassuring. "It's going to be okay. Everything is going to be okay."

After all they'd been through, she knew he wasn't going anywhere. The fear was hers alone to conquer. Once upon a time she had loved him so much that love had almost destroyed her. If it hadn't been for Danny, it very well might have destroyed her. But her son had kept her going. Her fear was the only wall left. It was up to her to knock it down.

She swallowed. "Let's take him to the carousel."

They opened the door, called to him.

A big smile broke over Danny's face when he saw them together, holding hands. "Hi," he said, running up, his face flushed from playing. "What's up?"

"How do you know something is up?" Gideon asked.

Danny canted his head. "You've got those looks on your faces."

"Looks?" Caitlyn asked. "What kind of looks?"

"Like you've got some important news."

Gideon shot her a glance. "He's very perceptive." *He gets that from you.*

Danny shifted his weight, his face pinched with concern. "Is it good news?"

"We hope you'll see it that way." She tousled her son's hair.

"What is it?" Danny asked.

"Let's take a walk," Gideon said.

"It's bad news. Did someone die?"

It killed her to think that was where his immediate thoughts went, to bad things. "No, no one died."

"So just tell me."

"Look," Caitlyn said as they stopped in front of the victory garden. "Let's take a ride on the carousel."

She and Danny got on. He headed for a horse, but she guided him toward one of the golden chariots with heliotropes painted on the side. "Why don't we sit here where we can talk?"

Her son shrugged, but plunked down beside her. Gideon started up the carousel at its slowest speed and climbed up on it. He came toward them, his gaze on them, reassurance in his eyes. The music started to play. "Tie a Yellow Ribbon."

Gideon settled in beside her on the chariot bench, their son sat across from them.

"You guys are acting just plain weird," Danny said, but she could tell he was nervous. He kept repeatedly rubbing his palm over his nose as if he would wipe away his anxiety like perspiration.

Gideon took her hand again. "We've got something important to tell you."

"Yeah. I got that."

They looked at each other. "You want to go first?" he asked.

They had already agreed that Gideon would tell him that they were getting married and Caitlyn would break the news that he was Danny's real father, but which should come first? Her announcement or his?

Caitlyn took a deep breath. "I suppose I'll take the plunge."

"Geez, you're freakin' me out, Mom, just tell me already."

Danny was right. She was putting too much into the buildup. "Danny . . ." She'd practiced breaking the news a hundred times since they'd gotten back from the Rocking J but she still couldn't make the words come out. "I know you loved Kevin very much. He was a good dad to you."

"Yeah." Danny's hands were fisted against his thighs.

"Caitlyn," Gideon said, "just rip the Band-Aid off. It's better that way."

"Danny," she started again. "Kevin wasn't your biological father. Do you know what that means?"

She didn't know what she expected. Shock? Outrage? Anger?

But Danny displayed none of those emotions. "I kinda figured," he said.

That stunned her. "What do you mean?"

Danny shrugged. "My dad . . . *Kevin* . . . had red hair, I've got black. He had blue eyes, mine are brown. He wasn't very handy, I am. Plus, I sorta heard people talking."

"Talking? What people?"

"Your garden club ladies. I overheard them say I looked exactly like my real dad." He stared her straight in the eyes. "Who is my real dad?"

"I am, son," Gideon said softly.

"Oh." Danny's glance flicked from Caitlyn to Gideon and back again. "Oh."

No one said anything for a minute or two. The carousel kept turning, the music kept playing. Then Danny wet his lips and stared at Gideon. "How come you left us?"

"I didn't know about you when I left."

Danny swung his gaze back to Caitlyn. There was that look. The one she'd feared, rife with accusation. "Why didn't you tell him?"

"I didn't know I was going to have a baby until after Gideon left town. I tried to contact him, but someone told me that he was dead."

"What about Da— Kevin?"

"He knew you weren't his son, but he couldn't have loved you more if you had been. He married me to give you a dad, give you a home."

Danny nodded, processing it all. "So, you're my dad now."

"I'm your dad now."

Danny leaned back against the seat, folded his arms over his chest, and for a long while he said nothing. They let him take his time. Finally, he said, "That's good. I'm glad I have a dad. I'm glad it's you."

"Can I . . ." Gideon looked so uncertain it punched a hole through Caitlyn's heart. "Give you a hug?"

That was all it took. Like a rocket, Danny was out of his seat and wrapping his arms around Gideon in a big hug.

Gideon smiled at her over the top of their son's head, a misting of tears in his eyes. Her eyes were misty too.

When the hug was over, Gideon put his arm around Danny, pulled him into the seat between them. "That's not all."

Comically, Danny smacked his forehead with a palm. "Don't tell me, I have brothers and sisters I've never met."

"No." Gideon chuckled. "That's not it."

"What is it?"

"We're getting married," Gideon said. "And we want your blessing."

"You're really, really going to be my dad?" Danny was smiling so wide it made Caitlyn's mouth hurt.

"I really, really am."

"That's cool."

"I love you, Danny. I loved you from the minute I saw you."

Tears were in Danny's eyes now. "I love you too, Dad. I love you too."

As the carousel slowed and the music stopped, Caitlyn knew that love really was capable of healing all wounds.

*Turn the page
for a sneak peek
at the first book
in Lori Wilde's fantastic new series.*

*Look for it in 2011
from Avon Books.*

The naked cowboy in the gold-plated horse trough presented a conundrum.

In the purple-orange light of breaking dawn, Mariah Callahan snared her bottom lip between her teeth, curled her fingernails into her palms and tried to assess him without panicking. It had been a long drive. There was a good chance she was hallucinating.

She reached to ratchet her glasses up higher on her nose for a better look, but then remembered she was wearing her contacts. She wasn't seeing things. He was for real. No figment of her fertile imagination.

Who was he?

Better question, what was she going to do about him?

His bare forearms, tanned and lean, angled from

the edges of the trough, an empty bottle of Jose Cuervo Gold dangling from the fingertips of his right hand. Even in a relaxed pose, his muscular biceps were tightly coiled. Mariah thought of hard, driving piston engines.

Like his arms, his legs lay slung over each side of the trough. He wore expensive eel-skin cowboy boots. She canted her head, studying his feet.

Size thirteen at least.

Hmm, was it true what they said about the size of a man's feet?

She raised her palms to her heated cheeks, surprised to find she'd made herself blush.

Question number three. How had he come to be naked and still have his boots on?

Curiosity bested embarrassment as she tracked her gaze up the length of his honed, sinewy legs that were humorously pale in contrast to his tanned arms. No doubt, like most cowboys, he dressed in blue jeans ninety percent of the time.

She perched on tiptoes to peek over the edge of the horse trough. The murky green water hit him mid-thigh and camoflagued his other naked bits. Robbed of the view. Rats. She didn't know if she was grateful or disappointed.

But nothing could hide that chest.

Washboard abs indeed. Rippled and flat. Not an ounce of fat. Pecs of Atlas.

A rough jagged scar, gone silvery with age, ambled a staggered path from his left nipple down to his armpit marring nature's work of art. The scar lent him a dangerous air.

Mariah gulped as captivated as a cat in front of an aquarium.

A black Stetson lay cocked down over his face, hiding all his features save for his strong, masculine jaw studded with at least a day's worth of ebony beard. His eyes had to be as black as the Stetson and that stubble.

Mesmerized, she felt her body heat up in places she had no business heating up. She didn't know who this man was, or how he'd gotten here, although she supposed that drunken ranch hands came with the territory. If she was going to be a rancher, she'd have to learn to deal with it.

A rancher? Ha! Big cosmic joke and she was the punch line.

Less than twenty-four hours ago she had been standing in line at the downtown Chicago unemployment office—having just come from a job interview where once again, she had *not* gotten the job—her hands chafed from the cold October wind blowing off the lake, when she'd gotten word that Dutch had died and left her a horse ranch in Jubilee, Texas.

Mariah's cell phone rang playing Wagner's "The Bridal Chorus". She fished it from her purse at the unemployment line and checked the caller I.D. When she'd seen her father's name, a tower of emotions tumbled in on her. Why was Dutch calling her after all these years? If he was broke and looking for money, he'd certainly picked the wrong time to call.

The weary woman in line behind her, holding a

runny-nosed kid cocked on her hip, nudged Mariah, and then pointed at the poster on the wall. It was a symbol of a cell phone with a heavy red line drawn through it.

"Hang on a minute," Mariah said into the phone, and then smiled beseechingly to the woman, "This'll just take a sec."

The woman shook her head, pointed toward the door.

"Fine." She sighed, never one to ruffle feathers, and got out of line.

A blast of cold air hit her in the face and sucked her lungs dry as she stepped outside. It was the first of October, but already cold as a Popsicle. She liked Chicago in the spring and summer, but the other six months of the year she could do without.

"Hello?" Head down, hand held over her other ear, she scuttled around the side of the building to escape the relentless wind.

No answer.

"Dutch?"

He must have hung up. Great. She'd gotten out of line for nothing. Huddling deeper into the warmth of her coat, she hit the call back button.

"Hello?" a man answered in a curt Texas accent. It didn't sound like her father.

"Dutch?"

"Who's this?" he asked contentiously.

"Who is this?" she echoed on the defensive.

"You called me."

"I was calling my father."

A hostile silence filled the airwaves between them.

"Mariah?" he asked, an edge of uncertainty creeping in.

"You have the upper hand. You know my name, but I don't know yours. Why are you answering Dutch's cell phone?"

He hauled in a breath so heavy it sounded as if he was standing right beside her. "My name's Joe Daniels."

"Hello, Joe," she said, completely devoid of warmth. "May I speak to Dutch please?"

"I wish . . ." His voice cracked. "I wish I could let you do that."

A sudden chill, that had nothing to do with the wind, rushed over her. She leaned hard against the side of the building, the bricks poking into her back. "Has something happened?"

"Are you sitting down?"

"No."

"Sit down," Joe commanded.

"Just tell me," Mariah said, bracing for the worst.

"Dutch is dead," he blurted.

Mariah blinked, nibbled on her bottom lip, felt . . . *hollow*. Hollow as a chocolate Easter bunny.

"Did you hear me?"

"I heard you."

Joe's breathing was harsh in her ear.

So her father was dead. She should feel *something*, shouldn't she? Her heartbeat was steady. A strange calmness settled over her, but she didn't realize that she'd slowly been sliding down the brick wall until her butt hit the cold cement sidewalk.

All she could think of was how she'd cruelly run

away from Dutch that afternoon fourteen years ago.

"Mariah?" A whisper of sympathy tinged Joe's voice.

"Yeah?"

"You okay?"

"I'm fine. It's not like my life is going to change," she said quickly.

"I know you weren't close. But he *was* your father." Joe's tone shifted, barely masking anger.

Oh, who was Mr. High-and-Mighty Joe Daniel's to judge her? "How did it happen?" she asked, ignoring her own shove of anger.

"We were at an event, Dutch swung off his horse, staggered, coughed. I could tell he was suffering. His face was pale and sweaty. He looked me in the eyes and said, 'Don't call Mariah until after the funeral'. Then he just dropped dead." Joe's voice cracked again. "He died with his boots on, doin' what he loved."

A long pause stretched out between them. Chicago and Texas married over the airwaves.

"Joe," she said softly, "Are *you* okay?"

"No," he said. "Dutch was my closest friend."

Joe's words finally hit her, a hard punch to the gut. Her head throbbed and she felt as if a full-grown quarter horse had just squatted on her shoulders. Dutch was dead and the last thing he'd said was "Don't call Mariah until after the funeral." Her father hadn't wanted her there.

"You've already buried him?" A soft whimper escaped her lips.

"At Oak Hill Cemetery in Jubilee. It's what he wanted."

"I see." She turned to stone inside. Iced up. Shut down completely. "Well then, thank you for calling to let me know."

"Wait," he said. "Don't hang up."

Her hand tensed around the cell phone. "What is it?"

"Dutch left you his ranch."

Dutch left you his ranch.

The words echoed in her head, bringing Mariah back to the present.

She blinked, seeing Stone Creek Ranch clearly for the first time in full daylight.

It was a country and western palace.

The main house sprawled over acres and acres of rolling grassland. On the drive up in the predawn, it had looked like a fat dragon sleeping peacefully after a heavy meal of virgins and villagers. In the daylight, it appeared more like a lazy, but handsome king lounging on his throne. Not unlike the lazy cowboy draped insouciantly over the horse trough.

Mariah had parked just short of the main entrance, pulling her rental sedan to a stop by a planter box filled with rusty-red chrysanthemums. Numerous other buildings flanked the house. Horse barns, sheds, garages, all well maintained.

Dutch had owned this?

She now owned this?

All these years her father had been living in luxury while she and her mother scrimped every penny. The emotions she'd kept dammed up flooded her—hurt, anger, sorrow, regret, frustration.

Yes, frustration. She had no idea how to run a ranch. She was a wedding planner's assistant for crying out loud.

Correction. She used to be a wedding planner's assistant. *Used to* being the operative phrase.

What was she going to do with the place? And on a more immediate note, what was she going to do with the man in the horse trough?

Tentatively, she inched closer.

He didn't move.

The shy part of her held back, but the part of her that had learned how to slip into the role of whatever she needed to be in order to get the job done—and right now that was assertive—cleared her throat. "Hey, mister."

No response. Clearly it was going to take cannon fire to get through his stupor.

You've got to do something more to get his attention. Hanging back and being shy puts you in hot water. Take the bull by the horns and—

Okay, okay stop nagging. She poked his bare shoulder with a finger. Solid as granite.

Nothing.

Come on. Put some muscle into it.

She poked again. Harder this time.

Not a whisper, not a flinch.

What if he was dead?

Alarmed, Mariah gasped, jumped back, and plastered a palm across her mouth. Dread swamped her. She peered at his chest. Was he breathing? She thought he was breathing, but the movements were so shallow she couldn't really tell.

Please don't be dead.

In that moment, the possibly deceased naked cowboy was the cherry on top of the dung cake that was her life. Three weeks ago, in one fell swoop she'd lost both her boyfriend—the rat bastard—and her dream job working for the number one wedding planner in Chicago. And now Dutch was gone too and she'd been left a ranch complete with a dead naked cowboy.

Be rational. He's probably not dead.

Maybe not, but clearly he was trespassing and she didn't want him thinking that it was okay for him to go around stripping off his clothes and falling into other people's horse troughs during his drunken sprees.

Be bold, do something about this.

Bolster by her internal pep talk, she stepped up to flick his Stetson with a thump of her middle finger. "Yo, Cowboy, snap out of it."

She was just about to thump the Stetson again, when one of those sinewy arms snapped up and his steely hand manacled her wrist. The tequila bottle made a dull pinging sound as it fell against the ground. Big fingers imprinted into her skin.

"Eep!" Oxygen fled her lungs. Panic mushroomed inside her. So much for being bold.

"Never thump a man's Stetson," he drawled without moving another muscle, his voice was as rich and luxurious as polished mahogany. "Unless you've got a death wish. You got a death wish?"

"N . . . n . . . no." Mariah stammered. She tried to pull away from the Clint Eastwood clone, but pushing against his grip was like trying to bully marble. In fact, her struggling seemed to only ensnare her tighter.

With a lazy index finger, he slowly tipped the brim of his cowboy hat upward, revealing eyes as black as obsidian and studied her with a speculative scowl like he was the big bad wolf just aching for a reason to eat her alive.

Oh man, oh wow, oh just kill me now.

He was one hundred percent alpha male, the kind who staked a claim on a woman with one hard sultry stare and who would fight to the death to hold onto her. The kind of man whose self-confident arrogance had always unsettled her.

She shivered

His gaze lasered into her as if he could see exactly what she looked like with no clothes on, his intelligent eyes full of mysterious secrets. He didn't seem embarrassed in the least. In fact, he had an air of entitlement about him. As if he had every right to sleep off a berserk bender in her fancy horse trough.

Strangely enough, he made her feel as if *she* was the naked one.

Unnerved, Mariah marshaled her courage, gritted her teeth. "Please let go."

His smile exploded, exposing straight white teeth. This cowboy possessed serious star quality. "What if I don't?"

"I'll dunk your Stetson in the water."

His devilish eyes narrowed. "You wouldn't dare."

Her knees wobbled. She was scared witless, but she'd learned a long time ago to tuck her fears behind bluff and bravado and act brave whether she felt it or not. Ignoring her sprinting pulse, she swept the cowboy hat off his head with her free hand. A thick tumble of inky black hair, two months past the point of needing a trim, spilled out.

"Try me," she said as tough as she could, hoping her voice belied her trembling legs.

His hard laugh clubbed her ears as he slowly released her. Mariah slapped his hat down on his head and snatched her arm back, held it across her chest. He hadn't hurt her at all, but his sizzling body heat branded her.

"What's the deal?" She glared. "You don't have indoor plumbing?"

"You're funny," he said. "Who are you?"

"I should be asking you that question."

"Oh yeah?" An amused smile played at the corner of his mouth. "Why's that?"

She drew herself up to her full five foot one. "Because my name is Mariah Callahan and this . . ." She swept a hand at the land around them. "Is my ranch."

"Oh yeah?" he repeated.

"Yes, and you're trespassing."

"Am I?" He lowered his eyes to half-mast. Bedroom eyes the exact same color as the cup of strong coffee she'd snagged at the Starbuck's drive through in the last big town she'd passed through.

"You are."

He studied her as if she was the most comical

thing he'd ever seen. As if he wasn't lying naked in a gold-plated horse trough looking as sexy as three kinds of misdemeanors.

Not that she cared. Not really. She had no room in her life for men—especially those of the cowboy persuasion. She knew just enough about cowboys to know she never wanted one.

"You sure about that?"

His words gave her pause, but determined not to let him intimidate her, she plunged ahead. "I just inherited this ranch from my father, Dutch Callahan and I'd appreciate it if you'd remove yourself from the premises immediately."

"Okay." He made a move to hoist himself up.

"No wait." She shielded her eyes with her hands. "I don't need to see that."

He chuckled, clearly finding her amusing, and sank back in the trough. But beneath the incongruous smile, she spotted the shadows that dug into the hollows beneath the blades of his cheekbones.

"Your father, huh?" he said.

"Yes."

"That's funny. I don't ever recall you coming to visit him."

Was that an intentional dig? Or just an innocent observation? Mariah glanced over at him. There was nothing innocent about this guy. "You knew my father?"

He crossed his middle finger over his index finger. "We were like that."

She felt envious, melancholia and irritated. "We were estranged."

"And yet, he left you this impressive ranch. I wonder why."

Sarcasm. From a naked cowboy. The guy was cocky.

Mariah shifted her weigh, feeling like she was being indicted or mocked. "I didn't say it made any sense."

"That's because it doesn't."

"Look," she said. "Could you just go?"

He shook his head. "I'm just not buying it."

"Buying what?"

"That you own this ranch. Look at you all Gucci and Prada and whatnot." He waved a hand at her outfit. "You look like a Barbie doll."

"I'm not tall enough to be Barbie."

"Barbie's sidekick then."

"Sidekick?"

"I don't know what they call Barbie's sidekick. Tonto Barbie. Doc Holliday Barbie. Sundance Barbie. Pick one."

"Are all your references movie cowboys?

"Pretty much."

"It's Chanel."

"What?"

"The suit. It's Chanel."

And the only decent outfit she still owned. Once upon a time she'd had several designer suits. Destiny had insisted she look like money and given her a generous clothing allowance. But that was in the past.

"Like I give a damn."

Seriously annoyed, Mariah sank her hands on her hips. "Do I have to call the cops?"

"Do you?"

What a jerk. "I'm calling the cops," she threatened, pulling her cell phone from her purse.

"Are you always this friendly?"

"Whenever I find a naked cowboy in my gold-plated horse trough I am. I'm pretty sure there's laws against public nudity, even in this backwater place."

"First off, I'm not naked," he said.

She couldn't stop herself from raking a gaze over his amazing body. "You look naked."

"Appearance can be deceiving. For instance you look stuck-up."

"Sometimes appearance can be deceiving but on the whole, I've found that what you see is what you get."

"So you're saying you *are* stuck-up?"

"I'm saying you look like a drunken derelict."

"Hung-over derelict," he corrected. "I'm not drunk anymore."

"Excuse me for missing the distinction. I'm sure your mother is so proud."

"I have underwear on," he offered.

"How comforting." As if a little strip of soaking wet cotton cloth hid anything. Why she should find that even more tantalizing than full nudity, she had no clue, but she did.

And that bothered her. A lot.

"Secondly, this isn't public," the cowboy continued. "It's private property."

"I know," she said. She couldn't believe this was happening. Having a conversation with this semi-naked, hung-over cowboy in a gold-plated horse trough. Had she fallen down a rabbit hole when she wasn't looking and ended up in Wonderland? She half expected to see the Mad Hatter pop up at any moment. "*My* property."

"Thirdly, it's not your horse trough."

Her finger hovered over the keypad. Before she could make up her mind whether to call the cops or not, a Sheriff's cruiser motored up the road.

"Ha! Apparently someone has already reported you," she said.

"I wouldn't gloat too hard," he observed. "The deputy will be on my side."

"Why's that? Just because you know each other? The good old boy network in action?" Mariah clenched her teeth. She'd had enough of cronyism in Chicago.

"Nope. The deputy is a woman."

"Then why are you so sure she'll side with you? Did you sleep with her?"

"Does that bother you?"

"Why should it bother me? I don't care who you sleep with. Why would I care about who you slept with?"

"You tell me."

"Tell you what?"

"Why you're upset at the idea that I slept with a lady deputy."

"I'm not!" She snorted.

"You look upset."

"I'm upset because you're naked in my horse trough."

"This conversation is going around in circles."

"No kidding."

"It's not your horse trough."

"It is."

"Nope, because it's not your ranch."

"It is and I can prove it.

"It's not and here's the reason why. My name's Joe Daniel's, this here is Green Ridge and I have a sneaking suspicion you're looking for Stone Creek Ranch."

Next month, don't miss these exciting new love stories only from Avon Books

Midnight's Wild Passion by Anna Campbell
Blinded by vengeance for the man who destroyed his sister, the Marquess of Ranelaw plans to repay his foe in kind by seducing the man's daughter. But when her companion, Miss Antonia Smith, steps in to thwart his plans, Antonia finds herself fighting off his relentless charm. And she's always had a weakness for rakes…

Ascension by Sable Grace
When Kyana, half Vampyre, half Lychen, is entrusted by the Order of Ancients to find a key that will seal Hell forever and save the mortals she despises, she has no choice but to accept. But when she's assigned an escort, Ryker, a demigod who stirred her heart long ago, she knows that giving into temptation could mean the undoing of them both.

A Tale of Two Lovers by Maya Rodale
Lord Simon Roxbury has a choice: wed or be penniless. Surely finding a suitable miss should be simple enough? But then gossip columnist Lady Julianna threatens his reputation and a public battle ensues, leaving both in tatters. To rescue her good name and his fortune, they unite in a marriage of convenience. Will it be too late to stop tongues wagging or will it be a love match after all?

When Tempting a Rogue by Kathryn Smith
Gentleman club proprietress Vienne La Rieux has her eye on a prize that would make her England's richest woman when a former lover, the charming Lord Kane, disrupts her plans. Neither is prepared for the passion still between them, but with an enemy lurking in the shadows, any attempt to mix business with pleasure could have tragic consequences.